Amid the Echoing Canyons, the Kindling of Eternal Desire...

"My lady," Ranse said teasingly, and lifted her down from the saddle. He did not step away.

Looking up, Kathleen saw the banked fires burning in Ranse O'Neil's dark eyes, and felt an answering blaze ignite inside her.

His mouth was gentle at first, then his arms pressed her against the full length of his strong body, and the world dissolved away. Wave after wave of urgent longing swept through her as she responded with all her being.

"Dear God . . . Kathleen," he groaned, tearing his mouth from hers, but holding her even closer.

"Ranse . . ." she murmured as softly as the distant murmuring of Cybille Creek, her fingers luxuriating in the soft warmth of his thick hair.

"My darlin' . . . my love." His voice was muffled against her throat. "God, how I love you . . ."

Always Tomorrow

Elisabeth Macdonald

PUBLISHED BY POCKET BOOKS NEW YORK

An *Original* publication of POCKET BOOKS

 POCKET BOOKS, a division of Simon & Schuster, Inc.
1230 Avenue of the Americas, New York, N.Y. 10020

ISBN: 0-671-60292-6

First Pocket Books printing September, 1986

10 9 8 7 6 5 4 3 2 1

POCKET and colophon are registered trademarks of Simon & Schuster, Inc.

Printed in the U.S.A.

FOR KAREN
My daughter, My friend

Brunfelsia calycina: A compact evergreen shrub with glossy ovate four-inch leaves. Earns its common name "yesterday-today-and-tomorrow" through its three-day flower color change from purple to lavender to white.

BOOK I

·⊷❧Ⅰ CHAPTER 1 Ⅰ❧⊷·

Ireland, 1866

First light turned the sky into a silver bowl. Across green
meadows still wet with morning dew, horse and rider took
the jumps as though they were one being. One after another,
they leaped the stone fences that snaked across the rolling
hills, leading at last to the cliffs above the Irish Sea.

Fiona Browne's auburn hair streamed loose behind her as
she rode, and her young face lifted toward the sky with an
expression of utter exhilaration. She wore an old sweater of
her father's, and the skirt of her worn riding habit was
tucked up so that she could sit astride the groom's saddle.

The stableboy had protested sleepily when she saddled
Agincourt, but she paid no attention. They both knew her
father would be furious to see her riding his prize stallion.
She had her own horses . . . all gentle mares or well-trained
geldings. But Agincourt was the challenge. He knew her, for
this was not the first time she had stolen a forbidden ride on
him.

How she loved the sleek power of him, the feel of his great
body moving beneath her. She loved the sweet smell of the
earth torn by his pounding hooves and the feel of the wind
rushing past them.

The dark mane tossing before her filled her eyes for a brief
flash with an image of Sean McLoughlin, his black hair
blowing in the wind as they raced each other across the
meadows of Morning Hill. Sean . . . her knees and thighs
tightened. Agincourt surged forward.

"I love you, Sean McLoughlin," she shouted into the
wind. The words lost themselves in the silvery morning air.
If she could steal away with Agincourt and make him her

3

own, she would do the same with Sean. She had always known it would happen one day . . . no! . . . now . . . today! The decision filled her with a wild stab of joy. Today, she would entice him to lie with her, and then he could not deny her. Then they must wed, and he would be hers forever.

The horse moved sinuously beneath her, and her heart seemed about to burst. She wanted to weep, and shout . . . and most of all, she wanted Sean.

Suddenly, she became aware that the highest jump was before them. Collecting her tumultuous thoughts, she leaned forward, her whole being united with her mount. Agincourt stretched his great body, as wild with the sense of freedom as his rider. Together, they soared over the high rock wall, seeming for a moment suspended in midair. Agincourt landed, gathering himself to run again. A breathless cry of triumph and fulfillment burst from Fiona's aching throat.

When she settled back in the saddle, Agincourt seemed to know the ride had ended. He turned homeward at a smooth even trot.

A faint sheen of perspiration covered Fiona's body and her chest heaved with emotion. Some rite of passage had ended there in the silvery morning on Agincourt's back. Today, her life would change. Today, there was Sean . . . today and forever.

Back at the stables, she turned Agincourt over to the unhappy stableboy. Assuming an air of unconcern, slapping her riding crop against her boot, she strolled into the house to change for breakfast.

Gnarled ancient oaks surrounded the mellow brick manor house, casting their shade across the artfully informal garden. Those shadows lay long in the morning sun as Fiona's booted feet fairly danced along the graveled paths. Her dark blue velvet riding habit swirled about her slender figure as she moved.

The morning was bright with promise, the air scented by the myriad blooming shrubs . . . the sweetness of lily of the valley, the spicy scent of the geraniums tumbling over the rock wall between the upper and lower gardens. The azaleas and rhododendrons were past their prime, with only vestiges of spring's blaze of color remaining. It was a garden of small enchanting vistas . . . the cobbled circle surrounding the sundial, fragrant with lavender . . . the broad stone steps leading to the second level where Mama's prized fuchsias lined the rock wall against the background of a clipped laurel hedge. Bees mumbled among the flowers, and a flight of starlings whirled up from the hawthorn tree like leaves before the wind.

Suddenly Fiona paused, bending gracefully over a glossy green shrub. With a quick glance to make sure her mother, whose life's passion was this garden, was not watching, she picked three blossoms from the shrub. Each of the small trumpet-shaped flowers was different . . . one purple, one lavender, one white. Yesterday-today-and-tomorrow, her mother called it.

Holding the flowers to her nose, she inhaled their faint, elusive fragrance. A smile curved her young pink mouth, and the hazel eyes danced as she made the three blossoms into a miniature bouquet. What did yesterday or tomorrow matter? There was really only today. Sean McLoughlin was waiting, for she had sent word to him at the stables before breakfast.

The flowers seemed an appropriate token for Sean. They had been together all their yesterdays . . . growing up here on her father's estate . . . learning to ride the fine Irish hunters Cedric Browne bred and trained . . . taking their first jumps together. With a wry twist to her mouth, she remembered that Sean had even been the one who comforted her and explained when her first woman's flow came. In her ignorance, she had been terrified, afraid she was dying. He had found her crying in the coach house and demanded indignantly, "Why didn't your mother tell you?" Then he had taken her to the stablemaster's stone cottage where his mother and three sisters had instructed her further until her fears ended in laughter.

Shy and scholarly, Margaret Browne's world was bounded by her garden. So intense was her preoccupation she failed to realize that a daughter required attention too. Fiona often told herself she didn't miss a mother's counsel, since she had Sean, she needed no one else.

Hurrying up the path toward the stables, she looked across the vast fields and green meadows of Morning Hill. Low clouds lay to seaward, but the sky above was a glorious sparkling blue, and the summer air was filled with the scent of flowers.

Sunlight glinted off the east windows of the manor house. It had been built by her great-uncle in the modified Georgian style so popular in eastern Ireland in the eighteenth century. The front wing of the house was unique for its ellipse shape. A front door of elegantly carved mahogany, with an exquisite Georgian fanlight above, opened into the great hall that was flanked by two drawing rooms shaped like half circles. It was a house open to the sun, with tall twelve-pane windows on both floors and a glassed-in conservatory on the east side.

Too many windows, Fiona thought now, glancing back at the house, hoping her parents hadn't noticed her departure. Not likely, for her parents seldom took much notice of her.

Catching sight of Sean waiting for her, Fiona's steps quickened, and her throat tightened painfully. Early sunlight poured over the whitewashed stables, over the two saddled chestnuts moving restlessly . . . and Sean. At eighteen, the stablemaster's son was a man. With his six-foot frame, his broad shoulders and the straight back of a horseman, Sean McLoughlin combined the best of the many tribes that had bred the Irish race. He was tall like the Viking northerners, and dark like the Black Irish of the west country, with thick black hair above an olive-skinned, finely chiseled face.

When Sean's blue eyes met her eager hazel ones, it seemed to Fiona the very air between them pulsated with longing. "Good morning, Sean," she said in a lilting voice. How wonderful he looked, his rough wool trousers tucked into leather boots, the white linen shirt open at the throat to reveal a glimpse of dark chest hair.

The mobile mouth that always curved so enticingly at the corners broke into a smile. "Fine morning, Miss Fiona."

"Miss?" She frowned at him. He had called her Fee for half her life . . . then Fiona . . . but Miss?

"Look at your hair," he added, his admiring eyes belying

the chiding tone. "Didn't your mother say you must wear it up, now you're sixteen?"

Fiona's hand went guiltily to the thick mane of dark auburn hair she had tied back with a length of blue ribbon. "It's far too much trouble," she protested. Then she realized he was teasing, and she laughed. "I shall have to do it next week when we go to the Horse Show in Dublin. Do I have to put it up for you, Sean?"

Sean McLoughlin looked down into the heart-shaped face regarding him with teasing innocence. God, how beautiful she'd come to be, with that wonderful glowing hair against her clear transparent skin, the beguiling pink mouth that made him ache to kiss it. The insatiable yearning that had tormented his nights for months now almost overwhelmed him. When had it happened, he wondered? When had they stopped being friends and companions, when had he started wanting to possess her in every way a man can possess a woman?

"You're perfect as you are," he replied softly. Her face softened at the words, the pink mouth trembled. Dear God, Sean thought, she feels it too. The knowledge filled him with terror and delight.

"Here." Fiona held out the flowers. "This is yesterday-today-and-tomorrow. I give them all to you."

At the words, Sean's face changed in a way that made the breath stop in Fiona's throat. Before she could take a step toward him, he turned to the horses. His voice was choked, and so low she barely heard the words. "Would to God it were possible."

"Sean?"

Without looking at her, he took the flowers and stuck them in the band of his worn tweed cap. "I brought Angel for you," he said tersely, handing her the reins.

"Dear Angel . . ." The words sang from Fiona's lips. Sean loved her. He'd tried, and couldn't hide it. Now, she had only to make him say the words. A great happiness filled her as she rubbed her forehead lovingly against the horse's muzzle. Reaching into her pocket, she offered the lump of sugar she had brought. With a loud wet slurp, Angel took it from her hand.

"Spoiling the horses," Sean said with mock ferocity, once more in control of his feelings.

"So your father would say." Fiona laughed and produced another lump of sugar for Sean's horse.

Watching Sean check the saddles, she knew he dared not look at her. Later . . . later, there would be a time for looking and for loving. Oh, she knew the McLoughlins were Irish, not Anglo Protestant aristocrats. They were not listed in Debrett's peerage as her parents were, but she cared nothing for that. With her entire being singing with love for Sean McLoughlin, she refused to consider the fact that her parents would object strenuously to her feelings for the stablemaster's son.

Cedric Browne was the younger son of a noble English family, and intended for the church, so he had often told Fiona. He had been saved from that undesired career by the death of a childless uncle who left him his estate in Ireland, Morning Hill. Here, Cedric had been able to turn his love for fine hunting horses into a profitable enterprise.

Catching a glimpse of Colin McLoughlin working inside a nearby stall, Fiona thought that it might have been very different for her father without McLoughlin. He was a kind of nobility himself, this finest horse trainer in all of Ireland. Periodically, other horse farms tried to lure him away. Colin would appear before Cedric Browne and tell him of the offer. Cedric always met it, knowing well that without Colin his prospering estate would not prosper. Turning back to meet Sean's warm eyes, Fiona knew that this young McLoughlin bid well to be even better than his father.

When Sean helped her mount, Fiona's whole body seemed to take fire from the touch of his hands. Looking down into his shaken face, she reached out and gently touched his cheek. Today, she thought, today. Then she spurred Angel forward, shouting over her shoulder in the old wild way, "Catch me if you can!"

Colin McLoughlin leaned on the half-door of the horse stall. A big man like his son, his face was lined by years in the sun and rain, his dark hair streaked with gray. He shook his head despairingly as the two riders began their usual fiercely competitive race across the Big Meadow. Didn't the master and mistress realize Fiona was a woman now, not a madcap ten-year-old to be racing about with the stable-master's son?

Gloom settled over Colin as he watched his son laughing down at the beautiful girl racing beside him. There would be trouble from this . . . sure as the sun rose over the Irish Sea. He must make a time to speak frankly and firmly to Sean.

The blue sweep of Killiney Bay glittered in the sunlight below the hill where the two riders reined up. In the distance, a misty green point of land jutted into the sea, and on the rocks below the surf broke in an endless fugue of sound.

On the point of the hill, the ruins of an ancient round tower fell into emerald grass studded with mayflowers. Stone walls lay tumbled into a tangle of whitethorn and yellow gorse.

Breathless from her furious ride, Fiona gave the landscape only a brief glance before she turned to Sean. He had dismounted and come to stand beside her horse, looking up at her with his handsome mouth curved in laughter.

"Welcome to Cuchulain's castle, my lady," he said, giving her a mocking bow.

At the words "my lady," something within Fiona stilled. Of late Sean's mother had taken to addressing her in that manner, stiff and formal where she had once been warm and loving. Of course she could no longer run to the stable-master's stone cottage with every hurt as she had done in childhood, but surely Bridget hadn't stopped loving her just because she had grown up? She would not think of it today . . . not this special day.

"My Lord Cuchulain," she said, laughing down into Sean's eyes, "Queen Maeve accepts your hospitality." With that, she tumbled from the saddle so that Sean had to catch her in his arms.

Suddenly, they were both very still, as though the moment were frozen in time. She felt his heart thundering, felt the warmth of his hands clasping her waist. This would be the day, she had been sure of it. But now that the moment had arrived, the intensity of her emotions overwhelmed her.

Instinctively, she pressed closer to him, sliding her arms about his neck, lifting her mouth to his.

Sean drew a deep shuddering breath. His arms tightened, crushing her breasts against his hard chest. His blue eyes darkened, deep and fathomless as an ancient pool as his lips took hers in a kiss that erased the world around them.

When Sean tried to break the embrace, Fiona clung to him, her mouth devouring his. She had wanted this for so long, planned this day so carefully, she would not be denied now. But Sean's hands were on her shoulders, bruising her with their strength, pushing her away.

"Fee . . . Oh God, my sweet Fee . . . we can't do this. It's wrong." His face was tortured by the denial of the hot longing in his eyes.

Aching for the feel of his strong body pressing against hers once more, Fiona tried to shrug off his hold. "It's not wrong," she cried in desperation when he would not yield. "I love you, Sean. I've loved you always. We belong to each other."

Sean groaned as though in pain. For a brief instant his grasp loosened, and she flung herself against him with such violence that he fell backward on the green. His cap fell off and rolled away. The horses shied and whinnied, then quieted, nibbling at the grass.

Fiona hesitated only a moment as she looked down into Sean's astounded face. He lay in the shadow of the remaining wall of the round tower. A thousand times they'd played here as children . . . fighting again the Gaelic wars against the Vikings, and reliving the adventures of Cuchulain and Queen Maeve . . . all the ancient tales told to them at Bridget McLoughlin's fireside. As he recovered himself, Sean began trying to sit up. At once, Fiona flung herself upon him so that her body covered his, pinning him to the earth. Her searching mouth claimed his in reckless abandon.

He couldn't stop. The sweet taste of her mouth was like a drug destroying his will. Her hands were like fire on his neck, his back, his chest, stroking the hardness that bulged his trousers. She turned then, pulling him with her, pushing away her clothing as they moved. Looking down into her eyes, he saw that the hazel lights had darkened into pools of passion. Her voice was low and husky. "Love me, Sean . . . please, love me."

Sean McLoughlin knew he had lost this battle. With her body pressing urgently against his, he tried to hold back. He must be easy for he was the first, even though any girl who rode as recklessly as Fiona had surely long ago torn her maidenhead. His strong gentle hands caressed until her moistness and her soft cries told him she was ready.

The discomfort surprised Fiona. When she gasped and winced, Sean lay still, holding her close until her body accommodated itself to his invasion. There was a stirring inside and she instinctively lifted her hips to meet his thrusts . . . wanting him closer . . . closer.

Afterward, they lay beside each other, staring up at the clouds drifting in from the sea. Fiona lifted her head from Sean's shoulder to look into his face. Bending, she touched her lips to his, her tongue flicking teasingly along his mouth.

"Happy, love?" she asked softly, smiling at him.

Sean did not smile. "It was wrong, Fee." His voice was unsteady. "A mortal sin."

"Which you shall have to confess to Father Cleary, I suppose." Her tone was light and teasing.

Sean's eyes were serious, as he reached one big hand to gently smooth a stray lock of hair back from her face. "Either that or not take Communion."

"I'm glad I'm not a Catholic," she announced, refusing to join in his remorse. "How anything so heavenly could be a mortal sin is beyond me."

"Ah, Fee . . . sweet love." He kissed her with such longing she nearly wept. She lay across his chest now, her breasts taut and aching, her whole being suddenly on fire to possess him once more.

Her mouth pressed hot against his throat, as she murmured, "If you have to confess anyway, we might as well do it again."

He was silent, caught in a guilt she refused to acknowledge. Fiona kissed him, again and again, his mouth, his ears, his throat. At last, as her tongue flicked in soft passionate urging against his lips, Sean opened to her. His hands stroked her soft flesh, gathering her up to possess her.

Beyond the ruined tower, the Irish Sea thundered a wild accompaniment to their joining.

The horses had wandered off. Struggling to put her clothing back in order, Fiona watched Sean as he led them back up the hill. Her whole being leaped with longing when she looked at him, wanting him as intensely as though they had not made love just a half hour ago. She was so wildly happy at the consummation of all her desires; she wished Sean did not seem so sad. In the throes of passion, he had cried out his love for her, as lost as she in the heavenly madness they shared.

Coming up to her now, one hand holding the horses' reins, he reached to smooth her rumpled hair, bending to kiss her forehead softly. "Are you all right, Fee? Did I hurt you?"

"Dear love," she said, sliding her arms about his waist and looking up into his solemn face. "In all our lives, you have never hurt me. Now, I'm yours forever, and you are mine."

"Oh God, Fee!" he cried as though in pain. "We're not playing games now. We're grown up, and I'm still the stablemaster's son and you're still the nobleman's daughter. Not all the love in the world can change that or make what we feel for each other possible."

"We'll be married," she replied confidently. Her face softened and her eyes grew dreamy. "We'll have a great white bed. I'm sure making love in a bed will be even better."

"Fiona!" Sean jerked away from her. "For the love of God, stop pretending like a child."

Tears brimmed in her eyes at his tone. She turned and reached down to retrieve his cap. "Yesterday, today, and tomorrow," she murmured pensively, taking the crushed flowers in her fingers. "That's how long I will love you, Sean."

As he looked into her eyes swimming with unshed tears, his face softened and he drew her back into the embrace of one arm. "I shall love you until I die," he whispered, his mouth against her hair.

"Swear it!" she demanded fiercely, taking his face in her

two hands and looking into his eyes. "Swear you will love me always."

"I swear," he answered reluctantly, "because I cannot help myself."

"And I swear that I shall love no one but you, Sean McLoughlin, for all my life. Until the day I die, I shall love you."

Sean groaned at the words and buried his face against the softness of her neck. "My love." The words were lost as Fiona's lips found his. He could argue with her no more. The social barriers between them would part them soon enough. Their love could have this moment.

Rain streamed down the French windows of the morning room. Beyond the whitewashed stables and the glasshouse, the hills were wreathed in gray mist. Fiona pressed her forehead against the cold window and sighed.

"Fiona." Her mother gave her an annoyed glance from where she sat working at her desk. "All this pacing about and sighing is most distracting. Do something with yourself . . . needlework or reading."

"I want to ride, Mama." Fiona sighed again.

A frown appeared on Mama's face as she impatiently smoothed a strand of graying brown hair back into her plain coiffure. Her hours in the garden tending the beloved fuchsias she bred and crossbred had aged her skin, and there were lines at the corners of her light brown eyes. "What nonsense. You can't ride on a day like this. It's impossible."

Impossible to be with Sean, Fiona thought, and impossible to stop thinking about him. Why had she thought that lying with Sean, loving him, would ease her yearning? It had only intensified the ache, now that she knew exactly what magic there was in the loving.

She crossed the room to the turf fire in the fireplace manteled with green Connemara marble, stretching her hands to its warmth.

On the polished parquet floor lay the jewel-colored carpets brought long ago from France. Her mother's desk was beautifully carved mahogany, with a matching chair upholstered in red leather. Two flowered wing-back chairs stood on either side of the fireplace, with a tea table between. Above the mantel hung a portrait of Sir Horace Browne's wife, her great-aunt, who had hated Ireland and lived here with her husband only briefly. Perhaps, Fiona mused, that was why they had had no children and Morning Hill had come to Papa.

Seated at her desk, with her plant records strewn about her, it seemed Mama had already forgotten her daughter's presence. Papa had once told her proudly that her mother was a genius. Did she not correspond with famous botanists around the world and take full charge of the glasshouse and the garden? But Fiona failed to appreciate his pride. With a wry smile, she recalled her mother's long scientific lecture on cross-pollination when she had asked where babies come from. After that experience, she took her questions to Bridget McLoughlin, who answered them honestly in matter-of-fact tones. Anyway, a country girl could scarcely fail to know the facts of life if she was at all observant.

The longing centered, hot and aching, between her thighs, and Fiona turned impatiently from the fire to pace the length of the beautiful room. She needed to be with Sean. Just to touch him would ease her.

Even as a child, she had found sedentary tasks difficult. Sitting still made her feel as though she would burst out of her skin. Mr. Bean, the tutor her father had hired, had been driven to distraction by her restlessness. It was only when Papa had allowed Sean to share her lessons that she became quiet. With Sean beside her, it became a lovely game. Sean . . . Sean . . . every cell of her body cried out for him.

"Fiona." Her mother sighed, putting aside her pen to gaze at her restless daughter. "Please go upstairs and play cards with Nanny Quinn. You've disturbed me so, I shall have to rewrite this whole passage."

"Sorry, Mama," she muttered, not sorry at all except for herself. If only Mama were like Bridget. If only she could talk to her about how it hurt to love someone.

Upstairs, in the little sitting room that had once been the nursery, Nanny sat napping in her chair before a blazing turf fire. Fiona paused to smile fondly at the sleeping woman. Nanny had grown plump in the years since she had come to Morning Hill to care for the Brownes' only child, but her hair in its tight bun was only lightly touched with gray, her broad face barely lined. Papa would be most annoyed to see a servant with her own turf fire, but Nanny had never kept her place. She took her privileges for granted. It was whispered in the village that Nanny was the love daughter of Lord Burton and the gombeen-man's widow. Although it had never been acknowledged, it was certain she had been raised to think herself above her neighbors.

Mary, the little village girl who had come to Morning Hill to be Fiona's maid, sat on the other side of the fire. She started up from her chair guiltily. "Do you wish something, Miss Fiona?"

"No, Mary," Fiona replied quickly. "Stay by the fire. It's an ugly day." Crossing the room, she sat down in the wide window seat and drew the pale green velvet curtains to shut out the room. This had been a favorite hiding place when as a child she had spent hours there reading or watching the workers in the stables and the gardens.

On the velvet cushion, her prayer book lay where she had left it last night. Carefully, she turned the pages to the marriage ceremony, and felt tears brim in her eyes as she gazed at the three blossoms pressed on the page . . . white, lavender and purple.

Beyond the rain-drenched windows, she could see the hazy image of the whitewashed, thatch-roofed stables and the horses in the paddock, their coats shiny wet. Sean came from one of the stables, his head bent against the rain, his tall body encased in a black macintosh. Everything inside her seemed to leap toward him. Closing her eyes tightly against the immensity of her longing, Fiona leaned back against the cushions with a sigh. Then she felt the warm moisture between her thighs, and sighed again. Her flow had started. She could not have been with Sean today anyway. But there would be another day. The sun would shine. The larks would sing above Cuchulain's ruined castle, and she would lie in the arms of her love.

·◦❉| CHAPTER 2 |❉◦·

"You've been to the bloody priest," Fiona accused, looking into Sean's anguished face. It terrified her to realize that the priest had the power to part them.

Yesterday's rain clouds still lingered, and the stable was dark and cold. This familiar place with its pungent odors and quiet sounds . . . the horses munching hay, the doves cooing in the loft . . . seemed suddenly alien. A trembling began inside her. But she glared at Sean as he held her away from him at arm's length.

His jaw tightened, and his big hands were like a vise on her shoulders. As soon as she could decently leave the house after breakfast, she had come running to the stables, aching to touch him after a day apart. Then, when she'd thrown her arms about him, he'd immediately pushed her away.

Sean's voice was low and harsh. "Father Cleary only told me what I already knew. That it's hopeless, that I must stay away from you."

"Damn Father Cleary," she cried. "What does he know about love? Why should he tell you what to do?"

"You're not Catholic, Fee, so you couldn't understand." Sean at last met her eyes, his mouth curving in a sad smile. The hands on her shoulders relaxed. "It isn't just Father Cleary and mortal sin, Fee, my love. It's that you're a lady. Ladies don't fall in love with the stable groom."

"Groom be damned!" Fiona burst from his grasp, throwing her arms tight around his waist. "You're Sean. My friend. My lover." She'd won, she thought joyously as his arms came around her shoulders, holding her close against

16

him. But when he cupped her face in one hand and looked down into her eyes, she felt defeat fall over her.

Sean gave her a wry smile. "Swearing like a stable hand won't change anything, Fee. I'm to leave tomorrow early, with Da and the others to drive the horses up to Dublin for the Horse Show. It's best we're apart for a while."

"I don't want to be apart . . . ever," she protested, holding him tighter.

"Don't," he muttered, as she began kissing his throat wildly. "Don't tempt me, Fee. God knows I want you."

"Then hold me. Just once before you go to Dublin. Kiss me goodbye." Standing on tiptoe, she pressed her lips to his.

Sean groaned as though in pain. His arms crushed her against his chest, and his mouth took hers in a devouring kiss.

"Sean!"

"Da!" They sprang apart to stare at a furious-visaged Colin standing in the stable doorway.

"Go to the house, Miss Fiona." Colin's voice was hard and commanding.

With one brief glance at Sean, who seemed frozen with guilt, Fiona turned and fled.

In the dim light of the stable, father and son stared at each other. Sean's misery was so apparent, Colin's anger nearly melted. For the boy's own good it couldn't go on, he told himself, and when he spoke his voice was harsh.

"You've forgotten yer place, lad. If you weren't a man grown, I'd whup yer bloody arse."

Sean drew a deep breath. "I've been to the priest, Da. I know what I must do."

"She'll not let go, that one," Colin muttered gloomily. "Nothin's been denied her since the day of her birth. She'll ruin ye, lad."

"You're wrong," Sean replied quietly. "Fee loves me, as I love her." Clenching his fists, he looked into his father's eyes. "But I'll stop, Da. I promised Father Cleary."

Colin shook his head. "As well say ye'll stop the sun from risin'. No lad, it's goin' away from here ye'll be. You an' Agincourt win the Cup at the Horse Show, everyone'll see how good you are. I'll find another place for ye."

* * *

The great Dublin Horse Show, each August, was the social event of the year in Ireland. Colin and the grooms and trainers drove the horses up to Dublin. A day later, the Brownes came in their closed carriage, with all their luggage, maids and footmen following in the jaunting cars. Since Cedric frugally refused to maintain a house in Dublin for this once-a-year occasion, they were always guests of his old friend, Lord Curran.

Cedric was early at the showgrounds with the other horsemen. Accompanied by Fiona, Margaret moved through the endless teas and receptions with a sort of preoccupied dignity that gave her the reputation of being rather cold. She had little in common with these women whose entire life was centered on the social round, and she only longed to return to her glasshouse and her beloved fuchsias. This year, Cedric had been unusually firm with her, saying she must take more interest in the social scene, since it was important to begin addressing the problem of a suitable husband for Fiona. Only if she made the right social moves, would Fiona be invited to the presentation at Dublin Castle.

Sounds of music, talk, and laughter drifted upstairs to Lady Curran's sitting room, which had been set aside for the ladies attending the Curran's annual ball, one of many that filled the evenings during the Horse Show.

Fiona stared at herself in the long pier glass. Her new ball gown was as fashionable as any at the ball, she was certain. Of peacock blue silk, the elegant drapes at her shoulders and hem were caught up by white silk roses. Mary had done her hair up in the latest style, quickly learned from Lady Curran's maid. Its rich auburn length was lifted from her slender white neck and piled high, with gleaming ringlets over her ears. There seemed nothing to set her apart from the other young girls in the ballroom below. Yet she had been subjected to the indignity of standing against the wall, waiting for the invitation to dance that never came. Like the horses paraded for bidding, she'd told herself angrily, and she'd escaped upstairs at the first opportunity.

How tedious it all was, she thought miserably, listening to

two young girls behind her discussing their presentation at Dublin Castle. She cared nothing for the Lord Lieutenant's invitation to the Castle, or even for being presented to the Queen in London as one girl had boasted of. With all her heart, she longed for the high meadow at Morning Hill, for the sea wind, and Sean's arms about her.

Her mother was in the card room, her one concession to social graces, and her father was no doubt discussing horses with his cronies. If she never returned to the ballroom, they wouldn't miss her.

Moving through the chattering crowd of ladies, their maids repairing hairdos and gowns, she found a chair in a quiet corner of the room. Arranging her full silky skirts about her, she sat down to dream of Sean. Although Papa took them each day to join the parade at the Horse Show grounds, she hadn't had a glimpse of Sean since they had come to Dublin. He would be riding Agincourt in the jumping competition tomorrow, and she longed for the time to be quickly gone, longed for the moment she could see him again.

"It's not surprising the girl has no social graces," she heard a woman's haughty voice on the other side of the curtained alcove.

Mrs. Reynolds, Fiona thought, recognizing the voice. The Reynoldses' country estate, Windward, was not far from Morning Hill, so that the lady and her daughter, Marianne, who was a year older than Fiona and had been presented at Dublin Castle, occasionally came to call. The calls were social duty of course, for Mrs. Reynolds found Mama as tedious as Mama found her.

"Margaret has none herself, to be sure," the voice continued. "And Cedric . . . imagine a brother of Lord Mountford becoming such a provincial. He thinks of nothing but his horses. They never go to London, and to Dublin only for the Horse Show. And, my dear, to breed horses for the market—" She paused only to sniff disparagingly before she added, "It simply isn't done."

"You cannot blame the poor child then," was her companion's mild rejoinder. "I'm sure she knows no better."

"One cannot cut them entirely." Mrs. Reynolds seemed

not to hear the comment. "But my dear, you never saw such countrified people."

Provincial perhaps, Fiona thought in fury, but not a vulgar gossip like you. She began to consider ways to get even with Mrs. Reynolds for her snide comments.

"You're so fortunate to have Lord Hadley with you for a holiday," the unknown companion made an obvious attempt to change the subject.

Self-satisfaction was evident in Mrs. Reynolds's reply. "Lord Robert is Mr. Reynolds's cousin, you know. Inherited the title from his father only last year."

"Quite a catch for some young lady," came the reply.

"He seems very interested in Marianne, my dear. Although I wouldn't want you to repeat it, I'm certain he'll offer for her before he returns to England."

Her smug assumption that Lord Hadley was as good as trapped by the disdainful Marianne infuriated Fiona. Then she allowed herself a conspiratorial grin. Maybe here was a way to get even with the spiteful Mrs. Reynolds. Even though she had behaved like a sullen child, refusing to flirt with the young bucks, and so had been ignored at the ball, she knew she looked beautiful. If she took the trouble to practice her wiles on Lord Hadley, perhaps she could ruin Marianne's chances and save that unknown gentleman from a miserable life.

Laughing softly, she jumped to her feet. With one last reassuring look in the mirror, she paused to bow to the discomfited Mrs. Reynolds before she returned to the ball.

Pausing at the head of the wide sweeping staircase, Fiona looked down into the great ballroom of Lord Curran's town house. At the far end, the musicians were playing the lancers. The whole room seemed a mass of whirling multicolored silken skirts, like a huge rainbow trapped there beneath the glitter of the crystal chandeliers. Richly dressed ladies, and gentlemen in stiff formal evening wear, observed the dancers from the sidelines. Despite Mrs. Reynolds's assertion, Fiona had been given all the advantages, including dancing lessons, and her feet began to move to the strains of music.

There was dear Papa, she thought, drinking port with the other men near the door to the supper room. Surely, he would know this Lord Hadley, or someone who could introduce her. Making her way through the press of people, she held her ivory fan modestly before her small white bosom, partially exposed by the décolleté neckline.

"Papa," she murmured, bowing and smiling modestly at his companions.

"What is it, my dear?" Papa's blue eyes glowed with pride as he looked at his lovely daughter, looking so proper now as opposed to her usual hoyden appearance. The remains of auburn hair fringing his bald head, and his heavy sideburns, were streaked with gray. Fiona thought he looked quite elegant in his new black formal wear, his trip to the tailor necessitated by his expanding waistline.

When she whispered her request behind her fan, he looked at her in pleased astonishment. "My pleasure, indeed. Shall we dance first?" He gallantly offered his arm. As well-bred as any gentleman present, Fiona thought, despite Mrs. Reynolds's snobbish conclusions. Excusing himself from his companions, he led his daughter to the floor.

To her surprise, he danced very well. Although she knew it was unseemly to be reduced to dancing with one's father, she didn't care. It gave him a chance to tell her he had met Lord Hadley at the horse sale that afternoon, and his lordship was interested in buying some Morning Hill hunters. When the set ended, Papa managed very adroitly to accost Lord Hadley, who had just returned his partner to her chaperone.

"I say there," Papa said, as though surprised at this meeting. "I'd hoped to see you tonight so I could tell you my stallion, Agincourt, will be in the jumping competition tomorrow. If you're interested in my hunters, you'll want a look at their sire."

"Indeed, I will," Lord Hadley replied almost absently, for his gray eyes were considering Fiona intently.

So this was the great catch of the season, Fiona thought, smiling at him over her fan. He was tall and lean, impeccably tailored in his dark evening clothes. His straight blond hair was combed back from the face of an outdoorsman, his fair complexion reddened by sun and wind. His blond moustache looked positively rakish.

"And who is this ravishing young lady?" Lord Hadley inquired.

"My daughter, sir. Fiona, may I present Lord Robert Hadley."

Papa looked so bland and offhand, Fiona almost giggled. He had managed the whole thing so smoothly she could scarcely believe it.

"May I have the honor of this dance, Miss Browne?" Lord Hadley bowed, his gray eyes never leaving her face.

He did not leave her side the rest of the evening, even escorting her in to supper. It was there that Fiona caught Mrs. Reynolds's hostile look, as well as Marianne's vengeful glances from where she ate with an escort far less desirable than Lord Hadley.

Yet before the ball finally ended, Fiona would have gladly given him to Marianne if she could have done so. Lord Hadley lived and breathed hunting. He had little else to talk about. He seemed quite entranced when she allowed him to discuss endlessly the various hunts and horses at his estate in England. Trying not to show her annoyance at the tiresome conversation, Fiona smiled entrancingly and murmured appropriate comments whenever he paused expectantly.

Her mind wandered across Dublin to Sean. Was he drinking poteen in some low tavern with the other horsemen? Was he with another woman? The familiar aching longing rose in her until she could no longer attend Lord Hadley's words. Let him win tomorrow, she prayed silently. If he wins, perhaps it will make a difference. Perhaps then, her father would consider the possibility of Sean as a son-in-law.

Beneath their parasols, fashionable ladies paraded the graveled paths around the Horse Show arena. They were attended by immaculately groomed gentlemen, as aristocratic as the horses being shown on the greensward. Fiona and her mother stood together beneath a huge spreading oak waiting for Papa. He had gone to the stables to check with Colin on his horses. Although Fiona had begged, he'd refused to allow her to accompany him.

"No place for a girl," he'd muttered gruffly as he departed.

Now, she suddenly felt giddy with joy at the sight of Sean and the other riders competing for the Breeder's Cup as they came into the arena to pace the distance between jumps. How handsome he looked, so tall and straight in the well-cut Donegal tweed jacket and gray moleskin breeches her father's tailor had made for him. He was bareheaded, his helmet and riding crop in his hand, and the wind ruffled his hair in a way that made her ache to touch it. He wouldn't see her in this crowd, she thought, her eyes following him as he and the other riders moved across the sunny arena toward the stables. But he would know she was there, her heart taking the jumps with him.

"Magnificent!" Lord Hadley exclaimed. He had returned with Papa and remained to watch the competition from the owners' enclosure. He cut a splendid figure, Fiona saw, impeccably groomed in his silk hat and morning coat. But as far as she was concerned, Marianne was welcome to him. There was something about him she found repellent, his cold arrogance perhaps.

"Indeed," Cedric responded proudly, his eyes gleaming as he watched Sean ride Agincourt into the arena. Sunlight gleamed on Agincourt's chestnut flanks as the riders lined up.

"Magnificent," Fiona murmured softly, with eyes only for Agincourt's rider.

Sean was fourth in a field of six, each of the riders preceding him having made at least two faults. How beautiful they were together. Fiona's heart caught painfully as she watched horse and rider float over the jumps. They made the first turn without a fault, smoothly moving back to take the most difficult jump of all, the treble. Her whole being tightened. She leaned forward, wanting to help them over. The two of them seemed to move as one, as Agincourt gathered himself to clear the treble. His hind hoof caught the last rail. The rail trembled for a moment as though about to fall. When it remained in place, Fiona let out a great sigh of relief and applauded wildly.

She was certain no other rider could duplicate such a

marvelous performance and no one did. At the announcement that the winner was Agincourt, owned by Mr. Cedric
Browne, with Sean McLoughlin up, she shouted "Bravo!"
so enthusiastically that both her father and Lord Hadley
looked startled.

When Sean rode into center ring, her heart leaped out
toward him, and she would have run to his arms were it not
for her mother's restraining hand. Did Mama guess how
wildly she loved Sean? It didn't matter. Nothing would keep
them apart now. She even felt a surge of resentment when
her father proudly accepted the trophy Sean had won for
him.

"Congratulations." Lord Hadley smiled at Papa. "I am
most impressed." He smiled warmly down at Fiona.
"That's a fine stallion your father has there." Fiona only
nodded, her eyes following Sean.

"A fine stallion," he repeated to Mama.

"And a fine rider," Fiona told him in a spirited tone. She
did not miss her mother's veiled look of warning.

"Indeed," Lord Hadley agreed blandly. "One of your
grooms?"

"The stablemaster's son," Mama interjected quickly,
seeing Fiona's eyes blaze.

"Yes . . . well, perhaps I'll have a chance to try Agincourt
myself," he said with a smile that encompassed both
women. "Your husband has invited me to Morning Hill for
a few days to look over his horses." Pausing, he bowed
slightly to Mama. "I hope you don't mind."

"Delighted," Mama replied quickly. "An honor." All the
while, she wondered how on earth she would entertain this
lord. But of course she knew Cedric hoped to make a fine
match for Fiona, and this handsome man seemed eminently
suitable. She would make every effort, just as Cedric would
expect.

Fiona suddenly felt the weight of her petty revenge on
Mrs. Reynolds. The wages of sin, she told herself wryly as
Lord Hadley went on and on about the Morning Hill horses.
If she had been Christian and forgiving toward Mrs. Reyn-
olds, perhaps she wouldn't now be burdened by Lord
Hadley's company at Morning Hill. Still, maybe he was

truthfully only interested in horses. She could soon quash any plans her parents might have for an alliance.

At this moment, as she watched Sean ride Agincourt around the arena on a slow, majestic victory lap, she wanted only to be with him . . . home again at Morning Hill, with his arms about her and his mouth hot on hers.

CHAPTER 3

Lord Robert Hadley was indeed a tedious man. Fiona struggled to suppress a yawn as he began yet another account of the many hunts he seemed to recall in endless detail. She wished he were seated in the Reynoldses' drawing room at Windward, taking tea and paying court to Marianne instead of being here at Morning Hill.

Her mother poured the tea with a smile and appropriate pleasantries. Only the absent expression in her eyes indicated to Fiona that she would rather be in her garden, taking advantage of the fine August weather.

Riggs, the butler, had set the tea table in the curve of the east drawing room where the tall windows looked out over the garden. Even in the shadows of late afternoon, the garden glowed with late summer flowers. The gold damask draperies reflected the warmth of the day. It was a lovely room, with paneled walls painted a pale gold and a carved oak fireplace, where they had dispensed with a fire today. The furniture in Chippendale style was upholstered in a tapestry pattern that caught the gold of the draperies.

From beneath her lashes, Fiona watched as Hadley continued to regale her father with stories of the hunt. She thought him rather handsome, in a foppish, aristocratic British sort of way. Too bad there was only one subject on his mind. Yesterday, when Mrs. Reynolds had come to tea, she had plied him with questions about the season in London, which he answered as though he had passed through the whole social scene in a daze. Even when they rode about the estate, Lord Hadley seemed unaware of its beauty. Only the quality of the horses had caught his attention.

"I hope you'll join me for a gallop this afternoon, Miss Browne," he said now, with a smile that indicated his certainty of her acceptance.

With her parents' eyes on her, Fiona nodded. "Of course." What else could she do, she told herself in desperation, suddenly filled with a great dislike for this supercilious Englishman? He had kept her from Sean ever since they'd returned from Dublin. There had been more entertaining at Morning Hill than she ever remembered. All the neighboring aristocrats and gentry had been to tea, and Papa had even organized a hunt to entertain the visiting lord.

She had already come to dislike Lord Hadley for his casual cruelties. On the day of the hunt, she saw him give one of the Reynoldses' ill-trained hounds a vicious kick, so that the animal howled in pain and limped away, dragging its hind legs. Mary had whispered to her that his lordship had struck one of the grooms across the face with his riding crop for not obeying quickly enough. It had all built up into a faintly uneasy feeling Fiona had about the polite drawing room façade of Lord Robert Hadley.

She had seen Sean only when the horses were brought around for her daily ride with Lord Hadley and her father. How boring those rides were, and how she hated having to keep the horse at a decorous pace even though Lord Hadley repeatedly admired her horsemanship. If only she could be with Sean, thundering across the meadows with her riding habit tucked up, taking the stone fences as though she and the horse simply flowed over them.

With a suppressed sigh of relief, she watched the maid come to clear away the tea things. Papa and Lord Hadley adjourned to the library to peruse the stud book, while Mama hurried to the greenhouse, happy to get back to her beloved fuchsias.

Upstairs, Fiona flung herself on the bed and stared disconsolately up at the lace canopy. Thank God, he was leaving Saturday, and life could return to normal. There would be a dinner party on Friday, with all the neighboring estate owners in attendance. Maybe she could turn Lord

Hadley's attention to Marianne and redeem herself for her spiteful behavior at Lord Curran's Dublin ball.

Mary had followed her into the room, retrieving the slippers she had kicked off. Now she stood beside the bed, slippers in hand, a pleading look in her blue eyes. She was a slight girl, with an elfin face, her dark brown hair in a neat bun.

"What is it, Mary?" Fiona asked impatiently, quite out of sorts with the whole world.

"If you won't be needing me tonight, Miss . . ."

"Why on earth wouldn't I?" Fiona demanded.

"It's Fergus O'Brien, Miss Fiona. Tonight's his American wake. He'll be goin' to Cork on the morrow to sail for America."

Fiona sat up, suddenly interested. "Is he the young man I've seen you walking out with?"

"Aye, Miss." Tears glistened in Mary's eyes. "And he's goin' away to make his fortune." She stifled a sob. "He says he'll come back for me, but no one comes back."

"Of course you shall go!" Fiona jumped from the bed and flung her arms about the weeping Mary. The sudden thought struck her that Sean would be at the wake, for he and Fergus were friends. "And I'll go with you."

Mary's eyes widened with shock. "But, Miss . . ."

"Shhh . . ." Fiona urged. "I shall have a headache after dinner, and you and I will go to the wake. But you mustn't tell anyone. Swear it."

Drying her eyes, Mary swore secrecy, and Fiona presented her with a lace and linen bodice to wear to her sweetheart's farewell.

Fergus O'Brien's family had been tenants at Morning Hill from time immemorial. Although his uncle had had a bad reputation as a rackrenter, Cedric Browne had proven to be the best of landlords, never demanding rents when the potato crop had fallen to the blight, for he did not depend on the rents for his livelihood. Margaret was an heiress with a tidy income, and the horse business had proven profitable. Still, with twelve children in the O'Brien cottage, Fergus could see no way to better his lot in Ireland.

He told all this to Fiona as they danced to the lively sound of the flute and fiddle at the crossroads near his father's cottage. All the tenants were there, as well as some of the villagers, the women dressed in their best red flannel petticoats. Jars of illegal poteen circulated. There were pots of boiled taties and bacon, and pudding stuffed with sloe plums. A feast for these people, Fiona realized sadly, remembering the spread at tea this afternoon . . . and half of it wasted.

Where was Sean, she wondered, glancing around at the laughing faces? She and Mary had sneaked down the back stairs, Mary clad in her new finery and Fiona in her plainest gown. But the reason for her presence here had not appeared. Surely Sean wouldn't miss his friend's American wake. Standing on the sidelines after her reel with Fergus, she watched the love glowing in Mary's face as she danced with her departing sweetheart. Tears stung Fiona's eyes. Mary was right . . . Fergus would likely never return from the golden shores of America, where so many had gone since the terrible famines of the forties. Would the two of them lie in each other's arms one last time tonight?

Shouts of welcome greeted Sean's arrival. Colin, and Bridget, and the three girls accompanied him. He carried a jug of poteen. Even though her heart seemed about to burst from her chest, Fiona stood quite still, watching, as Sean moved among his friends, responding to their joyful greetings. When he surrendered the jug to Mrs. O'Brien, he turned and looked straight into Fiona's eyes. Frowning, he pushed his way through the crowd toward her.

"What are you doing here?" he demanded.

Fiona lifted her chin defiantly. "I came to say goodbye to Fergus. Mary brought me."

"You're the landlord's daughter," he said in a low furious voice. "You've no place here with these people."

"They don't seem to mind any more than they did when I was a child," she replied shortly. "Fergus gave me a glass of poteen, and we danced a reel together." Slipping her hand into his unresponsive one, she added, "Don't be angry, Sean. I came because I knew you'd be here. I've missed you so terribly."

"You were occupied with your fancy lord," he answered stiffly, not looking at her.

"He's my father's guest. I have to be polite even though he is a pompous ass."

Sean's face broke into a wide grin. His hand tightened on hers. "Where did you learn to swear like that?"

"From you, love," she said with a laugh, moving closer to him. "And now, you must teach me to dance the jig."

Oh, it was good to feel his arms about her again, to smell the clean warm scent of him like summer heather, to look into his handsome smiling face, to drown in those loving blue eyes. Ignoring Colin's frowns, Fiona lost count of how many times she sipped from the jars of poteen. She only knew that when the last reel had been danced and the last farewell speech made, her head was swimming. Perhaps it was the poteen that made Sean laugh so loudly and hold her waist so tightly as they stood around the dying fire to sing a last song to speed Fergus on his journey. How clear and true was his deep voice, as the melancholy notes of "Come Back to Erin" lifted into the night air.

Mary and Fergus disappeared as Fiona had expected. Colin and Bridget had gone to take their young daughters safely home. Waving farewell to the little group still lingering beside the fire, Sean led her away, his arm about her shoulders as though he didn't care if the whole world knew she was his sweetheart.

The poteen had loosened Sean's reserve, and he sang to her as they walked slowly along the dark track leading back to Morning Hill.

> *"Put your darling, darling, darling,*
> *Your darling head my heart above;*
> *Oh, mouth of honey, with thyme for fragrance,*
> *Who with heart in breast could deny you love?"*

"Darling, darling," Fiona answered, stopping in the middle of the roadway. They were beside the haggard, where the dark bulk of the hayricks loomed in the starlight. Her arms went about his neck, her body pressed against his, and her face lifted for his kiss.

His kiss devoured her, as though he had been starved for her all the days they had been apart. Fiona clung to him, fire coursing through her body. All of her aimed at being one with this man. "Come with me, love," she whispered when they broke apart breathlessly.

She ran, clinging to his hand, wanting him with such urgency her body seemed to scream out for him. They stumbled in the darkness, across the graveled courtyard of the stables. Fiona went ahead of him, up the ladder into the hayloft. She fell into the bed of fragrant hay, holding her arms out to Sean as he covered her body with his own.

His mouth tasted of poteen, and she clung to it, savoring his flavor with her tongue. Sean's hands were everywhere, caressing her as they tugged away her clothing. She pulled at his shirt until they lay with her bare breasts crushed against the coarse hair of his chest. Then her skirt was gone, and his trousers, so that at last there was nothing to dull the touch of his hot skin against hers.

"Darling, darling," she repeated, as his mouth spread fire everywhere . . . on her pounding throat, her taut aching breasts, down the planes of her flat stomach, to the soft secret inner thighs. "Oh, Sean . . . please." She arched toward him . . . and gasped with relief at the sense of completion as he entered her.

Sean moved against her, and her body answered his as they ascended a dizzying spiral of sensation. Higher and higher, until her whole body seemed to explode with ecstasy. She heard herself cry out, a long-drawn cry of incredible joy. Then Sean's mouth covered hers to quiet her. Slowly, they drifted down from the heights until they lay utterly spent, their bodies still entwined.

Sean cradled her head on his broad shoulder, reaching out for her shawl to cover them. "Fee, my sweet love," he murmured sleepily.

"Darling . . . darling," she answered, as though she had forgotten all the other words she ever knew. She felt him relax, his heartbeat slowing beneath her head, his breathing deep and even. He was asleep, and she felt herself drifting after him. But she didn't want to sleep. She wanted to savor their loving, to commit every movement and every sensation to memory. As lovely as their joining in the meadow had been after that first sweet pain, it hadn't held the wild and searing power of tonight. It would be like this always now, and she could not bear to be parted from him.

Sleepily, she pressed her lips against his throat and murmured one last time . . . "Darling."

"Miss Fiona! Miss Fiona!"

An urgent whisper penetrated the dim recesses of sleep. The first gray light before dawn gleamed beyond the loft window. Fiona shivered and pulled her shawl about her, suddenly aware that she wore only her chemise. Sean lay sprawled beside her in profound slumber.

Holding the shawl close about her, Fiona peered down the loft opening into Mary's terrified face.

"Oh, please, Miss Fiona. Hurry! Nanny Quinn sent me to find you. Please come before it's light, or there'll be terrible trouble."

"Wait!" Fiona commanded, at once aware of the precariousness of her situation. God only knew what would happen to Sean if they were found like this. She would only be disgraced, but he . . . Quickly pulling on her clothes, she bent over him where he was already stirring sleepily.

"Sean. Darling love, wake up."

"Fiona!" He looked horrified as full awareness came over him, and she wondered how much of last night could be attributed to the poteen.

"I must get back to the house before light," she said, kneeling beside him as he sat up, holding his head with a groan. "Get dressed now, before the stableboys come to feed the horses."

"Oh, dear God, Fee . . . I'm sorry—" he began and she hushed him with a kiss.

Smiling into his eyes, she said, "I love you, Sean McLoughlin. Never forget it." Then she fled with Mary, across the graveled courtyard, through Mama's garden where the colors were muted in the dim light, and up the back stairs to a disapproving silent Nanny Quinn.

Leaving the unhappy Mary to deal with her disheveled and hay-stained clothing, Fiona fell into her bed and was immediately asleep.

When she awakened, the full effects of last night's poteen descended on her. A blinding headache pulsed behind her eyes, and her stomach roiled uneasily.

"I told the Mistress you'd taken a chill," Nanny snapped,

jerking the bedclothes straight. The odor of the toast and tea she'd brought made Fiona gag, and she turned her face away.

Nanny sat down by the bed and stared at her. Suddenly, Fiona wondered why her parents had never dispensed with the services of this uppity retainer. Maybe because Nanny filled the place Mama had never really wanted, mothering Fiona even after she was grown, taking the place of a governess, even a bit jealous of the tutor, Mr. Bean.

Her broad face twisted into a disapproving frown, Nanny commanded, "Now you listen to me, young woman."

"Leave me alone." Fiona pulled the sheet over her face.

"Needn't try to hide from your misdeeds." Nanny kept her voice low, but forceful. "You ain't the first lady of quality to bed with a groom. But you're my own, my little love, and I won't have you ruin yerself for the likes of Sean McLoughlin."

"I love Sean," Fiona said, lowering the sheet to stare defiantly at Nanny.

"Ah, what could you know of love at your age?" Nanny sighed. "Believe an old lady when I say love dies quick when all the world's agin ye."

"Nothing could make me stop loving Sean," Fiona cried, tears starting in her eyes.

Nanny took her hand, stroking it comfortingly. "Dear lass, your parents have it in their minds to wed you to Lord Hadley."

"I hate him!" Fiona burst out.

"He's a gentleman," Nanny protested mildly. "You'd live the life of a lady, among your own kind. It's best you do as Master and Mistress wish, love."

"Never . . . never!" Fiona pounded her fist into the pillow, then collapsed into its creamy linen depths, sobbing. For a long time, Nanny sat beside her, gently stroking her back, until Fiona slept again. Then Nanny went down to the Mistress to report that Miss Fiona was no better and would not be down to dinner.

The dinner party on Friday seemed endless to Fiona. Torn with guilt, she had surprised her mother by assisting with the preparations, and even coming downstairs early to help greet the guests. It was a relief when finally the ladies withdrew to the drawing room to leave the gentlemen to their brandy and cigars.

All evening, Mrs. Reynolds had struggled to conceal her annoyance that Lord Hadley had spent the week at Morning Hill, rather than at the Reynoldses' estate. Settling herself beside Fiona on the settee, she gave her a piercing look and said in a sly voice, "And what do you think of my dear Lord Robert?"

Fiona smothered a giggle. "He's a very proper gentleman," she replied blandly.

"Charming," Mrs. Reynolds insisted. Her small dark eyes searched Fiona's face, as though trying to pry out just what relationship had developed this week. "We'll be taking a house in London next year so Marianne can have her season. Lord Robert has promised to spend some time there with us."

"How nice for you . . . and for Marianne." Fiona's smile was sincere, and she thought Mrs. Reynolds sighed with relief.

When the gentlemen joined them, Fiona noted Mr. Reynolds's face was quite red, and he seemed to be in a temper. While the other gentlemen circulated among the ladies, passing compliments and making innocuous remarks, he planted himself before the fireplace.

"The government will have to take a stand," he said in a voice made loud by too much brandy. "They let Stephens escape from Richmond jail last year . . . now the b——" He caught himself, then continued, "Now he's organizing the Fenians again. Mark my words, there'll be another uprising . . . as bad as 1798."

Mrs. Reynolds left Fiona's side swiftly, taking her husband's arm and murmuring that it was not a subject to be discussed in front of the ladies. Watching the big man's florid face, Fiona thought he was afraid. The Fenian brotherhood, fighting for independence from England, had made the landlords their first target. There had even been killings. Agents and owners. And, she thought, Mr. Reynolds was not well liked by his tenants. Perhaps he had reason to fear the Fenians.

She smiled when Mama quickly took control of the

situation by asking Marianne to perform on the pianoforte. Mr. Reynolds sat down beside his wife, looking sullen and abashed. Fiona would have liked to hear more about the Fenians. Sean would tell her. Her thoughts drifted back to the American wake. How gay everyone had been, with no one afraid they might say the wrong thing . . . everyone easy and comfortable. Looking around at the stiff company resolutely paying attention to Marianne's performance, Fiona wished herself back at the crossroads with the country people, or anywhere with Sean. But Sean had been sent to a neighboring estate on some errand . . . just when she needed him most.

"So glad you're feeling better today," Lord Hadley said, as he and Fiona strolled through the flowering gardens next morning. Sunlight filtered through the oak trees, laying dappled patterns on the garden path.

"Yes," Fiona replied absently, her thoughts elsewhere. She had sent Mary with a note for Sean, only to be told he had gone to Lord Curran's estate outside Dublin to bring back a mare to be bred to Agincourt.

Pausing, Lord Hadley cleared his throat and reached to take her hand in his. "I shall be leaving in the morning."

How cold his hand was, as though he had no blood. She remembered with a pang the feel of Sean's hard, warm hands. "We've enjoyed your visit, Lord Hadley," she replied politely.

"Please, call me Robert," he said with a smile. She nodded, wishing he would release her hand, and wondering why his smile never seemed to extend to his cool gray eyes.

"You're quite enchanting, you know," he said, lifting her hand to press his lips against her fingertips.

Something in her recoiled, and she longed to jerk her hand away. Only inbred courtesy held her back.

"Thank you, my lord." At his arch questioning look, she added lamely, "Robert."

Still holding her hand, he began to stroll again, talking all the while of his estate in England. Only half listening to his description of the beauties and delights of Hadley Hall, Fiona's mind wandered to Sean. When would he be back? Surely the rumor Mary had brought wasn't true, that Lord

Curran had hired Sean as his trainer. As soon as this dull and shallow man departed, she would confront her father and demand that she be allowed to marry Sean. After all, Papa had never denied her anything.

"I shall speak to your father," Robert was saying and Fiona absently replied, "Of course."

"Until later, then." He kissed her hand and hurried toward the house. She wondered why he seemed so pleased with himself.

After tea, Robert went for a last ride on Agincourt, accompanied by Colin and one of the grooms. Fiona had slipped up to her bedroom, and Cedric sent Mary to find her. Her parents wished to speak to her in the library.

Although she was not close to her parents, Fiona was fond of them. It pleased her to see them on the sofa before the fire, holding hands. They were both smiling as though extraordinarily pleased with themselves. There was a short silence. Fiona waited, watching the firelight reflect off the glass-fronted bookcases and gild the rich oak paneling of the room.

Mama rose and embraced her, an extraordinary act for her undemonstrative mother.

"My dear." Her father rose too and kissed her forehead.

"We are so happy, Fiona," her mother added.

Puzzled, Fiona could only stare as Papa began to pace before the fireplace. His face beaming, he rambled on. "It's always been a thorn in my side that my wastrel brother George should inherit my father's title. But now . . . now my only daughter will be Lady Hadley of Hadley Hall. Oh Margaret," he added, turning to his wife, "I've waited a long time for this."

The import of his words slowly dawned on Fiona. A chill of fear ran through her. "What are you saying, Papa?"

"Lord Hadley has asked for your hand, dear," her mother smiled triumphantly. She gave Fiona a puzzled look. "He said he spoke to you."

Fiona gasped, recalling the one-sided conversation in the garden. "Maybe he did . . .." Her voice rose as fear and rage filled her heart. "I never listen to his boring talk. I cannot stand the man, and I will not marry him. What do you know about him anyway . . . except that he has a title?"

"Fiona!" her father thundered, his face mirroring his shock.

"I don't want his bloody title," she cried. "I won't marry him. You can't make me!" Tears spilled from her eyes, coursing hot down her cheeks. Choking back her sobs, she faced her parents defiantly. "I'll marry no man but Sean McLoughlin."

Her mother gasped and sat down on the settee as though thunderstruck.

"Good God!" Papa cried. "Sean McLoughlin . . . the stablemaster's son?"

"I love Sean . . . and he loves me." Dashing the tears from her cheeks, she gathered her strength and faced her parents rebelliously.

"What nonsense!" Papa exclaimed, throwing up his hands and giving his wife a look pleading for her assistance. She could only stare at her daughter in silent astonishment. Seeing that there would be no help forthcoming, he continued. "You're so young to be talking of love, Fiona. For once in your undisciplined life . . ." and he gave his wife a significant look . . . "you will obey your parents. The marriage agreement will be signed this very day. Lord Hadley will go to England to settle some business, returning in a month's time for the wedding to be held here at Morning Hill."

"No! No! No!" Fiona screamed. Didn't her father and mother care about her feelings? Was Papa so obsessed with titles that he would really force her to marry this dreadful man? Fear squeezed her heart, but she summoned all her willful temperament to face them again. "I'll only wed Sean."

"Unthinkable," Papa replied coldly. She had never seen him like this . . . so unmovable and determined. "Even the notion is beneath you, Fiona. We'll hear no more of it."

Reduced to desperation, she flung herself weeping into his arms. It had never failed to work before, but now her father stood very stiff and withdrawn. "Call Nanny Quinn," he said to his wife over Fiona's head. "Tell her Fiona's chill has returned. She should be given a sleeping draught and put to bed."

* * *

She seemed to be floating in space with something strange and menacing nearby . . . something she could not quite recall. The white lace canopy above the bed kept drifting away, and the white linen sheets seemed endless. A lark sang above Cuchulain's ruined castle.

"We will make love in an enormous white bed," she said to Nanny, and wondered vaguely why Nanny burst into tears.

··❧I **CHAPTER 4** I❧··

A misty rain blurred the blue-green Wicklow hills. As misty as her mind, Fiona thought, as Mary and Nanny dressed her. The effects of the sleeping draught lingered, so that she felt groggy and ill. But Lord Hadley was departing this morning, with the Brownes' best carriage to take him to Dublin to catch the packet to England. Her parents had commanded that she come downstairs to say farewell to her fiancé.

"I shan't marry him, Nanny," she said, wishing they would leave her alone. She only wanted to lie down until her head stopped aching.

"Ah, darlin'," Nanny Quinn murmured. "Don't fret now. Wait until you're feelin' better." She straightened the bodice of Fiona's pale green tarletan gown, and stepped back to admire her charge. "A bit of rouge, Mary," she said, noting how pale Fiona's cheeks were.

"Now, love," she continued, as Mary carefully smoothed on the rouge and then patted a strand of bright hair into place. "This morning, you will be polite to Lord Hadley. That's all that's needed. Don't shame your parents. You can fight with them when the man's gone." She sighed. "And I know you always get your way."

Like a sleepwalker, Fiona descended the stairs, with Nanny hovering anxiously on the landing. The carriage waited at the door, Colin and the stablehands were away already, driving the horses Lord Hadley had purchased to Dublin to be shipped to England on the boat.

"My dear." Lord Hadley strode across the great hall

toward her, his tweed greatcoat flung over his shoulders. "I was afraid I wouldn't have a chance to say goodbye, but I'm delighted you're feeling better." He smiled, and Fiona vaguely noted that the smile did not reach his eyes. How strange, she thought, and then he was kissing her hand lingeringly, looking at her with admiration. "Even indisposed, you're quite lovely."

Still holding her hand, he strolled toward the front door. "Take care of her," he said to Papa and Mama, smiling that same cool smile.

"Of course," Papa huffed.

Again, Lord Hadley kissed her hand. "We'll be wed in a month's time," he said. "I shall count the days until my return."

"Everything will be arranged," Papa assured him, glancing at Mama for confirmation. She smiled and nodded. Then there was a flurry of farewells, Papa walking to the carriage with Lord Hadley.

Only when the coachman whipped up the horses and the carriage moved down the beech-shaded avenue, spinning up gravel behind its wheels, did Fiona realize she had not spoken one word.

"I won't marry him," she said to her father when he came back into the great hall.

Papa's face hardened. "You're not well, Fiona. We'll discuss this another time. Nanny . . ." and he turned to the woman waiting at the head of the stairs. "Put her to bed."

When Fiona awakened next morning, the lingering effects of the sleeping draught had worn off. She felt restless and apprehensive, but quite in control of her faculties again. Listening to Mary moving about in her dressing room, she stared up at the lace canopy, considering what she must do.

A decision made, she sat up and called for Mary to help her dress. First thing, she would go to the McLoughlin cottage and find Sean. Surely, he'd returned from Currancourt by now.

Unlike the cottages of many of the tenants, the stable-master's house was neatly whitewashed, its thatch tight. Inside, the stone floor had been swept, and a stew bubbled over the peat fire. A gilt-framed oleograph of the Holy

Family hung above the dresser where the family pottery was arranged. The table and three chairs had been discarded from the kitchen at the mansion, repaired by Colin and cherished by his house-proud wife.

Bridget McLoughlin looked up from the bowl of bread she was stirring as Fiona entered. She was tall for a woman, and big-boned, her gray hair drawn back from her round, sweet face. Her pleasant features crinkled in a smile.

"Miss Fiona. We had it you were sick."

"Fee!" It was the youngest McLoughlin, Dierdre, coming in with a handful of eggs she'd gathered. The two older girls, Maeve and Grainne, worked in the kitchen at the big house now. All of them had been given their names from the Irish legends, for Bridget loved the old tales and was considered a true *shanachie,* or storyteller among her people.

"I'm quite well, Bridget," Fiona replied and winked at Dierdre. "Now that Lord Hadley has departed."

"Colin thought him a haughty man and cruel to the horses," Bridget said, then drew in her breath as though she had spoken out of turn. "They say you're to wed him," she added, watching Fiona intently.

"Idle talk!" Fiona lifted her chin, thinking that it would be, once she had it out with her father. "Where's Sean? Isn't he back yet?"

Something closed off in Bridget's blue eyes. Dierdre turned excitedly to Fiona. "It's coming today, he is. With Lord Curran's mare to be bred. We're cooking for him." And she indicated the stewpot and the pudding steaming away in the stone fireplace.

Joy soared in Fiona's heart. She would wait for him at the gatehouse, to see him before anyone else at Morning Hill, and tell him they must wed at once. Running down the beech-lined avenue toward the great iron gates, she quickly dismissed from her mind the image of Bridget's unhappy face and the pain in her eyes.

But when he arrived, handsome as ever and riding Lord Curran's beautiful bay mare, there was Brock, the gatekeeper, and all the stable hands running to greet him and welcome him back.

Despite the fact that he only raised his cap and nodded to

her, she followed him to the stables. No one else could see the way his eyes blazed when he looked at her. No one could guess at the bonds pulling them together as inevitably as sunrise.

Agincourt waited impatiently in the breeding pen. Sean was soothing the nervous mare, and answering the barrage of questions about the stables at Currancourt. When he looked directly at her and jerked his head toward the house, she sighed and turned away. It wasn't seemly for her to be there and she knew it. Later, they would be together . . . after he'd eaten with his mother and sisters . . . after the late summer darkness had fallen over the vale.

Time dragged through an interminable day. Teatime finally arrived. Agincourt had performed admirably, and Papa was pleased. Lord Curran would be grateful, he said, and went on to catalogue the virtues of his horses. When his monologue drifted to a close, Mama smiled at him. "Lord and Lady Curran will be guests at the wedding, of course."

"Certainly," Papa gave her a self-satisfied smirk. "We'll even invite my worthless brother. Now that he's nearly ruined, he might condescend to visit us. And of course, the fact that our daughter is marrying a lord . . ."

"There'll be no wedding." Fiona's voice was quiet.

Mama patted her hand. "Now, dear. You'll grow used to the idea and in time come to anticipate it. Remember that your parents' marriage was arranged and see how well that turned out."

Margaret had been a spinster even though she was an heiress. Bookish and shy, she nevertheless had refused the fortune-hunting suitors who offered for her in her London season. When her parents and Cedric's hopefully brought them together, she had been drawn to the unhappy younger son, so obviously unsuited to an ecclesiastical career. If there had been no passion in their marriage, there had grown the warm kind of love that outlasts passion.

"Lord Hadley isn't like Papa," Fiona said in a tight voice, a knot of fear growing in her stomach. "His eyes never smile. He's cruel to animals and unkind to the servants."

"What nonsense," Papa blustered. "I've had the best of recommendations for him . . . one of England's oldest noble families. We'll hear no more of it." He rose, throwing his linen napkin on the tea table. "You can help your mother with the guest list."

Fiona saw that he was quite out of sorts with her, and the knot of fear tightened. For the first time in all her life, she knew her father would not give in to her. Oh, he loved a lord. He had embarrassed her more than once, the way he fawned on Lord Curran. The fact that he was the second son and would never be Lord Mountford had rankled all his life. Now, he intended to compensate for that by marrying her to Lord Hadley.

Not bloody likely, she told herself, staring furiously at his bland face. A deep wrenching fear tore at her insides. Somehow, she vowed, somehow she would go with Sean.

"I must write a note to Lord Curran for Sean to take back with him." He turned away with a meaningful look at his wife. "The guest list, my dear . . . Time is short."

Late afternoon sun broke through the clouds and mist, its golden radiance lay across the garden, gilding the green meadows beyond. Diaphanous streamers of light slanted through the fir trees surrounding the little stone chapel on the hillside.

In the morning room, Fiona turned from the window to watch her mother making up the guest list, discussing each entry as though she expected no reply. A great sadness came over her. She would have to go away from this place she loved now, for her parents did not love her well enough to hear her pleas. Only Sean truly loved her. Only Sean, now and always.

A long-ago day flooded her memory. They were children, acting out one of Bridget's tales. This time, it was the story of Dierdre and her lover, Naisi, who fled from Conar, the old king, who intended to make Dierdre his bride. They fled to Scotland and there they were wed. Fiona's eyes stung as she remembered standing beside Sean as his sister Maeve pretended to perform the marriage ceremony. So they had been wed long ago. She would tell him that tonight.

Summer was dying, the late August night had grown chill. Shivering, Fiona hugged the heavy shawl about her as she waited in the hayloft for Sean. Faithful Mary had delivered her note to him, waiting until he answered, "Yes."

She heard his boots on the gravel outside and everything

within her leaped into life. When he stepped off the ladder into the loft, she went into his arms. There were no words, only lips, and arms, and bodies pressing urgently together.

"Darlin' Fee," he said breathlessly when at last their mouths wrenched apart. "I can't care for the wrong of it anymore. I'm sick with wantin' you."

"Then take me," she whispered, turning to spread out her shawl and draw him down beside her. "Take me now . . . my love, my own darling love."

"My ma says you're to wed Lord Hadley."

They lay spent in each other's arms, bodies entwined. Fiona turned her head on Sean's shoulder, kissing his throat and savoring the salt taste of him.

"I'm already wed . . . to you," she murmured, drawing closer so that his coarse chest hair aroused her breasts. The pulse between her thighs began to beat again. "Remember the day we pretended we were Dierdre and Naisi."

In the dim moonlight filtering through the loft opening, she saw his rueful smile. Gently, he smoothed her disordered hair. "It's late for pretending now, love."

"No pretending," she said, kissing him fiercely. "I'll go away with you, and we will marry."

"And where'll we go, Fee?" he asked in a bitter voice. "Lord Curran would turn me out at once if I took you away from here." His arms tightened about her and he groaned in despair. "There's no way out for us, darlin'. But your parents won't force you to marry that bloody English bastard. They've always given you what you wanted. All you have to do is what you've always done with them . . . wheedle and tease."

"Don't laugh, Sean!" The desperation in her voice erased his grin. "The marriage agreement has been signed. Mama is making up the guest list for the wedding. I've tried everything." Her voice dropped, low and bitter. "You know how Papa loves a title."

"Aye." Sean gave a short bark of ironic laughter. "He almost forced me to go to Lord Curran." A note of sorrow came into his voice. "Me own Da had something to do with it, too."

"To keep us apart," she said.

"Aye," he agreed, and fell silent.

The knot of fear grew again in her stomach. Slowly, she moved her hands over his body . . . the hard, hairy chest, the flat planes of his stomach, and down to his hard, hot arousal. At once, Sean turned, covering her body with his as they blotted out the uncaring world with their lovemaking.

Even after they were surfeited, Sean embraced her fiercely, holding her body against his as he turned so they lay side by side, face to face. After a moment, he became aware of her tears falling on his shoulder. Cupping her face in one hand, he looked at her tenderly. Love for her seemed to turn his bones to water.

"Did I hurt you?" he asked softly.

Fiona clutched him to her, weeping wildly now. "I can't bear it," she cried. "I shall die if I have to marry him, lie with him . . . let him make love to me."

Pain shot through Sean, pain so intense he almost cried out. Darling Fee in another man's arms. The thought was unbearable. She was his alone. They had been bound together their whole lives. Nothing would ever part them, he vowed. Not an English lord, nor all the aristocracy in England and Ireland together. Not even the bloody Queen herself. Passionately, he held her, kissing her again and again, his lips tasting the salt of her tears.

Last light gleamed on the waters of the River Dodder when they crossed it at Ballsbridge. Already the Dublin lamplighters were about their work. Gaslights flared along Northumberland Street just as the sun's rays faded from the spire of St. Patrick's and the buildings along the quays of the River Liffey.

Sean's uneasiness in this strange city communicated itself to Fiona where she sat in front of him on Lord Curran's mare. He had been to Dublin only for the Horse Show, it was growing dark, and they must soon find a place to stay.

They had started from Morning Hill before dawn, Fiona creeping down the back stairs to meet Sean beneath the beech trees on the avenue. She carried an old reticule of Nanny's containing one dress and a few necessaries. Perhaps she would never be back, she thought, as Sean lifted her up in front of him and kissed her. Yet, she could not help but believe that once she and Sean were married her parents would forgive her and want her home again.

They had walked much of the way to spare the prize mare. The day had been a lovely adventure, warm with late summer sun, and Sean full of laughter and kisses, singing to her as they walked. Strolling along the old military road, they had passed donkeys pulling creels of turf, two nuns with a black-shawled old woman in a fine red petticoat. Several roadies, ragged and emaciated, had held out their hands for pennies. When none were given, they'd turned despairingly away. In the afternoon, there was a tinker's caravan filled with dirty red-haired children who called nasty words after them. But now, with the dark city around them . . . she shivered, and Sean's arms tightened about her.

"Where did you stay for the Horse Show?" she asked.

"The landlord knows me Da," he answered. "We couldn't stay there."

They had passed the menacing bulk of the Beggarsbush barracks and came out on Grand Canal Road just by the Grand Canal Docks, when Sean said, "We'll try there."

It was quite a different Dublin from the one she had always seen from Curran House on fashionable St. Stephen's Green, Fiona thought as Sean pushed open the scarred doors of the Canalside Inn. She shivered, waiting for him, looking fearfully at the dark figures moving in the shadows along the street.

"There's a stable for the horse," he said, when he came back. "Around back. And the room will do for tonight." He helped her down and kissed her forehead lightly. "Tomorrow, we'll find a better place after I return the mare to Currancourt."

With the mare bedded down and fed, they came in the back door of the inn. Involuntarily, Fiona drew back from the odors of stale food, liquor and tobacco, urine and dried vomit. Sean gave her a worried glance, his arm tightened around her as the fat landlord met them.

"Extry fer the peat, if ye want a fire," he said, and Sean paid him.

It was not such a bad room, Fiona told herself, when

firelight gleamed from the tiny fireplace. The bed seemed acceptably clean. There was a table with a pitcher and bowl, and a tin pot for a commode, and one chair. A narrow window overlooked the stables in the rear.

Sean turned from the fire, looking at her with unhappy eyes. "I'd want better for you, Fee."

"We're together," she said, moving into his arms. "That's all that matters. Tomorrow, you'll return the mare to Lord Curran and find another place to work. Then we'll be married."

Sean kissed her, then looked down at her gloomily. "No priest'll do it . . . and no rector of the Anglican Church, either."

"We'll find a way," she replied, refusing to give in to his melancholy. "Anyway . . ." she added archly, stepping back to smile up at him. "We're already wed, you know. Else why would you have tumbled me in the grass alongside the road this very afternoon?" There had been a singing waterfall in the leafy glade where they stopped to eat the bread and cheese they'd brought. With the mare cropping grass close by, and the sunlight barely filtering through the heavy old trees, they had surrendered to passion.

In spite of himself, Sean laughed, gathering her close against him, his mouth hot and eager against hers. "God knows how I love you, Fee." He ended the kiss with a long sigh. "And the Good Lord forgive me if I've done wrong by you, but I couldn't bear—"

"That I belong to anyone else?"

"Aye." His arms tightened so that her breasts crushed painfully against his chest. "I'd see us all in hell first."

It would be like a wedding night. Fiona smiled as she turned back the bedding. Sean had gone downstairs for tea and food, and she slipped out of her grass-stained gown, a sturdy cotton one she had chosen, knowing it must last. The thin linen nightdress trimmed with handmade lace clung to her slender figure. She put her shawl about her and sat in the chair waiting.

When Sean returned with the tea and two bowls of steaming broth thick with cabbage and potatoes, she could scarcely eat for wanting to lie with him in the waiting bed. It was there in his eyes too . . . the wanting. At last, they could bear it no longer. The tray was abandoned on the hearth, and they were together in the lumpy bed.

There was time now. No chance of being found or interrupted. Only the two of them alone in the world, their bodies joined in passionate abandon.

Fiona awakened slowly in the half-light to the sounds of Sean moving about the room, getting dressed. They had slept but little, awakening again and again in the night to take each other in love. Yawning, she stretched, wincing at the slight soreness of her body, flooded with remembrance of the joy she had shared with Sean.

"Darling," she said, reaching one arm out to him.

He came to sit beside her on the bed. At once, she drew him down into her arms, her mouth hot against his. His tongue responded to hers, his hands caressing her breasts. With a long indrawn breath, Sean broke away.

"I must be off," he said in a shaky voice. "It'll take the day to ride to Currancourt and walk back here." Grinning, he bent to kiss her again. "I'll love ye an extra tonight to make up for it."

"Promise?"

His face softened, and his blue eyes darkened with love. "Promise." He bent to kiss her softly. "Would I had nothin' else to do."

Quickly he stood up, and turned to put on his tweed jacket, the one her father had bought for him for the Horse Show. "I'll pay for the room for tonight," he told her, "since it'll be late when I come back. You'd best stay in. This part of Dublin is . . . well, it's not a place fer a lady t'walk the streets."

Taking a coin from his pocket, he laid it on the table. "This'll buy your lunch, Fee. We'll have supper together."

She sat up in the bed, her heart flooded with love for the tall man standing beside her. "Where did you get the money, Sean?" In all her life, she had never had need of a coin, nor had she seen her father use money. There was always Riggs, the butler, or Morton, Papa's valet, to take care of such things.

Sean shrugged and grinned at her, reaching to pull her into his arms. "I was savin' to buy a mare of me own."

Fiona laughed, tumbling from the bed into his embrace. "And so you did, Mister McLoughlin." She held him, kissing his ear, his throat, the strong line of his jaw, until his mouth took hers in a devouring kiss.

"Oh God!" Sean broke the embrace. "I love you, darling, darling Fee, but I have to go." He paused at the door to look back at her. "Wait for me, sweetheart."

She disobeyed him, of course. It was not in her restless nature to spend the day cooped up in the room at the inn. But she was careful to stay on the streets where she could find her way back. She did not stay long.

It was a Dublin she had never even glimpsed when she rode through it in a fine carriage between Curran House and the Horse Show grounds. The ragged, reeking beggars appalled her, and she shrank from the glances of the hard-eyed women of the streets. Lined old faces stared hopelessly from the broken windows of decaying buildings. Dirty children played on the littered pavements. Rough men looked at her with speculative eyes, and when one dared speak to her, she fled back to the inn.

Alone in her room, she drank the tea she had brought upstairs with her, and ate the last of the bread and cheese from the kitchen at Morning Hill. The low dark room seemed to close in on her, and for an instant she was assailed by nostalgia for home. For Riggs laying tea, and Mama pouring from the elegant silver pot, with the maid bringing scones and jam and plum cake. The squalor and human degradation she had glimpsed in the streets of this slum made the memory more poignant. But Sean had never been at that tea table, and her life was with Sean now and forever.

Darkness crept over the city. The flare of gaslights followed the lamplighter's progress. In the tavern below, the noise of men talking and singing, the clink of glasses, rose to her as she sat by the narrow window, waiting.

Night deepened. Sean did not come. Fiona paced the tiny room. Even if apprehension had not killed her appetite, she would not dare go down to the raucous tavern for her supper. Perhaps Lord Curran had delayed him for some reason. But he would come soon . . . soon.

* * *

49

Damn Lord Curran! Sean thought. The fool had insisted on examining the mare and questioning Sean interminably about her breeding. He had intended the mare remain with Agincourt for several days just to make sure she had conceived, and he was annoyed that Sean had returned her so soon. When Sean told him he intended to be married and would need a place for his wife, Lord Curran had turned quite frosty. He could not expect a place of his own here, His Lordship told him emphatically. After all, he had been employed at Currancourt only a short time. In the end, Sean collected his few belongings and set out on the road to Dublin, with the last of his wages in his pocket.

It had all taken too long . . . the waiting for his money, the listening to Lord Curran's endless complaints. Now, he was walking back into Dublin in the darkness, in the mean unlit streets along the Canal Docks where menace lurked on every side.

Sean quickened his steps. Fiona would be alone, waiting in the room with no money for a fire, afraid and waiting for him. Tomorrow he would look for work, but now all that mattered was to be with her, to hold her, protect and love her.

The sound of his own footsteps echoed back from the dark and silent warehouses lining the street. At the corner, Sean paused, looking around. Had he taken a wrong turn? Surely, he'd come on a pub soon and stop to ask, for there were pubs on every block in Dublin.

Unsure of which way to turn, he looked about. There . . . against the night sky he saw the masts of the ships anchored along the quay. He turned toward them, down the dark street, past the odorous hidden alleyways of the waterfront.

At the sound of running footsteps, he turned, his fists ready. But the blow came from behind, a sudden flashing pain at the back of his head. His legs dissolved under him as he fell face down into the filth of the street. Just as the blackness closed over him, he heard a rough voice mutter, "Bring the bloke along. The longboat's waitin' at the quay."

CHAPTER 5

An insistent knocking at the door awakened her. Fiona stared about the unfamiliar room, disoriented and afraid. She must have fallen asleep from sheer exhaustion toward morning, after the tavern closed and silence fell over the inn. Her dress was rumpled, and she felt chilled and sick.

Stumbling to her feet, she opened the door, all her hopes that it was Sean dashed when she looked into the porcine face of the innkeeper.

"It's another day, madame," he said with a sly smile. "I'll be needin' yer room rent."

At once, she was all too aware of her precarious position . . . a woman alone with no funds. Twopence was all she had left from the coin Sean had given her, far too little for the room rent. Squaring her shoulders, she boldly returned the man's stare.

"My husband's gone to Lord Curran's estate to collect his wages. He'll be back today, and he'll pay you then."

The man gave a snort of harsh laughter. "Not bloody likely." His small eyes gleamed with lust as his glance roved over her body, leaving her feeling soiled and revolted. "Ye ain't the first lady of the gentry to hoist 'er skirts fer a handsome Irish lad. Likely a few pokes satisfied him. He'll be off lookin' fer his own kind now."

Fiona glared at him, hating being at the mercy of this low creature. "Get out!" she demanded. "My husband will be back this morning, and he'll pay you what's owing."

"Hoity-toity, ain't ye?" The man continued to stare at her, licking his fat lips. Fiona stood her ground, giving him a look that was filled with fury. "Wal," he finally conceded, seeing that he was unable to shake her. "He ain't back by noon, I'll be paid one way or another . . . or out you go."

Shaking, Fiona slammed the door and slid the bolt. Tears filled her eyes. "Oh, Sean," she murmured. Despite the innkeeper's insinuations, she knew from her heart that Sean would never abandon her. A sick feeling of dread washed over her. Something had happened to him, something terrible that kept him from her side. Sean loved her as she loved him. Only some dreadful accident could have delayed his return.

The hours wore on as the sun climbed the hazy sky. Fiona's thoughts whirled in frantic circles. She could not leave the inn, for it was here Sean would look for her. But she had no money to stay. Now, she was as desperate as the poorest beggar on the dirty streets outside. As poor as . . . She remembered Bridget telling of the terrible days of the Great Famine, when the potato crops had blighted year after year. The starving people had been forced to pawn their furniture, and even their clothes, for money to buy food. And she remembered going with her mother at Christmastime to take baskets to the poor. Many of the families had no furniture except a few large rocks to sit on, and only the clothing they stood in.

With sudden decision, she drew her extra gown from the old reticule. It was sprigged muslin and far too elegant for these surroundings, but perhaps . . .

"Is there a pawn nearby?" she asked the ancient crone who was sweeping out the tavern.

"A pawn, she says," the old woman cackled. "Be one on every corner in poor Dublin town. Down the street is Paddy's." And she pointed the way, calling after Fiona. "He's a hard one, Paddy is."

Paddy was a cadaverous man whose mean eyes stared at her across the counter in his dim shop. It was hung with used clothing of every description, even shoes, all of it exuding the ripe odors of poverty. Furniture was stacked all in a jumble, covered with dust. The dress she lay on the counter seemed totally out of place.

The pawn man's face tightened. "Yer stole it frum yer mistress, likely."

"It's my own," she replied furiously, edging away from an

old woman in a ragged shawl who came up to stare and touch the gown.

"Can't give much fer goods the police might take frum me."

"It isn't stolen!" Her voice rose in half-hysterical fear that he would not buy.

"I'll give yer a shilling." When she began to protest, he turned away. "Take it or leave it."

She took it, clutching the coin in her hand and leaving behind the gown she had hoped to wear on the day she married Sean McLoughlin.

The innkeeper came around from the bar when he saw her enter the Canalside. Without a word, he took her money, giving her a few coins in change. Enough, she thought, for a turf fire to warm Sean when he returned, and a supper to fill him.

Slipping the shilling into his pocket, the fat man gave her a lascivious grin. "Ye could've kept yer fine clothes, milady, and sold what's between yer legs."

"Keep away from me," she said harshly. "My husband will kill you if you lay a hand on me."

"Husband," he shouted with a snort of laughter. "Husband, indeed. Fer all yer fine airs, yer no better than the rest."

Streetlights along the quays flared into life, making golden circles in the night mist. Fiona sat with her shawl drawn tight about her, staring out into the darkness. One candle lit the room, for she hadn't yet ignited the turf in the fireplace, wanting to save the fire to share with Sean.

At a knock on the door, her whole being leaped with hope. Surely it was him at last. Breathless with longing, she flung open the door. The old crone held a tray with the two bowls of broth and the pot of tea she had ordered earlier, thinking Sean would be here to share it.

Closing the door on the old woman, Fiona set the tray on the table. With a shudder, she drew her shawl tighter against the cold room. Sean would be here soon, she told herself. She would light the fire now to greet him.

She drank some tea and ate one bowl of broth as she watched the fire dwindle and die. The last coals gleamed in the dark as the candle burned down. Utter despair fell over

53

her. Sitting beside the hearth to catch the last of the warmth, Fiona bowed her head on her knees and wept. In all her life, she had never felt so completely alone. Surely Sean was dead, or he would have returned by now. How could she live in this world without him? How could she face another day?

Exhausted with weeping, she crawled into the cold bed and wept again until sleep claimed her.

The innkeeper gave her a knowing look when she passed him at the entrance early next morning. But she refused to acknowledge him as she walked down the street to Paddy's. The fine linen nightdress brought only enough to pay the room rent. Still, she had the one bowl of cold broth from last night to eat, and a halfpenny in her pocket. If Sean were alive, she knew he would come today.

Another night of waiting. She spent the halfpenny for a pot of tea, and the crone warmed the greasy broth for her. Far into the night hours, she sat, staring at the dark window, frozen in grief, too exhausted to weep.

Cold dawn light seeped into the room. Fiona awakened to the hideous certainty that her lover was dead. Sean was gone from her forever, and she wept again. She could only stir from her grieving lethargy when the innkeeper pounded on the door.

"He ain't comin' back," he told her with deadly finality. "Ye've nothin' more to sell, exceptin' yerself." He eyed her speculatively . . . the pale drawn face above a young and lissome body. "I kin arrange that, if yer willin'."

"Get out!" she shouted, furious that he would dare to speak to her that way. "You bloody pig!"

"Me get out?" He made an ugly noise, more threat than laughter. "It's me own inn, lady. And it's you that'll pay, or get out."

"I'm going." Shaking with anger, she picked up the empty reticule and brushed past him. Perhaps Paddy would buy the reticule.

"Ye'd be better off here than on the streets," he shouted after her.

The minute she started walking down the debris-littered cobbled street, she wondered if he was right. Ragged, stinking beggars accosted her, clinging, whining their requests, refusing to believe her when she said she had no money. Rough-looking men eyed her, and one of the hard-eyed street women spat at her. Suddenly, a child leaped from a doorway, tore the reticule from her hand and disappeared into the maze of filthy alleys. Shocked, Fiona stared after him in despair.

"How much?" A big man in seaman's clothes, with an evil seamed face grabbed her arm.

"Take your bloody hand off me!" she cried, and when he dropped her arm in surprise, she fled from him, terrified.

How far she ran, she didn't know, but at last the street came out at the River Liffey. Its waters flowed silver in the mist, the great buildings lining the quays all blurred and dim. At the corner, a policeman sat on his horse, watching the traffic of carts and drays and wagons. In his white helmet and dark uniform he looked so sane and real, she let out a cry as she ran toward him.

The desk sergeant looked at her with cool eyes. He was a short muscular man with thinning brown hair. "Ye've run from home, and now ye wanta go back?"

Fiona nodded miserably, shivering beneath her damp shawl.

"Wal," he commented unsympathetically. "It's lucky ye are if there's a place to go back to. Most lasses come here, there's no place for 'em but the streets."

"I know," she murmured, so filled with pain that even speech was excruciating. Sean was dead, and she had no choice but to go back now to Morning Hill.

"The Bianconi car driver will take a message to my father, Cedric Browne of Morning Hill," she said in a dull voice, adding, "I have no money, but Papa will pay him." She could no longer hold back and silent tears rolled down her pale cheeks.

Sergeant Rourke's eyes softened a little. He pointed to a bench in the corner. "Ye kin wait there, lass."

When the message had been dispatched, the sergeant brought her a mug of tea. "Poor lass," he said. "What happened to the lad what brought you here?"

Tears streamed afresh as she gasped out her story.

"It's best yer goin' home," he told her sadly. "Dublin's a

mean town. If he was abroad at night, with money in his pocket, he's likely with the fishes at the bottom of the river now."

When she broke into uncontrollable sobs, he sighed and patted her bowed head awkwardly. "Now, now, lass. It's best ye not harbor false hopes. It happens a hundred times a night here in the city . . . and him bein' a country lad . . ."

All day, the mist hung over the city. Policemen came and went in the station. Prisoners were hauled into the room, some torn and bloody and mean, some simply ragged and exhausted. They were booked and taken away to jail. Fiona stayed huddled on the hard bench, at last falling into an uneasy doze with her head against the cold wall of the station.

Sergeant Rourke shook her awake, and she saw that it was night again. "I'm goin' off duty now, lass. Ye kin use the lav over there." He pointed. "Here's the rest of the lunch me wife packed."

Tears blurred her eyes. "You are so kind, sergeant."

"I've a lass of me own," he replied gruffly. "Ye'd best not go out on the street. Wait here fer yer Da."

Would Papa come for her, she wondered, watching the sergeant's departure with regret. She knew he would be angry, more angry than he ever had been with her, but she had always been able to smother his displeasure with her hugs and kisses. Her eyes filled again. Surely they would take her back as before, for she was their only child. With Sean dead, she had no one else, she had to count on their love.

Sergeant Rourke awakened her when he came on duty next morning. Struggling up into full consciousness, she stared at his kindly face. "Ye've been here all night," he said, shaking his head sadly. She had slept on the hard straight bench, her shawl clutched about her for the little warmth it brought.

"They'll come for me today," she answered, with more confidence than she felt.

He brought her a mug of hot tea and some bread and butter after she had been to the lav and tried desperately to freshen her clothes and her hair. She had almost finished eating when the heavy oak door of the station swung open, and Colin McLoughlin came in. He went straight to the sergeant's desk.

"Miss Browne?" he asked, his voice harsh.

The sergeant gave him an incredulous look. "You're Mr. Browne?" he asked doubtfully, staring at Colin's rough clothes.

"I'm sent to bring her," Colin snapped.

"Oh, Colin!" Fiona ran toward him, tears pouring down her cheeks, her arms outstretched. His cold and angry face stopped her before she could touch him.

"So ye had yer way," he said in a strangled voice. "Now where's me lad, me own son?"

Violent sobs shook her as she buried her face in her hands. The accusation in his eyes filled her with guilt. Sean was dead, and she was to blame. If she hadn't begged him to go away with her, he would be alive now, alive and well at Currancourt.

"It's not the lass's fault," Sergeant Rourke said mildly. "He was a country lad, with money in his pocket and alone on the streets of Dublin at night."

"Where is he?" Colin shouted, as though unable to contain himself.

"It's only a guess I can give ye," the sergeant replied. "But surely he wouldna have left the lass alone if he could come back to her."

"Aye," Colin answered, standing like a man turned to stone. "Aye. It's dead he is, then, for he loved her more than life." His face sagged with sorrow as he stared into nothingness, shaking his head as though to deny his own words.

"Colin," she whispered, reaching out to touch him, aching with a sorrow doubled now by his. "Colin . . . I loved him truly, and I will never stop loving him as long as I breathe."

His iron reserve broke then. Colin gathered her into his strong arms, holding her with her face against his shoulder as they wept together.

At last he regained control, and he held her away, looking down into her face. He seemed to have aged by years since last she looked at him.

"Ah, lass," he said brokenly. "I could have told ye it would end this way."

·⊰[CHAPTER 6]⊱·

Queasiness came over her again as it had every morning since her return to Morning Hill. Fiona swayed dizzily until Nanny's strong hand steadied her.

"Only three more buttons, love, then you can lie down." She gave Mary a sharp glance as the maid's fingers hurried with the buttons of Fiona's wedding gown. "Hurry up, Mary."

"I can't bear it!" Fiona cried, helpless tears welling in her eyes as the two women eased her down on the bed.

"We bear what we must," Nanny replied steadily, hurrying to straighten the folds of white satin and lace so they would not wrinkle. She and the seamstress from the village had worked night and day to finish this creation, with its soft ruffled shoulder drape and skirt flounces of French lace, as well as the rest of Fiona's trousseau. "Bring a cold cloth for her head, Mary."

The wet cool cloth across her forehead and her eyes was comforting. Hot tears rolled from under her closed lids as the cold sweat gradually subsided. At least she hadn't had to vomit. Nanny had so cleverly concealed her morning sickness that only sympathetic Mary knew of it. Fiona herself hadn't really guessed the cause of it until Nanny asked if her flow was late. Then she realized it hadn't come since that last night in the hayloft with Sean.

With shaking hands, she wiped away the tears. She must gather all her strength now, for today she would marry Lord Robert Hadley and give Sean's child a name.

Her parents had never stopped their planning for her marriage, and they wouldn't, she knew, even if she had the courage to tell them she was pregnant. Oh, they had been angry when Colin brought her home from Dublin . . . angry and shocked and hurt. How they had managed it, she never knew, but her misadventure in Dublin had been kept a secret. And everyone thought only that Sean had returned to Currancourt.

"Colin will say that Sean has gone to America," Papa told her in that awful confrontation in the library. He said the words without emotion, as though Sean's death meant less to him than the death of a good horse. "There's no point saying he's dead when we really don't know," he added defensively when she stared at him with hatred.

"You'll be ruined if the truth gets out," her mother's voice was low and cold. "The staff thinks you went to Dublin to shop with the Reynoldses."

Beyond tears, almost beyond feeling, Fiona only stared dully at her parents, wondering why they loved her so little.

Papa cleared his throat. "There's no reason not to honor your marriage agreement with Lord Hadley. The invitations have already gone out for the wedding."

The words aroused Fiona from her exhausted torpor. "I'll not marry him," she said.

"Of course you will," her father replied sharply.

Her control broke. Tears poured from her eyes. "No," she screamed. "No! No! No!"

"Fiona, dear," her mother began.

"No!" she shouted again. "It's his fault Sean's dead . . . his fault and yours. If you hadn't tried to force me to marry him, I wouldn't have run away, and Sean wouldn't be dead."

Mama paled. With an effort, she straightened her shoulders and turned to her husband. "She's quite exhausted, Cedric. I think we should discuss this later."

As ever, it was Nanny who held her and comforted her. And it was Nanny who finally forced her to face the consequences of bearing a bastard.

"His Lordship ain't a bad sort," she said, cosseting Fiona with tea one morning after the nausea had subsided. "The wee one will have a name and a home and a place in the world." Her eyes held a pained and distant look as she added softly, "It's well I know the hurt of it, love. Wasn't I

Lord Burton's bastard to all in the village? And never heard the end of it till I came here."

"Oh, Nanny, how can I marry anyone but Sean when I shall never stop loving him?" Fiona sobbed.

"It's the child you must think of now, little love," Nanny murmured, soothing her brow with a work-worn hand. "Givin' his babe the disgrace of bein' a bastard won't bring your Sean back."

So it was that she told her parents she would no longer oppose the marriage. They joyfully went forward with wedding plans, unaware that she carried Sean's child and certain that this would be the best thing for their willful daughter.

Now, as the queasiness drifted away, Fiona stirred restlessly. Sitting up on the bed, she listened to the low murmur of Nanny and Mary talking in the dressing room. Outside, the crunch of carriage wheels on the gravel drive told of the arrival of more wedding guests. Belowstairs, the kitchen was bustling with preparations, and the great hall was cleared for the dancing afterward.

Carefully, she stood up, testing her strength, glad that the nausea had subsided for today. Sitting down on the window seat, she looked out into the yard. Fine carriages were lined up before the stables, grooms hurrying to unhitch and care for the horses. From the front of the house came the murmur of the guests greeting her parents and her bridegroom's family.

Reluctantly, she lifted her gaze to the little chapel on the hillside . . . gray rock against the inky green of the fir trees. The stone pathway was edged now by pots of brilliant fuchsia plants from her mother's greenhouse. The green of the beech and oak trees was fading into autumn's yellow. It was a fair day, as her mother had hoped. The sky was an azure blue, with only little wisps of cloud.

A fair day to be wed to a man I will never love, she thought sadly. Clasping her hands against her abdomen, she held Sean's child growing there. That child would be her life now. Safe with a name and a place, and a mother who would love it doubly for its lost father. She must be strong now. With Nanny's help, she could conceal her condition for a month at least, and then all would be well. Today she must simply endure. Perform the necessary motions for the wedding, say the right words. Simply endure until it was over and not think about tonight.

Someone was riding in the paddock behind the stables. Broad shoulders, straight back, an old tweed cap on his head. "Sean!" she gasped, and pain lanced through her, almost unbearable in its intensity. Then the rider turned and came toward her at a slow canter. It was Colin.

Fiona bent her head against the windowsill, and wept.

Like a sleepwalker, Fiona descended the stairs. Mary carried the long satin train of the wedding gown, arranging it carefully at the foot of the stairs.

Papa waited, erect in his black formal wear, holding his arm for his daughter's hand, his round face gleaming with pride, bald head shining in the light from a hundred candles in the Austrian cut-crystal chandelier. Mama, dressed in pink silk velvet, her hair arranged with unaccustomed intricacy, glowed with tearful joy. And beside her, Fiona's future sister-in-law, Martha Hadley, to whom she'd taken an instant dislike. At once, she looked away from Martha's pinched shrewish face, her elaborately arranged drab blond hair, and the gray eyes as cold as those of her brother.

Slowly, the wedding party paced past the waiting guests, through the front door and along the stone pathway to the chapel.

Lord Hadley, would she ever be able to call him Robert, waited at the altar with the Reverend Mr. Moore, vicar at the Hadley estate, who had come to perform the ceremony at the insistence of the Hadley family. Robert looked every inch the nobleman in his formal clothes of black superfine, his blond hair and moustache bright in the dim light.

The music of the chimes filled the tiny chapel, with half the guests outside on the path. The last notes died away, and the vicar began speaking. These were the words she had meant to say with Sean McLoughlin. The thought filled her with such pain, that it was only with an effort she could control her voice and make her responses.

Then it was over, they were moving back down the pathway, with people leaning to congratulate them, smiling, laughing. The tenants and the stable hands and country folk from the village stood about on the lawns, applauding, enjoying the spectacle the gentry paraded for them.

Inside the great hall, a string trio brought from Dublin played for dancing. Tables were laid in the dining room with the most elegant of food ordered out from Dublin and from London. Riggs, the butler, presided over it all, cueing the footmen and the maids who poured champagne.

Robert held her hand in the crook of his arm, his other hand covering hers . . . smiling and bowing to the guests. Then there were toasts . . . her father, Robert . . . and champagne glasses refilled again and again. It all became a blur.

"You're looking pale, dear." It was her Aunt Elizabeth, Papa's sister, come from her home in London with her newly knighted husband, Sir Reginald Mercer, and her young son, James.

"Come sit with me, Fiona. I want us to know one another." With one arm about Fiona's waist, Elizabeth guided her to a chair in the cool, flower-filled conservatory. Potted palms partially hid them from the other guests. The dancing had not begun, but the trio played softly against a background of chatter.

The music and the hum of voices faded dizzily. Fiona clung to her aunt's hand. She drew in her breath painfully, scarcely aware of her surroundings. Twelve-year-old James had followed them, staring in utter adoration at Fiona.

"Here, James . . ." Elizabeth drew her kerchief from her bosom. "Wet this in cold water and bring it back to me." The boy scurried away. "Weddings are such frightful affairs," she continued, patting Fiona's hand. "I'm sure you're quite worn out."

James was back at once. The cold kerchief applied to her wrists and the back of her neck revived Fiona. Desperately, she thought, she must stay in control. Only a few hours now. Her mind recoiled from the thought of the wedding night to come.

"Thank you, Aunt Elizabeth," she murmured. "I'm quite recovered now."

"You're so lovely, Fiona. I do wish your father had given you a season in London next year instead of hurrying you into marriage so young."

Fiona smiled wanly. "I'll be seventeen next month. Perhaps he thought I wouldn't have another chance."

"Nonsense," her aunt replied in a spirited tone. "Even Cedric must have been aware that you're quite a catch. As an only child, you'll inherit Morning Hill, as well as your mother's income." When Fiona did not reply, Elizabeth continued in an ironic vein. "Perhaps that's what piqued Lord Hadley's interest."

"And that is why he married me?" Fiona asked, looking into her aunt's stout kindly face.

"I doubt it, dear. You're very lovely, you know."

"He doesn't love me," Fiona replied fiercely. "And I detest him."

"Oh, my dear." Elizabeth took her hand in a plump warm one loaded with jewels. "Be patient. You can make a good life for yourself as Lady Hadley, and," she paused, quickly adding, "you will have the protection of his name."

Did her aunt guess her condition, Fiona thought in sudden panic. Dear God, no one must know.

There was a long silence, broken by Elizabeth clearing her throat. "I'm pleased to be with Cedric again. It's been far too long." Smiling fondly, she glanced at her son standing nearby. "And of course, James is quite infatuated with you."

"I'm glad you came, Aunt Elizabeth," Fiona said, warming to the woman. "Father was quite hurt when his brother, Lord Mountford, refused."

"Dear George," Elizabeth's voice was sarcastic. "He thinks we're all beneath him now that he's consorting with Dukes and Princes." Her voice fell to a whisper. "And running through his fortune for the pleasure."

She sighed, and patted Fiona's hand. "You must come to visit us in London, my dear." Smiling complacently, she added, "Reggie's just been knighted by the Queen, you know, for his services during the monetary crisis."

"Lord Hadley doesn't have a London house, I'm afraid," Fiona replied.

"No, indeed," her aunt sniffed. "It's said he sold it to pay his gambling debts."

Fiona's eyes widened. "Oh, Aunt," she murmured. "Surely not."

"Perhaps not," Elizabeth conceded. "Perhaps it's only idle gossip . . . not to be repeated. After all, the Hadley title and the Hadley fortune are very old. At any rate, we'll have you down for the season next year."

Fiona's heart contracted painfully. When next year's season came, she would be heavy with Sean's child, in a distant and fearsome place called Hadley Hall.

Her parents had redecorated this suite for the wedding. The large bedroom, with its mauve velvet draperies and fine mahogany furniture, overlooked the gardens. On either side, there was a dressing room. Fiona stood in hers, cold as a marble statue, letting Mary and Nanny undress her.

In the night beyond, she could hear the voices of the departing wedding guests and through the windows see the grooms running ahead with torches to light the road for the carriages. From a distance, the sound of a fiddler indicated the country folk were still celebrating the wedding of the master's daughter.

The white wedding dress fell about her feet, a mass of gleaming satin and lace. Then the underclothing . . . and Mary lifted a nightdress of finest China silk and Alençon lace over her head. She shivered as it fell about her body.

"It will be all right, little love," Nanny whispered as she tucked the fine linen sheets about her and bent to kiss her forehead.

Then she was alone in the vast bed, in the dim room, with a silver candelabrum glowing on the table. Bitterness welled in her heart. She was trapped forever now, lost in a world without Sean McLoughlin. Closing her eyes tightly, she tried to stem the tears.

Sounds in Robert's dressing room awakened her from a light doze. She heard him curse at his valet, his voice slurred with drink. Then he stumbled into the room, reeling, holding onto the furniture drunkenly as he made his way toward the bed.

Without a word, he threw back the sheets and climbed in beside her. In the faint candle glow, she saw that his blank glassy eyes did not even focus on her. Pulling her nightdress up above her breasts, he began to fondle them roughly. She cringed away from him in pain, but he held on to her, now thrusting his hand between her legs, hurting her again. He was breathing hard now, and he heaved himself on top of her. The hard length of his erection burned against her thigh. At once he ejaculated, hot liquid spilling over her legs and on the sheet. With a groan, he rolled off her and lay back on his pillow, mouth open, snoring heavily.

Fiona lay rigid beside him, her insides heaving in sick revulsion. It will be all right, Nanny had said, but it would never be all right. To have known the love of Sean McLoughlin, and now to lie with this drunken animal who could not even complete the act. Bile stung her throat as she stared at him in disgust.

Quickly slipping from the bed, she went into the dressing room where she washed herself and dressed in a clean gown. Dear God, how she hated him, she thought, looking at him through the open door. How could she ever lie with him again? Nanny had said to be careful, for he would expect a virgin. What difference would it make to this drunken fool, and how would he ever know?

Her eye fell on Nanny's sewing basket. Deliberately, she took a needle from the pincushion. Beside the bed, she pricked her finger and leaned over to squeeze a few drops of blood onto the wet spot of spilled semen on the sheet.

Taking a wool throw from the foot of the bed, she blew out the candles and lay down on the velvet chaise. Her whole being seethed with emotion: hatred for Robert Hadley, anger at her parents, and grief. "Ah, Sean," she whispered into the darkness, and her heart seemed to burst with pain.

·❧ CHAPTER 7 ❧·

The morning they sailed from Dublin was misty, with a heavy sea. Almost at once, the pitch and roll of the packet boat made Fiona desperately ill. Less sympathetic than annoyed, her husband escorted her into the salon. Between bouts of retching, she lay on one of the couches, administered to by Martha's maid. Outside, Lord Robert stood at the rail, smoking his pipe and gazing toward England as though he could hardly wait to get there. Wrapped in heavy tweeds, Martha and the Reverend Mr. Moore paced the deck together, obviously invigorated by the icy air and the heaving sea.

The maid, a tight-lipped Welshwoman, emptied the basins and bathed Fiona's face without a word. Lying back against the cushions, Fiona closed her eyes tightly, no longer caring who might see the tears slipping down her cheeks. If only Nanny Quinn were here. From the beginning, she had assumed Nanny would go to England with her. Mary wanted to stay in Ireland and wait for Fergus, but Nanny would never desert her. Neither she nor Nanny had a say in the matter.

"You're grown now, Fiona, a married woman," her father had said coolly. "It will be easier for you to adjust to your new life without Nanny to spoil you as she has always done."

"But I will have no one," Fiona answered in a small, hopeless voice.

"Lord Robert and I have already discussed this," was the reply. "He will provide all the maids you need at Hadley Hall."

"He didn't want Nanny to go," Fiona said flatly, adding one more resentment to the growing accumulation she held against her husband.

Her throat ached with loathing when she thought of how pleased he had been to see the blood on the sheet the morning after their wedding. And how the next night he had actually accomplished consummation. He had hurt her terribly, perhaps because he had been in such a hurry. Or perhaps, she told herself sadly, it was because she had no desire to share her body with him and could not welcome him as she had welcomed Sean.

He was a stranger to her still, after nearly a week of marriage. She had hoped he would be kind, so that their life together could be endured. While he was not truly unkind to her, she seemed to mean little more to him than his valet. She was merely someone else whose purpose in life was to accommodate His Lordship.

"We're coming in to Holyhead now," Martha said in her clipped voice, standing in the doorway of the salon, easily balancing herself against the roll of the ship. "Clara, help Lady Hadley get ready to disembark." She turned at the doorway to add, "Robert has ordered a special train to take us down to Brookfield. A terrible extravagance . . ." With a disapproving frown, she was gone.

The rattle and sway of the train did little to assuage Fiona's continuing nausea. When the footman opened a picnic hamper of cold chicken and ham, she had to leave the compartment.

Lights of little villages slipped past the train windows and then the massed lights of Manchester as the train roared through the stinking city. They were in the country again. She could tell by the odors and the depth of the darkness beyond. Then the uniformed conductor came through, smiling obsequiously at Robert and saying, "Brookfield right ahead, Your Lordship."

The station was small, with the village of Brookfield dimly seen by gas- and torchlight. Carriages were waiting, footmen and grooms hurried about gathering up the baggage.

Robert took her arm and held it tightly against his side. His voice was low and stern. "You must remember, my dear, that you are now Lady Hadley. This is the first time my people have met you, and however you are feeling, I expect you to act the part of a lady. Head up now . . . smiling and gracious. Come along."

Fiona caught Martha's sardonic glance as Clara handed her the vial of smelling salts. Determinedly fighting her queasiness, Fiona thought she would not use the vial, nor would she give Martha satisfaction by behaving badly before the villagers and servants who had come to cheer Lord Hadley and his bride.

But she clung desperately to Robert's arm as they walked slowly from the train to the waiting carriage. Forcing a smile, she kept her head high, glancing around at the people who shouted greetings and good wishes from the crowd.

Inside the carriage, she leaned her head back against the soft leather cushions with a sigh of relief. Robert gave her an unsympathetic glance. "The staff at Hadley Hall will be waiting to greet you," he told her. "It's even more important that you make the right impression with them. Servants must know at once who is in control."

Numb with pain, she nodded. It was harder than she had guessed to cling to the thought of the child growing inside her. Sean's child, who would make her life worth living again. Far from all familiar things, in a strange country with strange people who cared nothing for her, the child seemed an impossible dream, as impossible as her dreams of happiness with Sean.

Soon Robert was snoring, his head thrown back against the cushions, his mouth open. In the darkness of the rocking carriage, Fiona gave way to tears, ignoring Martha and the Reverend who sat opposite. If only she hadn't been so afraid, if only she had stayed in Dublin. Surely, it would have been better to join her lover at the bottom of the River Liffey than to live the life that stretched bleakly ahead of her.

The hounds set up a racket when the carriages rolled down the long drive to stop before an enormous house silhouetted against the night sky. Torches gleamed through the darkness. Dozens of servants waited to greet them, grooms to take the horses and carriages, footmen and maids for the baggage.

"Are you quite ready, my dear?" Robert asked, as he awakened from his nap and stretched.

Fiona unplugged the vial of smelling salts and took a quick whiff. With her kerchief, she wiped her face, hoping there were no traces of tears remaining.

The staff was lined up in the great hall, all starched black-and-white uniforms. First the butler and the house-keeper, who eyed Fiona with suspicion, but greeted Martha effusively. The footmen . . . the maids . . . the cooks . . . it seemed to Fiona the line was endless. None of the names registered through her exhaustion. She managed to smile and nod to each of them, always aware of the air of hostility that hung like a presence in the hall.

A log fire blazed in a huge, elaborately manteled fireplace flanked by leather-covered sofas. A gleaming refectory table was centered by a massed bouquet of chrysanthemums. The rich oak paneling, the plastered ceiling beams, the wide sweep of the carpeted staircase rising to the second floor, all spoke of an ancient and wealthy family.

Why had Robert married her, Fiona wondered as she took in the splendor of Hadley Hall. Surely there were others available, girls with titles and fortunes to bring him. Or had Aunt Elizabeth's careful words hidden more than they told? If he had indeed gone through his fortune, then the generous marriage portion her parents had provided and the inheritance from her grandfather would certainly entice him.

She was too tired to think of it. When the servants had all been presented to their new mistress, her husband turned to her and said, "We'll change for dinner now."

It was a bitter struggle to subdue the tears that threatened. Surely, he would not expect her to preside at the dinner table after the horrendous crossing from Dublin. He knew how ill she had been. The old willful Fiona flared inside her. Once they were in their bedroom, she would simply refuse to come down for dinner.

The bedroom was enormous, with paneled walls painted a pale ivory. The bed hangings and the cover were of blue damask with rich silk fringe. At the windows hung draperies of velvet in a matching shade of blue. All the furniture was mahogany, elaborately carved and ornamented.

Before she had a chance to speak, Robert said in a frosty tone, "You should have said something to the servants, my dear. Thank them for the welcome and all that. It is expected here in England."

The words brought a flush of embarrassment to her cheeks. He could have told her that ahead of time, she thought resentfully. And there was no need to bring it up now, with his valet laying out his dinner clothes, and the maid named Kate who had been assigned to her busily unpacking.

"You must remember," he continued in the same overly patient but slightly annoyed manner, "This isn't Ireland, and we don't treat the servants as part of the family."

Resentment roiled in her. How dare he treat her like a child, chastising her in front of the servants? Forcing herself to keep silent, she sat down on the blue damask chaise.

Gathering all her courage, Fiona looked up at her husband as he slipped his arms into the coat his valet offered. "I shall have some tea and toast here, Robert. I'm sick and exhausted and I simply cannot go down to dinner."

"Nonsense," he replied brusquely. "It's expected of you."

"Nevertheless," she answered in a tight voice, "I will not go down with you." Suddenly her lips trembled and her eyes stung. "I would have expected my husband to care more for my feelings."

He looked at her with eyebrows raised above those cool gray eyes, and she knew suddenly with certainty, and for all time, how little he truly cared for her. The threatened tears spilled down her face.

"Oh very well," he exploded in an annoyed voice. "Have Kate bring your tray up here." The gray eyes hardened as he looked down at her. "I won't allow this kind of defiance again, Fiona. As my wife, you are to do what I ask of you, at all times, and regardless of your personal feelings. Is that clear?"

Turning on his heel, he left the room, the taut carriage of his tall figure shouting his annoyance. Fiona caught the significant look exchanged by the valet and the maid. A deep and painful loneliness settled over her. In all of this great mansion, there was no one who loved her, no one she could call friend.

down the hallway and through the oak-paneled library. Again the indulgent smile, and Fiona thought that *she* did not know Robert at all. "Hunting and horses are his passions, and he couldn't stay in the city for long, especially after our father died and the title came to him."

The baying of the hounds and the rattle of hooves on the drive came through the open window. "I do believe the hunters have returned," Martha said. "I'll ring the kitchen." Then she seemed to catch herself, and with obvious condescension turned to Fiona. "Oh, sorry, I suppose that's your prerogative now."

Fiona bit back a sharp reply. "Go right ahead, Martha dear," she said coolly. "You've had much more experience at this than I."

It was after noon before the hunters finally rode away. They were all near neighbors to the estate, and all great drinkers, to judge by the number of empty port and claret bottles the maids removed from the dining room.

Martha was closeted in the morning room with the housekeeper, and she had not invited Fiona to join them. Ringing for a servant, Fiona asked that a fire be laid in the library. There, she closed the windows and searched the shelves for something to read. There was little but ancient history books, stud books, and some romantic novels she suspected belonged to Martha. Restlessly, she paced the room, trying to not feel sorry for herself. But, staring into the blazing log fire, she thought of a tiny turf fire in a room at a Dublin inn . . . and Sean. As always, the thought of him filled her with almost unbearable pain. It was all she could do to keep her countenance when her husband came in and said, "Oh, there you are, Fiona."

He was obviously exhilarated by the hunt and, she thought, perhaps too much port. "Would you like to see the stables?"

It was the first gesture of welcome he had made to her since their arrival at Hadley Hall, and she seized on it. "I'd love to."

While they waited for a maid to bring her shawl, she asked about the horses shipped from Morning Hill, how they had survived the ocean voyage. To her surprise, he seemed to have forgotten them, but promised they would have a look at his purchases.

They went out through the French doors leading to the formal garden, a maze of clipped hedges and green lawns. Hadley Hall was even more enormous than she had guessed last night. Its three stories were crowned by stepped gables and steep roofs, the brick-and-stone walls softened by ivy and age. Situated on a slight rise, it looked down on the surrounding parkland of meadows and fields dotted by huge oak and beech trees. The wooded scene seemed endless, with only the roof of the dower house showing through the trees, and the faint gleam of the distant river.

A shrub-edged walk beneath a row of chestnut trees led to the stables. They passed the kennels, where the hounds lay sleeping in exhaustion, and the kennelmaster touched his cap to them. The long row of stables had been newly painted white, with green trim about the doors and windows. In the paddock beyond, horses grazed and frolicked.

"Where are the new horses?" Robert asked a stableboy who was cleaning out a stall.

"Mr. Holt put 'em at the end, yer Lordship," the boy replied, touching his cap. "Danny's workin' with 'em."

As they rounded the corner and came on the exercise yard, Fiona saw that Danny was having trouble. She recognized the horse. Agincourt's offspring always bore the elegant stamp of their sire. The horse reared away from the trainer, throwing its head, then kicking out behind. Danny clung to the reins, trying desperately to soothe the furious animal.

"Bloody fool!" Robert shouted. "I pay you to train horses, not let them get the best of you." Stepping forward, he pulled both reins and riding crop from the trainer's hands. Fiona suddenly realized that her husband had indeed indulged too heavily in port at the hunt breakfast this morning.

When the horse did not respond to his sawing at the reins, Robert's face flushed with anger, his eyes glittered furiously. He jerked on the reins so violently that the foam about the animal's mouth stained red. Lifting the riding crop, he began to beat the horse about the head, jerking the head down to meet his blows.

Horror poured through Fiona. She had never seen a horse handled in such a brutal manner. At Morning Hill, they were trained with gentleness and love. The sight clogged her throat with bile. She stood stunned for a moment before she grabbed at the reins and cried out. "Stop it! Stop it! For God's sake, Robert . . . stop!"

He stopped only because the poor creature had quieted, standing trembling, its mouth edged by bloody foam.

Throwing the reins to the trainer, Robert gave him a whack across the shoulders with the riding crop. "Do I have to show you your job, you bloody idiot?" he shouted. "That's how you deal with an unruly animal. Remember it!"

Turning on his heel, he stalked off toward the house, leaving Fiona to stare in pity at the trainer and his ruined animal. Slowly, she moved after her husband. Her heart seemed frozen within her. What kind of man was this her parents had married her to against her will? Behind that cool and detached façade, she had glimpsed a penchant for drunken violence that left her appalled and frightened. How could she ever manage to survive living with him, being his wife, an appendage to his life with no real purpose but breeding?

In the weeks that followed, Fiona was made aware over and over that, although she was Lady Fiona Hadley, she was not the mistress of the manor. Martha's occasional remarks that "perhaps this is your job now," did not lead to her relinquishing any of her power in the household. Very well, Fiona told herself, let Martha run the house. It's nothing I care to do anyway. I shall have my horses . . . and eventually my child.

Having made that decision, she broached the subject of the horses to Robert one night as they prepared to retire. "I'd like to have my own horses, Robert, and my own groom, if you don't mind." She looked him full in the face, ready to defy him if he should deny her request.

Robert had just come in from his dressing room, wrapped in a purple velvet robe against the chill of the autumn night. Firelight shimmered off the blue damask hangings and the crystal candelabra.

To her surprise, he smiled indulgently. "As Lady Hadley,

that's certainly your right." He patted her shoulder. "We'll choose them tomorrow, if you like."

Happiness welled in her, only to be dashed when he turned and added, "Of course, as soon as you become pregnant, I shall have to insist that you not ride at all." Stroking his moustache, he arched an eyebrow. "Can't endanger the heir, you know."

She watched as he blew out the candles and took off his robe. A little ray of hope rose in her. Perhaps they could learn to care for each other just a little. Robert was not deliberately unkind except when he drank too much. There had to be some kind of understanding between them if they were to spend their lives together.

When he lay beside her, she turned to him, determined to make the effort. She kissed him tenderly, even though she found the scratchy moustache and the stale taste of port unpleasant.

When he began to knead her breasts in that rough way which brought her no pleasure, she took his hand in hers. Hesitantly, she murmured, "Please, Robert . . . touch me here . . ." And she guided his hand down her hips to the warm moist spot between her thighs.

He did not reply, but drew his hand away. Holding her shoulders against the pillows, he thrust into her, and she gasped at the hurt of it. A few more violent thrusts and he was finished, groaning and rolling off her, breathing heavily.

Firelight flickered on his relaxed face, the eyelids closed. All the nights she had wept in pained frustration, while he slept a satisfied sleep, rolled back into her mind. She had tried, truly tried to care for him, and now she felt only loathing for this man she had married. Anger swept over her in bitter waves.

Suddenly, she sat up, throwing the covers back, startling him awake. "What . . .?" he muttered sleepily.

"I'm sick of it!" she cried, throwing a pillow across the room. Eyes blazing, she turned on him. "My father's stallion, Agincourt, cared more for the mares he covered than you care for me. There's no love in it. You're simply servicing me."

At once she regretted the words when she saw the fury rise in his face. His eyes were like gray ice as he reached across the bed and slapped her so hard her head snapped back. Rising from the bed, he threw on his robe.

"You talk like a bloody Irish whore," he shouted. "You're my wife, and I'll do with you as I please."

He started toward the connecting door between their bedrooms, then turned, looking at her with something akin to hatred. "Is your flux late?" he demanded.

"Yes," she answered, lifting her head, deliberately dropping her hand so that he could see the scarlet imprint of his palm on her cheek.

"Thank God that's taken care of." He stalked through the doorway and slammed the door behind him. She heard the bolt slide in the lock.

···❦[CHAPTER 8]❦···

"Why is it taking so long?" Fiona gasped the words, looking up through sweat-bleared eyes as the midwife wiped her face with a cold damp cloth.

"You've only been in labor eight hours, my lady," the midwife said in matter-of-fact tones.

"A mare delivers in an hour," Fiona protested. She sucked in her breath as another pain cramped through her. "Oh God! I didn't know it hurt so much."

The windows of the birthing room were closed against the fine spring day, and a fire roared in the fireplace. She had protested the heat and asked that the windows be opened, but both midwife and doctor assured her it was important to keep the room as warm as possible.

Now, the doctor stood up at the foot of the bed where he had been examining Fiona. He was a short stout man, with kind eyes. Smiling at her, he said, "You aren't a mare, my lady . . . and this child will not be a colt."

In spite of the pain rolling over her, Fiona smiled back. "How long?" She almost begged him to say it would be soon.

"It's hard to say with a first baby," he replied.

"And this one is early," the midwife added quickly. Fiona caught the knowing glance they exchanged.

Of course it wasn't early, but Fiona was sure neither of them would tell Robert so. It would be like accusing His Lordship of taking his marriage privileges before the ceremony.

"Take the straps now." The midwife placed them in her

hands. "They'll help you push harder, and we'll soon have the babe in your arms."

Soon . . . soon, Fiona thought, through a haze of agonizing pain. Soon Sean's child would lie beside her, and her life would begin again. The loneliness would be ended.

In the months of her pregnancy, her husband had been polite, but he never came to her bed again. There was little to occupy her time, for Martha ran the house and she had been forbidden to ride. She took long walks, talking to the child within, and sometimes weeping for its lost father.

Drenched with sweat, racked with pain, she pulled on the straps and pushed . . . again and again. There was a great tearing pain, and she heard a high wailing cry.

"A girl," said the midwife, the falling tone of her voice indicating her disappointment, as she turned to hand the babe to the nurse.

"If it weren't for girls, there would be no boys," the doctor replied in a jocular vein. But Fiona knew from the midwife's long face that Robert would have been more generous had she delivered a son and heir.

Pain began to subside. The midwife directed the cleaning up, and the doctor stepped to the basin to wash his bloody hands. "I'll tell Lord Hadley," he said, and the midwife nodded in eager agreement.

"Bring her to me," Fiona demanded when the bed had been changed and the maid had dressed her in a clean bed gown.

"Nurse will care for her," the midwife replied, gathering her tools into a worn leather bag. "Your husband asked me to bring a wet nurse from the village, and she's waiting in the kitchen."

"Send her away!" Fiona sat up in the bed, wincing at the pain, furious that she had not been consulted. "My daughter will have no wet nurse. I intend to nurse her myself."

"My lady!" the midwife said in shocked tones, staring at her wide-eyed. "It just ain't done. Not a lady in your position."

"Bring her to me at once," Fiona shouted, suddenly terrified that she might be deprived of the child.

The midwife rolled her eyes at the nurse as though to say,

what can you expect from someone raised in the wilds of Ireland. But the nurse obediently laid the tiny bundle in Fiona's arms.

Carefully, Fiona turned back the blanket and looked into her daughter's face. Like the kittens back at Morning Hill, she thought with a smile. The tiny eyes were screwed tightly shut and a soft mewling sound came from the rosebud mouth. Freed from the blanket, tiny fists made little circles in the air.

As she left, the midwife paused at the door. "I'll send the wet nurse up," she said. "The maid and the nurse will stay with you too."

Anger flared in Fiona, and her voice rose. "You bloody fool, didn't you hear me? I'll not have a wet nurse. Send her away."

The woman's expression seemed to say, we'll see about that, and Fiona knew she would report the exchange to Robert.

Peaceful silence descended on the room. The maid and the nurse stood stiffly, watching Fiona with wary eyes. The crackle of the fire and the soft murmur of the baby were the only sounds. A faint odor of blood and sweat lingered still. Fiona longed to have the windows open, but if it might harm her babe, she would leave them closed.

Searching the rosy little face for some resemblance to Sean, she decided that would come later. Now, the baby's fine hair was a light sheen of gold over her softly pulsing head. Suddenly, the eyes opened and seemed to look deep into her own. A sweet and precious sense of bonding flowed between mother and child.

"I love you, little one," Fiona murmured, gently kissing the tiny face. Silently, she added, I love you for the man who fathered you, for the love we bore each other that will never die.

Tears stood in her eyes, as she looked into the baby's dark unfocused eyes. The nurse's voice startled her. "Have you chosen a name?" she asked.

"Only for a boy," Fiona replied wryly. "And that was no choice, for he'd have been named after all his ancestors."

Looking into the baby's sleeping face, she asked silently, "What shall I name our child, Sean? Will she have your gift for song, and your loving heart?" The pain of loss that came over her was as fresh and wounding as the day she knew Sean was dead. But as she thought of him, an answer seemed to come from out of the past. Indeed, the Irish were a race of songsters, and Sean McLoughlin had been as fine as any of them. There was a song he'd sung that golden day on their way to Dublin.

> "*Kathleen Mavourneen, the gray dawn is breaking,*
> *The horn of the hunter is heard on the hill;*
> *The lark from her light wing the bright dew is shaking;*
> *Kathleen Mavourneen, what slumbering still?*
> *Or hast thou forgotten how soon we must sever?*
> *Oh, hast thou forgotten this day we must part?*
> *It may be for years, and it may be forever;*
> *Then why art thou silent, thou voice of my heart?"*

The sad, prophetic words brought the tears from Fiona's eyes. Pressing her lips to the baby's cheek, she murmured, "Sweet Kathleen . . . you will be the voice of my heart now."

"Katherine?" Robert said, when he came upstairs. "A proper enough name." He seemed ill at ease, but had done the expected thing by kissing Fiona's forehead with his cold lips.

"Kathleen!" was her spirited reply.

He frowned, then shrugged. "I don't suppose it matters greatly, since she's a girl." He continued to look at her in a disapproving manner. "Mrs. Skiles said you wanted the wet nurse sent away."

"I will nurse her myself," Fiona replied, ready to do battle with him over this.

"Really, my dear." He gave her a supercilious smile. "Only the lower classes do that!" When she continued to regard him in hostile silence, he shrugged once more. Glancing around the room, at the maid and nurse still in attendance, and the doctor standing in the doorway, Robert assumed an air of forced jocularity. He bent to kiss her forehead once more. "When our son is born next year, I shall have more to say about such things."

Fiona stared after him as he and the doctor went downstairs to tea. Exhaustion was falling over her, and she felt herself drifting. The thought of sharing his bed again brought a sourness to her throat. She had overheard enough of the servants' gossip to know that he had not been celibate during their months apart. He hunted every day of the week, except for a brief trip down to London. Oftentimes, she knew, the hunt ended at a village tavern, the Horn and Hounds. There, the hunters drank the night away and enjoyed the favors of the barmaids.

In these lonely months, she had learned much about the young male heirs of the English nobility. Robert was simply a product of his class and times . . . totally selfish, living only for pleasure, extravagant and shallow. When his friends came to stay at Hadley Hall for the hunting, she had observed that there was little to tell them apart except for physical differences. They had the same preoccupations, and the same lack of concern for the world beyond their elite little circle. But she had learned little about Robert's private business and sometimes felt a brief panic when she recalled Aunt Elizabeth's words.

"My lady, you should rest now." The nurse bent over the bed, her hands reaching for the baby.

Reluctantly, Fiona let Kathleen go. "Bring her to me when she's hungry," she ordered, fearful that Robert still might deny her this.

Her eyelids were heavy and her whole body sore and aching. Turning her head on the pillow, she sighed one word softly before she fell asleep. "Sean."

Leaning back on the velvet chaise in the nursery, Fiona gave herself completely to the sensuous pleasure of the baby's mouth at her breast. "Sweet Kathleen," she murmured as the baby sighed, released the nipple and fell into a satiated sleep.

"She's such a dear," Fiona's mother said from her chair beside the fire, watching as Nurse took the baby to change her and lay her in the gauze-draped cradle. "My hair was that color when I was a child," Mama went on, touching a hand to her graying light brown hair. "But it darkened as I grew up." She looked pleased. "She has my hair and Cedric's blue eyes, isn't that lovely?"

They were not *her* father's blue eyes, Fiona thought, although it was no doubt best to let everyone think so. Papa's eyes were light blue, and Kathleen's, like her father's, were a brilliant azure. Sean's eyes looking out of that tiny face were a constant source of both joy and sorrow to Fiona.

Adjusting her chemise, Fiona smiled at her mother. It seemed to her they were closer than they had ever been, closer than she could have hoped. There had been tears in Mama's eyes when she descended from the carriage to embrace Fiona for the first time since the wedding. Papa had harrumphed and tried to act gruff and unconcerned, but his eyes were moist too.

Robert had thought their coming for Kathleen's christening quite unnecessary and had told Fiona so after she had already sent the invitation. Vindictively, she thought that perhaps he didn't want them to know their daughter was not happy with the husband they had chosen. Not that Robert was concerned whether or not she was happy. It was the appearance of things that counted with him. She debated long about what she would tell her parents, deciding at last to wait for their questions.

Her parents had visited Aunt Elizabeth and Uncle Reggie in London before coming on to stay at Hadley Hall. Papa had joined enthusiastically in the hunting with Robert. Mama had brought some new fuchsia plants from the Royal Horticultural Society in London which required her special care to bring them safely home to Ireland. But there had been time for the talking they had never done before.

Now, Fiona joined her mother by the fire where the maid was laying tea. She hadn't invited Martha to join them, wanting this time alone with Mama.

"I'd hoped Aunt Elizabeth would come up from London with you," she said, indicating Mama should pour. "I liked her so much when I met her at the wedding, and I hoped we would know each other better."

Mama gave her a considering look, then turned to dismiss the maid. When they were alone, she said, "I'm afraid it's quite impossible for Elizabeth and Reggie to visit here now."

"What do you mean? I've invited them several times."

Gazing down into her teacup, Mama hesitantly continued, "I see, Fiona, that your husband doesn't share with you as Cedric does with me. I'm sorry for that, but in this case perhaps it's better." She sighed and looked at Fiona. "It seems Robert went down to London and demanded Reggie give him access to the capital of the inheritance your grandfather left you. As administrator, Reggie rightly refused. There was a dreadful quarrel, and Elizabeth said that Robert cut Reggie dead when they met at White's Club later." Her voice fell. "Robert was quite in the wrong, of course."

"He only married me for the dowry and the inheritance, Mama," Fiona replied, "and to breed children."

Mama flushed and looked away. "You mustn't be bitter, dear." She sipped her tea. "No marriage is perfect. I'm sure things will work out for the best."

Fiona saw that her mother wanted to believe that. Even though there was a deepening of affection between them now, as always her mother and father did not want to deal with unpleasant things. Nothing had changed there. She let it go, and presently Martha came in with the Reverend Mr. Moore, who had been taking tea with her downstairs.

The Brownes stayed a fortnight at Hadley Hall. By the time they departed, Fiona was well aware how restive her husband had become. Perhaps when her father was along, he couldn't end his hunt with whoring at the Horn and Hounds. She was sure he thought her parents as provincial as Martha obviously did, although he put on his best manners and even treated her with consideration in their presence. A flash of anger went through her at the idea that two such shallow people as Robert and Martha should think her parents beneath them.

"Could you come to Ireland for Christmas?" Mama's pleading look was directed at Robert as she stood before the carriage waiting to take them to the village station.

Robert laughed with that false jocularity Fiona hated. "It's a long time until Christmas, dear lady. We shall have to make that decision when the time comes."

Fiona and her mother exchanged glances, both knowing full well that he would never bring her to Ireland for Christmas. And her heart seemed to shatter in the certainty that she might never see Morning Hill again. Tears stood in her eyes as she embraced her parents and said goodbye. When the carriage disappeared among the trees lining the long drive, she felt a deep sense of loss, as though some part of her life had ended forever.

"They're gone," Robert said, and she sensed the relief in his tone. He turned to walk back into the house.

"Did you pay my father for the horses?" Fiona asked abruptly, drying her tears on her kerchief. Her mother had let it slip that the horses Robert had brought from Morning Hill had never been paid for.

"What!" Robert turned on her, his eyes blazing. "Those horses were part of your dowry, Lady Hadley."

"They weren't, and you know it." Her voice lifted as anger responded to his accusing look. "You've cheated my father, and I think it's infamous of you."

"It's none of your bloody business," he said in a hard angry voice. With that, he turned and walked toward the stables, effectively ending the conversation. She stood alone and cold in the June sunshine pouring over the elaborate entrance to Hadley Hall.

"Good night, my lady." Kate took up a candle to light her way and closed the bedroom door behind her, leaving Fiona in darkness and silence.

Fiona sighed, turning restlessly on her pillow. It had been a difficult day . . . parting from her parents, learning again that her husband was not an honorable man. Her tension must have affected Kathleen for she had been colicky, and Nurse had finally taken her away to soothe with a sugar-teat.

The scrape of the bolt in the door between her bedroom and Robert's brought her upright. Sitting there, she clutched the sheet in front of her, closing her eyes tightly against the shaft of light that fell through the door as Robert entered, all her being rejecting what was to come.

He crossed to the side of the bed and stood for a moment staring at her without expression. Then he began to disrobe.

"Well, my dear," he said in a cold and dispassionate voice. "Now you shall give me a son."

···᠙᠊ CHAPTER 9 ᠊᠙···

But, in the years following there was no son. Fiona seemed unable to carry a child past the third month, and there were three miscarriages . . . to Robert's undisguised displeasure. Without Kathleen, she knew her life would have been unbearable. But she could always turn to that small, loving creature, even when Robert and Martha chastised her for spending so much time with the child, and for spoiling her.

Seven days a week, Robert rode to the hunt, either from Hadley Hall or from the estates nearby. For a fortnight at a time, he would be gone to Sussex, or Devonshire, to the estates of his friends to hunt. There were almost always guests at Hadley Hall, aristocrats as obsessed by the hunt as Robert. Try as she might, Fiona could not make herself like any of them. The men were either bluff, red-faced and overweight, or languid pale young men who had been sent-down from Oxford and drank too much. The women seemed to occupy much the same position in their husbands' lives as Fiona occupied in the life of Lord Robert Hadley, they were all mere appendages, married for economic or family reasons. They obviously found Fiona's preoccupation with her child common and lower class. She found them tedious and silly, talking of nothing but clothes and society gossip. Still, she played the part of hostess, dressing well, wearing the family jewels which now were only paste replicas of those gone to pay Robert's debts. Behind the scenes, Martha managed the house and planned the entertainments, always taking her place at Fiona's side as co-hostess.

At last, the Reverend Mr. Moore's extended courtship of Martha culminated in marriage. His father, Lord Veith, had died and left him a considerable sum. Enough, he said to keep a woman of Martha's breeding in the comfort to which she was accustomed.

"The vicarage is quite impossible," Martha said one evening as the three of them sat before the drawing room fire after dinner.

Robert merely grunted, pouring himself another glass of port. Fiona concentrated on her needlepoint.

"I thought perhaps the dower house. It's been empty since grandmother died, and . . ."

"You'd like it?" Robert asked, turning to study his sister's expression, which was unaccustomedly humble. "Then take it, although I expect it's in a bit of a state."

"Dear Robert!" Martha rose from her chair to embrace Robert, who immediately backed away. Her hands fell to her sides, and she smiled into his annoyed face. "Bertram will be so pleased." Her stout face flushed like a girl's, and she glanced shyly at Fiona. "He does so want me to live as I've been accustomed to living."

"Surely, there will be a lot of repairs and redecorating to be done," Fiona said mildly. Just this afternoon, she had overheard Mr. Holmes, Robert's agent, telling him he must cut back on expenses. Rents had fallen off, and the potteries he invested in had failed.

"Martha can handle it," Robert replied, condescending to pat his sister's shoulder. "You have a free hand, my dear. Anything you want . . ."

"Thank you, Robert dear." Martha gazed at him fondly, then sighed. "I only hesitate because I fear what might become of Hadley Hall."

"Fiona can learn to run it," Robert growled, giving his wife a hard look. "That's her position."

The free hand Robert had given Martha was freer than even he guessed, Fiona thought as she stood in the church the dull February day of Martha's wedding. The cold and snobbish Veith family occupied the pews on one side, all of them seeming to think Bertram was marrying beneath him. Fiona sat on the other side, with the aunts and uncles and cousins she had never met before, or even heard of. Robert escorted the bride down the aisle to the strains of the new organ donated by Bertram's family.

Martha's wedding gown was of heavy imported silk satin, festooned with the finest French lace. When Robert got the bill for wedding clothes and trousseau, Fiona knew he would be livid. Not to mention the bills coming in for repairs to the dower house and furnishings. Many of the finest antiques from Hadley Hall had been carted away to the dower house, but Robert scarcely seemed to notice. If Martha had taken his horses or his hounds, it would have been quite another story.

At least, she was free now of Martha's oppressive presence. When she concentrated on the running of the manor, she soon knew what must be done, never doubting she could handle it, although Martha hadn't relinquished control until this very day.

"Dearly beloved, we are gathered here . . ." The visiting vicar from the Veith estate droned out the words of the marriage ceremony.

Fiona clasped her cold hands in front of her, against the sweep of her pale green silk gown. She was pregnant again, and this time, she told herself, she would be so careful. She would not ride, or even run through the gardens with Kathleen. When she finally gave Robert a son, perhaps he would be content to leave her bed forever. It would be worth the sacrifice.

The July weather turned hot and steamy. Robert had invited a great crowd for the hunt. They spent the afternoons and evenings complaining of the weather and drinking iced wine until Fiona was certain the wine cellar must be empty.

After tea, she felt quite ill. Perhaps it was the little salmon cakes Cook had made especially for today. Yet none of the other guests seemed unwell, and they soon dispersed, some to play croquet on the sweep of lawn east of the manor, others to ride—as though they hadn't spent the morning on horseback riding to the hounds. Feeling nausea rise, Fiona quickly climbed the stairs, not taking time to make her excuses.

It was her sixth month now, far too late in term for morning sickness she told herself as she vomited into the commode, then rang for her maid. Just as Kate appeared, Fiona doubled over with cramps.

Not again, she thought, dear Lord, not again. The pains of miscarriage were too familiar, but this baby was six months along. Kate helped her undress, and into bed, where she brought a cold compress for Fiona's head, and a warmed flannel for her abdomen.

Humid July air filled the room. Sweat poured from Fiona's body as she tried desperately to stop the cramping. She had wanted this child only because it represented a truce in her unhappy relationship with her husband. Not as she had wanted **Kathleen**. She had loved her daughter from the moment she knew she existed, because she was Sean's child, and all she would ever have of him in this life.

Pain rocketed through her, and tears stood in her eyes. Poor innocent babe. Perhaps it knew there was no love awaiting it. To Robert, it was his heir. To its mother, it was only a living sacrifice to her husband.

Gritting her teeth against the pain, Fiona willed it away. She must not lose this baby.

"Your guests are asking for you." It was Martha, standing in the doorway, fanning herself and looking very disapproving.

"My Lady is taken ill," Kate said as Fiona seized her hand in a convulsive grip.

Martha came round the bed, staring down at Fiona with not the slightest semblance of sympathy. All her good works as the wife of the vicar . . . the fund-raisers and parties for the orphans . . . yet she had no compassion at all for someone in pain. She had even seemed to take delight at Fiona's troubles in running the house, stopping by frequently to offer advice and consult with the butler and the housekeeper.

None of it mattered now, as pain rolled over Fiona. Sweat stung her eyes and the room was a haze. She gasped for the breath to speak. "Someone must go for the doctor at once."

It was over. Fiona lay in dazed exhaustion as the doctor and the maids cleaned up. A footman took away the tiny unmoving bundle that would have been her son. Silent tears streaked her face, as downstairs she could hear the voices of her guests at dinner.

"I shall have to tell Lord Hadley now," the doctor said, his kind face regarding her sadly.

"Yes," was all she could reply, knowing that the pattern of her life remained unbroken. He would demand a son again . . . and again. Perhaps she didn't love him enough to give him a child. Oh, if only she could go away from this hated place. Take Kathleen and flee back to Ireland where the ghost of Sean McLoughlin awaited her.

"A son," Robert said in an icy voice. He came into the birthing room, his face a mask of cold fury. "Born dead." Before she could respond, he continued in a voice that was like the lash of a whip across her heart. "It seems I've made a poor choice in a wife to give me an heir." Without so much as a touch to share her sorrow, he turned away with the final cutting words, "I'll expect you to perform better next time."

Resentment boiled in her, and she cried after him, "Damn your bloody heart. Maybe you should acknowledge some of the bastards you got on the village whores if you want an heir so badly."

In two long strides, he was beside the bed. Reaching out, he struck her across the face with such force that she cried out. The servants in the room gasped, but stayed in their places. Robert slammed the door behind him.

The house party broke up next morning. Fiona could hear the luggage being carted down the stairs, the farewells and then the carriages driving away. Good riddance, she thought, and demanded that Nurse bring Kathleen to her in spite of the protestations that the child should not be in a birthing room.

She did not see Robert again. Perkins, his valet, came to her room, shamefaced but trying to put on an expressionless mask. "His Lordship wishes me to inform you that he will be leaving for Scotland today."

"Murthly Castle?" Fiona asked tonelessly, looking at the nervous man over the golden head of her daughter snuggled beside her in the bed.

When he nodded, she said simply, "Good!" and dismissed him. Robert had taken her with him last year when he went to hunt at the vast estate of Lord Drummond in the highlands of Scotland. She had hated every moment of it, hated the vapid women and the men preoccupied with hunting or sex. Most of all, she'd hated being so long away from Kathleen.

Fiona lay back in her wicker chair, enjoying the warmth of the September sunshine. Chrysanthemums tumbled in a colorful riot around the edge of the lawn. The trees in the woods beyond had lost their sheen of green, with some already turning golden.

With a tender smile, she watched her daughter playing ball with her nurse. Surely, she was an extraordinary child, Fiona told herself. At two and a half she was everywhere, and into everything, her sturdy legs exploring the world of Hadley Hall. Sunlight caught the gleam of her golden hair as Kathleen ran across the expanse of green to fling herself against her mother's knees.

"Come play, Mama," she demanded.

"Mama is resting," the nurse chided, trailing breathlessly after her charge.

"Give me a kiss," Fiona laughed, lifting the child into her lap. Kathleen took her mother's face in two chubby hands, and Fiona's heart twisted as it always did when those brilliant blue eyes, so like Sean's, looked into hers. The little mouth planted a moist kiss on her mother's lips. Fiona's arms tightened, so close she could feel the beating of her daughter's heart. "I love you, my little one," she said, managing to land a kiss on one ear as Kathleen struggled free and ran after a kitten who had wandered into the garden.

Watching the indulgent nurse show Kathleen how to hold the kitten, Fiona felt a deep sense of contentment. Moments like this were precious, moments when her life was her own, with only her daughter to share it. The autumn day seemed somehow charmed, with a misty blue sky above the woodlands, doves calling in the distance, and the odors of dying summer like spice in the warm air.

She well knew the contentment would be ended when

Robert returned, and she clung to the feeling now. But the thought of her husband had shattered her inner peace, and she caught back the sobs that threatened to rise in her throat. Now that she was well, she must not cry any more for a dead son and a purposeless life. There was always Kathleen.

Robert had been gone nearly two months. She knew it was wicked of her to wish some dreadful accident might befall him so he could never return. Without his cold uncaring presence, life flowed pleasantly along. She had arrived at an understanding with the butler and the housekeeper and had told Martha to stop meddling with her servants. It had been an ugly scene, ending by Martha's marching out of the room with the words, "We'll see what changes will be made when Robert returns from Scotland."

The autumn days moved gently into each other. Now that Fiona was feeling rested and strong again, she had begun to ride, taking Kathleen in front of her on the saddle. Kathleen, who sang nursery rhymes in a voice as clear and true as that of her father, was fascinated by the pianoforte. The two of them played it just for the sound of the notes, and Kathleen laughed with joy. Together, they played hide and seek on the stairs and in the garden. Fiona saw the servants shaking their heads at indulging a child in this manner, but the new nurse she had hired herself thought it wonderful that Lady Hadley spent so much time with her daughter.

All her life now was concentrated on this child. Long since, she had given up any hope of a loving, or even pleasant, relationship with her husband. Kathleen was everything to her . . . her life, her one remaining love.

As she had guessed, they had never gone to Ireland. She kept her parents informed of Kathleen's progress, letters filled with pride and love. Her mother's were filled with longing to see her grandchild. Dear Ireland and beautiful Morning Hill, with the horses frolicking in the meadows, and all the beloved memories of Sean. Suddenly, Fiona sat straight up in her chair, almost laughing aloud with joy.

Robert would be gone at least two more weeks, and could do nothing to stop her. She would have the butler make arrangements for their passage to Ireland next week, herself, Kathleen and the nurse, and Kate. Going home to Morning

Hill would, she knew, open the unhealed wounds of Sean's death. But all that remained to her were memories. Bittersweet it might be, but she would find her love again in Ireland.

One of the footmen came across the lawn, pausing beside her chair. Giving him an amused glance, Fiona thought he looked as haughty as though he were a lord himself.

"There's a lad from the village, my lady. He claims he has a message for you, and he refuses to give it to anyone else."

"Then let me see him," she demanded with a smile. His stiff carriage as he walked back across the lawn told her she had once again fallen short in the eyes of her servants. No true lady would take a message from the hand of a peasant lad.

The boy came toward her through the golden September light. He was dressed in rough clothes, with a ragged cap on his head. The footman followed, eyeing him suspiciously. When the lad stood beside her, she knew he worked in a stable.

"Thank you," she said, taking the note from his hand. Fiona Browne Hadley was scrawled across the folded paper. Looking up at the footman, she added, "Give him a coin for his trouble, Preece." The man frowned.

"I'll wait fer an answer, milady, if yer please." The boy swept off his cap, and his straw-colored hair stood up in unruly tufts.

Fiona did not reply, for she had opened the note. All the breath went out of her. The handwriting wavered before her, and for a moment she thought she might faint. In spite of the warm sunlight over the garden, she felt cold as though all the blood had drained out of her. Faintly, she heard her own voice cry out. As though in slow motion, she saw the nurse and Kathleen running toward her.

Surely it was not a cruel joke. Surely not. Standing up, she knocked over the wicker chair. She scarcely heard the concerned questions of the nurse. "Take care of Kathleen," she said.

Lifting her skirts, she ran . . . across the lawn . . . the drive . . . the graveled sweep . . . to the stables. Without waiting for a saddle, she mounted the bridled horse and galloped toward the village.

·◦❪ CHAPTER 10 ❫◦·

Sean McLoughlin stared out the dirty window of his room on the second floor of the Brookfield Inn. Beyond the low forested hills, the step-gabled rooftop of Hadley Hall gleamed in the autumn sunlight.

She wouldn't come, he told himself morosely, turning away from the window. Looking around at the low-ceilinged room, the bed still rumpled from where he had tossed after his late arrival last night, his certainty grew. Fiona was Lady Hadley now, and she lived in a luxurious mansion set in a beautiful wooded park. Why would she leave all that for even a few moments with him? He had nothing to offer her to compare with what she now enjoyed. After all this time, she might have forgotten him, forgotten the joyous moments they had shared, and learned to care for the man she had married. If Mary O'Brien had told him truly, there was a child . . . his own blood. But, he chided himself, there will be other children, and Fiona would be a fool to acknowledge her first as a bastard.

He was the fool, he thought bitterly. A fool to come here, and a fool through all the bitter years when his only goal had been to return to her. That night in Dublin, he had been hurrying back to her.

The pitch and roll of the ship had awakened him. His hands were bound, and he lay on the floor of the fetid hold, stinking of his own vomit. The lump on his head throbbed viciously.

There were other men groaning and stirring in the dim light. Sean struggled to a sitting position. Shanghaied, by God, he thought, seeing that the other men were bound too.

94

A hatch banged open, letting in a rush of cold sea air. "The bloody British Navy," Sean growled, seeing the uniform the mate wore. The sailor holding up a lantern for the mate kicked Sean in the ribs.

"You're aboard Her Majesty's man-of-war, *Marlborough,* you stinkin' Irish pigs." The mate looked at the miserable men with contempt. "When you sign your enlistment papers, you can come on deck and join the crew."

"What if we don't sign," Sean growled and received another kick in the ribs.

"You can rot here, you bloody arse." He glared at Sean. Turning, he mounted the steps to the hatch. With a sly grin, he motioned at the men. "Up the ladder now, mateys. To serve England and the Queen."

Thus had begun two years of hell, in which he had never set foot on land. The Captain of the *Marlborough* knew too well that a shanghaied sailor will jump ship at the first chance. He'd learned the trade of a sailor under the whips of the regular Navy crew and watched the longboats ply into half the ports in the world. From South Africa to Australia to Hong Kong, and then the endless voyage across the Pacific, where at last the harbor pilot guided the *Marlborough* through the treacherous reefs of the Golden Gate.

Beyond their anchorage, San Francisco climbed its endless hills. Through the dusk, lights gleamed along the busy Embarcadero and fog crept in through the Golden Gate, across the mountain-rimmed bay, sliding over the hills and misting the lights of the city.

Sean pulled at an oar of the longboat, part of its crew for the first time. In the bow, the Captain stood proudly in his dress uniform for he had been invited to dine this night with the mayor of San Francisco.

The boat scraped against the wharf. The mayor's carriage was waiting, and there were lackeys to assist the Captain from the boat. With his love of ceremony, the Captain had the crew alight from the boat and stand at attention along the wharf as he walked to the carriage.

"Get aboard," the mate shouted. "We'll come back for the Captain tomorrow."

For the first time in two years, the world was steady beneath his feet. Sean hesitated, turning to look at the crowds of people streaming along the busy waterfront . . . laughing people, free people. Such a fury surged through him that the gaslights turned blood red in his eyes.

"Git along there!" the mate yelled at him. Seizing the man's arm, Sean flung him off the wharf into the stinking mud of low tide. Then he was gone, leaping across the fence at the end of the pier, pushing his way into the throng. Behind him, the shouts of the mate faded in the noise of the crowd.

Damn the uniform, he thought. He had to get rid of it, or they'd find him soon enough. Turning a corner, he saw before him a waterfront tavern. Nothing distinguished the seedy looking place from all the other taverns except its name, spelled in peeling green letters: The Emerald Isle.

God help this Irishman, he muttered, slowing down so that he could enter the tavern without giving the impression that he was being pursued.

The tavern was crowded. A bar worn shiny by patrons' elbows had little pretension to elegance. Behind it was a cracked mirror with liquor bottles arranged on a shelf in front. At Sean's entrance, a hostile silence fell over the crowd. The publican behind the bar paused in pouring a drink to stare, open-mouthed.

"A bloody Britisher!" someone shouted, and they were upon him, pummeling him with fists, tearing his shirt as they tossed him from one to another.

"For the love of God!" Sean shouted over the din. "I'm an Irishman." When they ignored him, he shouted the words again, this time in Gaelic. The struggling ceased, and the man holding him by the shirt dropped his fist. "I'm runnin' from the bloody Brits," he went on, still speaking Gaelic. "I thought I'd find an Irishman to help here."

"Yer uniform?" The man eased his grip on Sean's shirt, watching him warily.

"Shanghaied me, in Dublin, they did," Sean answered.

"The bastards!" He let go the shirt and took Sean's arm. "I'll stand ye a drink, by God. And maybe Connor there," he pointed to the man behind the bar, "kin find ye a shirt what ain't got Her Majesty's mark on it."

"I'd be obliged," Sean said, letting out a long sigh of relief.

"Obliged, he says." The man grinned at the crowd around them. "Come into a meetin' of the Fenians in a Brit uniform, and ye'll be obliged by a knife in yer guts."

Sean took the whiskey he offered and drank it in a gulp. "My name's Sean McLoughlin, and they'll be lookin' for me. I jumped ship."

"I'm Pat Mulroony," the man said, holding out his hand. He was a head shorter than Sean, with crinkled blue eyes and graying red hair. His grip was like iron.

Connor came from the back room and tossed a ragged plaid shirt to Sean. "Gimme Her Majesty's duds," he said. "I'll sink 'em in the mud where they belong."

The Fenian meeting was forgotten as the men crowded around to hear Sean's story. One after another, they stood for drinks, until his head was swimming. Then the singing began as was inevitable in every place where Irishmen congregate. Sitting at the rough, drink-stained table, with Pat's arm over his shoulder, Sean joined them. He was aware he was still in danger, not clear away from the navy yet, but for the first time in two years he was happy and his voice rose with the others.

"Oh Paddy, dear, and did you hear the news that's goin'
round.
The shamrock is forbid by law to grow on Irish ground;
St. Patrick's day no more we'll keep,
His color can't be seen,
For there's a bloody law agin' the wearin' of the Green.
I met with Napper Tandy and he tuk me by the hand.
He said, 'How's poor old Ireland, and how does she stand?'
She's the most distressful country that ever you have seen;
They're hangin' men and women there for the wearin' of
the Green."

When the crowd began singing the melancholy words, "Come back to Erin, Mavourneen, Mavourneen, Come back a-roon to the land of thy birth . . .", Pat rose from the table. "I'll be gettin' home now, or the missus will throw me hat out the door." He grinned at his own jest, then sobered. "Ye'd best come with me, lad. Best get out of San Francisco soon as ye can. I live in Oakland, over the bay. Work fer the railroad on the ferryboats they run from the train station at Oakland."

"I got no money, Pat," Sean said apologetically.

"No matter," Pat replied quickly. "Yer frum the old sod, and the Brits have done ye bad. Come along."

As the ferry moved toward the lights of the Oakland terminal with a soft chunk of paddle wheels, Pat told Sean his own story, his words punctuated by the low moan of the foghorns in the distance. The terrible famine of the '40s had sent Pat across the ocean to seek his fortune in America.

"Got off the stinkin' boat," he said, drawing on his pipe, "an' we were dirty Irish scum. That's the welcome America give us." He gave Sean a sidewise glance and wryly added, "There were too many of us and all poor. But, by God." He sat up straight and grinned proudly at Sean. "We made it, we did. Workin' hard at anythin' come along. Now, I'm engineer on a ferryboat with a fine house up there on the hill." After a brief silence, he spat into the churning water alongside the boat. "'Come Back to Erin,' they sing. Not me, lad. Not ever. Not as long as the bloody British bleed Ireland dry."

Pat's house was on a hill above the central part of Oakland, in a street of neat three-story homes. At the gate, a sign swung in the cold night breeze . . . "Board and Room."

"A fine house," Sean said, a bit awed by his new friend's affluence.

"Aye," Pat said proudly. "Me wife runs the house and makes good money at it. We got eight bairns, an' all of 'em gettin' educated at the parish school." He grinned. "I'll help the Fenian brotherhood . . . but 'Come Back to Erin'? Me arse!"

In the next few days, Pat's stout, bustling wife made over some old clothes a boarder had left behind to fit Sean. And Pat found a job for him, as a railroad fireman, shoveling coal on the route from Oakland east to Omaha.

"If yer determined to go back to Ireland, ye'll be headed in the right direction," Pat told him, as they walked into the railroad yards on the day of his departure.

"There's a lass . . ." Sean let the sentence trail into silence.

"I thought as much." Pat grinned and held out his hand. "God go with ye, lad. Don't fergit to look up me friend Derry in Omaha."

Sean made his way across the incredible vastness of the United States of America, passed from one helping Irish Fenian to another. He shoveled coal as the freight train rattled over the burning Great Plains. Beside him, a newly freed black man sang spirituals incessantly and never said another word.

In Chicago, a Fenian named McBride found a job for him at the stockyards. He stayed two months, living in a tiny room near the yards so he could walk to work, saving his money for the passage home to Fiona. When the job ended, he took the train to Boston, with yet another Fenian name in his wallet.

Moran lived on the South Side, in a red brick tenement where the stairwell smelled of stale cabbage. Sean slept on a quilt on the floor of the kitchen while he looked for work.

Returning at dusk from a long discouraging day filled with signs that said "No Irish Need Apply," Sean trudged wearily up the stairs. He paused on the second-floor landing, debating what he must do. His presence was a drain on Moran and his wife, and he must move on. But where?

"I brought us a pint to celebrate, darlin'." The strangely familiar voice echoed from the second-floor hallway.

Sean turned back and peered down the long hall lit only by one flickering gas lamp. "Fergus?" he asked, not quite daring to believe it could be true.

"B'God," the voice rose. "Sean McLoughlin . . . it can't be." They met halfway down the hall, holding each other at arm's length and staring in disbelief. "Holy Mother of God . . . it is you!" The two men embraced fiercely, and Fergus turned to shout at the woman standing in the doorway of the flat. "Mary . . . it's Sean himself."

Over the bucket of beer Fergus had brought from the corner tavern to celebrate the news that Mary was expecting their first child, the friends exchanged stories. Fergus had a steady job driving a dray for a warehouse company at the docks. Last year, he had saved enough to send for Mary to come to America. Now, he told Sean, they would save to buy a little place of their own, a place with some land about it, and room to raise their own garden and their children.

"It's God's blessing yer alive at all," Mary said when they had heard Sean's story. She looked blooming and content, her slender face already filled out by pregnancy.

"'Twas the Fenian Brotherhood saved me," Sean replied. "From the time I jumped ship, they helped. I'll not forget it."

"Then it's back to Ireland ye'll be goin'?" Fergus asked, exchanging a look with Mary.

"Aye," Sean said, swallowing the last of his beer, which was better than navy rum but not as good as Irish stout. He sighed. "I must."

"She's wed, Sean," Mary said softly, her eyes dark with sympathy.

A tightness closed like steel bands around his chest, and it was a moment before he could reply. "Lord Hadley?"

"Aye." Mary gave Fergus a questioning look, and he nodded slowly. "She had no choice," Mary continued, reaching across to lay her hand over Sean's. He sat slumped in his chair, staring at the red-checked tablecloth. He heard her draw a deep, shaky breath. "There was a child . . ."

"Mine!" Sean's head jerked up, and he stared at Mary's agonized face. Tears filled her eyes, and she looked again to Fergus.

"Tell him," Fergus prompted.

"They all said you were dead." The words tumbled out of Mary now. "The police in Dublin, Colin, everyone. She was like a poor lost ghost, grievin' for you. The master and mistress kept pressin' her to wed the lord, an' when Nanny guessed she was with child, she pressed it too . . . so the babe wouldn't be born a bastard."

"Oh, my God!" Sean covered his face with his hands to hide the painful tears that stung his eyes. "Where is she now?" He looked at Mary, now unmindful of the tears streaking his sun-browned face.

"She's Lady Hadley, of Hadley Hall, Brookfield, Sean. You can't change that . . . nor can she."

"The babe?" He had to know it all.

"A girl. The master and mistress went to the christening and thought her a beautiful child, but . . ."

"But what?" Sean demanded, seeing Mary's sudden hesitance.

"When I left last year, there were no other children. It's said her husband neglects her for his hunting . . . that he spends money like water, and his fortune's nearly run through."

"The bloody bastard!"

"Ye'll not change things by goin' back, Sean," Fergus urged in a low voice. "Stay in America. It's been good to us."

"She thinks me dead," Sean answered, knowing he could never express to them the bond that bound him to Fiona. "I'll see her once more."

Fergus helped him to a job as stable hand at the drayage company. Sean's expertise with horses was soon apparent, and before long he was promoted to trainer. For the next few months, he lived with Fergus and Mary, sleeping on a cot in the kitchen and paying board and room to speed the day they might move to the country. When, at last, he'd saved for passage home, he was lucky enough to find a freighter to Liverpool on which he could work his way to England. The little hoard of money he'd saved went back with him . . . intact.

And now . . . and now . . . Sean turned to the window again, where the distant roof of Hadley Hall seemed as inaccessible as a fairy castle in one of his mother's legends. He should go now, take the train to Holyhead and sail to Ireland to see his parents. Then . . . His spirits sank. What did the future hold without Fiona? These past years, she had been his obsession, his one reason to continue living. She was his life, and now he was certain she had rejected him.

Sean groaned aloud. "She won't come." Shoulders slumped, he turned from the window. He would pack and leave at once.

There was a sound of running feet on the stairs. The door flung open and she was there . . . her bright hair gleaming in the dim passageway, her lilac-flowered gown rumpled, her lips parted breathlessly.

The door banged behind her. She was in his arms, and all the empty years apart had never been.

CHAPTER 11

"Sean . . ." Fiona rolled on her side to look down into his face. They had taken each other in such mad haste there had scarcely been time for words. Clothes were strewn wildly about the low-ceilinged room. A pale stream of light lay across the bare floor and the rumpled bed, gilding the dingy whitewashed walls. "All these years," she said softly, smoothing back his damp black hair. He smiled, cupping her face in his palm. "All this time, I told myself it couldn't be as wonderful as I remembered . . ."

"And . . .?" he prompted, lifting his head to kiss her bare breast.

"Oh Sean," she cried, overwhelmed by the immensity of her love for him. "A part of me was dead until you held me in your arms and brought me to life again." She lay across his chest, her nipples taut against the rough dark hair, kissing him fiercely. Sean's arms tightened about her, his mouth devouring hers. At last they broke apart, breathless.

"Darling . . . darling . . ." Fiona murmured, her fingers gently stroking his cheek. He had aged, for there were crow's-feet at the corners of his brilliant blue eyes, and deep lines about the wide mobile mouth, his skin darkened by sun and wind. Looking at the marks time had ravaged on that beloved face, she was filled with an impotent anger for the years they had lost.

His mouth against her throat, Sean eased her back on the pillow. Their lips met, and his kiss deepened. In the very depths of her being, desire flamed again. Running her hands over his wide shoulders, Fiona gasped, suddenly aware of the long white-ridged scars crisscrossing his back.

At once, she drew away and rose on her elbow to stare at the ugly evidence of his suffering. "Oh Sean! Darling, what happened to you?"

He lay back, hiding the scars from her view. Tenderly, he drew her down into his arms and pillowed her head on his shoulder. After a moment, he spoke in a carefully controlled voice. "That's how the Queen's Navy taught me to be a sailor." Then he told her of his odyssey . . . his enslavement to the Navy . . . his journey across America with the help of the Fenian Brotherhood.

When he spoke of his time in Boston, Fiona cried out in delight. "Dear little Mary! Mama told me she had gone to America to Fergus." Then she sobered, lifting her head to look into Sean's eyes. "I was glad she would have her love, even if I was sure then that I would never have mine."

Taking her face in his two hands, Sean kissed her softly. "Mary said there was a child . . . is . . .?"

"Your daughter," she interrupted, gazing lovingly at him. "Oh Sean . . . how you'll love her. She's so bright and so beautiful."

"Will I see her then?" he asked hesitantly, suddenly wondering what lay ahead for them. Until now, he had made no plans. He'd only known that he must see Fiona again.

"Tomorrow," Fiona said in positive tones, and Sean smiled, recognizing his old sweet willful love. "You must come to Hadley Hall in the morning. You're a family friend from Ireland. We'll ride together . . . Oh, Sean! It will be like always . . . the two of us . . ."

"Your husband . . .?" he began, hating the sound of the word.

"He's hunting in Scotland and won't be back for at least two weeks." Her face changed in some subtle way, and pain filled Sean's heart.

"Is he unkind to you?" he demanded, thinking he'd somehow make the bloody lord pay for any hurt he'd done this girl.

"He never loved me," she said with a dismissive shrug as though she no longer minded. "He married me for my money, and for Papa's horses. Now the money's gone, and

I'm only a brood mare to him . . . someone to give him an heir."

"The bastard!" Sean muttered, drawing her close to him.

"We'll not think of him," she insisted, and she began to kiss his throat, his eyes, running her warm tongue along his lips until they opened to her demanding kiss. Her hands caressed his chest, moved softly down his arms and across his belly to stroke the hot hard length of his arousal.

"Fee . . . sweet love," he groaned, his body quickening to her touch. Taking her shoulders, he turned her on her back and propped himself on one elbow to look down into her face. "Dear God," he murmured, "you're so beautiful." She was, he thought, more beautiful than he had remembered through all the aching nights he had longed for her. The soft young breasts had rounded into maturity so that they filled his hand as he held and caressed them. With gentle fingers, he traced the line of her waist where it curved into hips no longer girlish but still utterly desirable. His hand moved across the soft nest of hair between her thighs and insinuated gently between her smooth legs. At once she opened to him, her breath coming in soft panting gasps.

How could she have lived without this, Fiona wondered, as she gave herself completely to the exquisite sensations radiating through her body? Everywhere he touched, her body responded like a torch set ablaze. The taste of his mouth was intoxicating and the touch of his lips like a seething flame.

"Sean!" she cried, lifting her body to take him deep into her. They were one being, as they were always meant to be. Nothing would part them again. It was her last coherent thought before her body was enveloped in a frenzy of ecstasy, and the room seemed to explode in a white-hot light.

When Fiona awakened, the sun had gone. The room was dim and cold. Turning to look at Sean sleeping beside her, she felt tears of joy sting her eyes. A miracle, she told herself. It was a miracle that he had survived and found his way back to her. The sweet warmth of love flowed through her as she bent to kiss him.

At once, his blue eyes opened, looking into hers. "Oh Fee.

Thanks be to God . . . it's true." He gathered her into his arms. "Sure, an' I thought I was dreaming."

"No, love," she sighed as he began to kiss her throat and she felt the quickening of desire. "No more dreams now. We'll be together always."

"Always, Fee . . . my own sweet love." His mouth took hers fiercely, and she surrendered once more to the bottomless passion that united them.

"I must go," she whispered, when they again lay breathless and fulfilled.

Sean closed his eyes tightly, wincing with pain at her words. "Dear love."

"I must, darling. For Kathleen . . . she'll be missing me." Even though she longed with all her heart to stay there in his arms, she sat up. Gathering her clothes, she began to dress. Sean lay still on the bed, watching her, his hands behind his head.

"She won't go to sleep until I tell her a story."

Sean grinned, his eyes dark with love as he looked up at her. "Willful as her mother," he teased.

Fiona sat on the bed beside him, pulling on her stockings. She must not surrender to the enticing warmth of his hands caressing her back. "I tell her the old tales your mother told to us," she continued gaily. The tightness grew in her body, and she knew it would take all her willpower to leave him.

The sudden sadness in his expression tore her heart. "Darling, darling," she said, smoothing back his hair and looking into his face. "You shall have your daughter . . . and your love. I promise you."

He did not ask how that miracle would come about. He simply drew her down into his arms and kissed her long and lovingly.

Next morning, when the maid showed Sean into the drawing room, Fiona was waiting in front of the huge carved fireplace. She was dressed in her favorite riding habit of dark green velvet and silk, the color turning her hazel eyes to green. For the first time, she had even scolded Kate about the way she dressed her hair. In the end, she did it herself, tying it back with a ribbon as she had done in those faraway days when she rode with Sean across the meadows of Morning Hill.

"How nice to see you again, Mr. McLoughlin," she said, holding out her hand, her eyes dancing mischievously. How handsome he looked in the secondhand gentleman's clothes he had bought in Liverpool. The black wool coat, tailored for another man, pulled a bit across his broad shoulders, but the gray trousers seemed molded to his long legs. His silk vest was the height of fashion, as was the white linen stock about his neck. Amused, she knew none of her husband's aristocratic friends could guess that Sean McLoughlin once had been a stableboy.

Sean kissed her hand in silence. He could not bear to call her Lady Hadley. Even while the old sweet magic pulsated between them, he felt a shiver of apprehension. Fiona was, indeed, the lady of the manor, standing before the fire in this elegant room. Quickly glancing about, he took in the dark red velvet draperies with gold silk fringe, the heavy dark mahogany furniture upholstered in fine tapestry, the rich carpets on the floor. The maid lingered by the doorway, and it seemed to him this great gloomy house was filled with watching eyes.

His unease at once communicated itself to Fiona. "You wanted to see the horses," she said. "We may as well go to the stables now."

She had sent orders early that two mounts be saddled for her and her visitor. Just being near Sean, walking across the garden with him, making inconsequential conversation had set the fires burning in her. Urgent need surged through her. She could not even make the gesture of pretending to show him the stables. The groom helped her mount, and she galloped off, leaving Sean to follow.

There was a place she knew, off the track, a little pond surrounded by reeds and tangled undergrowth. Ducks swam undisturbed on its glassy surface, and weeping willow trees trailed their branches in the water. Dismounting, she tethered her horse, then turned to Sean. For a long moment, he sat on the blowing horse looking down at her eager face. When he slid from the saddle, she flung herself into his arms.

His mouth covered hers. His breath was quick and hot in her ear as she pressed herself fiercely against him.

"Oh darling, darling," she cried as his big hands cupped

her hips and pressed her against the hardness of him. "I couldn't sleep the whole night for wanting you."

"Nor did I." His hands moved up her back, then caught her in such a fierce embrace the breath seemed to leave her lungs.

"Here." Breaking the embrace, she took his hand. Willow branches hung to the ground in long sweeping fronds, green-gold now in early autumn. "I come here sometimes when I need to be alone," she told him as the branches dropped about them with a soft rustle. The circle of branches created a canopy filled with green-gold light. Only the slight autumn breeze disturbed this private sanctuary. From the pond came the faint sounds of water creatures, punctuated now and then by the harsh quack of the ducks, and the beat of wings as they took flight.

"Fee," he said, taking her shoulders in his hands as they stood face to face. "It's a madness we have for each other."

"Darling Sean," she smiled up at him. "It's a madness called love." And she began to unbutton his vest.

They took each other again and again, there on the mossy ground, their hunger for each other insatiable. Utterly spent, Fiona lay in Sean's arms, half-asleep, at last dimly realizing that the horses had grown restless, and the sun had passed its zenith.

With a sigh, she rose to lean across and kiss Sean's closed eyelids. "Darling love, wake up. You must go have tea with your daughter now."

His eyes flew open, and she thought she might drown in those dark blue pools of love. A slow smile spread across the strong mouth softened now by a thousand kisses. "Fee . . ." he murmured, drawing her close so that their lips almost touched. "Shall I ever get enough of you?"

"Never," she promised with a laugh, and kissed him.

Tea had been laid in the garden. Maids and footmen hurried down from the house with the trays when they saw her coming. Around the edge of the sunlit lawn, chrysanthemums glowed in a thousand autumn shades. Black rooks called from the branches of the ancient beech trees. The clear crisp air tasted like wine . . . or, Fiona wondered, was it the taste of Sean still on her lips? Walking down from the

107

stables, she had kept a distance from him because she wanted so desperately to touch him. Her whole body glowed with life, a feeling so intense she was certain it must be visible.

Kathleen and Nurse were waiting beside the white wicker tea table. Nurse sat in a wide chair, holding the little girl on her lap as they leafed through a picture book.

"Mama!" Kathleen cried, looking up. Scrambling down, she ran across the lawn toward them.

Bending, Fiona held out her arms, marveling as always at the beauty of the child rushing toward her, light brown hair gleaming gold in the sunlight. "Mama . . . Mama . . ." The chubby arms wound tight about her neck as Fiona stood up, holding the beloved little body close against her.

Over the child's head, her eyes met Sean's, and she felt a great rush of pain for him. Tears glistened in his eyes, and his face worked with the effort to repress emotion. How she hated all the servants standing about. With all her being, she longed to be alone, to be free to include him in her embrace, the three of them bound by a love that would never end.

"This is my daughter, Kathleen," she said in a shaky voice, holding the child away. "Say hello to Mr. McLoughlin, dear."

Kathleen put a thumb to her mouth and glanced shyly up at the tall silent man staring at her with a stunned expression. To Fiona's surprise, for Kathleen was timid with strangers, the little girl suddenly leaned away from her, holding her arms out to Sean. Darling . . . darling, Fiona thought, as Sean's arms tightened convulsively about the child and he closed his eyes to squeeze back the tears. She will be yours, and we will be together always now, far away from this place. This morning, she had asked Baines to book passage for three to Ireland.

The moment passed. Sean composed himself, and they sat down for tea. How hideous it was to have all these listening ears, Fiona thought, seeing the open curiosity of the nurse. Nothing could be spoken but inanities, nothing that could be passed on for gossip belowstairs or carried to Martha in the dower house.

They concentrated on Kathleen, who clung to Sean's knee

while he drank his tea. Aware that she was the center of attention, the little girl began to show off, turning somersaults for Sean's applause. Watching Sean's face, Fiona wondered whether the servants saw the fierce adoration in his eyes as he watched the child. Love for him flowed through her. How warm and gentle he was with Kathleen, and when her demands went too far, more firm than she could ever be. Promise for the future seemed as golden and perfect as the sunny autumn day.

At last they were alone, as Fiona walked with Sean to the stables to say goodbye. Kathleen clung to her hand and reached the other hand to Sean.

"She's near as beautiful as her mother," Sean said in a choked voice.

"And her father," she answered, looking up at him with the eyes of love.

They were nearing the stables now, where a groom waited, and she said the words hurriedly. "You'll take a horse with you to use. I told the stableboy to saddle him."

"I shouldn't come here again," Sean said, one eye on the approaching groom.

"I'll come to you tonight at the inn, love," she whispered.

"You mustn't," he protested. "You'll be seen."

"After dark," she insisted. "Wait for me."

Obsessed by her passion for Sean, it seemed to Fiona that the remainder of the day dragged with leaden slowness. When darkness fell at last, she dismissed Kate, dressed in her plainest gown. With a shawl covering her head, she hurried to the stables. The hounds set up a racket so that there was no time to saddle her horse. She simply mounted astride and raced toward the inn.

Fearful that the stableboy at the inn might recognize her, she tethered the horse in the woods nearby. Stumbling through the darkness, she slipped in the back door of the Brookfield Inn, ignoring the raucous sounds from the tavern, praying she would meet no one coming down the back stairs.

Sean aroused from a waking dream of love at the light tapping on his door. "You shouldn't have come here," he said as Fiona flung herself into his arms.

109

"How could I stay away from you, darling?" she murmured huskily, covering his face with hot kisses.

"Someone might recognize you." Even while he protested, his body was responding to hers, burning with delight that she had come to him.

"No one saw . . . no one knows," she assured him, hurriedly unbuttoning her gown, her thighs already damp with longing.

There, in Sean's tiny room, the world ceased to exist. There was only the fulfillment of long-denied dreams, only arms, and kisses and sighs, and eager bodies melded together.

Before first light, Fiona rode back to Hadley Hall, telling the grooms she had gone riding early. She scarcely noticed them whispering and snickering behind their hands as she moved toward the house in a haze of fulfilled passion.

Two days later, Lord Hadley's agent, Mr. Holmes, brought the tickets to Ireland she had asked for. Thanking him pleasantly, she silently cursed him for the delay. She had no money for tickets, and Sean's American savings were nearly gone. Two days without Sean, waiting for the tickets, for he had adamantly refused to allow her to come to the inn again.

Mr. Holmes was obviously uneasy that she had asked him to do something without His Lordship's orders.

"My father is unwell," Fiona lied. "I'll be met in Dublin, so I'll take only Nurse and Kathleen with me."

With a dubious frown, Mr. Holmes departed.

She was glad to see him go, for Sean was coming to tea. Even though it was risky, inviting him here, she needed to be with him, and he would not allow her at the inn. Nor could she deny him the company of the daughter he adored.

Glancing out the window, she saw Mr. Holmes talking to Baines, then driving away in his trap. It was a gloomy day, with a dark low sky, and a cold wind blowing. They would have tea in the nursery. At least there, they could do with fewer servants, for she had become aware that the servants watched her with wary eyes, exchanging smirking glances as they waited on the tea table where she sat with Sean and Kathleen.

"Your bath is ready, my lady," Kate called from the dressing room.

Fiona slid into the depths of the iron tub, letting the warm water flow sensuously over her body. Glancing down, she wondered if there weren't a glow emanating from her. The fires ignited by Sean's love must surely be visible. With a soft moan, she closed her eyes, feeling need for him rush through her.

When the water cooled, she stepped from the tub and Kate wrapped a thick towel about her. While Kate bustled about setting out her underthings, Fiona turned to the tall pier glass, letting the towel drop so she could look at the body where Sean McLoughlin created such magic.

Her breasts seemed heavier. Did she only imagine that the areola around the nipples had changed from pale pink to deep rose-brown? I'm pregnant, she thought with irrational certainty. A breathless joy soared through her. Sean's child . . . the child of their love . . . lay in her womb. Reason told her it was too soon to be sure, but her heart knew its truth.

The possibility of a child brought a sense of urgency. They must leave England at once. Today, their departure for Ireland must be settled. She knew Sean longed to see the family who had thought him dead, and she wanted to see her parents again even though she would have disgraced them. After that was time to decide about America.

"The Reverend and Mrs. Moore are waiting for you in the library," Kate said, turning from the door where the downstairs maid had brought the message.

Dear God, Fiona thought. What if they stay to tea? No . . . Sean would not come to the house if he saw their carriage. But damn Martha's interference. She seldom came to call since their confrontation over the servants.

Quickly she dressed in a gown of pale gold flowered challis, impatiently hurrying Kate with her hair. Perhaps she could be rid of the Moores before teatime.

Martha dismissed the maid peremptorily and told Bertram to close the library doors. Then she turned her coldly hostile eyes on Fiona and stared for a moment in grim silence.

A chill of apprehension fell over Fiona . . . a coldness not

111

dispelled even when she moved closer to the fire glowing in the huge stone fireplace. Could Martha have learned about Sean?

"You common slut!" Martha hissed, and Fiona knew.

Trembling, she wondered how she could live through this interview. The bitterness her sister-in-law bore her had begun at their first meeting. With sudden insight, Fiona knew the reason for Martha's hatred. She had wanted to keep Robert for herself. The marriage to Bertram had been merely a substitute and a sham. Fiona glanced at Bertram, who stood with hands folded, staring miserably at the floor.

"You've disgraced my brother's name," Martha continued in a low voice seething with repressed fury. When Fiona opened her mouth to protest, Martha interrupted. "Did you think it would go unnoticed that you spent the night in that low Irishman's room at the inn?"

Only now did Fiona realize how indiscreet she had been. With eyes only for Sean, she hadn't seen the eyes watching them. Her need for him had been so ravenous and so compelling she had thought of nothing else. Clenching her fists, she determined to get through this interview in silence. Tomorrow, she would be gone from here.

"I've sent word to Robert. God knows how he'll deal with your scandalous behavior, but I promise you, you Irish whore, you'll pay dearly." With that, Martha swept from the room, holding aside her skirts as though touching Fiona might soil her. Reverend Mr. Moore followed meekly.

Distractedly, Fiona paced the room, sick with the realization that the servants, the stable hands, and even the villagers were aware of her meetings with Sean. Damn them all, she told herself, lifting her chin. Tomorrow, she would leave them behind and . . . please God . . . never see any of them again.

When Sean arrived, she was waiting for him at the nursery tea table. There was no point any longer in trying to dissemble or pretend, so she sent the maids and the nurse from the room and closed the door firmly behind them.

"God help me," Sean said when she told him. "I've brought trouble on ye, love."

"Not you, darling," she answered slipping her arms about his waist and looking into his face. Kathleen stared up at them with wide eyes. "It's my fault for not going away with you the very first day. Now, we'll go tomorrow."

Sean drew her close and kissed her until Kathleen tugged at her skirts for attention. Happiness glowed in Sean's face as he stooped to lift his daughter in his arms and kiss her cheek. "Tomorrow," he said.

While she waited, almost frantic, after Martha's departure, Fiona had made plans. Now, she gave Sean the tickets to Ireland for safekeeping. "We'll take the early train to Holyhead," she told him, "and catch the packet for Dublin."

"Aye," he agreed, smiling as Kathleen reached up to rumple his hair.

"I'll pack what we'll need and bring my bag to the inn tonight after dark." She drew in her breath sharply. "I couldn't stand another confrontation with Martha. In the morning, we'll slip away quietly and meet you at the station."

Holding Kathleen in one arm, Sean reached out the other to draw Fiona into his embrace. Eyes glowing with happiness, he bent to kiss her. "Thanks be to God," he murmured against her lips. "We'll never part again in this life."

She shouldn't have stayed at the inn with Sean, Fiona knew, handing the horse's reins to the smirking groom. Ignoring his look, she said, "Hitch the gig right away. I'll be going into the village."

A contented sigh escaped her as she hurried toward the house. It was impossible for her to be alone with Sean without wanting to lie with him, to join their bodies in that perfect unity that sent her soul soaring beyond the stars. She drew a deep breath, her heart filled with the incredible knowledge that from today she would be with him always.

There was nothing to be done now, but collect Kathleen. Fiona was already dressed for traveling, and she had asked Nurse to dress her charge warmly this morning for a trip into the village.

Faint sobs came to her as she pushed open the nursery door. Nurse sat rocking by the fire, her apron pressed to her eyes. Startled by Fiona's entrance, she sprang to her feet. Guilt washed over her tear-stained face.

"Where's Kathleen?" Fiona demanded, a sense of dread creeping over her as she glanced about the strangely silent room.

"Oh, my lady!" Nurse began to sob uncontrollably.

"Stop it!" Fiona cried, seizing the woman by her shoulders and shaking her. "Where's my daughter?"

"They took her," Nurse sobbed. Terror stabbed through Fiona, and she scarcely recognized her own voice in the awful cry torn from her throat.

"Who?" and she shook the nurse roughly.

"The Reverend and Mrs. Moore," Nurse gasped out the words. "They took her away." Her eyes slid away from Fiona's. "Mrs. Moore said you're not fit to be mother to Lord Hadley's child, and she'll not let you have her back."

·◁| CHAPTER 12 |▷·

Blinding rage erased her first panic. Fiona ran down the stairs, shaking with fury. How dared Martha touch her child? How dared she play God and pass judgment? Brushing aside the surprised groom, she leaped into the waiting gig and whipped up the horse.

At the dower house, she jumped down, handing the reins to a gardener, who seemed to be the only person about. The cold wind tore at her cape, and the oppressive gray sky seemed to lie against the soaring roof of the house.

Martha's formidable butler answered her ring. He was a large man, with a face set in blank stolid lines. "Madame is not home to you, my lady," he intoned in an expressionless voice.

"Damn your bloody mistress!" Fiona cried, trying to force her way past him. "She's stolen my child, and I want her back."

"You are not to be allowed in the house, my lady."

His hands were like a vise on her shoulders, his large body blocking the wide doorway. Fiona's rage dissolved into a bottomless fear. "Let me in, you fool! I'll have my daughter." Her cry of panic might as well have been shouted into the autumn wind for all the impact her words had on the man.

"I'm sorry, my lady." With a rude shove, he pushed her out of the doorway and slammed the great carved oak door in her face.

Sanity seemed to desert her. Fiona screamed and wept and pounded upon the unforgiving door until her hands bled. Exhausted, she sank down on the stone step, weeping wildly.

At last, she became aware of the gardener, still holding her horse and staring at her in open-mouthed astonishment. She must go to Sean. A sense of relief flowed through her at the thought. The butler's strength would be nothing against Sean. Together, they would take their daughter back from these conscienceless child stealers.

Sean was waiting for her in his room at the inn. Their bags stood ready for the journey, but already he was pacing the floor. Apprehension gripped him like an icy hand when he heard the train whistle from the village station. Had Fiona changed her mind? Or had something happened to her?

The door flung open, and he cried out at the sight of her. The dark blue merino dress was disheveled, her hair blown awry, and her face ravaged by tears.

"Fee!" Sean took her in his arms, and she began weeping hoarsely. "For the love of God, darlin', what's happened?"

"They've stolen Kathleen," she gasped out between sobs.

"Who?" His apprehension hardened into fear.

"That wicked bitch, Martha, and the Reverend Moore. They took Kathleen to the dower house, and they won't even let me see her."

"God curse their bloody souls!" Sean held her close, trying to quiet her uncontrollable weeping. "Fee . . . Fee . . . sweet love, stop now. It'll be all right. I'll go with ye, and we'll get her back if I have to murder them all to do it."

Slowly the weeping faded into gasping sobs, as Fiona clung to him. "She called me a whore, Sean. She said I'm not fit to be a mother."

"God send her to the fires of hell for what she's done," Sean growled. Holding Fiona away from him, he looked fiercely into her face. "We'll go now and take Kathleen away."

A sense of his strength flowed through Fiona. Looking up at his stern face, she felt reason return. Taking a kerchief from her sleeve she began to wipe her tear-wet face. Sean bent to kiss her gently, and her arms tightened about him.

"Are ye all right, darlin'?"

"Yes, my love . . . now I am all right." The warmth of his

embrace, his deep voice soothing her, and his gentle kisses brought a sense of calm. They must not do anything foolish now, she thought, or they would lose Kathleen forever.

"We'll steal her back tonight," she told him, her confidence rising as the plan formed in her mind. "I know the house and we can go in the dark when everyone's asleep. I'll come for you in the gig . . . we'll get Kathleen, then take the night train."

"We can go now," Sean protested. "I'll beat the bloody hell out of anyone who tries to stop me."

"No," she said, pressing a finger against the angry set of his mouth. "At night will be best . . . then no one will follow us. We'll be aboard a packet to Ireland by the time they know we've taken her away."

"Aye," he conceded reluctantly. "But ye'll not go back to the Hall."

"I must," she sighed. "I nearly killed the poor horse for whipping him in my panic. I'll take him back and get another."

"First you rest." Sean lifted her in his arms and laid her on the bed. "I'll bring some food from the tavern, and a wee drop of whiskey to calm you."

"Darling . . . darling . . ." Fiona let out a long sigh of relief. Reaching up, she cupped his face in her two hands and drew him down to kiss his mouth. "Tomorrow . . ." she murmured. "Tomorrow, we will be in Ireland, together for always."

Hours later, Fiona wept again, for pity of the bloody stripes on the horse's back. In all her life, she had never treated an animal so. Back at Hadley Hall, she followed the groom into the stable to make sure he cared for the creature properly. Then, ordering him to hitch another horse to the gig, she went into the house to repair her clothing and her hair.

Kate could not meet her eyes when she answered Fiona's ring. "Yes, my lady," she said in a low voice when asked to take away the torn and stained traveling dress and bring another. This gown was of dark green velvet trimmed with beading. It was more elegant than Fiona would have chosen, but it would do.

Kate had nearly finished with her hair when Fiona heard

the rattle of a coach driving onto the gravel sweep. A chill of fear swept through her. Dear God, she thought, not Martha again . . . and she wished she had brought Sean with her. Yet, if it were Martha, perhaps she had brought Kathleen. Fiona stifled the urge to flee down the back stairs. She would face it out.

The scrape of the bolt in the door separating her bedroom from her husband's startled her. Drenched with horror, she met the icy gray eyes of Lord Hadley in her mirror.

"Robert!" she gasped, standing up so quickly that Kate dropped the hairbrush to the floor.

"Yes . . . Robert." There was an ugly tone to his low voice. "Your husband, remember?" For a long harrowing moment, he stared at her with cold hatred. "Get out!" he said to Kate, who stood trembling behind Fiona, and the maid scurried from the room.

Dark dread filled her, and she recoiled from Robert as he moved slowly across the room toward her.

"You whore!" he shouted, his face contorted with fury. When he raised his arm, she knew she must get away. The odor of whiskey was strong on him, and she had seen his violence when he was drunk. He had struck her many times, and beaten animals into submission. Whirling, she ran toward the door.

Robert was quicker. His hand caught her shoulder and flung her backward. She stumbled, one cheek hitting the edge of the dressing table as she fell. Warm blood dripped onto the beaded velvet.

Quickly, he bolted the outside door, then turned toward Fiona where she struggled to rise from the floor. The expression on his face made her flesh creep. The gray eyes gleamed like those of a madman, and his thin mouth was twisted in a hideous grimace.

"Cuckold me, will you . . . you bloody Irish bitch!" His hand smashed across her face, knocking her head back against the dressing table. Fiona cried out in pain, lifting her arms to ward off his blows.

Seizing one shoulder, he jerked her to her feet. "Whore!" he shouted again, his fist striking her full in the face. Blood spurted from her nose. Crying out, Fiona covered her face with her hands, trying to staunch the flow.

Eyes glittering strangely, Robert grabbed her with both hands and flung her onto the bed. Horror poured over Fiona as he pulled down his trousers, and she saw that he was sexually aroused.

"Monster!" she screamed, struggling with him as he ripped away her clothing.

Robert was a man of the outdoors, and Fiona was no match for his superior strength. He heaved himself on top of her, pinning her to the bed, while his hands tore away her skirts. The white pillows were splotched red with her blood as she tossed her head from side to side, trying to free herself from him. All the years when he had shown her only the most perfunctory attention had not prepared her for such violence.

Finally freeing her arms, she clawed at his face, pushing, tearing his shirt and tugging at his hair. Robert grabbed her arms, pinning them to her sides. He thrust into her with such violence she thought her body would tear apart.

Fiona screamed until her throat ached. No one came . . . no one would. Again and again, he forced himself into her, hitting her when she tried to resist. Never in all the years had their sexual union lasted this long. With a guttural cry, Robert threw back his head, his eyes tightly closed, his lips curling back over his teeth. She felt him explode inside her, and prayed that it was over.

But when he rolled off her, he rose and began to beat her again. Methodically this time, over her whole body, with special abuse for her breasts and pelvic region. Pain flowed over her in great agonizing waves, until she could bear no more and sank gratefully into unconsciousness.

Sean stared out through the bars at the tall gables of Hadley Hall silhouetted against the sunset. It had happened so quickly he hadn't had a chance. He'd thought it was Fiona returning when the door burst open, and three men rushed him.

"Horse thief," one of them muttered as they pinned him to the floor and bound his hands behind him.

Struggling to shake them off, Sean shouted a demand for an explanation.

"Yer riding a horse from the Hadley stables," the stout

constable told him. "Without permission or a bill of sale. That's horse stealing, and His Lordship's put out a warrant for ye."

"His Lordship?" Sean gasped, struggling to his feet.

"Right, mate. Lord Hadley's back and wants his horse, as well as the thief who took it."

"Likely wants the thief who took his wife, too," one of the men snickered. He fell silent at a look from the self-important constable.

Now, Sean stood in the ancient, stinking jail, half-crazed with not knowing what had happened to Fiona.

"Horse stealin's a hanging offense," the constable had informed him as he turned the key in the tiny cell.

Damn that bastard Hadley . . . and Sean's hands tightened about the bars in fury. A bit of loose brick fell to the floor. Sean's heart rose as he shook the bars and found them loose in the centuries-old brick. The fools hadn't bothered to search him. Reaching into his boot, Sean drew out a stout knife and began to dig the bars loose from the rotten window sill.

Struggling up through a haze of pain, Fiona turned her head on the bloody pillow to look at the room. She was alone, still lying in her torn and ruined gown on the bed that was dark with blood. Tears ran from her eyes when she looked down at her bruised and battered body. Blood flowed in a hot pulsating stream between her thighs.

Desperately, she gathered her strength to reach for the bell pull. Some one must come to help her, or she would bleed to death here alone. With all her waning strength, she pulled at the bell rope . . . again and again.

Fear clotted her chest. Painfully, she lifted herself into a sitting position. If no one would answer the bell, she must go find help. Her whole body cried out in agony as she placed her feet on the floor and tried to stand. Blackness poured over her and she felt the carpet scrape against her face.

Carefully, Sean eased the last bar from the window. The constable had left no guard, and there was no one about to hear. But the tavern down the street was filled with roisterers, and one might chance by.

Barely squeezing his wide shoulders through the narrow window, he jumped to the ground, allowing himself a long sigh of relief. He had no doubt that Lord Hadley, who owned this village, had the power to have him hanged. Every cell of him longed to seek Fiona, to hold her safe and take her away with him. Yet, he knew the odds against him. A lifetime of subjection to the rule of the English nobility had taught him the absolute power of their authority. No one could dare question Lord Hadley or his motives.

Fiona! He almost cried the name aloud. If he were caught again, there would be no waiting for the hanging. His death would not help her. She was strong and quick. She would find a way to escape the bloody lord with their daughter. Perhaps she already had.

He would go to Holyhead and wait for her there . . . send a message to her to come to him. The decision made, he kept to the shadows as he crossed the village. The late train stood puffing in the station. Sean broke into a run as its departing whistle sounded. Leaving the protective shadows, he ran across the station and swung aboard.

"Dear God!" The sound of Kate's cry brought Fiona up into a wavering consciousness. She was dimly aware that she lay on the cold floor of her bedroom, and that the carpet was soaked with blood.

"Oh, my lady!" Tears poured down the maid's plump face as she struggled to lift her limp mistress onto the bed. "The wicked, wicked man," Kate sobbed, pulling away the bloody bedclothes and looking down into Fiona's glazed eyes. "He told me to clean you up and keep my mouth shut if I valued my position here." When she started undressing her mistress's battered body, she cried out.

"He's a devil," she told Fiona who lay limp and unresponsive. "God will punish him . . . oh, surely God will punish him."

Through a deepening haze, Fiona watched Kate changing the bedclothes, washing away the blood, binding a pad between her thighs where the blood still flowed. She wanted to speak to her maid . . . to ask about Sean, about Kathleen. But there was no strength for the words.

Still weeping, Kate carefully tucked a warm comforter about her. Fiona felt herself drifting, dimly aware that there was no more pain.

Sean's face seemed to float in the candlelight. Gathering all her strength, Fiona reached a hand toward him. "Darling . . . darling . . ."

"What, my lady?" At once Kate was there, bending over her, straining to hear the garbled words.

"Tomorrow . . ." The words seemed to come from far away, from another body in another place. "Tomorrow, darling . . ."

Her soul flew out across the dark Irish Sea and soared with the larks above Chuchulain's ruined tower.

BOOK II

···❧⟨ CHAPTER 13 ⟩❧···

Brookfield, England, 1877

Because it was her birthday, Travis, the governess, had allowed Kathleen to wear a new spring gown of sprigged muslin. She'd even cancelled lessons for the day.

But no one would remember now that it was her tenth birthday.

Huddled in the shadows on the landing of the great curving staircase, Kathleen pushed back her long, honey-colored hair and covered her ears against the screams from the birthing room. The doctor had been sent for this morning, and everything else at Hadley Hall seemed to have come to a halt. If her stepmother, Deborah, produced the son and heir her father so desperately desired, her birthday would be forgotten forever. Only her governess had remembered, and tears of self-pity welled in her blue eyes as she realized there had not even been a package from her grandparents in Ireland.

The dark Persian carpet on the staircase scratched her legs, and she pulled her skirt about them, looking down into the great hall with its elaborately manteled fireplace. Loneliness wrapped about her like a dark thick blanket as she dreamed of the Ireland she had never seen and the grandparents who wrote loving letters. They would never again come to Hadley Hall. Deep in her being, she knew that, even though she had been only three when they were last here.

It was after her mother's funeral, and she had sat on the stairs as she did now, alone and afraid. The memory of loud, angry voices saying bitter, ugly words haunted her. She could not comprehend the reason for the quarrel then, any more than she could comprehend the real meaning of death, or that she would never see her mother again.

Now, try as she might, she could not conjure up a true memory of Mama. There was only a sense of warmth and security, loving arms holding her, and a faint scent like summer roses. Every trace of her mother had been banished from Hadley Hall, even before Papa married Deborah. There was no portrait hanging with the rest of the Hadleys, who glowered from the walls and the hallways, no clothing or jewelry. It was as though Fiona Browne had never lived at Hadley Hall.

Kathleen remembered when her father had brought his bride home. She had been six years old and beside herself with excitement. She must have been sure that now she would have a mother to love her, as the father she seldom saw did not. Travis saw to it that she was dressed in her best to greet the bride and groom when they returned from their honeymoon in London.

Earlier, Travis had been shocked when Lord Hadley took a steel mill owner's daughter as his second wife. "Money!" she sniffed to Baines, the butler.

Baines had given the governess a condescending look. "The girl seems acceptable enough . . . and healthy enough to bear His Lordship an heir." With a shrug, he added, "Her money will pay your wages." Travis seemed about to say more, but Baines had spotted Kathleen listening, wide-eyed, and shushed the governess.

How she had wanted Papa to hug her that day in the great hall, where all the servants were lined up to greet their new mistress. But he had merely nodded toward her, and said, "This is my wife, Lady Deborah, Kathleen."

Dropping the curtsey she had practiced all week, Kathleen stared up at the woman who would be her mother now. Deborah wore an elegant gown of blue silk, ornately trimmed with ruffles, lace and silk flowers. Kathleen had thought her beautiful then, with the wide-brimmed lacy hat on her dark blond hair.

Without expression, she looked down at the child staring at her. "Fiona Browne's daughter?" she asked.

There was the faint sound of indrawn breath along the line of servants. Kathleen glanced at their suddenly impassive faces, wondering why the very mention of her mother's name brought such a reaction.

"That will be enough, Deborah," Papa had said through clenched teeth. Kathleen thought he looked like he wanted to slap his wife . . . exactly the way he'd looked when he had slapped her for talking of her mother. She had seen his hand grip Deborah's elbow tightly. "Let it die," he had gritted in a low voice.

Deborah had winced at his touch, but quickly regained her poise, smiling and greeting the servants as though nothing had happened.

In the years that followed, Kathleen puzzled over the relationship between her father and his wife. Deborah was always unsure of herself in his presence, constantly trying to please him and gain his attention. At first, it seemed Papa would be disappointed in his longing for a son and heir. It was over a year before Deborah became pregnant and miscarried. Next, there was a premature girl who died, then another miscarriage. The baby now arriving upstairs had gone full term, with Deborah in bed most of the time.

Kathleen shuddered as the gasping cries rose. Did it hurt so terribly? She knew it hurt the mares too, but it was soon over, and they always seemed so pleased when they turned to look at the baby horses they had borne.

She hoped this baby lived . . . boy or girl . . . although Papa would certainly be kinder to Deborah if the child were a boy. Perhaps now, there would be someone to love Kathleen, she thought with a sigh, a small brother or sister. She had already made friends with Higgins, the new nanny. A smile touched Kathleen's lips. The baby would be her birthday gift!

Kathleen lifted her head, listening to the silence. Deborah's cries had ceased. Down the hallway, behind the closed door, she heard a baby crying lustily. Joy leaped in her heart, and she ran up the stairs, into the hallway to confront one of the maids who came from the birthing room carrying a basin of bloody water.

"Is the baby all right?" she demanded.

The maid looked at her in surprise. "The doctor will be down to tell His Lordship at once." Then she relented, smiling. "A fine healthy boy."

Kathleen raced down the stairs, holding the skirts of her sprigged muslin gown high. At the bottom, she stopped suddenly. This news was the only thing that would make Papa happy, other than the day's hunt, yet she instinctively knew he would be annoyed if she were to burst in to tell him. Even at his most ingratiating, he was cold, and when he was annoyed, he could freeze her with one look. With a sigh of resignation, she sat down on the stairs. Shortly the doctor, Mr. Wyatt, came down, patting her on the head as he passed.

Excited, wanting to share the news, Kathleen popped up from her seat and followed him down the long hallway to where her father waited in the library. The doctor left the door ajar, and she could see Papa turn toward him from where he was pouring a glass of port from a nearly empty decanter.

"Congratulations, Your Lordship," the doctor boomed. "You have a fine, healthy son."

A look of triumph filled Papa's face. His pale eyes gleamed as he turned to fill another glass with port, handing it to the doctor. "To my son," he said, raising his glass. "Heir to Hadley Hall and Viscount of Brookfield. Lord Robert Edward Hadley. At last!"

Unable to contain herself, Kathleen ran to him, throwing her arms about him. He stood stiff and unresponsive, but she was used to that. "Oh, Papa," she cried, almost dancing as she looked up at him. "Isn't it wonderful! My brother Edward was born on my birthday, and we will be like twins."

The doctor's booming laugh filled the room as he reached to pat her head again.

Even her father smiled indulgently. "It is a special day, Kathleen. You may eat dinner with me tonight. Tell Baines I said cook must fix whatever dessert you want for the occasion."

"Oh Papa!" She attempted to hug him again and saw him visibly withdraw. He did not like to be touched. She guessed she had always known that. In the future, she would remember.

How lovely the table looked, Kathleen thought later, looking down the long expanse of snowy linen. Candles in silver candelabra gleamed on the sparkling crystal, the heavy silver, and the centerpiece of spring lilies. Travis had made her change into her best silk gown of pale rose. The maid had brushed her hair and tied it up with a matching ribbon. Even Aunt Martha had said she looked quite presentable.

Papa sat at the head of the table, drinking claret now. Aunt Martha was on his right, across from the doctor, and Uncle Bertram sat opposite Kathleen.

"Everything is so perfect!" Kathleen exclaimed as the soup was served. Never before had she been allowed at the adults' table.

"Everything is as it should be," Aunt Martha said coldly. "One should never accept anything less from one's servants."

"Yes, ma'am," Kathleen murmured, her spirits dampened, a reaction Aunt Martha always seemed to evoke.

The meal became interminable. Every time she tried to enter the conversation, which turned from the new heir inevitably to the hunt, Aunt Martha shushed her. Her appetite gone, Kathleen stared at her aunt across the table. They had never liked each other, although she kept hoping someday things would change. Yet, even Deborah was not fond of Martha . . . wary of her, but certainly not fond.

Her aunt sat straight upright in her chair. Even here, at a family dinner, she held her mouth in a hard straight line. Her corseted breasts covered by plum-colored silk looked hard too, as though the whole woman was carved of stone.

Uncle Bertram was always quiet. He was a little deaf, or at least pretended to be, and sat abstractedly through dinner as though thinking of otherworldly things, as befitted the Vicar of Brookfield.

"Kathleen!" her aunt's sharp voice brought her quickly back from her thoughts. "Where are your manners? You're making a dreadful mess of your fish. Baines . . . take it away."

Papa glared at her. "Perhaps I shouldn't have allowed you to eat with the adults," he grumbled.

Shamed, Kathleen stared down at the disappearing plate, her stomach roiling. When the roast and Yorkshire pudding were set before her, she looked at it with loathing. The sounds of cutlery against china, the adults' conversation seemed to come from a far distance.

"Kathleen!" Papa's sharp voice brought a cold sweat to her skin. "Sit up straight," he snapped. "Your manners are atrocious. Not even good enough for the children's table!"

They hated her. All of them, Papa, and her aunt, and Deborah. She could never do anything to please them and make them love her. Despair settled over her, and her stomach heaved. Before she realized what was happening, she had vomited into the Yorkshire pudding.

Knowing she was in disgrace, Kathleen stayed in her room next day. Even Travis could not coax her out for a walk. For the first time, Papa had offered her the privilege of the adult dinner table and she had proven herself unworthy. The certainty that he would not offer a second chance settled bleakly over her.

The clouds of despondency lifted when the post was brought from the village and there was a package for her from Ireland. With the package was a letter in her grandmother's precise hand. Kathleen curled up on her bed to read it, postponing opening the package, savoring the anticipation.

"Darling Kathleen," the letter read. "Your present is late because your grandfather, my beloved Cedric, passed away in his sleep last Monday night. I knew Ireland was too far to bring a ten-year-old for a funeral, but I have written to your Papa, asking him to let you visit me.

"With your present are some things of your mother's. Perhaps it would be best if you did not show them to your father. I long to see you, for you are all that's left of my family. I want you to love Morning Hill as I do, and as your mother did. Your loving grandmother, Margaret Browne."

Quickly, Kathleen tore open the package, her delight in the gift dimmed by the death of a grandfather she could not remember. With a sigh of disappointment, she lifted out the fine wool shawl, woven in shades of blue. It was new . . . not her mother's. But wrapped in tissue beneath, she found a gold-framed miniature. On the back her grandmother had written, "Fiona Browne on her sixteenth birthday, 1866."

Love flowed through Kathleen as she stared at her mother's beautiful face, the shining auburn hair, and the hazel eyes. A faint memory stirred of a beautiful laughing face looking into hers, warm kisses, loving arms.

There was something else in the box, and she carefully removed the tissue, her eyes drawn again and again to her mother's image. It was a book, the English Book of Common Prayer, bound in ivory-colored leather with a worn gold filigree design on the cover. "Fiona Browne" was written on the title page in a round girlish hand. The book fell open then, to the marriage ceremony. Puzzled, Kathleen carefully touched the three tiny flowers pressed there, round with scalloped edges, colored white, and lavender, and purple. Her mother had placed them there, long ago, for reasons she could never know. Tears filled her eyes, along with a sense of loss so profound she could hardly bear it.

"My grandmother sent this from Ireland," Kathleen later told Higgins, holding up the blue shawl. "Do you think Edward would like it?"

The wet nurse handed the baby to Higgins, wiped her breasts and silently left the room. Higgins cooed to the child as she changed his nappy, then tucked him into the carved mahogany, satin-lined cradle. Smiling, she turned to touch the shawl gently. "It's lovely, miss. But I'm afraid Edward would only spit up on it. It's your gift, dear, keep it for yourself."

Even her gift was rejected, and Kathleen sighed inwardly. "May I hold him?" she asked uncertainly.

"Well . . ." Higgins hesitated, glancing around to make sure they were alone. Kathleen settled in the rocking chair, holding out her arms.

As she carefully placed the blanket-wrapped baby in Kathleen's arms, Higgins added, "He's quite a beautiful child."

Turning back the blanket, Kathleen looked into the chubby little face. The baby yawned and opened his eyes. It seemed to her those eyes smiled at her and love for him welled up inside her.

Carefully, she touched one of the waving fists, and felt a rush of joy as he clasped her finger tight.

"He likes me!" she cried, looking up at Higgins with shining eyes. "Oh, he's so strong and beautiful." The wide dark baby eyes seemed to regard her intently as though a message of love and bonding flowed between them.

"Dear little Edward," she whispered, overwhelmed by love for him. "You are my birthday twin . . . and I will love you always."

CHAPTER 14

1885

"An eavesdropper never hears good of herself," Travis had often said before her tenure at Hadley Hall ended on Kathleen's fourteenth birthday. The words flashed through Kathleen's mind now, as she paused outside the drawing room door. She had stayed to watch Edward's riding lesson, and now she was late for tea. Her hair and clothes were rumpled from her headlong rush into the house. Vainly trying to smooth the wrinkles from the dark brown foulard riding habit that managed to disguise her slender figure, she listened unwillingly. Her deep blue eyes clouded with old hurts as she pushed her heavy hair back into the neat chignon with a trembling hand.

Inside the drawing room, Deborah made no attempt to lower her voice as she scornfully said, "She's a mousy little thing . . . always riding off by herself. Never opens her mouth except to Edward."

"Nevertheless, my dear," Papa interrupted impatiently. "She shall have a season in society. I've told my solicitor to take a house for us in London."

"A waste of money . . ." Deborah began.

"We'll hear no more about it." There was an edge to Papa's voice. "Since your esteemed father saw fit to tie your fortune up so that we've nothing but the annual income, I must look for other ways to settle my debts."

"If only you hadn't gone through Fiona's money and my dowry." Deborah's voice was a low, complaining whine. "My father says that using capital is inexcusable."

"Your father be damned!" Papa replied harshly. "He's left me no alternative but to arrange an advantageous marriage for Kathleen. A rich son-in-law can be a great asset. She'll be eighteen this spring. We can't wait any longer."

"But I don't like London." Deborah's faint words sounded a bit shaky.

"You'd better learn to like it," Papa growled, "since you have Victoria and Georgiana, daughters of your own, to marry off one day."

In the strained silence that followed, Kathleen sighed, composed her face and stepped into the room, slipping into her place. Tea had been set next to the tall windows overlooking the lawn that swept down to the woods where the river gleamed through the trees. The windows stood open, for the spring day was unseasonably warm. Brilliant-colored tulips gleamed in the sunlight, and robins called from the budding apple trees.

"You're late." Papa frowned at her.

"I was riding with Edward and forgot the time." Taking a teacup from Deborah, she sipped her tea, hoping her face did not reveal the pain the overheard conversation had caused her. "Alston says he's doing very well." She said it not only to please Papa, but because she was proud of Edward.

"Humph," Papa replied, sipping his tea, and staring out the windows.

Deborah cleared her throat in a familiar diffident manner. She was no more at ease with Papa than was the rest of the family, Kathleen thought sympathetically, hoping whatever husband might come her way would not be so cold and distant. There was a dark bruise on Deborah's left cheek, and Kathleen idly wondered if she had slipped in her bath again.

"Your father has decided you'll have a season in London, Kathleen." Deborah glanced uneasily at her husband, who continued to stare at the window in silence. "We must call in the seamstress and begin work on your gowns." Again she glanced at Papa, as though seeking his approval for her words.

"Quite right," Papa said, turning to regard the two of

them speculatively. He had grown quite heavy, his once handsome face tending to jowls now, and flushed with the bloom of wine, the once bright blond hair dulled by a mixture of gray.

"I'll leave you two to your plans," he said, rising. "I'd like to have Alston show me Edward's progress."

Silence fell in the room at his departure. Kathleen stared at the silver tea service, gleaming in the afternoon light. The familiar heavy feeling pressed inside her chest. Try as she might, she could not win the affections of her father or her stepmother. If Mama had lived, perhaps it would have been different. But it was useless to dream of that. At last, she became aware of her stepmother's distress.

Deborah sat perfectly still, staring at the door where her husband had exited the room. Her pale blue eyes glistened with unshed tears, and her hands nervously worked the handkerchief she held.

Compassion filled Kathleen's heart. Although Deborah never made an effort to be kind to her, she had often felt sorry for her stepmother. Papa treated her only a little better than he treated the housekeeper, and he was often quite disdainful of her in the presence of guests. And there were all those lamely explained bruises . . .

"What is it, Mother?" she asked softly, half afraid of the anticipated rejection.

At once, Deborah straightened in her chair, making a valiant effort to control her tears. Turning, she filled the teacup again, and took another slice of plum cake, a habit that was rapidly ruining her once fine plump figure.

Kathleen waited, not surprised that Deborah did not reply. She had often enough indicated she felt her stepdaughter was beneath her confidences.

After a moment, she lay down the half-eaten cake, setting her teacup down so abruptly the tea sloshed onto the linen cloth. "I've never been in society in London." The note of despair in her voice astonished Kathleen.

"Neither have I," she replied, without thinking.

"It's quite a different thing," Deborah said crossly, frowning at her. "I don't . . . I don't . . ." Despite her efforts at control, she dissolved into weeping.

"I shan't know what to do," she sobbed. "I'll embarrass

135

Robert and ruin your chances for a rich husband." Kathleen stared at her in astonishment. "I wasn't born to the aristocracy, you know," Deborah added, lifting her round chin defiantly. "I had no season in London. I don't know where to begin . . ." She began to weep again.

Rising from her chair, Kathleen tentatively patted Deborah's heaving shoulder. "Never mind," she said. "I'll tell Papa I don't wish to go to London to be displayed on the marriage market."

"No! No!" Deborah protested, clasping her hand and staring up at her with wide frightened eyes. "Robert would be furious. He'd think it was my fault, and I couldn't bear it."

"I truly don't want to go." Kathleen looked seriously down at her stepmother.

"It won't do." Deborah's voice took on a note of panic. "We must go. Robert has said so."

Kathleen sighed, sorry for this woman whose whole world turned on her husband's approval. With an ironic twist to her mouth, she thought that if she lived for approval, she would have died long ago. In all this great house, there were only two people who cared for her: Edward, who loved her as truly as she loved him; and Francine.

When the time had come to dispense with the services of a governess, and Travis had departed, Kathleen had been inconsolable at what seemed the loss of her only friend. It was Aunt Martha who had said, "Give her a French maid like all the fashionable young girls have, and she'll soon get over Travis."

So Francine had come to Hadley Hall. She was five years older than Kathleen, born in France, and sent into service at the age of thirteen. After she came to Hadley Hall, she was ill for a long time, finally confiding to Kathleen that one of Lady Veith's sons had made her pregnant, then sent her to a village midwife for an abortion which was badly bungled. Filled with compassion, Kathleen cared for her, covering up her neglect of her duties and winning the girl's undying loyalty.

Lonely for the company of other girls, Kathleen enjoyed the sprightly Francine, with her sparkling dark eyes and dark curly hair, her round bosoms and hips that made the menservants stare. They became friends as well as mistress and maid. Kathleen delighted in the evenings curled up by her bedroom fire while Francine plied her with all the backstairs gossip. Even after she was well, she was not an efficient maid and would have soon lost her position if Deborah had known the truth. Too often, Kathleen did for herself, knowing that Francine was dallying with a handsome footman or one of the grooms. It was worth it to have the ebullient young girl as a friend.

"Don't tell your father," Deborah implored now, still clinging to Kathleen's hand. "Please."

"It will be all right," Kathleen assured her, determined that she would find the opportunity to speak to her father. What did she have to lose, since he disliked her anyway? She had heard enough of the social season in London from the guests who frequented Hadley Hall to realize that disaster lay ahead for Deborah, and for herself.

But when Kathleen approached her father in the library before dinner, her courage failed. For once, there were no house guests and Lord Hadley was alone. In the seventeen years they had lived together, they had never had a private conversation. He was unfailingly gruff and uneasy in her presence, and she was aware that she was an annoyance to him. Long ago, she'd realized that he cared little for family and that his obsession with the joys of the hunt went beyond the normal. Now, the Prince of Wales had started the fashion of shooting, and her father had joined in avidly. It was worse than fox hunting to Kathleen. At least in the hunt, one had the joy of fine horsemanship, but to simply slaughter wild animals seemed to her cruel and stupid.

She saw that he had nearly finished a bottle of port, and his eyes were not quite focused. It took all her courage to speak, and the words came out in an ill-considered rush.

"Papa, I wanted to tell you that I don't wish to have a London season. I'd rather stay here at Hadley Hall with Edward and the little girls." Her voice wavered, for this was the boldest she had ever been with him.

He glared at her. "If I'm willing to go in debt to find a rich husband for you . . . you'll damn well do your part. We're going to London!" The words had such a ring of finality, it was a moment before she could bring herself to speak again.

"Deborah doesn't want to go either. She feels incapable, since she's never been in society."

Papa filled his glass with the last of the port, muttering to himself. When he turned to face her, she saw that he was furious, and she shrank within herself as she always did in his presence. "Stupid woman," he growled. "How I could have lowered myself . . ." The words trailed off as he stared into his wine. "Well," he finally said. "Nothing to be done about it but to contact my relations in London. They'll find a sponsor to help guide you and Deborah through the season."

"But, Papa . . ." Kathleen dared a final protest.

"It's decided!" He glared at her. "You've done nothing else for me," he added in an accusing tone. "I expect you to find a wealthy husband."

She had always obeyed him, and everyone else, fearing that disobedience might cost her what little status she held in this household. "Yes, Papa," she replied meekly.

The London house was a small, but elegant, Georgian mansion on Grosvenor Square. It was a cold and rainy May evening when they arrived in the traveling coach, Papa, Deborah and Kathleen, with the servants and luggage following in the wagonette. The coachman had trouble finding the address, and Papa cursed him roundly before they stopped at a tavern to ask the way.

All during the weary coach ride down to London, Deborah had speculated nervously about the young woman who was to be her mentor in society. She seemed to have completely dismissed from her mind the children who had been left with their nannies and the servants. Kathleen sighed, already missing Edward.

Lady Serena Neville's services had been obtained through Martha's contacts with her in-laws. In her first season, Serena Ainsworth had made a brilliant marriage to the elderly Lord Neville, yet when he died a few years later she had been left penniless. Lord Neville's heirs, his children from his first marriage, had bitterly resented their father's young bride and had conspired to see that she inherited nothing from his vast estates.

Papa refused to say how much Lady Neville's services were costing him. Martha, a bit put out at not being invited to join them for the season in London, had sniffed and said, "She's thankful for anything that comes her way, according to my sister-in-law, Lady Veith."

Shivering from the cold and damp, Kathleen could feel only relief when the butler escorted them into the drawing room. A fire blazed in the fireplace, reflecting off the polished furniture and the glittering crystal chandeliers. An Aubusson carpet lay on the gleaming floor, and in one corner a rosewood piano displayed a huge vase of spring blossoms. The room was finished with paneling painted a pale gold. Draperies in gold velvet hung at the tall windows, and the furniture was upholstered in a gold velvet with green satin striping.

Lady Neville stepped forward to greet them, while footmen took their wet cloaks. Kathleen stared in surprise at this young woman who would be her guide through the feared social season. She had expected someone as formidable as Aunt Martha. Serena Neville was still under thirty, Kathleen was certain, and she seemed to belong here; she was as small and exquisite as the house itself. Her oval face was like delicate porcelain framed by clouds of dark hair done up in the latest fashion.

Smiling, she came toward them, holding out her hand. "Lord and Lady Hadley, and Miss Hadley, how nice to meet you." She wore a pale green gown that matched her eyes. Looking into those eyes, Kathleen saw a reserve there, as though Lady Neville had learned to guard her feelings.

"Nasty night, what?" Papa said gruffly, while Deborah nodded nervously.

"I'll ring for some port," Lady Neville said, as graciously as though it were her own port, not paid for by Papa. "Shall I have the servants lay out a cold supper for you?" She looked inquiringly at Deborah, who struggled to assume an air of authority and replied, "Yes, do."

While they ate the cold supper Lady Neville had thoughtfully had laid before the fire, she talked of how she had opened the house, hired the servants, stocked the pantry, and laid her plans for Kathleen's presentation to society.

"I'm pleased to see such a lovely young woman," Lady Neville said, smiling at Kathleen. "That makes everything so much easier."

Deborah glanced doubtfully at Kathleen, then said effusively, "The house looks very nice."

"It's a beautiful little house," Lady Neville replied, glancing around. There was a sadness in her eyes, and lines of pain at the corners of her mouth. Kathleen wondered where she had been living since her husband died, if she had been reduced to a room in the house of some begrudging relative.

"Certainly cost enough," Papa said gruffly, already well into his second bottle of port.

"Your solicitor and I agreed it's the best we could find with a suitable address." Lady Neville was obviously trying to conceal her annoyance, a feeling Kathleen found herself sharing.

"According to your instructions, Lord Hadley," she continued, "I've made arrangements for a reception here for Kathleen the first of June. Since the house is small and there is no ballroom, I thought that the best alternative. Caterers, musicians, flowers, have all been arranged for. If a seamstress is required, I have one we can call upon. First thing tomorrow, we should go over the guest list so that the invitations can go out at once."

Kathleen glanced at the young woman's bland face, secretly amused at the adept way she was handling Papa.

"Umnn." Papa's face was flushed, his eyes drooping. With a sigh that was barely audible, Lady Neville turned to Deborah.

Nervously, Deborah adjusted the skirts of her rumpled carriage gown, then looked up at Lady Neville with a wavering smile. "That will be quite satisfactory," she murmured.

"Miss Hadley?" Lady Neville turned to Kathleen with a pleasantly inquiring look.

What clods she must think them, Kathleen told herself as she nodded, admiring the young woman's aplomb, longing for such lovely self-assurance, and wondering miserably how she would live through the next two months.

Lady Neville had prepared a guest list that was obviously the cream of society. It included numerous Hadley relations, as well as the aristocratic Veith family, for Aunt Martha and Uncle Bertram were to come down for the reception.

The three women sat in the morning room going over the list. It was a small room, but light and airy with white painted Chinese Chippendale furniture, draperies and cushions in a bright chintz printed with blue Chinese motifs. Outside, the dreary London weather misted the green of the square across the street. Papa had gone out in the coach, saying only that he would return for supper.

"I thought perhaps you'd want to add some of your relations, Lady Hadley?" Serena Neville sipped her tea, smiling at Deborah.

"Oh my, no!" Deborah flushed miserably, looking down at her hands clasped in the lap of her plum silk morning gown. "They're in trade, you see," she mumbled, refusing to meet Lady Neville's inquiring glance.

How sad that Deborah felt she must deny her parents, Kathleen thought. They seemed so fond of her and of the grandchildren on their infrequent visits to Hadley Hall. Her mother was an older replica of Deborah, but with far more sparkle and spirit. Mr. Macabee, tall and handsome, with thick gray hair, a huge drooping moustache, and a commanding presence, looked more the aristocrat than Lord Hadley.

"Pity." Lady Neville's face was carefully bland. Speaking quickly to cover Deborah's obvious embarrassment, she turned to Kathleen. "And your mother's relatives, wasn't your grandfather a brother of Lord Mountford?"

"Grandpapa died some years ago," Kathleen replied, carefully not looking at Deborah. "Grandmama still lives in Ireland, and she's not at all well. I'm afraid we've lost contact with any other of my mother's relations."

"I see."

Of course she would see, Kathleen thought. They were mere country bumpkins, come to London to try for a wealthy husband, and nothing at all to offer in return.

"There was an aunt of Mama's," Kathleen suddenly remembered her grandmother had mentioned them. "She and her husband live here in London, he's Sir Reginald Mercer."

"Wonderful!" Lady Neville brightened for the first time. "They're in the best society since Sir Reginald is so highly regarded by the Queen." Quickly, she added the name to her list. "There's a son, I believe, and he must be included of course."

Stacking the invitations on the desk, she said, "I'll have these delivered this afternoon. And now, we should look over your gowns. Why, Lady Hadley, whatever is the matter?"

Deborah was weeping quite openly, her handkerchief to her face. "I shall never learn it all," she sobbed. "It's quite impossible."

"Nonsense." Lady Neville came around the desk to take Deborah's hand and pat it comfortingly. Kathleen warmed toward the young woman when she saw that the concern in her eyes was genuine. "It's all quite strange now, dear lady, but I'll be right beside you. Then, when you bring your own daughters down for their seasons, you will wonder why you were ever so frightened."

Under her soft encouraging words, Deborah's sobs subsided. The butler announced the arrival of the seamstress, and Deborah's fears were forgotten in the exquisite fabrics and the elaborate patterns she had brought to show.

The days that followed were busy ones, filled with fittings for the new gowns, shopping in the elegant Regent Street shops for hats, and gloves, and evening slippers. It was another world from Hadley Hall, and in spite of her fears, Kathleen found herself caught up in it. Serena had a lively sense of humor that overrode all of Deborah's complaints, and would not even allow Kathleen to retreat into her customary shyness.

Francine was beside herself with delight at the new adventure. New gowns and plans for entertainments kept her agog with excitement. Eyes sparkling mischievously, she confided to Kathleen, there was a whole new crowd of admiring males to conquer backstairs.

With a twinge of envy, Kathleen watched as Francine dabbed carmine on her lips, preparing for an assignation with a handsome footman. Gaily flinging a shawl about her shoulders, Francine departed, and Kathleen sighed. Sometimes, she would have gladly traded places with her maid.

CHAPTER 15

It was all so futile and ridiculous, Kathleen thought as she stood beside Deborah and Papa to greet the guests come to her reception. Glancing down at the rose-colored silk gown with its lace fichu and tiny silk rosebuds holding the flounces about the hem, she sighed. Serena had chosen the gown, even though Papa had grumbled at the additional expense of a London dressmaker. Serena had also supervised the dressing of Kathleen's hair, with its thick length carefully drawn up to the back of her head to fall into a cascade of shining honey-colored ringlets.

Kathleen scarcely recognized the girl looking back from her mirror.

"Lovely," Serena murmured. "Lovely."

But even Serena's compliments could not give her the self-confidence to cope with all these strangers. To her dismay, she stammered her responses to introductions, and when guests paused for conversation, her mind became a confused blank.

With Papa as an example, the idea of a husband of any sort filled her with dismay, but to be displayed like this, like a mare at auction, was almost more than she could bear. Bear it, you must, she told herself, her lips frozen in a permanent smile. Perhaps if she were to find a rich husband, Papa would love her at last. Yet none of the young men who kissed her hand and passed on resembled the dream lover she had conjured up from the novels she read and from Francine's fanciful tales of love. She must not think of it now, she told herself severely, and turned to greet Lord Wright and Mr. Tarleton.

Lady Neville drifted in and out of the room, discreetly keeping the guests entertained and circulating. She looked so beautiful in her plain gown of ivory brocade that Kathleen sighed with envy.

All the guests were strangers who seemed to speak another language, greeting each other with shrieks of excitement or languid acknowledgments. There were pale-skinned young men who looked her over in cool appraisal, then proceeded to the buffet laid out in the dining room. And there were stout matrons and portly husbands, and haughty young women whose presentations the Hadleys would be expected to attend.

The musical trio played discreetly in the background while the guests wandered about consuming the champagne Deborah had thought far too costly.

At last, Serena drifted over to them; smiling, she bent near Deborah's ear. "I think you should join your guests now." At once, Papa moved toward the champagne. Deborah sighed and turned gratefully away just as the butler announced, "Mr. James Mercer."

"My dear cousin," James said, seizing Serena's hand and kissing it enthusiastically, his dark eyes admiring. "You're nearly as lovely as your esteemed mother." He was a well-built young man of medium height with dark hair already receding above a face that just missed being handsome by the irregularity of his features.

"Sir . . ." Serena objected, withdrawing her hand, an amused quirk at the corners of her mouth. "You mistake me . . . this is your cousin . . . Miss Kathleen Hadley."

James flushed, but it was a moment before he could tear his bright dark eyes from Serena to greet Kathleen. "My mother sends her regrets," he said, after kissing Kathleen's hand. "Papa is ailing, and she feels she should be with him." Stealing another glance at Serena, he smiled at Kathleen. After cocking his head to study her, he grinned. "I can see Fiona in you. When Mama and I went to her wedding, I quite fell in love with her, and I've never forgotten her, although . . ." Once more he glanced at Serena, and Kathleen smiled, certain that Serena could make this charming man forget any other woman he'd ever known.

Inwardly, she sighed, thinking that if she must choose a husband, someone like James would do very well. But how could she expect to compete with a woman as beautiful and self-assured as Serena. From the way James's eyes kept returning to Serena, even after she had excused herself to see to another guest, Kathleen could tell he was already deeply infatuated.

"Mama hopes you will come to tea, Kathleen," James interrupted her melancholy thoughts. "She was very fond of your mother, and she regrets losing contact with you."

"I should like that," Kathleen murmured shyly. "No one at Hadley Hall ever speaks of Mama. Perhaps Aunt Elizabeth could tell me about her."

At once, James flushed and looked away. Kathleen felt the old sinking pain she always felt when people refused to talk about Fiona Browne. As a child, she had been haunted by a sense of guilt, as though she had done something wrong, so that she was not allowed to speak of her dead mother. Perhaps Aunt Elizabeth would tell her what James obviously would not.

"I thought it went well," Serena told them after the guests had departed. The family stood yawning before the drawing room fire, as Papa finished a brandy.

"Did you really?" Deborah quavered, and Aunt Martha sniffed in deprecation.

"It was lovely, Serena," Kathleen hastened to assure her, wishing Papa and Deborah would show a little more appreciation of Serena's efforts. She felt exhausted and immensely relieved that the ordeal was over.

Smiling, Serena took Kathleen's hand. "You looked beautiful, dear. Tomorrow should bring a host of invitations for you. Of course," she said, turning to Papa who regarded her with a bleary eye, "we must have a dinner party soon. I'm sure that tomorrow the drawing room will be filled with promising young gentlemen come to call."

As Kathleen wearily climbed the stairs to her room, where Francine waited to be told all about the reception, Kathleen tried to recall what had gone so well. The names and faces of the guests were a blur, and she had the feeling she had not been a great success. The highlight of the evening had been meeting James. Faintly, she wished he had found her as attractive as he obviously did Serena. He had promised she would meet his mother, Aunt Elizabeth, who had known Fiona. As so often before, Kathleen tried to conjure up a memory of laughing eyes and warm loving arms, all lost long ago.

In the days following the reception, many of the guests returned to call in the afternoons. Serena served generous teas, which the young gentlemen devoured with alacrity.

Sitting stiff and ill at ease, Kathleen attempted to follow conversations that made no sense, peppered as they were with the latest London slang and filled with sly gossip.

She always felt relieved when the guests departed, although they must begin at once to dress for whatever ball, reception, or party they were bid to that night.

For the first great ball they attended, at Criddle House, Serena inveigled another gown from Papa, this one of French blue brocade. The rich fabric made Kathleen's eyes glow like sapphires, Serena said.

In the carriage en route to Criddle House, the helpful young woman repeated her instructions. "Never dance with the same man more than twice. You must remain with Deborah until asked to dance, then return to her side. Never accept a dance with one man after you've refused another."

Kathleen felt a surge of exasperation. It was all so complicated and, she was certain, quite hopeless.

Sitting beside Deborah, she watched the colorful kaleidoscope of whirling ball gowns, felt the call of the music, and waited to be asked to dance. No one approached her. Deborah grew restive. Shame poured through Kathleen, and she longed to flee from this miserable place.

Suddenly, James appeared before her, smiling and bowing, drawing her onto the floor to whirl her in a waltz.

"Dear James," she said. "You are kind to be Samaritan to a wallflower."

"Nonsense," he protested, smiling at her. "I only dance with my favorite lovely ladies, you and . . ."

"Serena," she finished for him, smiling when he flushed.

"She's quite adorable," he managed to say, then blushed furiously.

Amused, Kathleen laughed softly. "You have wonderful taste, James. I'm flattered to be included on your list."

"You are included, dear cuz, and I won't allow you to be a wallflower," he promised.

She had no sooner returned to her seat beside Deborah when Mr. Tarleton appeared, asking for a dance. He was an aging dandy who talked incessantly about himself, so she needed only to smile and nod.

Lord Wright was next. Kathleen was grateful when that dance ended, for His Lordship held her closer than necessary, and his hands had a tendency to wander far from her waist.

When James came to escort her in to supper, she smiled as she took his arm. "You kept your promise, James. I've danced all night. Shall I ask how you did it?"

"Merely pointed out my beautiful cousin," he said gaily, then confided sotto voice, "Some of these gentlemen don't see too well."

Kathleen did not believe him. She was too gauche and shy to be sought for her fascinating company, and she had no great fortune to lure men to her. It seemed quite probable then that James had somehow pressured those gentlemen into dancing with her so that she would not be the evening's wallflower. Well, she told herself, perhaps I should just consider this evening a gift from James and enjoy it.

After that, they saw James often at the many balls, and receptions and parties and teas they attended. One fine afternoon in early July, he came to take Kathleen and Serena in his barouche to join the fashionable parade through the park. He was amusing and attentive, but Kathleen was soon aware that he was holding Serena's hand beneath the folds of her gold merino carriage gown.

Papa had not been pleased at the number of guests bid to Serena's "small" dinner party. With a practical air, Serena assured him they must entertain all the young eligibles who had called on Kathleen or shown an interest in her at the balls and receptions they had attended.

Aunt Martha and Uncle Bertram had stayed on, and they were present at the table tonight as, inevitably, was James. Mr. Tarleton, who seemed to make a career of London seasons, was there, Lord and Lady Markham and their gangling son, Percy, who was taken with Kathleen, perhaps because he was as shy as she, and the rakish Lord Wright.

Even though he sat across the dinner table from her now, deep in conversation with Papa, Kathleen was aware of Lord Wright's bold glances. He was a fine-looking man of medium height, but his eyes gave evidence of dissipation, with dark circles beneath them and a hardness not unlike Papa's in their pale gray depths.

Serena had told her that Lord Wright was immensely rich, but notorious. "He'll not offer for you," Serena said, "but he'll undoubtedly try to seduce you."

Avoiding Lord Wright's eyes, Kathleen kept her attention on James, who was telling of the gold discovery in the Transvaal and the rush to Johannesburg. As a banker, any new supply of gold was of interest to him, he said.

"A chancy investment," Lord Wright pronounced with certainty. With a supercilious smile, he turned his full attention to Papa. "You're a gambling man, Robert, what have you heard about the American cattle business?"

Deborah frowned at the word "gambling" and James interrupted in an annoyed tone. "It's a wild craze among British investors, and very risky, since none of them know anything about cattle ranching."

Lord Wright bent his head toward Papa, rudely ignoring James. "I'm in the process of helping form a syndicate to go into the cattle business in Wyoming this year." With a sharp look at James, he continued persuasively, "You have only to check the history of the companies already in business there. The Prairie Land and Cattle Company paid a dividend of 200% last year. You're not likely to make that kind of return from gold mines . . . or banks." He added the last in a significant tone with a sly look at James, who turned coolly away and began to speak to Aunt Martha who was seated beside him.

Kathleen saw that Papa's eyes had taken on a glazed greedy look as Lord Wright continued to ply him with details of huge profits for little investment in America. A coldness came over her, for she was certain that whatever funds Papa did not gamble away at Crockford's Club would be gambled with this smooth-tongued lord.

Aunt Elizabeth's invitation did not come, for Uncle Reggie continued to be very ill. Kathleen longed for the meeting with her aunt, but knew she must wait until the time was right. She missed Edward's company desperately. With him, she could always be herself, not pretend to be the belle, which she assuredly was not. With the aid of his tutor, he wrote to her weekly, telling how he missed their rides together and her help with his reading lessons. Soon, she thought, soon it will be over, and we can go home, for she was certain now she would find no husband in London.

Kathleen had made a valiant effort to enjoy the balls and receptions, but she never felt comfortable anywhere except with James, who obviously had no designs on her. It was James who took them to the opera, using his father's box at Albert Hall. Kathleen sat engrossed in the singers on stage and the magnificence of the audience, aware that, behind her, James was kissing Serena's hand and whispering into her ear. Serena had changed, the wariness gone from her green eyes when she was with James, a certain glow about her. How ironic, Kathleen thought, that she had been brought to London for Serena to help her find a husband, and it was Serena who would be offered for, in spite of her lack of a dowry. But the happiness glowing from those two enveloped her in its warmth. She watched the progress of their romance with growing affection for the participants.

"Mama will send the carriage for you tomorrow," James said one night as he left them at the house after the opera. "For tea. She regrets she hasn't been at home for calls during Papa's illness, but he is improving now . . . and she's anxious to meet you." He hesitated, glancing conspiratorially at Serena. "I say, cousin, would you mind a bit of a plot?"

Kathleen giggled. Poor love-struck James was so obvious. "You two want to be alone," she teased, then sobered when she saw the yearning look on Serena's face.

"I'll come with the carriage," James said, "and we'll leave you off with Mama."

"Done!" Kathleen laughed. "But you must assure me

149

your intentions are honorable, cousin. After all, I am responsible for Serena's reputation."

James laughed aloud. "You're more like your mother than I'd guessed. She was a bit of a devil, that one."

"It's all been a terrible waste of money," Deborah hissed the next morning as they sat at breakfast.

Serena looked pained and hastily excused herself. Kathleen sighed and steeled herself for what was to come. They were to leave for home next week, and no young man had yet sought out her father to ask for her hand. In her shyness, she had failed to fulfill her father's hopes for a good marriage. She wondered if now she would have to go back to Hadley Hall and remain a spinster for the rest of her life.

Deborah's face looked pinched and pale. The pressure of the social season was telling on her to such an extent that she even dared confront her husband. Last night, Kathleen had overheard them quarreling about Papa's activities.

"Cockfights, Crockford's gambling club, and the Haymarket whores too, no doubt!" Deborah's voice was bitter. "Throwing money about, while I'm expected to keep expenses down and lure some rich gentleman into offering for your hopeless daughter."

Humiliated by what she had overheard then, and what she knew was coming now, Kathleen closed her eyes in pain.

For once, Papa did not shout at Deborah. He simply rose from the table, threw his napkin down, and stalked from the room, calling for the coachman.

The strained silence was broken by Serena's soft voice as she returned to the breakfast room. "James will be here today to take you to meet his mother."

Eyes stinging, her throat tight, Kathleen merely nodded.

Serena glanced at the tight-lipped Deborah. "Are you going along to visit Kathleen's aunt?"

"I have a sick headache," Deborah said, with a withering look at Serena. "The woman is no relation of mine, anyway."

The two girls' eyes met and Serena's were flooded with relief.

Just a few hours later, the carriage with James and Serena

inside rattled away as Kathleen was admitted to Burnham House's stately hall. The uniformed maid took her calling card and disappeared down the long hallway. Apprehensively, Kathleen looked about at the richly furnished house. Elegant statuary stood on the marble floor of the entry hall, and the walls were adorned by enormous oil paintings of unknown ancestors, the ceiling a wonder of frescoed plaster. A tremor shook Kathleen as she wondered what dreadful revelations might lie before her this day.

Aunt Elizabeth sat by a black marble fireplace in the elegantly appointed drawing room. Tea had been laid with the ornate silver and thinnest bone china. She apologized for not rising to greet Kathleen, pleading the pain of her arthritic knees. A stout, pleasant-faced woman, Elizabeth regarded Kathleen with shrewd brown eyes.

"You are quite as lovely as James has told me," she said, smiling.

"Thank you," Kathleen murmured diffidently. No matter how often she had been told these last weeks that she was beautiful, she could not believe the words. For too long, she had been the mouse in the corner at Hadley Hall. That poor drab child, as Aunt Martha was wont to sigh.

"James has been very kind to me," Kathleen said politely, pouring the tea as her aunt had indicated she should. "My great season would have been quite a failure without him."

"Ummm," murmured Elizabeth, sipping her tea. "And why do you suppose that is?"

They exchanged knowing looks, and Kathleen smiled, liking her aunt more than she had expected. "Serena is a wonderful person, Aunt Elizabeth. I hope you don't object to her because she has no money."

Elizabeth sighed. "James will inherit everything we have, and of course, he's taking over the bank from his father already. I'm rather pleased, actually, that he won't need to marry money."

For a while, they spoke of the social season, the weather, the activities of the royal family. Then, a silence fell between them. Kathleen was aware that her aunt was regarding her rather quizzically. Seeing her guest's questioning look, Elizabeth smiled. "As I said, dear, you're quite lovely. But not at all like your mother, although there is a tinge of her auburn in your hair."

Pleased, Kathleen touched her hair. "I'd hoped you'd tell me about my mother," she began hesitantly, almost afraid of what she might learn. "No one speaks of her at Hadley Hall. It's as though she never lived there."

"The bloody . . ." Catching herself, Elizabeth swallowed the oath, flushing in a manner reminiscent of James. With a long sigh, she turned to stare into the fire. "Fiona was quite beautiful," she said. "And quite spoiled and willful. Yet, she had a passionate and loving heart." Again she sighed heavily. "Your father . . ." she paused, seeming to search for words. "He didn't understand her," she finished lamely.

Silence closed over them, with only the soft rippling sound of the flames in the fireplace and the distant voices of servants. A pain caught at Kathleen's throat. What had happened so terrible that even her great-aunt, who loved Fiona, could not speak of it?

Reaching across, she laid her hand over the older woman's plump bejeweled one. "Please tell me the truth, Aunt Elizabeth. All my life, she's haunted me in a way I can't explain. At Hadley Hall, she's like the ghost of someone who never existed." Tears started in her eyes. "I feel as though a part of me is lost because I can't have even a memory of my mother."

"Poor darling." Elizabeth's hand clasped hers tightly. "I'll tell you then, though it may break your heart to hear it."

"Please." Kathleen felt suddenly frightened, as though she stood on the brink of some terrible abyss from which there would be no turning back.

"The marriage was arranged," Elizabeth began, settling herself more comfortably in her chair, her large brown eyes gazing sadly at Kathleen. "Fiona didn't want it. I knew that when I met her at the wedding, and I knew what the Brownes did not. That your father's reputation was not the best." She paused, clearing her throat. "I hate to speak ill of your father, child."

"He's dreadfully extravagant, Aunt Elizabeth," she said stiffly, smothering all feeling of disloyalty as this morning's unhappy scene replayed in her mind. "Even though he's terribly in debt, he's talking now of investing in the American cattle business. He gambled on bringing me to London for the season, hoping I'd find a wealthy husband."

"Poor child," Elizabeth said sadly. "Wealth marries wealth, and James tells me your father has offered no dowry for you."

"I didn't know that!" The words burst from Kathleen, and her face burned with the shame of it. "No wonder all the beaus have passed over me. Except Lord Wright, who tried to lure me into the garden alone." Her voice dropped, and pain filled her chest. "He said I'd not be offered for, so I might as well be my mother's daughter and enjoy it."

Elizabeth's eyes blazed. "That despicable swell will never be welcome in my house again, and I'll see that James cuts him dead."

"So there is a scandal," Kathleen cried. "I guessed it, Aunt . . . and I'd rather know it all. Please, I feel so alone."

"Very well!" Elizabeth sat up straight, her lips compressed. "Then I'll not spare Robert Hadley, for he never spared your Mama." She motioned for Kathleen to fill her teacup again, then settled back, sipping her tea.

Kathleen stared at her aunt, immobile, waiting.

"I didn't know it when I saw how unhappy she was at the wedding, but there was a young Irishman, a commoner, that she loved. It was said he had been killed, and that was how she was willing to marry Lord Hadley. Then the young man came back. He'd been in America, but he came to her at Brookfield."

Something clicked inside Kathleen's head, flooding her mind with a memory of golden sunlight and a tall man who hugged her fiercely, tears gleaming in his blue eyes.

Elizabeth sighed and stared into the fire for a long moment before she continued. "As I said . . . there was a wildness in her, and she loved him in a way she could never have loved Lord Hadley, who neglected her shamefully. She showed no discretion, going to her lover at the village inn, having him to tea while her husband was hunting in Scotland. It was a terrible scandal, and Lord Hadley did nothing to hush it up. Then . . . ." Elizabeth's voice fell and her expression saddened . . ."we heard she had died. The young man had gone away, perhaps to America again. Reggie and I went up to the funeral because we were fond of your grandparents." She sighed deeply. "There was no grief in that house, my dear. We didn't stay, but Margaret wrote me afterward that they had quarreled with Robert and broken with him."

"So that was why they never came to see me?" Kathleen asked in a low voice. The spark of anger at her father that seemed always to have burned inside her burst into flame.

"He'd forbidden them," Elizabeth said sadly, "and although Margaret begged him, he wouldn't allow you to visit her . . . even after Cedric died, and she was alone."

Tears spilled over and streamed down Kathleen's cheeks. "He's never loved me," she choked out the painful words, bitterly angry now. "I guess he blames me for what she did . . ."

"Nonsense," Elizabeth said brusquely, handing her a kerchief since Kathleen couldn't locate her own. "That man is quite incapable of love. It isn't your fault that he's the way he is, any more than it is your fault that your mother threw her life away for love of a commoner."

The words soothed an old wound that had troubled her heart for as long as she could remember. "It's not my fault . . ." she repeated, and wiped her eyes. Suddenly, she felt as though a great burden had been taken from her. "It's the scandal then, as much as the dowry, that means I won't be offered for?"

"I'm afraid so, dear."

"Papa will be furious," Kathleen said, looking into her aunt's sympathetic face. "He'd so hoped for a rich son-in-law to help pay his debts." To her dismay, she giggled hysterically. "He gambled on me, and lost." She covered her face, unable to stem the tears.

"Perhaps he'd let you come to stay with me, dear. I'm certain James will be married soon. Reggie and I'll be alone here. I've always wanted a daughter."

"Oh, Aunt Elizabeth!" Kathleen rose and flung her arms about her aunt's stout shoulders, hugging her close, treasuring the warmth of the embrace her aunt returned. But, even as the tempting dream of living in this great house with the caring presence of Elizabeth filled her mind, there came the remembrance of Edward's letters. He missed her desperately, his last letter said. He couldn't bear it if she didn't come home soon. And she knew at once that she could not leave him there alone in that gloomy house where there was no love.

CHAPTER 16

Cheyenne, Wyoming, 1886

Kathleen and Edward stood on the drab and ugly platform of the train station at Cheyenne, Wyoming, far removed, to Kathleen, from the safe familiar green of the English countryside. Behind them, the train still huffed quietly, disgorging passengers and taking on new ones.

She felt Edward's hand tighten on hers, and she looked down at him in commiseration, knowing he was as apprehensive as she. He was tall for nine years old, and thin from his winter's illness, so that the Norfolk jacket and tweed knickers seemed made for some other boy. To her surprise, she saw that his hazel eyes were shining with excitement as he took in the incredible surroundings. Strangers glancing at the boy smiled involuntarily in response to Edward's unconscious charm.

The cloudy early morning light did nothing to soften the bare angular lines of the unpainted frame buildings. There were few trees, and no grass or flowers to be seen. All kinds of rigs . . . wagons, rough coaches, and drays moved down dirt streets littered with horse droppings. A motley crowd swarmed about the station and the platform. No wonder Edward was so wide-eyed, she thought, staring herself at the Indians wrapped in colorful blankets, their long black hair lying in plaits on their shoulders. Some of them cheerfully posed for the cameras of travelers, holding out their hands for payment for their trouble. There were a few well-dressed people of the better class, but most were roughly dressed, speaking in that harsh American accent.

"Papa isn't here," Edward told her, and Kathleen felt a twinge of fear.

After the long and exhausting train ride, surrounded by all kinds of strangers, surely Papa would not fail to meet them. Deborah had thought the whole trip madness, daring to argue with Papa that Edward's lung problems would clear up eventually in England. A trip to the Wild West was an unnecessary danger to the child. But after the year he had spent in Wyoming, Papa was certain the climate there was exactly what Edward needed.

Somehow, Papa had raised the money to invest in Lord Wright's British and Far West Cattle Company. He'd even been able to persuade the syndicate to place him in charge of the Wyoming operation. It was a legitimate reason to flee his hounding creditors while he tried to recoup his fortune.

Papa had spent last winter at Hadley Hall. On his return to Wyoming, he'd determined that the house he'd ordered built was ready, then sent for Edward to join him. Because Deborah was pregnant and dared not travel, Kathleen had been sent to America with her half brother.

"If the British had kept control of America, this place wouldn't be so savage. Why, it's worse than India."

At the sound of the familiar complaining voice, Kathleen glanced at her traveling companion. Stout Mrs. Tydings, with her cold gray eyes, her gray hair pulled into a tight bun, and a faint moustache on her upper lip. She was the widow of an army man, having traveled the world with him until his death. Deborah had thought her the ideal guide for Edward and Kathleen and hired her for the year. But Mrs. Tydings had never really left England behind. She had produced a teapot, tea caddy and alcohol burner from her reticule to fulfill the daily ritual of teatime, on shipboard as well as on the train, to the amusement of the Americans.

Kathleen gave her an annoyed glance, weary of her complaints. How she wished Deborah had allowed Francine to come along. She would have made a lark of the trip. Too young, too flighty, Deborah said, and there was no appeal.

"Look!" Edward interrupted her thoughts, tugging at her hand. "Real cowboys!" He had been devouring everything written about the American Wild West, and as Kathleen's eyes followed his pointing finger, she saw the illustrations come to life.

Three horsemen rode past the station, roughly dressed

157

and wearing wide-brimmed hats above weather-beaten faces. Even their saddles were strange cumbersome affairs with a horn in front and a high cantle behind.

When she met Edward's shining eyes, she was caught up in his excitement. It was an adventure. Never mind that they were merely obeying a whim of Papa's, they were in an exotic place, a world away from England.

"Miss Hadley?"

At the sound of her name, spoken in a deep masculine drawl, Kathleen whirled to meet a pair of dark eyes that seemed to see right through her. The man stared in so bold a manner, she felt a flush rise to her cheeks.

"Y . . . yes?" she stammered, then annoyed at herself, squared her shoulders and stared back at him.

He was tall, his lean saturnine face weathered and brown. One thumb hooked through his belt, he stood regarding her in a quizzical manner. His clothing was similar to that of the cowboys she had just observed . . . denim pants, a wool plaid shirt with a kerchief tied about his neck, and a leather vest. The gun belt he wore seemed to be as much a part of attire in this country as a belt to hold up a man's trousers. When he politely removed his wide-brimmed gray hat, she saw that his hair was black, thick and unruly. There was a strange sort of familiarity about the man, as though she might have known him in some other place.

"I'm Ransom O'Neil," he said. "Foreman for the British and Far West. Your father asked me to meet you."

Behind his courteous façade, she sensed annoyance, as though meeting His Lordship's family at the train station was not in the line of his ordinary duties, and he resented it.

"Where is my father?" Kathleen demanded, suddenly painfully aware that in this unfamiliar place they were in this man's power.

O'Neil gave her a sardonic look, settling the wide-brimmed hat back on his head. "His Lordship is fox-hunting at Powder River with Moreton Frewen." He did not trouble to hide the contempt in his tone.

Kathleen stared at him in astonishment at his attitude. Mrs. Tydings gaped, open-mouthed.

"Old Mortal Ruin!" Edward chortled. "Papa told me Frewen was out to make a fortune in cattle, too."

"Too?" Mrs. Tydings gave the boy a warning look which he chose to ignore.

"Certainly," Edward turned his dazzling smile on O'Neil. "That's why Papa is here . . . to recoup his fortune."

"That will be enough, Edward," Kathleen said, uncomfortably aware of O'Neil's grin. She turned to the man, determined to treat him like the servant he surely was, although he obviously didn't know his place. "Is there someone to help with the bags?"

"In Wyoming, everyone helps himself," O'Neil answered, giving Edward a wink. "Where are they? The buckboard's waiting just around the corner."

O'Neil found a black man in a railroad uniform to help load their trunks, and Edward manfully joined in helping carry bags to the buckboard. The baggage loaded, O'Neil climbed up into the driver's seat and took the reins, planting his high-heeled boots against the dash.

A far cry from the liveried coachman at Hadley Hall, Kathleen thought wryly, glancing with amusement at Mrs. Tydings. Her stout traveling companion had settled herself in the open buckboard with a grim expression indicating she had endured primitive cultures before and would endure this one.

What was it about O'Neil that disturbed her, Kathleen asked herself, as he snapped the reins? He was not impolite or rude, but there was a hint of arrogance. All the years of servants bowing and peasants tugging forelocks had not prepared her for such a man. Even Papa's agent, Mr. Holmes, never failed to act subservient. Perhaps it was simply the way of Americans, she thought, smiling to herself as she wondered how her father dealt with this man's independent and irreverent attitude.

Cheyenne was soon behind them. The buckboard bounced and swayed along a dusty primitive road, its passengers huddling against the discomfort of cold and threatening weather. Under a sullen gray sky, the sagebrush plains seemed to stretch away forever, broken at last on the west by a faint line of blue mountains dominated by one tall peak still glistening with snow. A chill wind blew unceasingly.

Edward had chosen to sit beside the driver, with Kathleen and Mrs. Tydings in the second seat. Dismayed at riding in an open carriage in such weather, Kathleen had insisted the boy don his heavy tweed greatcoat. Now, she sat shivering inside her own woolen cloak, listening as Edward plied O'Neil with questions.

Glancing from the boy's pale eager face to the man's pleasantly tolerant one, she felt herself warm toward this American for his kindness to Edward. Self-confidence exuded from the man even in the way he sat on the hard board seat, his broad shoulders relaxed, his big gloved hands holding the reins with an air of complete competence.

A faint longing stirred somewhere deep inside, and Kathleen sighed softly. After her disastrous London season, she had given up any hope of romance or marriage in her life. She would be the spinster older sister, a role assigned to her by Deborah and Aunt Martha. Forcing away any discontent when she saw other girls marrying and making a life for themselves, she devoted herself to her books, to Edward and his two little sisters. Now, there was to be another child. Edward's illness made his mother hope for another boy, another heir . . . just in case. But when Deborah confided that hope, Kathleen had been furious that anyone could even entertain the possibility of losing Edward. She'd hated the idea of bringing the boy to Wyoming, but now she was here, she thought perhaps the clear dry air might truly work a cure.

"Will I be a cowboy?" Edward was asking eagerly.

O'Neil gave him a sidewise grin and drew a pouch of tobacco from his shirt pocket. "It's not as easy as those Wild West novels you've been reading would have you believe." Shaking tobacco into a curl of paper held in his fingers, O'Neil rolled a cigarette, sealing it with a flick of his tongue. Edward watched in fascination. When the cigarette was lighted, O'Neil broke his match in two and dropped it on the floor of the carriage.

"It's a hard and dirty job, herding cows," he continued, blowing a stream of smoke into the cold air. "I doubt His Lordship would think it suitable for you."

Once more, Kathleen was aware of the subtle change in

the man's tone at the words "His Lordship" ... almost derisive. Arrogant, she thought again, then turned, startled by the sudden weight of a sleeping Mrs. Tydings against her shoulder.

"Alston says I'm an extraordinarily fine rider," Edward insisted.

"Who's Alston?" O'Neil glanced at the boy.

"My riding master at Hadley Hall."

O'Neil's laugh was definitely derisive this time. "Has Alston ever punched cows?"

"No." Edward's voice held a quaver of doubt. "But he's teaching me to ride to the hounds."

"Two damned different things." O'Neil's reply was abrupt. He drew hard on his cigarette.

Edward's face was a study in dashed hopes. At once, resentment flared in Kathleen. How dared this insolent creature speak to Edward in that manner? After all, he was little more than a servant.

"When Papa returns," she said in a loud, sharp voice, "you may do as you wish, Edward, no matter what the servants may think."

With a low sardonic chuckle, O'Neil glanced back at her, the dark eyes piercing, strangely disturbing. Lifting her chin, she refused to meet his look, turning to stare after a jackrabbit that leaped across the road and ran into the sagebrush.

Ranse O'Neil inhaled deeply, then dropped the cigarette butt onto the floor of the buckboard, grinding it out with the toe of his boot. Impatiently, he snapped the reins at the horses, urging them to a faster pace. That arrogant, insensitive bastard, Hadley, he cursed to himself. As a friend, he would have been happy enough to meet the old boy's daughter and son at the station. But to be ordered to do it, as though he were a menial ... It was the damned English attitude that rankled him. So many of the titled bastards had descended on Wyoming intending to grow rich in the cattle business with no effort on their part, overstocking the ranges while looking for the profits of 200% that the prospectuses for their companies promised. He wouldn't have stayed at Cybille Creek Ranch if it hadn't been home.

Damn! He'd promised himself he wouldn't think of that. The past was dead and gone, and there was no way to turn things back to the way they'd been.

That worthless valet of Hadley's should have met the train, but His Lordship couldn't get dressed by himself, so the man had gone along to Powder River. At least the old boy gave him a free hand with running the cattle and the cowhands. He had to, since he knew nothing about it. What was he to do now, with three more helpless Britishers on his hands?

The boy seemed bright and willing, though he looked like death warmed over. That snotty old bag was a servant, so she'd be no problem of his. But the girl . . . Just now, when he'd glanced back at her, he'd caught a flash of unexpected fire in her startlingly blue eyes. Were all Englishwomen so drab, he wondered? She was only nineteen, so her father said, but here she was dressed in an ugly tan-colored gown that made her look at least thirty. He hadn't had time to really study her, although just now, beneath the hood of her cloak, he'd glimpsed a pale oval face smooth as carved ivory, a rose-colored mouth that was soft even as she spoke sharply to him, putting him in his place. What was it he'd sensed in that brief exchange, he asked himself? A disturbing sense of depths unplumbed, passions hidden, a temporarily banked fire . . .

Letting your mind wander, Ranse, he chided himself, then grinned. He'd had one compensation for the long ride into Cheyenne to pick up the "master's" kids, he'd shared Maud's bed last night. It wasn't that he found celibacy difficult, but it was nice to break it up once in a while.

After a pause near midday to relieve themselves and to eat the lunch Ranse had brought from a Cheyenne café, they continued the weary ride. There was little change in the countryside, sagebrush plains with occasional low rolling hills, small springs surrounded by willows bursting with new catkins, cattle cropping bunch grass among the brush.

Late in the afternoon, Cybille Creek Ranch came in sight at last.

"A hunting lodge," Edward cried, rousing from his nap

where he had joined Kathleen on the rear seat. "Papa has built a hunting lodge."

The big two-story house was built of chinked logs, with a gray shingled roof, and limestone chimneys on each side. A veranda, supported by peeled-log pillars, covered the entrance on the north and turned the corner along the east side. The house itself was enclosed by a pole fence behind which a few spindly trees struggled for life in a land where it seemed only sagebrush thrived. Beyond the house were log corrals and outbuildings, some of the buildings roofed with dirt. The yards were bare and dusty, extending eastward to a line of trees that indicated the presence of Cybille Creek. Undulating sagebrush-covered hills rose toward distant mountains beneath a dark and lowering sky.

"Storm coming," O'Neil announced as he drew the horses to a halt before the house. A man dressed in cowboy clothes appeared from nowhere to take the horses' reins. Another man came out of the house and began to unload the trunks. O'Neil helped Mrs. Tydings down from the buckboard, and she rushed to the shelter of the veranda. Edward leaped down by himself and began helping carry in the luggage.

Gathering her cloak about her, Kathleen looked down at Ranse O'Neil where he stood with arms uplifted to help her descend. For a long moment, she stood transfixed by the depths of his dark eyes. Her heart began to beat in a way that almost suffocated her as the strong hands closed about her waist and lifted her effortlessly to the ground.

There was a distant rumble of thunder, and the wind brought the sweet smell of wet earth. Somehow, the moment held a portent she could not fathom, as they stood face to face for what seemed an endless moment.

Then O'Neil stepped back. Sweeping off his wide-brimmed hat, he bowed deeply. "Welcome to Wyoming, my lady Kathleen."

··•❑I CHAPTER 17 I❑•··

Kathleen paused before the French doors that led from the dining room onto the east veranda. Evening was coming on. The trees lining Cybille Creek were faintly gray in the falling rain. Sipping her tea, she watched the thin smoke rising from the chimneys of the outbuildings.

"That's the bunkhouse and the cookhouse," Mrs. Sanders offered, gathering the tea things from the dining table, for Mrs. Tydings had insisted on having tea at once upon their arrival. "And the foreman's cabin . . ." She gave Kathleen a tentative smile, her pale blue eyes wary in her stout, plain face.

Mrs. Sanders was both the cook and housekeeper, for she told Kathleen at once that servants were difficult to get or keep in Wyoming. Her husband was the thin, hawk-faced man who had unloaded the baggage, his position seeming to be a sort of houseman.

When Kathleen merely nodded, the woman continued, "My niece, Tessie, is the housemaid. Lord Hadley thought you'd be bringing your own maid, but since you didn't, Tessie can help you out, if you want . . ." Her voice trailed off indecisively.

With a weary sigh, Kathleen managed a smile. "We'll work things out tomorrow, Mrs. Sanders. Could we have an early supper, please. We're all very tired." Glancing out the windows at the torrents of rain pouring from the dark skies, she added, "I've never seen such a storm."

"Not unusual in Wyoming," Mrs. Sanders grinned, seeming to take personal pride in the weather. "The winters here are the worst in the West. I hear you won't be staying the winter."

Kathleen nodded absently. "Yes, we're to return to England with Papa this autumn."

In the last of the light, she saw a man come from the smallest of the buildings and walk toward the lighted cookhouse. His black mackinaw billowed in the wind. As the door opened, he stood in the square of lamplight, shaking the water from his hat. The sight of Ranse O'Neil's rugged profile brought an odd catch to Kathleen's throat. At once, she shrugged off the feeling, turning impatiently to Mrs. Sanders.

"There's unpacking to be done. Will you send Tessie upstairs at once." With another wary glance, the woman departed. Kathleen sighed. Mrs. Sanders didn't know what to expect from the English guests any more than they knew what to expect from Wyoming.

Looking about the dining room, with its wainscoting of green-painted paneling, the long pine harvest table surrounded by ornately carved chairs, she moved out into the vestibule. The floor there was paved with the same limestone as the fireplaces. It seemed small and crowded after the great hall at home, and it opened at once through an archway into the sitting room. A fire crackled in the huge stone fireplace, gleaming on the polished floor where rugs in primitive designs of red and black and gray were scattered about. The furniture was rustic and plain, but upholstered in a dark red velvet, the same material as the drapes at the tall windows. The walls were simply the inside of the logs, highly varnished. On the stairwall stood an intricately carved mahogany sideboard. Papa's study was on the other side of the stairs.

Shaking her head at the strangeness of the place, she mounted the curving staircase to the second floor. There, she found a harassed Mrs. Tydings trying to help a tired and unruly Edward with unpacking.

"What's the matter with you, Tydings?" he demanded sulkily, as Kathleen looked at the bedroom in dismay. Opened trunks and bags stood about with clothing spilling onto floor and bed.

"I'm sure Mrs. Tydings isn't responsible for this mess." Kathleen gave him a severe frown.

"I wanted my night clothes," Edward replied, his lip trembling. He plopped onto the bed and stared at her, his eyes glistening, so that she saw he was about to cry from sheer exhaustion.

Mrs. Tydings let out an exasperated sigh and looked questioningly at Kathleen. At that moment, the door opened.

"Mrs. Sanders said you wanted me." Tessie was young, probably still in her teens, with the same drab light brown hair and pale blue eyes as her aunt, and already tending to plumpness.

"Will you draw a bath for my brother?" Kathleen said, knowing from past experience that a warm bath would settle the boy down for the night.

"Draw a bath?" Tessie tried to stifle her giggle.

Annoyed and tired, Kathleen frowned at her. "Where is the bathroom?"

Tessie giggled outright. "There's a bathroom next door, but we have to bring the water from the kitchen."

"Then do it . . . at once." Tessie looked surprised at the severity of Kathleen's tone, but she hurried away.

Mrs. Tydings rolled her eyes expressively. "A primitive country."

Shrugging, Kathleen moved about the room, trying to bring some order to the chaos. Primitive country, perhaps, she thought, but it was only five years ago that Deborah had had running water and bathrooms installed at Hadley Hall.

The bedroom assigned to Edward had draperies of dark printed chintz, and the furniture was elaborately carved curly maple. Chastened by his sister's attitude, Edward jumped up from the bed and began trying to help pick up clothing.

"Here's your nightshirt," Kathleen said, retrieving the garment from under a chair. "Go take your bath, now," she added, as Tessie passed the open door carrying two buckets of steaming water.

"Miss . . ." Behind her, Mrs. Tydings gave a shaky cry and sank into a chair, fanning her flushed face.

"We're all much too tired," Kathleen assured her, patting

the stout shoulder. "Tomorrow, we'll deal with unpacking." Tessie had returned to stand in the door, her face questioning. "Show Mrs. Tydings to her room, Tessie . . . and help her get ready for bed. Then you can bring her supper on a tray."

"Oh, Miss." The gratitude on Tydings's face was almost amusing after the haughty attitude she had maintained toward Kathleen for most of the trip.

The two women departed. Edward returned, warm and flushed from his bath, clad in the flannel nightshirt.

"I don't want supper," he said in a small tired voice, as Kathleen tucked the covers about him. "Tea was quite enough."

"For me, too." Kathleen smiled and bent to kiss his damp forehead. "Good night, Edward." Reaching out, she began to turn down the bedside lamp.

Edward sat bolt upright, his multicolored hazel eyes pleading. "Leave it on, Kathleen. I know I stopped having a light at home, and I will be brave . . . but . . . just for tonight."

"Just for tonight," she agreed with a tender smile. Tucking the quilts about him, she kissed his forehead again, then went out of the room, leaving the door open a crack.

She found Mrs. Tydings wrapped in a gray woolen robe, performing her ablutions in a china basin set on a washstand of garish bird's-eye maple. Assuring the older woman that everything would seem more manageable in the morning, she turned to go, meeting Tessie at the door with Tydings's supper on a tray.

"Will you want me to help?" the girl asked.

"When you're finished here," Kathleen said, wondering whether it would be worthwhile to teach the girl the proper way to address her mistress.

Her own bedroom, next to Edward's, was furnished in dark mahogany, the bed with carved posters, an ornate gilt-framed mirror over the dresser, braided rugs on the floor, and dark blue flowered chintz draperies at the windows. Rain poured steadily against those windows, flashes of lightning were followed by low rumblings of thunder.

As she placed a bag on the dresser and began to empty it into the drawers, she suddenly realized how she had taken charge since their arrival at Cybille Creek Ranch. Deborah would be amazed at her retiring stepdaughter, she thought with a low chuckle. Perhaps in Wyoming she needn't play the role of spinster older sister. Maybe here, all the impulses stifled for so long would find expression. She thought of Serena managing the house in London with seemingly effortless ease, and she hoped she could emulate her.

Serena was managing that same house on Grosvenor Square now, for she and James had moved there after their winter wedding. A faint sense of resentment rose in Kathleen as she remembered how Papa had refused to let her go to London for the wedding. Deborah had been ill—another miscarriage—and he had insisted she could not go unchaperoned.

A sudden sense of freedom washed over Kathleen. Deborah was far away. Here at Cybille Creek, only Kathleen was mistress of the house.

In the drawer with her neatly ironed linen handkerchiefs, she carefully placed the miniature painting of Fiona Browne on her sixteenth birthday. "Mama," she murmured softly, as always admiring the beautiful young face. "Why couldn't I have been like you, beautiful and free?" Her eyes stung as she carefully covered the picture with the handkerchiefs, for she had learned long ago that Papa would be angry if he saw the miniature.

Withdrawing her other treasure from the bag, she opened the pages of the Book of Common Prayer to the mysterious blossoms pressed on the marriage ceremony. Purple, lavender and white, they must have come from Ireland, for there was no such plant at Hadley Hall. Perhaps it was something rare and exotic. Her grandmother had been an avid botanist before her death two years ago. What had they meant to the beautiful Fiona? Were they a link to the mysterious young Irishman she had loved so passionately she had risked disgrace to be with him?

Sighing with regret at the unfathomable past, Kathleen laid the book on the dresser. A sudden impulse seized her. Taking the miniature from the drawer, she sat it upright on the dresser, so that she could look into her mother's face each morning when she awakened.

"Miss Hadley." Kathleen started, and turned to Tessie

who had come into the room without knocking. "Ranse is downstairs. He wants to talk to you."

"Ranse?" Unbelieving that a maid would use the first name of a man in a position of authority, Kathleen stared at the girl.

"Ranse O'Neil," the girl repeated impatiently. "You know, the foreman."

"I know," she replied and sighed tiredly. Tomorrow was soon enough to begin Tessie's training.

"Shall I tell him you'll be down, or do you want him to come up here?"

Astounded, Kathleen stared at her. "I'll come downstairs, of course."

"Good. I'll tell him." Tessie bounded away, leaving Kathleen staring in disbelief.

Looking down at herself, clad only in her petticoats, she imagined greeting Ranse O'Neil in such a state, and in her bedroom. Inexplicably, she began to giggle.

Opening her trunk, she drew out a morning robe Aunt Elizabeth had given her. She had seldom worn it, thinking it much too luxurious, for it was of heavy silk brocade in a rich deep rose color with tulle ruching about the neck and wrists. Still amused at the incongruity of it in Wyoming, she drew it on and looked in the mirror, amazed at the way the color brightened her face and added a gleam to her dark blond hair. She would not have dressed so for any man in England, she thought, certain that she should take it off and don her old dark green wool robe. Impulsively, she tossed her head at the image in the mirror and swept from the room, down the stairway.

It was well worth taking the chance, she thought, to see the astonishment on O'Neil's face when he turned from the fireplace to greet her. His slicker hung in the hallway, dripping onto the stone floor. He had changed his wool plaid shirt for a cotton one of light blue, and he no longer wore his gun belt.

There was a long silence while his dark eyes seemed to take inventory of her, covering her from head to toe. Outside, the sweep of rain and wind beat against the house, here, the fire crackled, and she could smell the wet wool of the big gray hat lying on a nearby table. Those dark eyes held her transfixed, as unfathomable as the past she had just been trying to probe from the flowers in her mother's prayer book. Why should this man she had barely met make her think of her mother's mysterious lover? Forcing herself to break eye contact, she told herself she had left all her manners and all propriety in England.

"You wanted to see me?" she asked, forcing herself into the condescending tones one used with inferiors.

A grin broke across his dark tanned face, revealing white even teeth. It flashed through her confused mind that he had a beautiful mouth, wide and sensitive, quite at odds with the rugged lines of his face.

"I wanted to make sure you'd settled in all right, your majesty," he said.

Flushing at the words "your majesty," Kathleen realized how officious she had sounded. Ranse O'Neil was an American, not an English servant, and he obviously did not consider himself inferior to anyone.

"Thank you," she murmured, turning to stare into the fire so that he could not see her embarrassment.

"Can I do anything to help?"

She looked up at him, seeing that his grin had faded now that he had put her in her place. "We'll finish unpacking tomorrow," she answered, annoyed that she couldn't control the trembling in her voice. "You're kind to inquire."

The dark eyes softened, holding hers. "Wyoming must seem a wild place to you. I've seen pictures of your home in England. Very grand."

"Yes." She was surprised by the faint unhappiness she felt at the mention of Hadley Hall. "Can I offer you some port?" Distractedly, she looked about the room, certain that her father would have port at hand.

"No," he answered, his eyes still intent on her face. "You're tired. I won't keep you." He picked up his hat.

"When will my father return?" she asked, suddenly reluctant to have him leave her.

"Not until the weather changes and the roads are dry." Again, she sensed a faint hostility, as he added, "Can't believe chasing a damn fox is more important to him than being here to meet his kids."

Stung by the implied criticism of her father, fair or not,

she shrugged. "He's often away hunting for months in England. Hunting is his life's passion."

There was unveiled contempt in the dark eyes. "A pretty trivial passion," he said in a hard voice.

Suddenly, her eyes burned. She wanted to cry for all the empty years without her beautiful mother, with her cold uncaring father and the repressive Deborah. But not here, not before this self-assured American.

Squaring her shoulders, she said in her best "mistress of the house" voice, "Thank you for your concern, Mr. O'Neil. Good night."

This time, his grin was a bit uncertain, but the dark eyes were as intense as ever. "Good night." Walking into the foyer, he took his slicker from the hall tree.

Standing there in the flicker of firelight and the faint glow of the glass-globed lamps, Kathleen saw him turn to stare at her once more.

"You're a beautiful woman," he said in a low voice. "I can't figure why you don't know that."

···❦I CHAPTER 18 I❦···

The morning sky was mottled with the last of the storm clouds scudding wildly eastward on the wind. Kathleen looked out her bedroom window on a landscape as strange and foreign as any Mrs. Tydings could have seen in her travels. The distances were immense, stunning the eye with their scope. Blue mountains scalloped the horizon to the westward, and it seemed to her they might mark the edge of the world.

As she watched, four horsemen rode out the gate onto the main road. Only the tall, straight-backed figure in a gray hat held her eyes. Last night, Ranse O'Neil had told her she was a beautiful woman, and her cheeks warmed in remembrance of his bold stare.

The horsemen galloped across the sagebrush plain, disappearing over a rise. Turning to the mirror, Kathleen considered the face reflected there. Serena, and James and Aunt Elizabeth, had told her she was lovely, but she had thought they only meant to be kind. "Beautiful" was the girl in the miniature, staring up at her . . . with shining auburn hair, hazel eyes, a proud chin, and a willful mouth.

Perhaps it had been the robe, and she held the rose-colored silk up to her chin, marveling at how the color brightened the sheen of her dark blond hair.

The mustard-colored gown she had chosen for the day was laying across her bed. Deborah had picked the material, saying it was practical and would wear well. On an impulse, Kathleen tossed it across the room. Opening her trunk, she drew out one of the gowns Serena had chosen for the months in London. Deborah had insisted she bring them,

172

since they'd hardly been worn, and it would not matter in America if they were out of style.

Holding up a sky-blue merino gown trimmed with darker blue braid, she marveled at how it deepened the color of her eyes. Why had she let Deborah, who had no taste at all, choose her gowns all these years? What a wretched little puppet she had been, doing everyone's bidding simply to avoid Papa's anger and Deborah's displeasure.

Moving furiously, she began tossing everything Deborah had ever chosen into a pile in the corner. She would give them to the poor . . . or burn the ugly things. Finished, breathing quickly, she felt a deep sense of freedom, even though she realized she had only a minimum of clothes left . . . those she had saved from her London season, and they were at least a year out of style.

"What are you doing, Kathleen?"

Startled, she turned to see a tousle-haired Edward standing in the doorway, rubbing his eyes sleepily.

"I'm unpacking," she informed him lightheartedly.

Edward grinned impishly. "Last night, you reprimanded me for unpacking in the same way."

Laughing, she reached out to hug him and plant a good-morning kiss on his cheek. "You are too old now to walk into a lady's room without knocking," she said, trying to sound severe, but unable to contain her exuberance. "Now, get dressed and we'll go down to breakfast. Tessie and Mrs. Tydings will help us sort out the mess later."

Downstairs, Mrs. Tydings's heavy eyebrows rose in horrified astonishment when Mrs. Sanders poured herself a cup of coffee and sat down at the breakfast table.

They were seated at a round oak table in the small breakfast room just off the kitchen. It was a pleasant room, Kathleen thought, with its wainscoting of ivory-painted pine below the varnished logs. Morning sunlight poured through the lace curtains at the windows, laying intricate shadow patterns on the white linen tablecloth.

She struggled to suppress her smile at the cook's temerity and Tydings's reaction to it. America was, indeed, a strange country, where servants refused to use titles and the cook sat at the table with her mistress. She wondered whether Mrs. Sanders behaved in this manner when Lord Hadley was at home. He would certainly be incensed if she joined him at table. In speaking of Ireland, his greatest complaint was that the servants were allowed undue familiarity there.

"Will you have more tea?" Mrs. Sanders asked, hefting the silver pot from its tray in the center of the table.

"Please," Kathleen said.

"Me, too," Edward chimed in. Kathleen glanced at the boy, amazed to see that he had cleaned his plate of the fried ham, biscuits and gravy that had been served for breakfast.

Mrs. Sanders grinned at him. "Always like to see a growing boy clean his plate."

Maintaining a lofty silence, Mrs. Tydings gave the cook a frosty glare, then tried to catch Kathleen's eye, as though to say "do something about this person."

Kathleen's lips twitched. She found she was enjoying the American informality. Perhaps a person in Mrs. Tydings's position could not afford to enjoy it for fear of losing her own place.

"Mrs. Tydings," she began, "would you mind supervising Tessie and Edward in unpacking his things?"

"At once." She stood up, beckoning to Edward, an expression of relief on her face.

"Like to try American coffee?" Mrs. Sanders asked, pouring herself another cup when Edward and Tydings had departed.

"Why not?" Kathleen held out her cup, for the brew smelled delicious. But she winced at the strong flavor and set the cup down at once. This was not England, and she wondered how to begin to be mistress of the house in a society that seemingly recognized no class barriers.

"I would like to go over the menu with you each day, Mrs. Sanders," she began, trying to put some authority into her tone.

Tolerantly, Sanders went along with her requests, and they had soon organized duties, including the laundry Mrs. Sanders said was done twice weekly by the blacksmith's wife.

"Edward and I like to ride every day," Kathleen said finally. "Is Mr. O'Neil in charge of the stables, too?"

Her companion stared at her, then the stout face wrinkled into a wide grin. "He's in charge of everything, honey."

So much for her authority over Mrs. Sanders, Kathleen thought, almost bursting into laughter at being called "honey" by the cook. Struggling to maintain her poise, she asked, "Will you have Mr. Sanders tell him to arrange for horses for us, then?"

"Sure." Mrs. Sanders leaned back in the creaking bow-back chair. "Sandy'll see Ranse this afternoon."

"Thank you." In England, the words would have been a dismissal, but the woman only took another sip of coffee and sighed.

"He's a good man, Ranse O'Neil." The pale blue eyes looked steadily into Kathleen's. "Your Pa's damn lucky to have him. Best cowman in Wyoming."

Absently sipping at her own coffee, Kathleen nodded, undismayed by the woman's presumption, something in her wanting to hear more. An image of that tall, self-assured man filled her mind and she felt her heartbeat quicken.

"This ranch belonged to Ranse," Mrs. Sanders said.

Incredulous, Kathleen stared at her.

"That's right, Miss." The determined expression on Sanders's face seemed to say she wanted to put the English in their place. "He ain't nobility like your Pa, but this is America. His Pa was a scout with the Army and married an Army officer's daughter. Ranse grew up at Fort Laramie. Him and his wife homesteaded this place . . ." Her voice trailed off, and she stared out the window for a long moment, an expression of sadness spreading across her heavy features. "Ranse was gone on roundup when their cabin burned. Killed his wife, and their baby . . . near killed him when he come home. He just rode away . . . went up into Montana, so I heard . . . left everything behind . . . cattle, horses. Finally, the bank foreclosed and sold out to the British and Far West Cattle Company."

"Why did he come back?" Kathleen asked softly, thinking of those dark, shuttered eyes and the pain that must lie behind them.

"The syndicate offered him a lot of money to run the place for them and . . ." She sighed heavily. "I reckon a man has to face his ghosts sometime."

Kathleen was silent, staring out into the sunny ranch yard. Ranse O'Neil was lonely . . . perhaps as lonely as she had always been. Now she understood the brusqueness that lay over the gentleness that had showed itself to Edward.

"Well," Mrs. Sanders heaved herself up from the table. "Them dishes won't wash theirselves." And she began clearing the table.

Alone in her room, Kathleen gently touched the lovely face in the miniature. "Mama," she murmured softly, "why did I think I was the only person who had lost the one I loved . . . the only one who was lonely?"

Would her life have been different if Papa had allowed her to go live with Aunt Elizabeth in London? But he would not countenance any healing of the breach with her mother's family, except as it might benefit him. When they returned from London to learn that Grandmama had died, she had not even been allowed to attend the funeral in Ireland. Aunt Elizabeth had written to chastise him for such behavior, inciting him to forbid Kathleen even to correspond with her great-aunt. So, for the last year, she had simply devoted herself to Edward and the little girls, with no hope of ever finding a different life of her own.

But now . . . and suddenly she was smiling at her image in the mirror. Now she was in Wyoming, where the unbending rules of English nobility did not apply. She was free. The thought was at once exhilarating and frightening.

There was a knock at her door, and a flushed-faced Tydings reported Edward's unpacking finished.

It wasn't like him, Ranse thought, as he crossed the ranch yard toward the lights gleaming from the big house. The new white shirt he'd taken from his duffle scratched his neck, and the scent of bay rum from his recent shave filled his nostrils. All this because Lord Haw Haw's tony daughter had sent word by Sandy that she wished to see him. A good thing he didn't live in the bunkhouse. The cowhands would never be finished kidding him about dressing up for her ladyship.

Tessie answered his knock and led him into the big sitting room, announcing, "Mr. O'Neil is here, my lady."

"Mr. O'Neil?" Ranse inquired in a low voice, looking at Tessie in amazement.

Kathleen rose from her chair by the fireplace and faced

him. She wore a blue gown that made her incredibly blue eyes seem as deep as the lakes of the Tetons.

"Not my lady, please, Tessie," she said, with a soft laugh.

"But Mrs. Tydings said . . ." the girl began, flushing.

"My father is only a viscount," Kathleen explained, smiling. "Therefore, only his wife is addressed as 'my lady.'"

"I'll never understand it all," Tessie mourned.

"Don't try," Kathleen answered, and turned those marvelous eyes on him. "Good evening, Mr. O'Neil. Shall I have Tessie bring you some coffee?"

"No." He grinned at her, delighted and amazed at the scene just observed. This girl was certainly not a chip off her haughty father. "I might be persuaded to have some of His Lordship's good brandy."

He watched her pouring the brandy into crystal glasses, admiring her deft hands, the easy movement of her slender figure silhouetted against the firelight, the glow of her hair. When she turned to hand him the glass, she smiled and, startled, Ranse realized he'd been staring.

"What can I do for you?" he asked, when they were seated opposite each other in the two Morris chairs flanking the fireplace.

"It's about the horses," Kathleen answered, suddenly aware that she'd poured two brandies and was holding one in her hand. "Edward and I ride every day at home, and we'd like to continue here if you can arrange it."

"How good are you?" he asked bluntly, amused when she sat up straight, her eyes flashing.

"One has to be bloody good to ride to the hounds," she replied in a sharp voice.

"Bloody good?" he repeated, admiring the way her pale skin flushed when she realized she'd used an oath.

Flustered, Kathleen took a sip of the brandy and felt it sear all the way down to her stomach. "Can you arrange it for tomorrow?" she asked, determined now not to let him know how the unwavering regard of those dark eyes unnerved her.

Slowly, he turned the brandy glass in his hands, the amber liquid gleaming in the firelight. Her eyes fastened on those long strong fingers lightly downed with dark hair. A strange burning sensation that had nothing to do with the brandy poured through her.

"You have to realize," he was saying when she forced her attention back to reality, "that riding in Wyoming is not at all like England, even though your father and the Frewens keep insisting on fox hunts through the sagebrush."

In spite of herself, Kathleen smiled at the image of the Brookfield Hunt pouring across the endless sagebrush hills surrounding the house. "Edward and I won't be hunting . . . just riding."

"Good." Ranse drained the last of his brandy and stood up. "Is that all, then?" Suddenly, he needed to get away from this woman whose presence brought back feelings he had thought gone forever. He'd been young then, for God's sake, and Dorie only seventeen. She was gone, and the baby, too, and he'd sworn never to think of it again. Why should this slender English girl, totally different from Dorie, make him yearn for the warmth and gentleness and love he'd lost? Damn it all, a night in Maud's bed once in a while was enough for him. Missing that wouldn't tear him apart and leave him bleeding inside for years.

"Tomorrow morning, then?" she asked, standing up.

"Fine." His voice was strangled and harsh. The old pain was suffocating him. He had to get out of here.

Kathleen stared after him, surprised by the abruptness of his departure. Ranse O'Neil was unlike any man she had ever known. Tonight, he'd been first pleasant, even amusing, then suddenly she'd sensed a kind of anger in him. The dark eyes, his whole face had closed against her, as though he'd drawn a curtain between them. Shaken, she finished her brandy, then sat for a long time staring into the fire, trying to fathom the changes she felt surging through her.

Washed clean by the storm, the air was clear and crisp, almost intoxicating, the sky an intense blue. Feeling giddy with anticipation, Kathleen walked across the ranch yard with Edward skipping beside her. The huge log ranch house faced westward toward the blue Laramie Mountains. To the north, there were low hills topped by limestone rimrock. On the east, Cybille Creek flowed musically over the rocks, its banks lined with cottonwood trees and willow, the first tender catkins of spring just beginning to burst. The meadows spreading out from the creek bed on the flats below were greening. To the south stretched the endless sagebrush plain.

The ranch yard was a busy place with riders coming and going, the blacksmith working at his forge. Heading for the stables, they passed the bunkhouse, the cookhouse, the foreman's cabin, and the corrals.

"Good morning." Ranse O'Neil came out of the tack shed carrying a saddle on one hip. He smiled at them, his teeth very white in his dark tanned face. "Ready to go?"

There was no sense of the furious rejection she'd felt as he left the house last night. The dark eyes, so brown they were almost black, danced with amusement, quickly taking in the neat black superfine riding habit she wore with a white ruffled linen blouse.

"Good morning," she replied, determined not to lose her poise with him again.

"I want a western saddle," Edward demanded.

"Going native, huh?" Ranse's voice held a warm teasing note.

"But we're used to English saddles," Kathleen protested. "Surely you have some here."

"Damn postage stamps," Ranse said, failing to conceal his annoyance. "But you can have whatever you want."

"I want to be a cowboy," Edward proclaimed, running his hands over the western saddle Ranse held.

"Give the kid a chance," Ranse urged, looking at Kathleen.

"He might get hurt," she protested, knowing that if anything happened to Edward, she'd never forgive herself.

"For God's sake, he's half-grown, not a baby. If he can ride at all, he can handle this." His voice was curt. Without waiting for her answer, he strode into the stable and threw the saddle over a pinto horse tethered there.

"How about an Injun pony?" he asked Edward, who was almost dancing with excitement.

Flushed with anger at O'Neil's high-handed behavior, Kathleen could only watch while the horse was saddled and Edward boosted into the saddle.

"Ride him around the corral," O'Neil ordered, "so I can

see if you know how to handle him." Ignoring her, he walked over to the corral fence, leaning his arms on the top rail as he watched Edward walk the horse around the enclosure.

Trembling with apprehension, Kathleen joined him beside the fence. At once, she was aware of the man beside her in a way she had never before been aware of any man. There was a strong clean odor to him . . . horses, tobacco, sagebrush . . . an odor she could only describe as masculine.

"Rides well," he commented, as Edward urged the horse into a canter. Reaching into his shirt pocket for tobacco, he began to roll a cigarette.

"He's had lessons for years," Kathleen replied, beginning to relax, now that she saw Edward could handle the pinto.

"Lessons!" His dark eyebrows rose in amusement, as though riding horses were something instinctive that did not need to be taught.

In her annoyance at his air of superiority, Kathleen fell silent, asking herself how she could ever have felt attracted to him. After a moment, watching him smoke the cigarette, his eyes intent on the rider and horse, she said coolly, "Edward is a gentleman and has to learn the ways of a gentleman." When his only reply was a contemptuous look, she added boldly, "You wouldn't know about that."

Her heart plunged in despair at her own cruelty when she saw the wince at the corner of his mouth. The dark eyes were hard when he looked at her. "No," he said. "Perhaps I'm not a gentleman, but this is not a country for those who are weak, or cowards." Throwing down his cigarette, he ground it out with his heel. "Would you make your brother a coward? Right now, he fears nothing. He can do anything."

Tears stung her eyes. "I'm sorry," she said in a shaky voice, and regaining control, added, "He's all I have . . . I couldn't bear . . ." Once more, her voice failed her.

The dark eyes softened, but he looked quickly away. "Use your whip," he yelled at Edward, who at once forced the horse into a rocking gallop. "That's enough!" Ranse shouted, and Edward pulled the pinto back into an easy walk, around and around the corral.

In silence, Ranse watched the boy. Feeling chastised, wronged and quite out of sorts, Kathleen found herself covertly watching him rather than Edward. Slowly, his expression changed to one that seemed to her both sad and pensive. In a thoughtful voice, so low she barely caught the words, she heard him say, "My son would have been about that age now."

Somehow she knew he was not speaking to her, but the poignant words, the longing in his dark, saturnine face touched her vulnerable heart. "I'm so sorry," she murmured. "Mrs. Sanders told me."

"Oh yeah?" His lips twisted wryly. "Lil has a big mouth."

For a moment, their eyes met and held, and she wanted to weep for the loneliness she saw mirrored there. Then he looked away, reaching into his shirt pocket for his tobacco. As he lit the cigarette, she saw that all traces of vulnerability had vanished from his face. The mask was back in place.

Taking a deep drag on the cigarette, he blew the smoke out explosively. "Hey, Eddie," he called. "Get over here, and let's get your sister fitted out western style."

CHAPTER 19

Candles in tall silver candelabra shed a warm glow over the impeccable white linen, gleaming off the polished silver and the crystal glasses. Seated at her father's right, Kathleen allowed herself a moment of pride in the perfection of the table with its centerpiece of spring wildflowers Edward had helped her gather. The fine linen, the silver and crystal were all furnished by British and Far West Cattle Company, but she had put everything together, taking charge as she had never done at home. Preparations had occasioned a brief tiff between Mrs. Sanders and the complaining Mrs. Tydings, which she had managed to settle.

Lord Hadley's arrival that afternoon had set the ranch in an uproar. The entourage consisted of his own enclosed traveling buggy, followed by that of his friend, Dr. Charles Vickers, in turn followed by the cowhand who had charge of the hunting horses. Papa had greeted Edward and herself in his usual cool, noncommittal manner as though they had parted only yesterday. Then he told Kathleen that Dr. Vickers and his companion, Michael Fraser, would be staying overnight. Would she see that their quarters were made up and order an appropriate dinner? Ignoring her questions as to how she was to accomplish all this, he mounted the stairs to his bedroom, followed by Perkins, his elderly valet, who looked exhausted.

Glancing around the table now, Kathleen met Charles Vickers's admiring brown eyes. He was a middle-aged man with good strong features, his gray hair thick and leonine, his gray moustache neatly trimmed. He had a good tight-knit figure, clothed in a much wrinkled black broadcloth suit.

Mrs. Tydings sat beside him, dressed in her usual drab gray wool. Across from her was Mr. Fraser, a youngish man with thinning light brown hair and anxious blue eyes. He had already imparted the information that he was in Cheyenne awaiting his appointment to the state attorney's office, for he had recently graduated from Harvard Law School.

At the end of the table sat a sleepy Edward, who had been allowed to stay up for the occasion. Sighing, he glanced at Kathleen. He was bored, she knew, and disappointed once again at the way his father had greeted him. As soon as it was decently possible, she would send him off to bed.

The last of the guests sat across from her, where she found it almost impossible to avoid Ranse O'Neil's eyes. He wore a black broadcloth suit, with white shirt and a string tie. His dark hair had been cut and brushed in an attempt to control its unruliness. Dr. Vickers and he knew each other and seemed on friendly terms. She had been surprised that her father included him among the guests, although, she told herself, surely Wyoming held no more surprises.

In spite of her efforts, their eyes caught and held for a brief moment. It was he who looked away. Kathleen felt an inner trembling speed along her limbs. Why did this man she'd known only a few days disturb her so? She mustn't allow her inner turmoil to show, for she was playing the part tonight of Lord Hadley's hostess. When Dr. Vickers spoke, she turned to him with a faint sigh of relief.

"That shade of blue becomes you, Miss Hadley," he said, attacking the thick slice of roast beef on his plate. "Brings out your remarkable eyes."

"Thank you," she murmured, feeling the warmth climb her cheeks. "You're very kind."

"Not at all," he answered heartily. "I only speak the truth."

She was painfully aware of Ranse O'Neil's dark eyes regarding her in an enigmatic way. He did not add his compliments, but his eyes never left her face as he drank from his wineglass.

"Do you find America very different from England?" the doctor asked.

She knew he was making polite conversation, but was thankful to be diverted from the man across the table. "Oh yes," she said. "Quite different. Have you ever been to England?"

"Yes, I have." His eyes danced mischievously, and Kathleen suddenly liked him very much. "That's why it amuses me to watch the behavior of the English on this frontier."

Quickly, Kathleen glanced at her father, fearing that he might take exception to Dr. Vickers's remarks. But Lord Hadley was filling his wineglass again, his face already flushed. She had seen him so many times at dinner, present but not present.

Dr. Vickers took another slice of roast beef from the platter Tessie offered, smiling around the table. "There's a story the natives tell of two upper-class Englishmen arriving on the train in Cheyenne. Surrounded by mounds of luggage, they stood looking about for a porter. A couple of cowboys were nearby, watching the passengers, and one Englishman called to them, 'Here . . . you!' The cowboys looked at them curiously. 'Here you,' commanded the Englishman, 'take hold of these boxes.'" Dr. Vickers paused, obviously enjoying his own anecdote. "The cowboy looked the Englishman over, then said, 'Sorry, Your Lordship. I'm punchin' cows for the King of England, and he don't like me to do odd jobs on the side.'" He roared with laughter as he delivered the punch line. Mr. Fraser joined in, and Kathleen heard O'Neil's deep chuckle across the table. Edward laughed because everyone else was laughing. Mrs. Tydings tightened her lips and gave the doctor an icy look.

In spite of herself, Kathleen smiled. When her father looked about the table, saying, "Eh, what was that?" she covered his hand and answered, "Nothing at all, Papa."

"Speaking of the King of England," Mr. Fraser said, with a glance at Dr. Vickers. "I can't imagine he lives any better than the Frewens." Turning to Kathleen, he continued, "I hope you'll have a chance to visit them. It's quite an experience. Even in the finest homes in Boston, I've never seen such luxury . . . hothouse roses daily . . . caviar, champagne. The cost of living like that on the frontier must be exorbitant."

"They're in the cattle business," Papa unexpectedly broke into the conversation. "Fortunes to be made in the business. Last year, the Prairie Land and Cattle Company declared a dividend of 25%. We paid 20%, ourselves." Waving his wineglass recklessly, he went on. "Nothing like it. Turn the cattle on the range, sell them when they're fat. No overhead except for a few cowhands. Nothing like it."

"The range is badly overstocked," O'Neil said in a tight voice. His eyes were cold and his rugged face set in hard, disapproving lines. "The Englishmen are building paper castles. Their greed could destroy the whole industry."

Kathleen held her breath at his obvious insubordination, fearing he might have sparked Papa's anger. There was an aura of tension about the table, dispelled when Papa finished his glass of wine and seemed to lapse back into his alcoholic haze. Staring down at her plate, Kathleen felt a strange chill come over her with a sudden shattering insight. She could not help comparing her father with O'Neil, for in spite of his arrogance Ranse O'Neil was a man of strength and self-confidence. She saw Papa refill his wineglass and sighed inwardly. Lord Robert Hadley was a weak and selfish man, always looking for an easy way out of the financial troubles caused by his own imprudence. That was why he gambled . . . why he had taken a chance on this American venture . . . and why he drank to cover his own weakness.

Dr. Vickers cleared his throat. "Speaking as one not in the business, it would seem to me best to breed a better cow."

If he meant to divert the conversation into safer channels, Kathleen thought, he'd made a poor choice, although she was glad to be diverted from her own melancholy assessment of her father.

But O'Neil seized on the subject with enthusiasm. "I've ordered some Hereford bulls for just that reason. They should be arriving from the East soon. I hope next year we'll have a whole new crop of white-faced calves on the range."

Mrs. Tydings drew in her breath, obviously shocked at such subject matter at the dinner table.

Dr. Vickers gave her an amused look and said quickly, "All this talk of cattle business can't be very interesting to you, Kathleen. Tell me, has Ranse shown you any of the country around here yet?"

Before she could reply, Ranse frowned at the doctor. His voice was cool. "Running a ranch this size doesn't leave me much time for entertaining dudes."

Mr. Fraser and Dr. Vickers exchanged amused glances. With O'Neil's dark eyes riveted on her face, Kathleen drew in a painful breath. A slow resentment boiled in her. She hadn't asked to be entertained, merely for his help with the horses. Relieved for the excuse, she stood up, roused the nodding Edward, and excused herself to take him up to bed.

As they mounted the stairs, she heard behind her the chairs scraping as the men left the table and the low rumble of their voices as they moved into the sitting room for brandy and cigars. Hurt and anger warred within her. Even knowing Ranse O'Neil's past did not excuse his rudeness. More than a little of her anger was directed at herself for allowing herself to be drawn to him so quickly.

"I like Wyoming," Edward said, swinging his riding crop as he strode across the ranch yard beside Kathleen. "I wish Papa would let us stay here." He looked up at her. "Would you mind, Kathleen?"

Smiling fondly down at her brother, Kathleen observed the health beginning to glow in his once thin, pale face. Wyoming agreed with him. Her smile widened as he self-consciously tilted back the battered cowboy hat, imitating Bill, the grizzled old cowhand who had given him the hat. Ever since Papa's return, O'Neil had avoided them. Bill had been assigned to care for their horses and guide them around the countryside if they asked.

After their noonday meal, Edward had asked her to walk with him along Cybille Creek, where they had not explored before.

He gave an exaggerated sigh. "I do wish Papa hadn't hired Mr. Fraser to come out from Cheyenne to be my tutor. He's a bit of a stick."

Kathleen laughed, thinking that Michael Fraser was indeed a stiff and self-conscious young man. "Papa is really helping him out, Edward. The man needs to earn some money while he's waiting for his government appointment. Besides," she added, "it won't hurt you to get back to your lessons."

"Lessons are a bore," Edward announced. "Anyway, when I grow up, I'm going to be a cowman. Just like Ranse."

Kathleen's heart skipped painfully at the sound of the name. Why could she not erase those dark eyes from her mind, and push that tall figure out of her dreams? Why were her eyes always searching the ranch yard for the sight of him? Silly, foolish girl, she chided herself, suddenly desperately lonely for Francine. What would her friend, with all her romantic experience, have to say about the feelings that tormented her?

Spring had warmed the countryside, and Kathleen returned from each ride bearing a handful of the wildflowers blooming among the sagebrush. In her hand now, she carried a mixture of red Indian paintbrush, blue lupine, creamy sand lilies already wilting, and red penstemon. Looking down at the blossoms, so different from the carefully cultivated gardens of Hadley Hall, her mind suddenly flew to the flowers pressed in her mother's prayer book. Purple, lavender and white . . . she could not find them in Wyoming, she knew. Would she ever understand their significance, lying lost and fragile next to the marriage ceremony?

After dinner at midday, Kathleen and Edward took up their exploration of the creek. She still wore her riding habit of navy blue with smart brass buttons on the jacket, for the spring air was crisp.

Automatically, her eyes searched the ranch yard, and she drew in her breath almost painfully. Ranse O'Neil, mounted on Hawk, his favorite bay horse, was talking to a cowboy near the corral. Her throat felt dry, and her heart beat almost painfully. She had scarcely seen him since the dinner party for Dr. Vickers. Surely, he was avoiding her, and at that moment she knew it for the best, for her response to the sight of him was almost overwhelming. Her hand closed over Edward's shoulder, and she hurried him along, down the cutbank toward the creek.

Cybille Creek was full from the spring runoff of melting

snow. The clear water sparkled in the sunlight, its music loud as it tumbled over the rocky creek bed. Along the bank, they came on a spring half hidden among towering trees and willows. Puffs of cotton blew from the ripened buds of the cottonwood trees, drifting lazily through the air. The spring had been enclosed in a framework of logs, two high, bleached white as bones. Where the water trickled down toward the creek, moss grew thick and green, waving gently in the flowing water. A bed of grass spread along the sides, golden buttercups gleamed there, and watercress grew in the stream.

"Sandy says there are lots of fish in here," Edward said, tugging at her hand. "Let's go look. We might spot some."

"You go ahead," she urged, sitting down on the logs surrounding the spring. "I can't keep up with you." Bemused, she watched Edward's small figure disappear among the stand of willows along the creek. The sunlight on the water, the murmur of the stream over its rocky bed, the rustling of the cottonwood leaves . . . all filled her with a strange sense of *déjà vu*. The soft, sad cry of the mourning doves touched her empty, yearning heart.

The soft plop of horses' hooves in the wet grass aroused her from a waking dream. Standing up, she turned to face Ranse O'Neil and thought her heart would leap from her chest. Silent, she stared at him as though she had turned to stone in his presence.

"Miss Kathleen," he said, and swung his tall body down from the saddle, letting the reins trail on the ground. When he took off the wide gray hat, his black hair was so rumpled her hand ached to smooth it.

"I wanted to tell you . . ." He paused uncertainly, as though not sure what he wanted to say.

"Yes?" Kathleen attempted a frosty look, trying to deny the turmoil inside her.

The black eyes looked directly into hers. "I wanted to apologize for my rudeness at dinner the other night."

"Edward and I don't intend to bother you again," she burst out. "Bill has been most helpful."

"Damn!" he swore softly, his mouth twisting as he frowned. "I let your father get my goat every time. It was nothing against you and the boy . . ." His voice trailed off as his dark eyes searched her face.

Kathleen's heart was beating so wildly she was sure he could hear it. She was drawn by those eyes, that dark sardonic face, yet she feared what he might read in her own eyes.

"Forgive me." He said it hesitantly, as though they were words he did not often use. Reaching across the space between them, he cupped her chin in one gloved hand.

In those black eyes, she saw fires she knew might burn her beyond healing. Bending his head, Ranse lay his mouth gently against hers, and Kathleen knew she was lost.

"You mustn't," she murmured against his lips, her voice trembling, yet well she knew that he would.

As though all this had been rehearsed in some long-ago time beyond remembering, his arms came about her. When his lean body pressed against hers, she felt herself melt against him. An aching need that held both pain and pleasure filled her. Yielding to his kiss, she knew there were passions in her never guessed at, depths unrecognized and unplumbed. Time stood still. Eternity lingered there beside the rippling water, beneath the sighing trees.

"Kathleen!" Edward called.

For an instant, she closed her eyes tightly, for the first time ever wishing Edward far from her. Ranse drew away. His dark eyes looked into hers with such longing it was almost physical hurt when he wrenched them away.

"You're right," he said. "I mustn't." Without looking at her again, he mounted the horse and rode back up the creek bank.

Spring ripened into summer. The leaves of the cottonwoods changed from green-gold into a lush dark green. Fledgling bluebirds tried their wings from the nest in the eaves of the house. The days fell into a pleasant enough pattern. Kathleen and Edward rode each day, always finding new trails to explore in the endless expanse of the countryside. Michael Fraser had been installed in one of the guest rooms upstairs. He and Edward did lessons each morning in the study. Fraser was not a sociable man and spent most of his free time reading from the crates of books he had brought with him.

It was her father who concerned Kathleen. With little to occupy his time, he became restless and morose, starting on the port before noontime. At the slightest excuse, he would pack up and ride off to hunt with the Frewens or at a nearby ranch owned by an English family named Carrington. As was his custom at home, he would be gone for days or weeks at a time. It seemed to her that he should take some interest in the affairs of the ranch, but he did not show the slightest inclination to do so.

Ranse O'Neil and most of the cowhands were away for weeks. They had left early one morning with a canvas-covered wagon Edward told her was the chuck wagon, a herd of saddle horses, and another wagon carrying bedrolls and gear.

"It's time for calf branding," Edward told her, a bit pompous and proud of his newly acquired knowledge. Sighing, he stared at the cloud of dust hanging in the still blue air behind the train of men and horses. "Ranse said I'm too young to go along."

Kathleen looked at him in astonishment. "You mean you asked him if you could go?"

"Of course," he replied impatiently. "How else will I learn the cattle business?"

She had laughed indulgently then, and laughed now to see him running across the ranch yard to greet the returning wagons. They had come after supper to sit on the veranda overlooking the yard and the creek. Papa had been back since yesterday, and he sat in silence puffing on his pipe, the inevitable glass of port in one hand.

"Full of the devil," Papa observed, indulgent of his son as he never had been of his daughters.

"I'm so glad we came to Wyoming," Kathleen said. "Edward's health has improved unbelievably." Papa did not reply.

Kathleen's eyes probed the dusk, longing for a glimpse of Ranse O'Neil's tall figure. On their last meeting, he had kissed her, and the memory still sent shafts of fire burning through her. What could she say to him when they were face to face again? Would he know how she had yearned all these weeks to feel his mouth gentle against hers once more? Valiantly, she tried to suppress the feeling, then found herself overwhelmed by it as she watched Ranse swing down from his saddle to greet Edward with an arm about the boy's shoulders.

The coral and pink sunset faded into gray and the air cooled. Papa rose and went in through the French doors. She heard the clink of the port decanter on the dining room sideboard and sighed in resignation. If Papa wished to drink away his months in Wyoming, she could not prevent him.

Much later, when she came downstairs after telling Edward good night, she heard Papa's voice in the study. The words were slurred and his tone angry, as so often happened when he drank too much.

Ranse O'Neil's low voice answered evenly, "Since you're supposed to be in charge of this operation, I assumed you'd want to know the calf count." There was a sharp edge of annoyance to his words.

"What the bloody hell do I pay you for?" Papa snapped.

Kathleen paused where she stood on the stairs, shaking her head in despair as she heard the clink of glass and decanter once again. Papa was drunk and quarreling with Ranse.

"I've just had a look at the books, Your Lordship." Ranse's voice was angry now, and his use of the title had a sarcastic inflection. "If you're paying me to run this operation, then your damned extravagance at the Cheyenne Club has to stop."

Had Papa been in Cheyenne, she thought in surprise? She had been longing to go into town to shop, but when she spoke of it, he always put her off.

"None of your bloody business," Papa's voice rose.

"Like hell, it isn't!" The tone of Ranse's voice matched Papa's. "British and Far West hired me to run a ranching business, not a resort for you. The company isn't supposed to pay your gambling debts and liquor bills. Good God, you even signed chits for the services of your whores. I damned well want it stopped."

Kathleen fled up the stairs to her room. She could not bear to hear any more. Sitting down on the bed, she thought of the night of the dinner party, when she'd had that first shattering insight into her father's true character. He was not a man of honor, and nothing would change that. If Edward should grow up to be like him, she could not bear it. The realization that she neither respected nor loved her father was distressing, but somehow she had always known his true nature. She would see that Edward never followed in his footsteps, for Edward was the one person she loved in all the world. As soon as the familiar phrase came into her head, tears started in her eyes. It was no longer true. She loved the tall angry man quarreling with her father downstairs, and she had no control over him or whatever fate might hold for the two of them.

"Ranse said he'd show us the cliffs today," Edward said, trying to make Kathleen quicken her pace as they crossed the ranch yard together. She wore her black riding skirt and an ivory-colored silk shirtwaist.

The calf-branding crew had been home for two days, and

she had scarcely seen Edward in that time. Listening absently to Mr. Fraser's complaints about the boy's inattentiveness, she watched her brother trailing Ranse O'Neil about his work.

So much for lessons today, she thought, smiling as she tied a straw sunshade firmly over her neatly coiled hair. Far to the west, Laramie Peak stood blue and partially concealed by clouds. A few white cotton clouds drifted low in the azure sky, their shadows moving across the gray sagebrush plain. Along the road, yellow rabbit brush blazed, and the purple blooms of Scotch thistle swayed in the slight breeze.

A tremulous anticipation ached inside Kathleen. In the weeks Ranse had been away, she had, more than once, walked alone to the spring beneath the creek bank. Sitting there, she'd listened to the rustle of the wind in the cottonwoods, the musical chatter of the blackbirds riding the willows, longing to hear the sound of a horse moving down the sandy bank, wanting to turn and meet a pair of black eyes yearning toward her.

"Is that the new horse you promised?" Edward called as they approached the stables where Ranse was cinching her sidesaddle on the chestnut mare.

Ranse's favorite bay, Hawk, stood already saddled. Hitched to the rail beside him was a black gelding Kathleen had not seen before. The animal tossed its head and moved nervously as they approached. Faint apprehension quickened her heart.

"Why a different horse?" she asked Edward. "Didn't you like Chief?"

Ranse looked up. His dark eyes drew her like a magnet. A pulse began to pound hard at the base of her throat. After a long, tense moment, he spoke. "He'll never improve as a rider without a challenge. Chief's all right for beginners . . . right, Eddie?"

"Sure." Edward managed to swagger a bit as he picked up the saddle blanket and spread it on the gelding's back.

"Aren't you going to saddle up for him?" she asked, seeing Edward stagger under the weight of the western saddle.

"He knows how," Ranse returned easily. But she saw that

he was covertly watching Edward's struggle, although he did not move to help the boy.

The gelding shied and reared at the weight of the saddle. Kathleen caught her breath, and fear sharpened her voice. "That horse is too spirited for Edward," she protested. "After all . . . he's only a boy."

The black eyes riveted her. "Would you make *him* into a wastrel too?"

He meant Papa, she knew, although she was glad he had not said so in Edward's presence. The painful memory of the quarrel she had overheard came back. Trembling, she walked away, detaching herself, not watching until the gelding was saddled and Edward mounted.

"See, Kathleen," the boy called. "You don't give me credit. Ranse has taught me a lot about handling western horses."

The tall man reached up to squeeze Edward's shoulder, giving him an approving smile. Then he turned to help Kathleen mount, and her breath caught in her throat at the touch of his big hands on her waist. Even after she was seated, her skin burned beneath her riding habit where he had touched her.

For a while, they rode in silence along the wide gravelly bed of Cybille Creek. She saw that Ranse was watching Edward's handling of the horse intently, without making the boy aware of it. A deep sense of gratitude filled her that Edward should have the friendship and affection of a man like Ranse O'Neil—a man of integrity and honor. Shame for her father flooded through her as she watched O'Neil gently showing Edward how to handle the spirited gelding.

Where Cybille Creek poured into the Chugwater River, they paused to rest the horses. When Ranse helped her dismount, their eyes met and held for a long aching moment until the sound of Edward's voice drew them apart.

"What is that called?" he asked, pointing to the eroded cliffs towering above the river, buff-colored and pitted so that they resembled chalk.

"Squaw's Leap," Ranse replied, and with an amused glance at Kathleen asked, "Would you like to hear an Indian story?"

"Yes, please." Edward clapped his hands, once more the small boy.

Ranse sat down on a large rock, with Edward close beside him. Kathleen sat on another nearby. The horses cropped grass noisily.

"It seems there was a young and beautiful squaw, the daughter of a chief." Ranse drew out his cigarette makings and began to roll a cigarette.

"She fell in love with a young warrior who was very poor, for the Sioux had stolen all his ponies. When he came to claim her for his bride, he found an older warrior had brought many ponies to the chief in exchange for his daughter. The young girl had no choice, she would be wife to the warrior who brought her father the most ponies. Heartbroken, the young brave took his weapons and went away to steal ponies from the Sioux."

Ranse paused to light his cigarette, obviously enjoying being the storyteller. "The Indians used to camp along the creek where the ranch is now. At one time, you could still see the tepee circles in the sagebrush along the creek. They were a free people for a thousand years. Now, the white men have destroyed them." He paused so long, looking reflectively into the distance, Kathleen wondered if the story had ended.

"What happened?" Edward prompted eagerly.

"It was said the young man had been killed by the Sioux. The night of her marriage feast, the girl ran away from the camp and threw herself off the cliffs to die on the rocks below rather than marry the warrior she didn't love." A wry grin twisted his mouth. "Romantic story, isn't it?"

"Is that all?" Edward asked, obviously disappointed.

Kathleen looked down at her hands, strangely shaken by his simple tale of love and death.

"Like Romeo and Juliet," Ranse said quietly. She could feel his eyes on her. "I read a lot in the long Wyoming winters, you know."

Looking away, afraid to meet his eyes, she saw the vast prairies spread before her and the rock-rimmed low hills with the cliffs looming above the river. "Wyoming is such a big country," she said softly, almost to herself.

"They do say," Ranse answered with an easy smile, "that you can stand on a hill in Wyoming and see forever."

Quickly dismissing the sense of foreboding his story had provoked, Kathleen laughed. "How lovely . . . to see forever, no beginning and no end." Their eyes met in mutual delight at sharing this fancy.

Edward watched with a puzzled frown. The two people he adored most seemed unaware of his presence.

"Have you always been a cowboy, Ranse?" he asked, determined not to be left out.

Reluctantly tearing his eyes from Kathleen's, Ranse laughed, reaching out to rumple the boy's golden hair. "I've always been a Westerner, if that's what you mean," he answered indulgently. "The O'Neils have lived here since my grandfather came out from St. Louis with Colonel Ashley and ran his trap lines along the drainage of the Medicine Bow Mountains."

"And you were educated here, too?" Kathleen asked, wishing Edward hadn't destroyed that moment of rapport. It had always puzzled her that Ranse in some way differed from the other cowhands. His speech was a little more precise, even with the same Wyoming drawl. Or perhaps it was the easiness of his good manners.

"Yes, by my mother." A flicker of sadness crossed his dark face, and she knew he would understand her own irreparable loss. A faint smile played across his lips as he continued. "Her parents came of the best families in St. Louis. My grandfather would have been a general in the Army if he hadn't been killed in the Indian wars. My mother was educated at the finest girl's school in St. Louis, then shocked the whole family by running away with a half-breed Army scout."

Kathleen thought she might have been back in London, seated beside the fire with Aunt Elizabeth, listening to the tale of the willful Fiona Browne who had given everything for love.

Edward listened in wide-eyed silence, as though aware his question had opened unexpected doors.

"Life here was pretty uncivilized," Ranse went on, looking sadly into the distance. "It was hard on her, but she adored my father and would have endured anything for him."

"Then you have no family now?" She said the words tentatively, remembering his face when he had spoken of his dead son, not wanting to cause him pain.

"No." His voice was gruff. Reaching into his pocket for tobacco, he began to build another cigarette. She thought he meant to signal an end to the conversation and sat silent, watching him.

Lighting the cigarette, he blew smoke out explosively, his eyes on the distant cliffs. A breeze rustled the leaves of the cottonwoods, and somewhere in the distance a quail called for its mate.

Too much had been said, perhaps. She'd asked too many questions, come too close to old wounds he still bore beneath an outward shell of unbending strength. The ride back to the ranch house was painfully silent, for even Edward seemed to sense the constraint between his companions.

Summer dusk lay warm and still beyond the dining room windows, for Tessie had neglected to close the draperies. A lone man stood beside the corral fence smoking a cigarette. With a shock, Kathleen realized she would have known that silhouette anywhere . . . Ranse O'Neil. She wondered what he was thinking there alone. Even though she had observed his easy camaraderie with the men, she knew he could not be one of them, for he commanded them. He was alone, as she had always been alone. His cigarette flipped out across the dark ranch yard, leaving a trail of sparks behind it. Kathleen's heart contracted painfully. That gesture seemed to her a symbol of loneliness there in the darkness.

CHAPTER 21

"'Bye, Kathleen." Edward's disconsolate voice came from the French doors opening onto the veranda. Turning, she waved at him, smiling at the sight of Mr. Fraser's stern face behind the boy. There were too many interesting things around the ranch for Edward to care for lessons, and he had neglected them shamefully. When Mr. Fraser had finally demanded that Edward pay attention or he would resign, Kathleen had been glad Papa was away at the Carrington Ranch. He would have had Mr. Fraser packed and gone at once, but she had backed the poor beleaguered man. Edward's schooling was important, no matter how Papa might denigrate learning. Still, the sad little voice calling after her, as she left for her afternoon ride, made her resolution waver. No, she told herself sternly, Edward must catch up on the neglected studies.

"Edward won't be riding today," she told Ranse, seeing that he had saddled Blackie as well as her own mare, Babe.

He looked surprised, but grinned, nodding in agreement when she told him what had happened. "But you shouldn't ride alone," he said.

"Then perhaps you'll join me." She said the words boldly, although she was quaking inside. When she saw him hesitate, frowning, she was certain she would die of embarrassment if he refused.

At last he answered, with a shrug, "Sure."

The touch of his hands on her waist where he had lifted her into the saddle still burned, as he mounted Blackie and rode up beside her.

Afternoon sun lay warm and golden on the bare ranch

yard. The scent of sagebrush drifted on the breeze, aromatic and pleasant. In the distance, a blue haze lay close to the horizon, so that only the flatlands were in view, stretching to the end of the ancient earth.

In silence, they rode along the banks of Cybille Creek below the house, the lush green of the wild hay meadows spread out before them. The air was still and warm, so quiet the ripple of water in the creek could be heard clearly. A mourning dove called, sighing over and over.

"What caused that?" Kathleen asked, reining in her horse, and pointing to a dim circle in the sagebrush. Within the circle were young sagebrush and shortgrass, as though the vegetation had been trampled and was just growing back. There were other circles, she saw now, aligned along the creek bank.

"This was an Indian camp," Ranse said. "Each circle was a tepee."

"Yes, you told us. I remember." A stillness came over her then. Long ago, another people had been here . . . alive, laughing, loving, working. She could almost smell the horses, the meat roasting over the fires, hear the dogs barking and the children calling. It was as though she were surrounded by the shades of presences known and loved.

"Kathleen." Ranse's voice was soft, as though he were awakening a sleeper.

With a start, she came back to the present. "I could almost see them," she said, vaguely surprised at herself for sharing such an intense experience. "The horses coming and going, the papoose in his cradleboard on his mother's back, the black-haired squaws bent over their work . . ." She looked around to meet the steady gaze of his dark eyes.

"Nothing is ever lost," he said simply.

In that moment, Kathleen knew she loved him. Another man would have laughed, or dismissed her foolish fancy. Ranse O'Neil accepted and shared an experience that had shaken her deeply. Those dark eyes plumbed the depths of her soul. It took all her strength of will to remain silent, to spur her horse ahead on the trail.

"We've never been here before," she said, when he had led her across the creek and through a tangle of willows, red birch, and chokecherry bushes.

A spring bubbled from the hillside, making its silent way through a small flowered meadow to disappear among the bushes on its way to Cybille Creek.

"A good place for a picnic," he said in a teasing voice, and she laughed. The three of them had made a joke of Ranse's picnic lunches, for they inevitably consisted of dried beef jerky, hard biscuits, and fresh water.

When he dismounted, tethering his horse, and came to stand beside her, the laughter died in her throat. An unfamiliar tingling flowed along her veins, and a sense of wild excitement, as wonderful as it was, was frightening.

"My lady," he said, still teasing, and lifted her down from the saddle. He did not step away, so that her back remained pressed against the mare's flank, Ranse in front of her so close their bodies almost touched, his hands still hot on her waist.

Looking up, she saw the banked fires burning in his dark eyes and felt an answering blaze ignite inside her. Without thought, she slid her hands along his arms, across his broad shoulders. Almost brazenly, she lifted her face and felt his lips meet hers. His mouth was gentle at first, then his arms came around her, pressing her against the full length of his strong body, and the kiss grew more demanding.

It was as though the world dissolved away. For Kathleen, there was nothing but the sensation of his mouth claiming hers, the warmth of his arms and his lean body. It was as though she were a gas lamp someone had suddenly set alight. Wave after wave of urgent longing swept through her as she responded with all her being.

"Dear God . . . Kathleen," he groaned, tearing his mouth from hers, but holding her even closer, his cheek pressed against her hair. She clung to him, wanting this moment to last forever.

He drew a deep ragged breath, stepping away from her, holding her shoulders in his big hands. "Kathleen," he said again, and the sound of the word was like a caress.

The dark eyes searched her face, conjuring up in her such a tumult of emotion she was suddenly terrified by the depth of her own feelings. Trembling, she stepped out of his hold. Quickly, she moved across the tiny meadow, calling back in a shaky voice, "Where's the picnic?"

Behind her, she heard his chuckle. She could not turn toward him, although in her mind's eye she saw him taking the blanket, the canteen of water, the cloth sack containing jerky and biscuits from the back of his saddle. She heard the sound of his boots in the wet grass as he bent to fill the canteen from the spring.

"Damn!" he said, and she looked. He walked toward her, one boot sloshing water. "Slipped," he explained in obvious chagrin, and she laughed aloud, relieved that the moment had been defused.

Sitting down on the grass, Ranse pulled off his wet boots and socks, placing them in the sun to dry. Then he looked up at her with a grin. "Hungry?" he asked.

Kathleen shook her head, giving him a bemused smile. A warmth suffused her whole body that had nothing to do with the golden sunlight across the flowered meadow.

"Well," he said, offering her the canteen. "You'd better be thirsty after what I just went through."

"Water cold?" She took a drink from the canteen and handed it back to him.

"Hadn't you noticed I turned blue?" he asked in mock pain, grinning at her as he spread the blanket out on the grass, setting the lunch sack in the middle.

Kathleen untied her bonnet, laying it on the blanket beside her. His gray stetson joined her bonnet. She wanted to look at him, but dared not. Surely her eyes would reveal all the new and frightening emotions his kiss had aroused. A sigh escaped her as she struggled to control her feelings. Even as she stared into the distance, she was aware of Ranse watching her.

"Those are the cliffs you told us about the other day, aren't they?" She pointed toward the chalky outcropping in the distance.

"Yes, Squaw's Leap." His voice was low, questioning.

Filled with a bemused sorrow, Kathleen turned over in her mind the story Ranse had told that day. "Such a sad story," she began, wondering why it had affected her so. Then, with sudden shattering insight, she knew. Tears filled her eyes, and she heard herself saying, "Like my mother's story. She never loved my father. She was forced to marry him because he had a title and money." She gave Ranse a

201

sidewise glance and saw in his face only sympathy and gentle caring, and she went on with the words she could have said to no other human being. "There was a young man, so my Aunt Elizabeth told me." Again, she looked into his tender eyes, and she felt the hot tears coursing down her cheeks. "Like the young warrior, only he was a young Irishman. My mother loved him desperately. She would have run away with him when he came to England for her, but she died . . ." Her voice faded. "Doomed love . . . just like the Indian maiden."

Ranse reached across and drew her into his arms.

She yielded to him, burying her face against his shoulder. "She was a scandal, so they say . . . a wanton woman." A sob shook her. "They don't let me forget it."

"Kathleen," he murmured, gathering her closer, his mouth warm against her temple. Then he held her away, looking into her face, one finger gently wiping away the tears. "You are Kathleen," he said earnestly. "What she was has nothing to do with you. Yesterday is gone. Forgive her."

With those words, the terrible burden she had carried always seemed to be lifted. Ranse bent toward her, his mouth kissing away the tears. Carefully, he eased her back onto the blanket, looking down into her face. The tears ceased as she felt herself drawn into the depths of his eyes, and waves of longing washed through her.

"Ranse . . ." she murmured softly, her hands moving of their own accord along his broad shoulders, her fingers luxuriating in the soft warmth of his thick hair.

His mouth moved over her face, soft as the kiss of the wind, savoring her ears, her cheeks, the curve of her throat. When at last he reached her lips, she responded fervently, her hands tangled in his hair as she pressed against him. The soft probing of his tongue aroused a wild new sensation, and instinctively, she opened her lips to him. His kiss deepened, filling her mouth with the sharp masculine taste of him.

All her senses were sharpened, incredibly aware. The wide blue Wyoming sky seemed a blanket spread lovingly above them. Somehow, he had removed the pins from her hair. His hand, stroking through the loosened strands, sent a tingling warmth along her limbs.

"Ranse . . ." She murmured his name as softly as the

distant murmuring of Cybille Creek, reveling in the desire for her she saw in his dark face.

"My love . . . my love." His voice was muffled against her throat. "God, how I love you."

Intense joy poured over her at the words. Turning her head, she found his mouth and whispered against it, "I love you, Ranse." And she was lost in his deep, demanding kiss, as his arms gathered her fiercely against his aroused body.

An aching urgency suffused her entire being. Ranse's fingers fumbled at the buttons of her linen shirtwaist, and she helped him. As his hand slid gently inside her chemise and cupped her breast, she gasped and arched herself into his touch. Drawing away, he drew the chemise off over her head. With a glad cry, she welcomed his mouth against her breasts, the sensations aroused by his touch radiating outward into the hot pulsing of her blood.

Reaching down, she unbuttoned his shirt and pushed it off. His mouth claimed hers again, her hands drifting in delight along the strong muscled back, her breasts taut against his rough chest hair.

Lost in desire, they were scarcely aware of clothes hampering them. He fumbled with her skirt, and it was gone along with her pantaloons, and his jeans. There was nothing between their passion-filled bodies but the soft summer air.

His mouth explored her vulnerable softness, from lips to breasts, down the planes of her stomach, to the velvet of her thigh. Longing pulsated through her. With all her inexperience, somehow instinct and her love for this man combined to show her the way.

Ranse looked down into her face, his voice throaty with desire. "Sweet love . . . I don't want to hurt you."

"You could never hurt me, dearest Ranse." Her fingers gently stroked his dark face, which softened in a way that told her she had touched him deeply.

With gentle fingers, Ranse caressed the throbbing moistness between her thighs, carefully pushing aside her maidenhead, stroking until she cried out and arched against his hand.

"Oh love . . . please . . . please . . ." She gasped the incoherent plea, all passion centered now, aching for him to fill and complete her.

She felt him steeling himself, holding back to spare her pain as he came into her slowly, waiting until her body had accommodated itself to his invasion. Closing her eyes, Kathleen followed his lead until a throbbing desire rose from the very center of her . . . a need that would not be denied. With a soft cry, she arched against him, taking him deep inside her.

Ranse drew in his breath sharply. His mouth covered hers, devouring her in incredible sweetness. Wildly, she lifted herself against him, wanting, wanting . . . His hands cupped her hips, lifting her to meet his thrusts until reality fled. She was lost to the all-enveloping rapture exploding through her body.

Desire spent, they lay in each other's arms. The golden warmth of summer caressed their bodies. Faintly, as from a distance, Ranse could hear the horses cropping grass, and beyond that, the mourning doves' soft tones. Turning, he looked down into the face of the girl beside him. She lay there in the flowered meadow, her bright head like a lovely flower itself. Her deep blue eyes met his, and the love he saw reflected there filled all the scarred and empty places in his heart.

He had wanted her since that first night, when they'd faced each other before the fireplace. Even then, as she'd tried to put him in his place, he'd guessed at the loneliness in her that matched his own. But he'd told himself a hundred times it could never be, for she was the daughter of an English lord born to a world he could never know. As though fate had overruled his doubts, she lay here in his arms, she had given herself to him. And he knew that he had given himself . . . for all time.

"Kathleen," he murmured, bending to kiss her bare shoulder, loving the sound of her name in his mouth. "Darling Kathleen . . . did I hurt you?"

Her hand stroked his hair lovingly, and she smiled a satisfied smile. "The hurt was easily forgotten in what came after." When he chuckled and kissed the tip of her nose, her face changed. The blue eyes darkened with apprehension. "Am I a wanton too . . . like my mother?"

Ranse drew her close, her soft warm body arousing him again. With all his heart, he longed to erase the pain and

204

loneliness behind her innocent question. "Do you love me, Kathleen?" he asked, looking into her eyes.

"Oh . . ." The word reflected the joy flooding her lovely face. "I love you so . . . I didn't know . . . I didn't guess . . ." The words were lost as his mouth covered hers.

"Perhaps you are like your mother," he teased gently, his lips a breath away from hers. "A wanton only for the man you love."

CHAPTER 22

Kathleen lay awake far into the night, reliving every moment of the most glorious day of her life. Wanton and sinful she might be, but she did not feel any guilt. Only joy that Ranse O'Neil loved her and thought her beautiful. They had taken each other again, there in the summer meadow, blending their bodies in an ecstasy that welded their souls forever.

It had been scandalously late when they rode back to the ranch, almost dusk. Lights were already gleaming in the dining room, and she was sure she saw Edward's face peering from the windows. Ranse drew her into the tack shed, kissing her so that her knees were weak with longing.

"Tomorrow, sweet love?" he asked softly, and she had nodded, already aching to lie with him again.

Then Edward had burst in, demanding, "Where have you been? I was worried."

In the darkness of her room, Kathleen smiled. All these years, Edward had been her dearest companion, and now she lay here plotting how to escape him tomorrow. A glow suffused her body as she thought of Ranse, of how he had touched her, both body and soul. In the faint moonlight through the window, she could see the miniature on her dresser, and her heart reached out toward the woman painted there. Mama, she thought lovingly, for the first time free of guilt and shame. Dear Mama, now I know, now I understand.

As she was dressing next morning, she heard the rattle of a rig driving into the ranch yard. Looking out the window, she smiled at the figure of Mr. Fraser hurrying to take the mail sack from the driver. The poor man had soon thought better of his job as tutor and met each mail coach anxiously awaiting the letter telling of his appointment. He would be leaving soon, she was certain. With a sigh, she finished pinning up her hair, wondering how she and Ranse could ever be alone then.

Hearing her father's voice, she sighed again. He must have returned late last night after everyone had gone to bed. The barriers between Ranse and herself suddenly seemed insurmountable.

The atmosphere at the breakfast table was cold indeed. Kathleen glanced around, at her father's cold face, Mr. Fraser's hangdog expression, and Mrs. Tydings's firm angry mouth. Edward had not appeared.

"I'll be going back to England," were Tydings's opening words. "Just as soon as it can be arranged." She gave a long exasperated sigh. "I can't bear this country another day."

"I'm sorry to hear it, Mrs. Tydings," Kathleen lied, hoping her face did not reveal how the news pleased her. The bubbling animosity between Tydings and Mrs. Sanders must have erupted with a bang.

"I shall be leaving too," Mr. Fraser said. "My appointment came in this morning's mail." He looked unutterably relieved, and Papa frowned at him.

"Do you wish to return with Tydings, Kathleen?" Papa glowered at the woman.

"Certainly not, Papa," she protested, wondering what she would do if he insisted, for she could never leave Wyoming now. "I will stay with you and Edward."

He allowed himself a grim smile. "Edward seems much improved, but I think I'll have Dr. Vickers take a look at him."

"Then we'll be going into Cheyenne?" she asked, trying to hide her disappointment.

"Might as well make a trip of it," he growled. "You can do some shopping, I'll show Edward the sights, Mrs. Tydings can catch her train, and Mr. Fraser . . ." He frowned at the man again, and Kathleen knew he was simply annoyed because the man had inconvenienced him. "Mr. Fraser can assume his new position." He rose from the table, turning to

Kathleen as he started from the room. "Perhaps you could tell Bill to have the surrey ready in the morning."

Edward was still at the table demolishing a stack of Mrs. Sanders's pancakes when Kathleen walked across to the stables. Bill was in the tack shed cleaning saddles, and she delivered her message.

She hesitated, watching him rubbing saddle soap into the leather, wanting to ask and knowing how much her question might reveal. "Where's Ranse this morning?" She could not help herself. Already wanting to see him, touch him, be near him, underlay her every thought and movement.

"He's gone into Cheyenne," Bill answered.

In all her life, she had never felt so bereft. The gray front of clouds moving in from the west seemed an omen about to rob her of the only true happiness she'd ever known.

"Those Hereford bulls he ordered supposed to be in on the train today. He took a couple of the boys and went to bring the critters."

Relief flooded through her. Why had she at once assumed he was gone forever? "When will he be back?" Suddenly, she didn't care if Bill guessed her feelings, as he surely must.

"Coupla days," Bill replied, taking up a rag to polish the saddle in front of him. "Depends if the train's on time. Never can tell." He glanced up at her with a knowing grin. "We might meet him on the way into town tomorrow."

A storm that night rinsed the air clean. Early the next day, under the blue vault of sky, the odor of sagebrush rose from the plain, steaming in the morning sun. The miles into Cheyenne spun slowly out behind them. They met only a farmer, with his wagon full of children, reminding Kathleen of the tinkers who roamed England in their dirty caravans.

By a quirk of fate, Mrs. Tydings was able to board the eastbound train at once. She had finally admitted she'd quarreled with Mrs. Sanders, and that was the last straw in a long list of complaints. Clutching a British and Far West Cattle Company draft for her wages, she climbed aboard and settled in her seat. Without the slightest tug of feeling, Kathleen waved goodbye as the train chugged out of the station.

Dr. Charles Vickers came down the steps of his big square

brick house to greet them, shaking hands with everyone, effusively congratulating Mr. Fraser on his appointment.

"You'll all stay for supper, I hope."

Kathleen thought her father hesitated, but everyone else agreed at once. Bill and Perkins went on to leave the luggage at the Plains Hotel, with Bill to return for them later. Kathleen had refused to bring Tessie, for she had soon learned to do without her services except when her gown buttoned up the back.

"You might as well use my guest room, Michael," the doctor said pleasantly, "Until you can find suitable lodgings."

Mr. Fraser seemed immensely relieved by the arrangement and gladly carried his own baggage up the stairs.

The front of the house was given over to the doctor's offices, and he led them down a dark paneled hallway, lighted only by one electric bulb, to an equally dark sitting room filled with leather-covered furniture. Proudly, he pointed out the electric lights recently installed, with wires snaking up the walls and across the ceilings.

From a cabinet set in a wall of bookshelves, he took a bottle of whiskey and a bottle of claret, setting them on the low table before the fireplace. Then he called down the hallway, "Rachel, bring some glasses."

Seating himself, he looked around at Papa, Kathleen and Edward. "Well . . ." he looked quite pleased with himself. "I'm delighted to see all of you again and have the chance to return your hospitality.

"My housekeeper," he said when Rachel appeared, carrying the glasses in her hands. She was an ancient crone, clad in a black gown with stains on the skirt. Mumbling to herself, she set the glasses on the table, and nodding at the doctor, departed.

Dr. Vickers poured the wine, adding a little to the glass of water he offered Edward. For himself, he poured straight whiskey.

"You're looking beautiful, Miss Kathleen," he said, his brown eyes warmly admiring as he lifted his glass in salute to her.

"Thank you," she murmured, sipping the claret. Charles

was a lovely gentleman, always giving the impression that he cared greatly about the person he was addressing.

"And our young man seems to be blooming," he added, studying Edward, who was trying to look polite, although Kathleen knew he was bored.

"I'd like to have you take a look at him," Papa said, refilling his own glass from the wine bottle. "It seems I made a wise decision in bringing him to Wyoming for his health."

"Obviously," the doctor agreed, and smiled at Edward. "Come along into my office, young man. I can look you over while we're waiting for supper."

The two of them returned just as Rachel laconically announced supper. "Can't find a thing wrong with him," the doctor said, as they settled around the dining table.

It was a small room, paneled with dark wood. Its high curtained window caught the last of the daylight, and above the table an electric chandelier glowed through etched glass shades. The table linen was less than immaculate, accounted for, Kathleen saw, by the way Rachel plopped the food on the table. Dinner consisted of tough, fried mutton and fried potatoes, with the only bright spot of the meal being a dish of fresh peas, which the doctor told them had been brought to him by a patient as partial payment on a bill.

Mr. Fraser joined them. He had changed into a dark jacket and shaved again. Kathleen thought he seemed more at ease here than he ever had at Cybille Creek Ranch.

Feeling sorry for the man, she attempted to draw him into the conversation. "Have you known Dr. Vickers long?"

He smiled at Dr. Vickers, who answered for him. "Michael and I met when I was in my last year at Harvard Medical School. He was an undergraduate."

"And Charles befriended me," Mr. Fraser interrupted. "He's good at that."

Everyone laughed, although she saw that Papa's eyes were cold, and Edward looked puzzled at the reason for their mirth.

"You'll be returning to England this fall, Lord Hadley?" Dr. Vickers asked as Rachel poured coffee all around.

"After the cattle are shipped," Papa replied, looking at

the coffee with distaste. "The directors of British and Far West will expect a report from me."

"And a fat profit," Michael Fraser said, with an edge to his voice.

"That's what we're all in the cattle business for, Mr. Fraser," Papa replied testily.

At once, Dr. Vickers changed the subject again. He was very good at it, Kathleen thought with a smile.

"Edward's health has improved so remarkably here. I hope a return to England won't set him back."

"It won't," Papa answered complacently. "Besides, I've had good news from England that makes it less important."

"What news, Papa?" Kathleen asked, wanting to take Edward's hand, feeling the boy's pain as he stared questioningly at his father.

"Deborah has delivered a fine healthy son," Papa said. Smiling around the table, he lifted his glass. "To Thomas Hadley, second son of the viscount, Lord Robert Hadley."

Kathleen's heart contracted as she watched Edward visibly withdraw from his father's rejection. Cruel beast! she wanted to scream at her father. He had practically told them all that it didn't matter now if Edward's health failed, for he had begotten another heir.

"Congratulations." Michael Fraser's voice held an ironic note as they all lifted their glasses in salute to the newborn son.

"Will you be in town long?" Dr. Vickers changed the subject again. Kathleen glanced at Edward, relieved to see he was finishing his fried potatoes as though there had been no exchange with his father.

"We'll stay tomorrow night," Papa replied. "Kathleen will want to shop and I have business."

"Will you go to the railroad yards to see the new Hereford bulls?" she asked, hoping he would say yes, that there would be a chance she might see Ranse tomorrow. Just to see his face . . .

"Lord, no," Papa replied testily. "It's O'Neil's job to look after the animals."

* * *

211

Breakfast in the hotel dining room had been hearty and delicious, and Kathleen assumed they would take dinner there.

"You may have dinner at the hotel," Papa told her when she went to his room after the day of shopping. "I intend to take Edward with me to the Cheyenne Club."

Over his shoulder, she saw the expression of dismay on Perkins's face as he brushed his master's broadcloth jacket. "The Cheyenne Club!" she cried. "He's only a boy. That's no place for him."

"High time he started becoming a man," Papa replied contemptuously. "He's been mollycoddled enough by you and by that nincompoop Fraser."

"Papa, please—"

"I'll hear no more from you." His voice was hard and cold. "Now, leave so I can dress."

Anger seethed through her. It was clear Papa meant to lead Edward down the same paths of dissipation he had trod himself. Furious, she hurried to Edward's room to tell him he mustn't go with Papa. But Edward's unflagging curiosity about everything in the world won out.

"Don't worry, Kathleen," he comforted, patting her shoulder. "I won't get into trouble, or get drunk, or anything. I want to see this famous place."

She was too angry and worried to eat after they departed in the surrey with Bill driving. There were still a few shops open. Throwing her plaid wool cape about her shoulders against the chill of oncoming evening, she left the hotel and walked down the main street, pausing to study the shop windows. Distracted by her indignation over her father's behavior, she wandered several blocks before she realized dusk had fallen and the shopkeepers were locking up.

Although Cheyenne boasted electric lights, the streetlights were few and far between. She hurried from one pool of light to the next as darkness settled over the city, uncertain which direction to take to the hotel.

Now, she saw she had wandered into a business section, although the businesses seemed to be mainly saloons. The board sidewalks grew more crowded with people moving about, mostly roughly dressed cowboys, some of them very drunk. From behind the swinging doors of the saloons came the sounds of raucous voices, the tinny banging of pianos, and in some the monotonous sounds of the games of chance. The odor of liquor permeated each doorway. The few women she passed were dressed in garish fashion, and they looked at her with strange hard eyes.

Fear clutched at her chest as Kathleen realized she had strayed into the roughest part of town. Looking anxiously about, she hoped to see someone sufficiently sober and decent to ask directions.

"Hey, blondie." Two drunken cowboys turned to stare at her as she passed them. Cold with apprehension, she pulled the cape about her and hurried away.

"Aw, honey, don't be in such a hurry," one of the cowboys called.

They had turned to follow her. Terrified, she began to run with no idea of direction. Her heart raced in fear as she heard them running behind her.

Suddenly, one of them grabbed her roughly by the arm. "C'mon, sweetie," he mumbled, his voice thick with whiskey. "We'll show you a right good time."

"Leave me alone!" she cried, looking about in terror. In running from them, she had foolishly left the protection of the brightly lighted street and was now trapped in a blind alley.

"You could learn to like me," the man muttered thickly. His arms clasped about her like a vise, his hideous, foulsmelling face close to hers.

"Let me go!" she screamed, beating at him with her fists, twisting her face away from his, knowing with horror that her strength was futile against him.

"C'mon, Joe . . . hurry up," the other man urged, his lustful face staring at her over Joe's shoulder.

In answer, the man holding her seized the neck of her dress and ripped the bodice to the waist. His rough hand shoved inside her corset cover and grabbed her bosom.

In stark terror, Kathleen screamed and screamed again, even as the man shoved her against the wall and down into the dirt and filth of the alley. Struggling beneath his weight, she kept on screaming as he cursed and ripped at her clothing. The other man was laughing hideously in the darkness.

Suddenly, the laughter stopped, and she was dimly aware of another presence. Her attacker was flung away from her, crying out in pain. The last sound she heard before she fainted was that of men struggling in the darkness of the alley.

CHAPTER 23

Everything Kathleen could see was red: the heavy velvet draperies of the bed where she lay, the red-flocked wallpaper, the glass shade of the lamp glowing on a table at the foot of the bed. A thick odor of incense hung in the air.

Horror shot through her as full awareness returned. Surely she was in a bordello. She had heard enough gossip about such places, read enough in the London tabloids Francine delighted in, to know the sort of place that would be decorated like this. Drenched with a cold sweat of fear, she closed her eyes tightly. Those same tabloids often carried stories of the white slavers, those vile creatures of the underworld who kidnapped young girls and sold them into the slavery of prostitution.

She must find a way out of here. Opening her eyes, she scanned the room. A woman bent over the bed, staring down at her with cold blue eyes. Her hair was a dead dyed black, her mouth and cheeks scarlet with carmine, and her jewels flashed in the light. She wore a wrapper of heavy red silk, elaborately trimmed with black lace.

"She's come to," the woman said to someone behind her, as though she would not have cared one way or the other.

All the dreadful tabloid tales ran wildly through Kathleen's mind as she looked into those cold eyes. The other person approached the bed, and relief washed over her as Ranse O'Neil's black eyes looked down into hers.

"Better now?" he asked gently, taking her hand in his. As he leaned over the bed, she could smell the faint scent of whiskey on his breath. To her dismay, she burst into tears.

Ranse sat down on the bed beside her. Fishing a handkerchief from his pants pocket, he carefully wiped the tears. "You'll be fine," he said. "Thank God I was there and heard you. Those two bastards are in jail."

All the horror of the dark alley returned, like a hideous nightmare. In spite of her efforts at control, the tears continued. Ranse reached out one big hand to smooth back her disordered hair, and his face turned hard and angry. Following his glance she saw her torn gown, the great livid bruises glowing darkly against her white bosom. Carefully, he drew the blanket up to cover her.

"Where am I?" she whispered, swallowing a sob, wanting him to take her in his arms . . . wishing the woman would go away.

"Maud's place," he replied. "You were out cold, so I brought you up here, and Maud looked after you."

Her eyes swept around the garish room. "Is this place a . . .?" She couldn't say the word.

Ranse's black eyes crinkled in amusement. "Yes, it is." His strong fingers lay warm against her bruised face. "How the hell did you get into this part of town?"

"I was so angry at Papa," she began, taking his hand into hers tightly. "He took Edward to the Cheyenne Club. I didn't think he should . . ."

"Stupid bastard!" Ranse muttered.

"There were some shops open, and I was looking . . . but I was so upset, I didn't notice where I was going."

"A damn fool thing to do." His face was grim. "Do you realize you might be dead in that alley if I hadn't come along and heard you screaming?"

Maud gave a short bark of laughter. "Ranse is one of the few men I know would even pay attention to your screaming. It's every man for himself in this town, honey."

Kathleen was shocked to see her calmly light a small cigarillo. *Even if she were not a bad woman, I wouldn't like her,* Kathleen thought. *And she resents me.*

Ranse smoothed her hair again, giving her a warm smile. "Hope you've learned your lesson. Don't wander around Cheyenne alone at night."

"But why did you bring me here?" she asked, puzzled. "This awful place . . ."

His hand dropped hers. She felt his withdrawal, as his

voice came out flat and cool. "Maud's a friend of mine, and it was close by."

"But how could you—" she began.

"For God's sake!" Ranse stood up, a flush of anger across his dark face. "You're behaving like your idiotic father. Would you rather be in that filthy alley?"

"It's a house of ill fame," she protested, wanting him to pick her up and carry her away from this awful place. From across the room, she heard Maud's sardonic chuckle.

"And you are a stupid English girl who doesn't have sense enough to be grateful she's safe . . . in whatever kind of house." With an icy look, Ranse turned and stalked from the room.

Maud laughed, a hard-edged laugh, staring at the door Ranse had banged shut behind him, calmly smoking her cigarillo.

How dared he desert her in a bordello . . . with this awful woman? Kathleen sat up and flung the blanket off. It was obvious that all the good qualities she had attributed to him had been only in her mind. He was a man like her father, who consorted with low women, and she almost cried out at the ugly thought. He'd saved her honor and probably her life. But she felt bereft now, at the loss of the man she had thought he was.

"Feelin' better, honey?" Maud asked, watching her with detached curiosity.

"I'd like to go back to the Plains Hotel," she replied, holding her torn gown together.

The woman gave her a wicked grin. "If you hadn't put Ranse in such a temper, I reckon he'd have taken you." An odd shadowed look came into her pale blue eyes. "Never saw him get so riled up over so little."

Looking helplessly about, Kathleen realized that, without Ranse, she was at the mercy of this woman. She would never dare venture out into the street alone, and she could not anyway, with her gown in such disreputable condition. "If I could have my cape," she said, sitting dizzily on the edge of the bed, only now aware that someone had taken off her shoes.

"Don't get in such a fluster," Maud said with an amused look. "You're not likely to lose your honor here."

Kathleen's cheeks grew hot as she realized Maud was making fun of her. Forcing herself to speak calmly, she said, "I'd just like to get back to the hotel and change my clothes."

Maud shrugged and ground out her cigarillo in a cut-glass tray. "Ranse didn't bring your cape," she said. "By now, some streetwalker will have made off with it." Pulling the bell cord near the bed, she continued, "I'll have the maid fix a bath for you while I try to find some clothes." Looking Kathleen over as she rose unsteadily to her feet, Maud went on, "It's a cinch you can't wear mine."

Kathleen stared dully at the full-bosomed amazon of a woman, and her ironic smile.

When the uniformed maid arrived, Maud gave instructions to prepare a bath, then asked, "Is Clarice busy?" The maid nodded, and Maud said, "Well, tell her to see me when she's through." Turning, she looked Kathleen over once more. "Clarice is about your size."

Kathleen tried not to think about what Clarice was busy at, as she slipped into the gilt-trimmed porcelain tub. The warm water went a long way toward restoring her spirits, and it eased her aching body, which she saw was covered by bruises. She washed her hair too, for it stank of the filthy alley. As she stepped from the tub and wrapped herself in an enormous fluffy towel, the maid returned with the borrowed gown. It was a rather flashy style, but Kathleen grimly assured herself she was not in a position to be choosy. She dressed quickly, braiding her wet hair and pinning it around her head.

When she came out of the bathroom, Maud was sitting in a red velvet chair beside the fireplace smoking a cigarillo, a glass of liquor on the table at her elbow.

"Well," she said, looking Kathleen over. "That should get you back to the hotel all right. I've sent for my driver to take you there. You may as well sit down until he comes." She gestured toward the chair opposite her.

Sitting down stiffly, Kathleen was all too aware of her bruises. Draining her glass, Maud reached for the cut-glass decanter to refill it. "A little brandy?" she asked, and shrugged when Kathleen shook her head.

"Ranse told me his lordship's kids had come out for the

summer." The inflection of her voice when she said "his lordship" was familiar. Somehow, Kathleen knew, the words did not set well on Wyoming tongues.

Maud's pale eyes roved over her, speculatively. "He didn't mention you were a looker." Staring at the glowing end of her cigarillo, she said, almost to herself, "I wonder if he noticed."

Kathleen felt a jolt of surprise as the woman's face took on a yearning look. She seemed almost to have forgotten there was anyone else in the room. A feeling of sympathy crept into Kathleen's mind as she watched Maud. However rich she might be as the owner of this vile place, she was alone and lonely. It came to her that the yearning was directed at Ranse O'Neil.

"Have you known Ranse long?" She blurted out the words without thinking.

Maud's face changed at once. Her eyes were sharp, and her mouth lifted in a deprecating smile. "We've been friends for a long time." The inflection of the word "friends" made her meaning all too clear. They had been lovers . . . and Kathleen felt a pain knot in her stomach. The sickness grew inside until she feared she would faint again. The man she had given herself to, with all her heart and soul, was a man like her father, who lay with whores, then lied to the woman who loved him.

Through a haze of pain, she heard the driver arrive. As he took her elbow to guide her down the back stairs, Maud placed a fur cape about her shoulders, saying the night was chilly. Her driver would bring it back.

As from a distance, Kathleen heard herself saying coolly, "Thank you for all you've done. I'll see you're well paid."

Maud's blue eyes hardened. She looked insulted, and her voice was cold. "I don't expect to be paid for helping someone."

Somehow, the woman had managed to make Kathleen feel more gauche than she had ever felt among all the nobility in London. "Thank you," she managed to say again.

"Good night," Maud snapped.

As the elegant carriage sped through the dark streets of Cheyenne toward the Plains Hotel, Kathleen thought of the strange, almost envious look Maud had given her in parting. She was in love with Ranse O'Neil, and jealous of the attention he had shown Kathleen.

Alone in her hotel room, she quickly shed Clarice's dress. Dear God, she thought, as she lay in the darkness, I am as jealous as Maud, sick with anger that he loved another woman when I thought his love was mine alone. But she knew it was not just another woman, it was the kind of woman . . . the kind of woman her father and his dissolute friends reveled with. It was unforgivable, and she wept for the loss of a love that had scarcely bloomed.

"I didn't like it much," Edward told her the next morning as they sat at breakfast in the dining room of the Plains Hotel. He had been sent back from the Cheyenne Club last night with Bill, and Papa had still not appeared at the hotel.

Kathleen listened to Edward's description of his night at the Cheyenne Club, a deep anger at her father burning inside. She had not spoken of her ordeal, although her aching body reminded her constantly. Clarice's dress had been packed off by messenger. There was nothing left to remind her, except the deep and painful knowledge that the man she had loved was unworthy.

"There were lots of women there, but . . ." he frowned in puzzlement, "not like you. They wore flouncy dresses that showed their bosoms." Edward paused, flushing.

"And the men?" she prompted.

"They just gambled and got drunk," he replied, obviously repelled by what he had observed. "Papa . . ." Words seemed to fail him.

"What?"

In a low, shamed voice, Edward went on. "He got staggering drunk and went upstairs with one of the women. When he didn't come down again, Bill said I should go with him."

Fury at her father nearly blinded her. He could wallow in his own depravity, but she'd be damned if she'd let him drag Edward down to his level.

"Good morning." Ranse O'Neil stood beside the table, holding his gray stetson, his dark eyes intent on her face.

All the anger she had felt toward her father was suddenly

220

directed at Ranse. Surely, he had been in the red-light district on his way to visit Maud . . . and only a few days after he had seduced a virgin in a sunlit meadow. Irrationally, she wanted to scream at him, to hit him with her fists, to somehow repay him for the hurt that tore through her.

"Coffee," he said to the waitress's questioning look, and sat down at the table.

"Did the new bulls get here?" Edward inquired eagerly, unknowingly covering Kathleen's icy silence.

"Yeah," Ranse replied, with a sidelong questioning look at Kathleen. "I wanted to tell His Lordship we're leaving with the critters this morning, but it'll take us about two days to get back to the ranch. Wouldn't want the old boys to damage themselves."

"Could I go with you?" Edward asked, and his face fell when Ranse shook his head.

"You all right?" Ranse asked in a low voice, his eyes intent on Kathleen's face.

"Yes, thank you," she replied coldly, not meeting his eyes.

Ranse took a coin from his pocket and handed it to Edward. "Go in the lobby and get me a newspaper, will you, Eddie?"

Kathleen watched her brother, the future Lord Hadley, obeying the orders of Ranse O'Neil. A sick knot of painful disillusion grew inside her heart.

Ranse attempted to take her hand in his, and she jerked it away. She felt him studying her, and she thought she could not bear his nearness another moment.

"I wanted to make sure you weren't badly hurt," he said.

"Surely, Maud told you when you went back to finish your business with her." She put a vicious emphasis on the word business. At her words, Ranse jerked upright in his chair and stared at her.

"Well, god damn it," he said wonderingly. "You're still bitching because I took you where you'd be safe."

"A whorehouse," she said bitterly.

Ranse stood up, flinging some coins down on the table. "I thought you might have come to your senses this morning." His voice fell, low and filled with bitterness. "So that's what you English call love. Well, keep it, sister. I can do better."

Watching the tall figure cross the restaurant, she wanted

him with such intensity she felt sick and dizzy. Every fiber of her being longed to call after him, to bring him back, to recapture the brief incandescent joy they had shared.

He took the newspaper from Edward, clapped the boy on the shoulder and was gone through the swinging doors.

Tears clogged her throat, and she thought for a moment she could not bear the pain that poured through her. When Edward sat down across from her, his face questioning, she rose and fled to her room.

CHAPTER 24

Preparations for the fall cattle roundup got under way immediately after Ranse returned from Cheyenne. All through those last days of August, wagonloads of supplies came out from town. Newly hired cowhands appeared on the scene, filling the bunkhouse to capacity.

Fascinated, Edward spent every waking moment following Ranse at his work. Showing off his newly acquired knowledge, he reported to Kathleen what he had learned during the day. "They're stocking the chuck wagons," he told her, "and Ranse hired a new cook for the roundup." He sighed. "I wish I could go with them. I'd ride circle all day, bringing the cattle in to the holding herd, and then sleep out in my bedroll every night."

Kathleen looked at him, amazed at the amount of information his young mind had stored away. If Edward needed a hero at this stage in his life, she supposed Ranse O'Neil would do. But for herself, she could not bear to speak to him again. Since their return from Cheyenne, she had kept close to the house, reading, sewing, pacing her room, forgoing her daily ride simply to avoid seeing Ranse.

"It sounds like a rough life," she said, finally aware that Edward was awaiting an answer.

He laughed. "Someday, I intend to try it."

Soon, Kathleen thought, as they walked downstairs to the dining room together . . . soon, the chuck wagons would roll out to the roundup camps. Ranse would be gone, and then perhaps her wounded heart would begin to heal. She meant to shut him out of her life, certain that his moral values were as loathsome as those of her father.

223

Yet, in spite of her resolution, she often found herself at the French doors, staring out across the ranch yard, her longing eyes searching for the tall figure of Ranse O'Neil.

"Ranse hired a new bronc peeler today," Edward announced at the supper table.

Papa was nearly always silent at table these days, his face overlaid with an alcoholic glaze. Kathleen tried to ignore him and carry on a normal conversation with Edward. Her governess, and the minister, had taught her she must honor and respect her father. But she felt nothing toward him now except bitterness. He was a dishonorable man. She had never told him of her misadventure in Cheyenne. Only she and Ranse knew of it . . . and Maud . . . the name sent a sick pain stabbing through her.

Seeing Edward's bright expectant face turned toward her, she asked, "What's a bronc peeler?" The American slang he picked up so easily brought a smile to her lips.

"A horsebreaker," Edward replied. "We always need extra horses for the roundup because the men riding circle have to change horses twice a day. It's hard work," he added seriously.

Next day, he insisted Kathleen go to the corral with him to watch the bronc peeler at work. She didn't like the man, with his hard eyes and his seamed, weather-beaten face. Nor did she like his way with the horses, whipping them across the head, and spurring the recalcitrant ones until there was blood on their flanks.

"There are better ways to train horses," she said grimly.

"But there isn't time," Edward assured her. "The roundup crew is moving out tomorrow, and they need the horses."

"Eddie's right," Ranse said, leaning his arms on the top rail of the corral, his eyes on the horse plunging wildly about the corral. "There's not enough time."

Kathleen dared not look at him, although the familiar scent of his tobacco, the faint clean odor of his maleness filled her with such longing she was sure it must be visible. All these past days she had avoided him, and now she found that nothing had changed the way his presence affected her. Sternly, she reminded herself of the anger and resentment of their last meeting, of the humiliation she had felt in that house of ill repute where he had taken her.

"There's never enough time," Ranse added in a low voice.

Her heart pounded painfully against her ribs, and her whole being ached with regret. Ranse continued to look straight ahead, his face dark in the shadow of the wide-brimmed hat.

The horse in the corral was under control now, moving at the rider's direction, its mouth rimmed with foam. Ranse glanced back at his own horse, standing behind him. "Hey, Eddie," he said as he grinned down at Edward. "How about unsaddling Hawk for me?" When Edward eagerly reached for the bay's reins, Ranse added, "Walk him around a little to cool him off. We've had a hard morning."

Even with all the activity going on about them—riders moving back and forth, the bronc peeler throwing a saddle on a new horse, the blacksmith's hammer ringing as a horse was shod—they might have been alone. Slowly, he turned to face her. The black eyes riveted her, held her so that she could not look away.

"There are some things need to be said between us," he said.

"It's all been said," she answered, trying desperately to control the insane desire to throw herself into his arms.

"Once, you said you loved me, Kathleen." His voice was so low she could barely catch the words in the noisy ranch yard.

Pain rose from deep inside, bringing again the knowledge that this man was less than she had thought when she said those words to him. "That was before . . ." She managed to choke out the words.

"Before I saved you from rape?" he asked evenly. The black eyes were guarded now.

Kathleen cleared her throat painfully. "I never properly thanked you for that."

"No, you didn't," he replied, in the same expressionless tone. "But I'd have done as much for any woman."

If he had meant the words to hurt, he had succeeded. Kathleen gripped the corral rail tightly, dizzy with anguish.

Out of her pain came the bitter words, "I couldn't love a man like my father . . . a man who consorts with low women . . ."

His face blazed with anger. "Maud's been my friend through a lot of lonely years. If you can't forgive the past . . ."

"I can't!" The words burst painfully from her throat. "I can't forgive an ugliness I've lived with all my life!"

"I'm not your father." For a brief moment, his eyes begged for understanding, but when she hardened her face against him, the curtain came down once more.

There was a long aching silence. At last Ranse spoke, in a low even voice. "I'll be gone with the roundup for about a month, then I'll be taking the cattle train to Chicago for the sale there." He was silent again, seeming to grope for words. "I wanted to make sure you're . . . you're all right."

"I'm not pregnant." She spit the words at him. "You're off scot-free."

"Free?" The black eyes stared into hers as though plumbing the depths of her soul. His mouth twisted in a pained, ironic way that made her want to cry. "I'll never be free again," he said. Turning on his heel, he walked away, across the ranch yard to where Edward was rubbing down Hawk.

Stunned, Kathleen stared after him, overwhelmed by a sense of irreplaceable loss.

The ranch seemed oddly deserted in the days that followed. The bronc peeler still worked in the breaking corral, often with Edward watching in fascination. Bradley, the blacksmith, was still at his forge, shoeing the newly broken horses. Life went on . . . and yet, to Kathleen, it was filled with emptiness.

Summer faded as September came on. Nights were cooler, and the mornings brought a nip to the air. In the wide cobalt sky, skeins of geese honked their way southward. The willows along Cybille Creek were tinged with gold.

The pain of her parting with Ranse lay within Kathleen like a hidden wound, festering and deepening with every passing day. She and Edward had resumed their daily rides, even though every trail evoked a memory of Ranse that added to her lonely misery.

Papa was invited to a final hunting party at the Frewens, before their departure for England. He left at once, with Bill driving the surrey and an exhausted-looking Perkins struggling with the baggage.

Kathleen soon realized that her melancholy was wearisome to Edward. Even their rides together were no longer fun. Before long, he was spending most of his time at the corral, watching the horse-breaking, even learning a bit of blacksmithing from Bradley.

Annoyed by his desertion, she rode off by herself one day. Inevitably, she arrived at the meadow where she and Ranse had made love that summer day that now seemed eons ago. The willows had turned gold and russet, the green of the cottonwood leaves was fading. In the gold-tipped grass, only the starry blue of wild asters bloomed.

Dismounting, Kathleen sat there in the meadow and gave herself over to weeping and self-pity. In all the drab and lonely years of her life, she had found true happiness only here in this place, and with only one man. Even now, she knew there would never be anyone else for her.

Above the tops of the rustling cottonwoods, she caught a glimpse of the beige cliffs of the Chugwater. Ranse's story of the Indian maiden who died for love flooded through her mind. On that day, she had at once related the story to her mother. Was she doomed to repeat that unhappy fate? Even though she knew she would never fling herself from a cliff for love, would not returning to England and leaving her love behind forever be a kind of death?

Yesterday is gone. Startled, she looked around the glade, almost certain someone had whispered those words to her. Tears rose in her eyes, and she clasped her hands together in anguish as she remembered who had said those words to her. "Ranse," she whispered into the autumn wind, "I loved you so . . . I love you still."

Yesterday is gone. The words echoed in her mind. Ranse O'Neil was a man of honor; she had known that from the beginning. All the lonely years, he'd said of Maud. All that was yesterday, she told herself now. Could she, in her jealousy . . . and for the first time she recognized the truth of her emotions . . . could she deny whatever comfort Maud had given him? It was not like her father, lying with the village whores while his wife waited at home. Ranse had suffered a terrible loss in his young wife and son so long ago. If he had found some surcease from sorrow with Maud, how could she blame him?

Yesterday is gone. Kathleen jumped to her feet, brushing away the tears. Every cell of her being longed for him ... longed to touch him and hold him and tell him of her love. When he returned, she would go to him, shamelessly seeking his love and forgiveness. In all their tomorrows, they would never be apart again.

On the western horizon, the sun was a round red ball trailing tattered shreds of gray cloud. Already, nighthawks swooped through the chilly air. Strange, there was such a flurry of activity at the corral, Kathleen thought, this late in the day. Touching her horse's flank with the whip, she rode quickly from the creek bank and across the ranch yard.

Skirts flying, Mrs. Sanders ran toward her. "Thank God, you're back, Miss. Oh ... thank God!"

The ludicrous sight of Bradley and Sanders carrying the tack shed door into the corral struck Kathleen with a chill of fear. Sliding down from the horse, she flipped the reins around the hitching rack. "What is it, Mrs. Sanders? What's happened?"

Wringing her hands distractedly, the woman moaned, "It's the boy, Miss ... it's little Edward ... he's hurt."

Half-realized fear bloomed into terror. Without realizing what she was doing, Kathleen grabbed Mrs. Sanders's shoulders and shook her roughly. "Where is he—tell me?"

Her hair falling down from Kathleen's rough treatment, Mrs. Sanders mutely pointed toward the corral.

Heart pounding wildly with panic, Kathleen ran to the corral. A cry was wrung from her throat when she saw Edward's small figure crumpled in the dust of the corral. Pushing through the gate, she ran to drop on her knees beside him.

He lay like a broken doll, his bright hair stained with dust, a trickle of blood on his chin. Instinctively, she reached out to gather him into her arms. Bradley grabbed her shoulders to restrain her.

"Don't move him, Miss," he warned. "He's got a broken

leg and God knows what else. Me and Sanders'll put him on the door and carry him to the house." He stood up, taking her with him, his burly arm about her shoulders. Tears poured from her eyes as she looked down at the unconscious boy, his leg tucked under him at an odd angle. "We sent a rider for the doctor."

"Edward," she sobbed. "Oh, Edward." He lay so still, and fear ran along her veins in an icy flood.

Patting her back, Bradley bent to help Sanders gently ease the small body onto the door. The bronc peeler came into the corral, staring at the proceedings with an abashed look on his seamed face.

Struggling to control her weeping, Kathleen asked, "What happened?"

Both men glanced accusingly at the bronc peeler, who refused to meet their eyes. Kathleen stared at him in horror. "You let him ride an unbroken horse!" she cried.

"The kid begged me," was his defensive reply. "Said he'd done it before and could handle it, but one buck and he was gone."

"You bloody fool!" She was shouting hysterically. "You've killed him!"

"He ain't dead, Miss," Bradley tried to soothe her. "Jest hurt bad."

"Warn't my fault," the bronc peeler growled. "Damn English haw-haws anyhow."

In a fury, she turned on him, striking out at him until Bradley restrained her. "Get off this place," she screamed, aware that she was totally out of control. "If I see your face around here again, I'll kill you . . . you murderer."

"The kid ain't dead . . ." the man began, but Bradley jerked his head sharply toward the bunkhouse. The man fell silent, turned and walked away.

One of the ranch hands had brought a lantern to light their way through the dusk. Still weeping, Kathleen followed Bradley and Sanders as they carried their small sad burden into the house. Mrs. Sanders walked beside her, a comforting arm about her shoulders.

"He'll be all right, Miss. Why, Bradley's near as good as the doctor hisself. Many a time, he's fixed up a cowhand's broke leg or arm. Livin' out here like we do, so far from town, we have to learn such things." Mrs. Sanders's voice droned on, low and soothing. Kathleen's wild sobbing eased. When the door was placed across two chairs in the sitting room, she could look at Edward and be angry with herself for losing control.

As the boy began to regain consciousness, she knelt beside him, wiping his pale face with the wet cloth Mrs. Sanders had brought.

"Kathleen?" he whispered shakily, lifting his hand to touch her face.

"Oh, Edward," she cried. "I shouldn't have gone riding without you. I shouldn't have left you alone."

"Not your fault . . ." His voice trailed off, and she saw that he was drifting back into unconsciousness.

"Edward!" she cried, gripped by the terrible fear that he might never awaken again.

"It hurts," he gasped, as his eyes glazed over.

Kathleen burst into tears.

"Now, Miss," said Mrs. Sanders in a tone that told Kathleen she was losing sympathy with these wild paroxysms of grief. "It's best he's out of it, or he'd be in awful pain."

At that moment, Bradley returned with two boards and began putting a splint on Edward's broken leg. The boy cried out several times during the operation, but he did not awaken. Spent with grief and fear, Kathleen watched in helpless silence.

When he had finished, Mrs. Sanders covered the boy with a blanket. Sandy had built up the fire and lit the lamps.

"We'll have to leave him right there," Bradley told Kathleen. "If I know Dr. Vic, he'll be right here as fast as he can. We'll just watch the boy through the night."

"Yes," Kathleen replied in a flat voice, staring at Edward's still white face. "I'll watch him." Looking up into the three concerned faces surrounding her, she asked, "What if he awakens?"

"I have some laudanum," Mrs. Sanders answered. "Like I said, we have to be prepared for everything out here."

Sandy placed a comfortable chair near Edward's head for Kathleen. His wife offered to bring supper, but Kathleen shook her head, her eyes on Edward. The three of them spelled each other, watching through the night, keeping the fire going, talking in low voices. Kathleen refused to leave the boy's side. It was her fault, leaving him while she was off weeping for a lost love. Edward was her brother . . . her birthday twin . . . and the dearest friend of her life. Nothing must happen to him. And silent tears flowed down her flushed cheeks.

Noise in the foyer awakened her from her exhausted sleep. Her neck ached from sleeping in the chair, and she groaned softly as she turned to see Dr. Vicker's welcome figure coming into the room.

His brown eyes were warm as he returned her grateful embrace. "Who's the patient?" he asked with a smile, inclining his leonine head. "You look exhausted, my dear."

"No matter," she protested quickly. "It's Edward . . . we gave him some laudanum for pain during the night."

"He seems to be stirring now." Dr. Vickers bent over the boy, lifting his eyelids, his big hands checking the neck, the great bruise on his forehead, then moving carefully along his limbs searching for broken bones.

Straightening up, he turned to meet Kathleen's apprehensive eyes. "Probably a concussion from the bump on the head. He'll be in and out of consciousness for a few days. Broken leg . . . Bradley did a good job, but I'll put on a cast."

Relief flooded through Kathleen. Edward would be all right now that Charles Vickers was in charge.

At once, there was a bustle of bringing a bed downstairs for Edward . . . the messy business of applying a cast while Kathleen gratefully held the boy in her arms. It was only when Edward was settled and sleeping once more, when Mrs. Sanders had gone to prepare breakfast, and Dr. Vickers had ordered her to bed that Kathleen thought of her father.

"He's at the Frewens," she told Dr. Vickers, after Sandy had gone to send a rider with the news.

"Oh yes . . ." He gave her an ironic smile. "Those wildly extravagant English aristocrats. Their kind has made the name 'British' a bad word in Wyoming. They make one huge party out of their roundup, or a helluva mess as their foreman would say. Ranse wouldn't put up with it."

Ranse, she thought, as she moved wearily upstairs to her room. That thoughtless, criminally stupid horsebreaker might have behaved differently if Ranse had been here. But in this crisis, she had learned something about her own strength. And she had come to an understanding of forgiveness, without which love cannot live. Let go of yesterday, she told herself once more, as she fell across her bed and surrendered to exhaustion. Yet, she wanted Ranse here, needing his strength to lean on.

·❖I CHAPTER 25 I❖·

Papa returned from the Powder River ranch on the Frewens' fastest horse, leaving Perkins and Bill to bring the surrey and the baggage.

"I'll have O'Neil's hide for this," he growled, after he had seen the still-groggy Edward and heard the whole story.

"O'Neil had nothing to do with it," Kathleen protested, exchanging incredulous glances with Dr. Vickers. "It was that bronc peeler, Robinson, who let Edward get on an unbroken horse. And Sandy says he's already left the ranch."

"Be damned," Papa's voice rose, and he glared at her. "O'Neil hired the bloody bastard, didn't he?" Turning away, he filled a glass with port from the decanter, and downed it.

Edward moaned and thrashed about. Dr. Vickers hurried to his side. Kathleen stood staring at her father's back, horrified by his distorted thinking. O'Neil was less to blame for Edward's accident than a father who had never paid any attention to his son. It seemed to her that Papa was less concerned with Edward than with the fact that his hunt had been cut short. Turning away, she watched Dr. Vickers speaking to Edward in soothing tones. She knew what her father was. Why did his arrogance and selfishness never fail to surprise her? Why couldn't he have been a man like Charles Vickers, a man who cared about everyone?

Papa slumped into an armchair beside the fireplace, holding a fresh glass of port. Edward had quieted and fallen back to sleep. Dr. Vickers took the chair opposite Papa. Filling a glass with port, Kathleen offered it to him. He smiled his thanks, took a sip and fixed his gaze on Lord Hadley.

"Kathleen says you'd planned to return to England next month, early in November," he said.

"Yes." Papa stared morosely into the fire. "As soon as the cattle sale is completed. Passage has already been booked . . . and now this." He indicated Edward with a wave of his hand.

All the old resentments roiled up inside Kathleen. Try as she might, she could not love this man who had fathered her, for there was no love in him. Edward's brush with death was merely an inconvenience to him. She walked across the room and looked down at the sleeping boy, filled with pain for his hurts.

"Quite impossible," Dr. Vickers was saying in firm tones. "Edward can't be moved for several weeks. A trip of that length, especially an ocean voyage, could be disastrous."

Papa grimaced. "I shall miss the start of the hunting season."

All the suppressed anger of the years spilled over. Kathleen turned on him with blazing eyes. "You'll have other hunting seasons," she cried bitterly. "You won't have another Edward."

"Really, my dear." Papa looked at her with surprised disapproval.

Dr. Vickers frowned. "Whatever the inconvenience to you, Lord Hadley," he said with an undertone of lightly veiled sarcasm, "I'd suggest you put off your return to England until after the first of the year."

Papa's reply was to rise and refill his glass of port. Ashamed for him, Kathleen avoided Dr. Vickers's eyes, sighing with relief when Tessie came to announce that supper was served.

The news that Lord Hadley and family would be staying on after roundup was received with grim resignation by the staff. Their presence would require more wood for heating, more supplies from town, more months of catering to the needs of people totally unfitted for this country.

"I'm not sorry to be staying," Kathleen told Charles Vickers as the two of them drank coffee at the breakfast table next morning. A fire crackled in the small breakfast room fireplace, cutting the chill of the autumn day. Outside, the sun shone from a cloudless sky, the air was like crystal.

Perkins had returned from Powder River with the message that Papa was bid to Moreton Frewen's farewell party at the Cheyenne Club. He had finished breakfast quickly and gone to supervise Perkins repacking for the trip into Cheyenne.

"So you've learned to love our wild country?" Charles asked with a knowing smile.

Had he guessed that her real reason for loving Wyoming was embodied in one man? The thought of Ranse drew her restlessly from her chair. She pushed aside the lace curtains to stare out into the ranch yard.

Near the blacksmith's shop, Ranse O'Neil bent to examine a horse's hoof. Kathleen's heart seemed to shatter inside her chest. She hadn't known he was back. He had taken off his hat, and the wind ruffled his black hair in a way that made her hand ache to smooth it.

An autumn wind blew wisps of dust across the ranch yard as she stood still, eyes devouring his beloved figure. Would he forgive her . . . could he love her again? Or would the rest of her life be filled with this empty ache of loss?

Suddenly, she was aware that Charles stood beside her, his eyes following hers. Quickly, she let the curtains fall back into place.

Charles ran a hand through his thick graying hair, his eyes regarding her kindly. "His life is very different from that of an English lord, Kathleen."

"I've always hated the life of an English lady," she answered in a strangled voice. With trembling hands, she refilled her coffee cup, spilling the dark liquid on the tablecloth. She stared at the spreading spot, sick with shame that Charles Vickers had guessed her secret.

"Does he know you care for him?" His voice was soft and caring, not condemning.

Once he knew it, she thought, her mind flooded with the memory of a sunlit meadow and love beyond all her dreams. But she had thrown it all away with her stupidity and jealousy. Unless Ranse could forgive her . . . but he was a hard man in a hard world. Perhaps he could not love so foolish a woman. Eyes blinded with tears, she turned again to the window, wondering whether she had the courage to ask forgiveness.

"You must keep up with your lessons if you're to enter Harrow next year," Kathleen told Edward that evening, as she sorted through the schoolbooks Mr. Fraser had left.

Edward groaned piteously. Charles Vickers laughed. Leaning one elbow on the mantel of the sitting-room fireplace, he regarded the boy with tolerant amusement.

"Your sister may prove a harder taskmaster than Mr. Fraser," he said. "But I hope she'll wait to begin lessons until you're a bit less groggy."

The clink of the decanter refilling Papa's wineglass distracted them. Kathleen sighed. Charles pretended not to notice, bending to add a log to the fire.

Stacking the books on a table beside the fireplace, Kathleen heard Tessie answering the front door.

"Ranse!" Edward cried joyfully.

Such a turmoil churned inside Kathleen, she feared for a moment she might be ill. It required all her strength of will to turn and face the tall man standing in the archway leading to the foyer. He wore a black broadcloth suit, carefully brushed, his dark hair neatly combed. There was about him such an air of grace and warmth she was drawn to him beyond all reason. Clenching her fists tightly, she was able to steady her voice enough to say, "Good evening, Ranse."

The black eyes flicked over her, coming to rest on Edward, who was waving frantically from his improvised sickbed. Grinning, Ranse moved toward the boy, nodding at Charles and Papa. Papa muttered a greeting through his alcoholic haze.

"I'm glad you could come to supper," Edward said, grimacing with pain as he shook hands with Ranse.

"Supper?" Papa growled. Ranse flushed at the obvious intonation.

"You're welcome to stay," Kathleen hastened to add, giving her father an icy look. "Edward didn't inform us he'd invited you, but you are welcome."

"Thanks, no," he replied coldly, without looking at her.

"I came to see my buddy here." Sitting down beside the bed, he began questioning Edward about the accident.

Watching the dark head bent toward the boy, listening to the gentle tolerance in his deep voice, Kathleen yearned toward him. This man was her love . . . now and always. Somehow, some way, she must win him back. She was aware of Charles's eyes on her, but she no longer cared if all the world knew she loved Ranse O'Neil.

"I thought you had better sense," Ranse was saying, only half-teasing Edward.

Shamefaced, Edward looked up at him. "I heard the cowboys making fun of the English 'haw-haws,' and I wanted to prove I was as good as any of them. It looked easy when Robinson did it."

"Robinson's been at it a few years." Ranse smiled and clasped the boy's shoulder. "You don't have to prove anything, Eddie. If you're a good man, it shows, and you don't have to ride a bucking bronc to prove it."

Tears stung Kathleen's eyes, and she looked away. Charles was nodding his approval. Papa was stirring himself to pour another glass of port.

"O'Neil!" Papa's voice was loud, that ugly, commanding voice she had often heard him use with servants.

Ranse turned toward Papa, his dark eyes flashing.

"If you've been tending to business," Papa said harshly, slurring his words, "I want a report."

Slowly, Ranse rose to his feet, facing Papa. "We're ready to start the drive to the railhead," Ranse's voice was cool and even. "I'll be going to Chicago with the cattle to try to get the best price possible."

"Bloody well better get a good price," Papa growled, glaring at Ranse. "The syndicate expects a better dividend this year."

"They're likely to be disappointed," Ranse told him evenly. "It's been a long, hot summer with poor grass. The cattle haven't fattened. Every company on the range is making heavy shipments, and that will make prices even lower."

"Excuses!" Papa broke in. "Excuses for your bloody poor management."

"You can replace me any time you want." Ranse's eyes were black ice.

Papa drained his glass and rose from the chair, weaving a little. "Your fault . . ." he slurred the words. "Your bloody fault the boy was hurt. You hired the fool who caused it. Now, I'll miss the hunting season . . ."

"You son of a bitch!" Ranse's voice was like the crack of a whip. "You drunken son of a bitch! Find yourself another foreman." He stalked across the room, slamming the front door behind him.

"Ranse!" Edward called after him desperately.

Kathleen and Charles stood in stunned silence. With all her being, she longed to run after him, hold him and tell him of her love. But all the years of rejection and repressed emotions held her immobile.

Papa slumped into his chair, his chin resting on his chest, breathing heavily.

Gray and gloomy skies matched Kathleen's mood as she dressed next morning. Supper last night had been tense, uncomfortable, and brief, with Charles attempting to make light conversation. Papa had retired early, mumbling that he would be driving into Cheyenne tomorrow for the Frewen party. Charles had made Edward comfortable for the night, then with a commiserating look at Kathleen withdrew to the guest room.

Descending the stairs, she could hear Tessie joking with Edward as she helped him with breakfast. Papa and Perkins had departed before dawn, driving ahead of Charles's carriage. How like Papa, she thought now, to drive away in search of his own pleasures, leaving chaos behind him. She knew he would not apologize to Ranse, for he had never apologized to anyone in his entire life. Surely, he must know, as she did, that without Ranse O'Neil the British and Far West Cattle Company would be in ruins.

Tossing through the sleepless night, she had decided that there was no one to face Ranse O'Neil except herself. Her mouth twisted in an ironic smile as she thought of the Kathleen Hadley she had once been . . . doing everyone's bidding, trying desperately and futilely to please. Now, she was about to circumvent her father's orders and beg the man he had fired to stay.

There was no answer when she knocked at the door of the foreman's cabin. A cold wind tugged at her shawl as she knocked again and waited. He'd gone, she thought, and was desolated at the thought of losing him forever. Peering through the window, she saw his bedroll and duffel bag lying on the floor. The one-room cabin seemed stripped of every personal thing. He was making ready to leave.

Across the yard, she saw Bradley working the bellows at his forge, and she ran to him. "Have you seen Ranse this morning?" she asked breathlessly.

From the cold way he looked at her, she guessed he knew Ranse had been fired, and he resented it. "He rode down by the creek there a minute ago." Without a word, she ran in the direction he pointed.

Golden cottonwood leaves drifted earthward, twirling in the cold wind. Flocks of south-winging birds resting in the bare red-brown willow branches rose at her approach, wheeling away to pursue their journey. Cybille Creek was low, the water moving silent among the stones.

Ranse's bay horse was drinking at the spring. He stood with one booted foot resting on the silvery log edging the spring, watching the horse with a grave face.

"Ranse!" she called, running toward him. When he saw her, his face hardened, and she was certain then that she had lost him. Not only her father's foolishness had driven him away; she had been equally foolish in her unreasonable jealousy of his past.

"I was afraid you'd gone," she gasped breathlessly, coming up to him.

"I planned to stop at the house to say goodbye," he said stiffly. He stood straight, the reins still in his hands, his eyes avoiding hers.

"You mustn't go!" she cried and to her horror felt the tears spill from her eyes. "Papa was so drunk, he doesn't even remember last night. Charles told me so before he left this morning."

"I'm no man's slave," Ranse replied in a cold voice.

"And I won't toady to an incompetent fool like Lord Hadley."

"If you leave, we'll be ruined," she sobbed, hating her father for demeaning this man. She lay a hand on his arm in supplication. "Only stay through the cattle sale . . . please, Ranse. For me, and for Edward."

"Don't!" For a second, his mask seemed to fall, the dark eyes shadowed with pain. "You must know . . ." his voice sounded strangled as she took his other arm, holding him with both hands.

Kathleen's pride fell to the ground with the autumn leaves as she looked up into the pained face of the man she loved. Her mouth trembling, she asked, "Do you love me, Ranse O'Neil?" The shawl slipped from her shoulders as her arms slid about his neck.

Ranse groaned softly. Then his strong arms were crushing her against him, and his mouth sought hers. All her pent-up longing was poured into that kiss. The world about them was obliterated as she gave herself over to the wild sensations of joy drenching her.

"Kathleen, sweet Kathleen," he murmured against her ear. She lifted her face to look into his devouring eyes. Slowly, that passion faded, his arms dropped away from her. Once more he was under rigid control.

"I can't love you, Kathleen," he said in a flat voice. "We come from different worlds. If you can't accept what I've been, how can you accept what I am?"

"I love you, Ranse." Through tears blurring her eyes, she stared up at him, clinging to him.

Gently, he pushed her away. "Whatever was between us once, Kathleen . . . your life is in England, and mine . . . " He let out his breath in a long sigh, one strong finger softly tracing the line of her cheek, wiping away her tears.

"I won't desert you now," he continued . . . "or Edward. I'll go sell the cattle in Chicago, and then . . ."

"Ranse . . ." Kathleen moved toward him, longing for the comfort of his arms, but he held her away.

"Then I'll move on. I should have gone before." His voice choked as their eyes locked, burning with longing. His control shattered, Ranse seized her in his arms, holding her fiercely against him, his mouth devouring hers.

As suddenly as he had embraced her, he let go, turning to mount his horse. Reaching up, Kathleen laid her hand on his knee. "I'll be waiting for you," she said.

There was no answer as horse and rider topped the creek bank and disappeared from sight.

CHAPTER 26

It was snowing the November day Ranse O'Neil returned from Chicago, the first tentative snow of the season. Tiny flakes drifted down through the cold gray air as Kathleen watched from the French doors of the dining room. Her heart pounded erratically as she watched him jump down from the loaded buckboard, greet the ranch hands, give orders in that easy manner of his for unloading the supplies.

The weeks he'd been gone had been uneasy ones for her. Papa had stayed on and on in Cheyenne, and she was certain his bill at the club was enormous. In the days he'd been home, she'd been aware that his drinking was now totally out of control. Most days he was drunk before noon, sleeping it off during the afternoon to rise and begin all over again before supper.

"Kathleen." Edward's fretful voice came from the sitting room, and she sighed. The boy's enforced idleness weighed heavily on him. The lessons she insisted he do each morning had become a chore for both of them. All the storybooks had been read more than once. Every game she managed to think of soon palled.

Reluctantly, she turned away from watching Ranse to go to Edward. Smiling, she nodded at Sandy, who had just filled the woodbox beside the huge fireplace.

"Ranse is back," she told Edward and chuckled to see his discontented face break into a grin.

"Tell him I want to see him at once," Edward said imperiously.

Kathleen frowned, annoyed that he sounded so like her

242

father. "He'll see you when his work is done, young man. Stop acting like an English 'haw-haw.'"

Edward looked abashed, then chortled. "You're getting to be nearly as bossy as old Aunt Martha." Settling back on the pillows, he flicked his riding crop at his leg cast. "When will Dr. Vickers come to take this odious thing off?"

"Before Christmas, I should think," Kathleen replied, glancing in the beveled mirror above the table to tuck a stray lock of hair in place.

Edward watched with a knowing grin. "You're glad he's back too, aren't you?"

"Who?" she asked with labored innocence.

Edward broke into delighted laughter. Watching her distractedly straighten the books on the table, he asked, "Will you marry Ranse and stay in Wyoming, Kathleen?"

To her dismay, tears started in her eyes. How could she answer such a question when Ranse had offered her no choice? I'll be moving on, he'd said, and the thought burned all the bruised places in her heart.

"I wouldn't mind," Edward continued, serious now. "If you lived in Wyoming, it would mean I could come back here, wouldn't it?" When she did not reply, his voice became tentative. "I like it here, Kathleen. I want to come back."

Not as much as I want to stay, she thought, staring into the blazing fire. Everything inside her seemed to be poised, waiting . . . waiting for Ranse to ask her to stay with him.

It was late afternoon before he came to the house, helping carry in supplies for Mrs. Sanders's kitchen. Papa was sleeping off his morning drunk, and Edward had finally fallen asleep while she read to him. Kathleen sat beside the fire, the book still open on her lap. At the sound of boot heels coming down the hallway, she knew who it was. When he entered the room, she stood up quickly, letting the book fall to the floor.

"Ranse . . ."

"Hello, Kathleen." His expression was as distant as a stranger's. With a glance at the sleeping Edward, Ranse stepped across the room, taking a leather folio case from beneath his arm. "I wanted to go over the cattle accounts with your father."

She stared at him helplessly. Why had she let herself dream that the weeks apart would make him change his mind? He had set her out of his life, and she ached to be in his arms, to let his kisses wipe away all the frustration and anger and hurt.

"He's sleeping," she answered tonelessly.

"Drunk?" he asked in a voice filled with contempt.

She nodded, in shamed silence. Knowing her heart was in her eyes, she turned to look into the flames. Summoning all her courage, she asked quietly, "Will you be going away, Ranse?"

For a long moment, she thought he would never answer. At last, he cleared his throat, and she turned to face him, shocked by the black anger in his eyes.

"God!" he exclaimed, making a gesture of futility. "The bastard!" He took a deep breath, looking past her, carefully not meeting her eyes. "I can't leave you and Eddie at his mercy. I'll stay until you leave for England." Turning away, he added, "Tell Lord Hadley to send for me when he's sober."

I've lost him, she thought, listening to him walk back down the hallway to the kitchen, to the sound of his voice talking with the Sanderses. No matter how much I love him, he'll not love me again. Because he is Ranse O'Neil, he won't desert me and Edward here in a land strange to us. He'll stay until he knows we're safe. A faint hope rose from the depths of her despair, a hope that somehow she could win his love once more.

After the first November snowfall melted, a belated autumn lingered again in Wyoming. The last leaves fell reluctantly from the nearly bare cottonwoods, the wild rose bushes bloomed with red berries, the sky was a flawless azure blue and Laramie Peak gleamed with new snow.

Ranse did not come to the house again except for brief visits with Edward. His business meeting with Papa, behind the closed doors of the study, had been a heated one.

"No bloody dividends this year," Papa said afterward, between drinks. "The syndicate will have me drawn and quartered."

He was afraid, Kathleen thought with sudden insight.

What Ranse had once called the paper castles of the English cattle companies were crumbling. From talking with the Sanderses, Kathleen knew that cattle prices had fallen everywhere. It was not Ranse's doing, it was the greed of investors overstocking the range, hungry for fast and huge returns on their money. The syndicate members would be angry, that was certain. She was equally certain that at home in England all the fault would suddenly be laid on Ranse, and Papa would play the victim.

The days seemed endless as she waited for his infrequent visits, aching for just the sight of him. When he came, he had little to say to her as he and Edward played their ongoing tournament of gin rummy. She brought him coffee, with tea for Edward and herself, and sat beside the fire filling her eyes with the look of him to carry into her dreams.

"There, young man," Charles Vickers said, carefully massaging Edward's shrunken leg muscles. "Almost as good as new."

"Will I be able to walk again?" Edward asked, staring at his leg in apprehension.

"Certainly," came the confident reply as the doctor signaled Sandy to remove the tub filled with broken plaster cast. "Crutches first, then a cane, then shank's mare."

"How about riding?" Edward persisted. He grinned at Ranse, who had come to the house to help with the removal of the cast. "Ranse brought Blackie in when they moved the horses to winter pasture, and he's just waiting for me."

Charles winked at Kathleen. "I'll let Ranse decide when the time is right for that."

Delighted at being freed from the cumbersome cast, Edward sat up in bed, swinging his feet over the side of the bed. At once, he grabbed his forehead, groaned, and fell back on the bed. "Dizzy . . ." he gasped.

"I was about to say, let's not rush this," Dr. Vickers said with a smile, pulling the covers over the boy.

"Blackie's not going anywhere without you," Ranse assured him, standing at the foot of the bed, grinning at the disappointed Edward.

Handing the basin of water to Tessie, Kathleen let her

eyes turn to Ranse. Never once had he looked at her since he'd entered the room. With all her heart, she longed to see in those dark eyes the light that had once blazed there for her alone.

Gathering her courage, she said, "Charles will be staying for supper, Ranse. Won't you join us?"

He seemed startled by the sound of her voice. It was a moment before he turned to her, and her heart plunged when she saw his cool, shuttered eyes. In a silence that seemed to last forever, the tension between them was almost palpable in the room.

It was Ranse who looked away. His voice sounded almost angry as he said, "Afraid not. I've got some riding to do today and won't be back until late."

"I see." Struggling to maintain her composure, Kathleen was determined no one would know how his rejection had wounded her.

She caught the compassionate glance Charles gave her before he turned to Ranse. "I'll be leaving early tomorrow, perhaps I'll see you then."

"Sure." The two men shook hands, and Ranse left the room as though demons pursued him.

Papa had stumbled off to bed soon after supper. Worn out by the day's ordeal, Edward slept noisily. With the two Morris chairs drawn near the fire, Kathleen and Charles shared a companionable silence.

Charles puffed on his cigar, sipping at his brandy, seeming in a contemplative mood. "Is Robert always like this?" he asked at last.

She sighed. "It seems to grow worse and worse. He's deathly bored here and can't seem to find any other way to pass the days." Her voice dropped, low and bitter. "He should never have left England."

Charles shook his leonine gray head resignedly. "No, but a man should . . ." He left the sentence unfinished, but finally added, "I'll talk with him before I leave tomorrow. I doubt it will help, but he should be aware of his duty to you and Edward."

"Ranse promised me he'd stay on until we leave for England," Kathleen told him. "He knows the situation."

There was a long silence. She was aware of the kindly brown eyes studying her, and she avoided looking at him.

"You love Ranse, Kathleen?"

To her dismay, she felt tears burn her eyes. She looked down at her hands twisting together in her lap, and nodded her head.

"Something has happened between you . . . a quarrel?" Charles prompted in a low voice.

Again, she could only nod, afraid to trust her voice.

"He's a proud man," Charles continued, leaning back in his chair, his eyes on the cigar smoke curling upward in the firelight. "Men like Ranse O'Neil are the aristocrats of Wyoming. He was in the cattle business early, and he might have been a millionaire now if it weren't for the tragedy of his wife's death. Now, he's trying to make a comeback, and it isn't easy."

He finished off the brandy, turning to stare into the fire. "You'll have to understand his pride, Kathleen, if you love him. If you were wrong in the quarrel, have the courage to tell him. Wrong or right, men like Ranse put up a wall when they've been hurt." Looking up, he smiled at her. "You can't batter it down, but maybe you can undermine it with love."

"Oh, Charles," she cried, letting the tears come now. Reaching across the space between them, he took her hands and held them tightly. "Dear Charles, thank you for understanding."

"Go to him, Kathleen," he smiled and patted her hand. "You'll have to go to him."

"I know." Her voice was faint as she wondered whether she had the courage to chance rejection once more.

It seemed that after Charles's departure, the Wyoming winter settled in to stay. Day after day, the snow drifted down from lowering skies. Each morning, the ranch hands shoveled paths across the ranch yard so that they could go about the work of caring for the animals. The majority of the cowboys had been let go for the winter, with only a maintenance crew in residence to look after the horses and work at repairing equipment.

Edward began the painful business of learning to walk

again, determinedly making his way about the house on crutches. Caring for the boy took a great deal of Kathleen's time, but not enough to ease the restlessness burning in her. She could not ride, as the snow continued to pile up until there was two to three feet bordering the shoveled paths. Edward complained that Ranse had not been to see them. Kathleen failed to share with him the time she spent staring out the French doors, treasuring every glimpse she caught of Ranse O'Neil. At last, bored to distraction, she threw away all her years of aristocratic upbringing and went into the kitchen to help Mrs. Sanders bake fruitcakes for Christmas.

"We won't have a Christmas at all," Edward said morosely, watching the women at work from his seat at the kitchen table.

"In America, we make our own Christmas," Mrs. Sanders informed him. "I'll bake all kinds of goodies. Sandy will bring in a tree to decorate. And you will have to think of gifts you can make yourself for your sister and your father."

Edward groaned and fell silent. After a minute, he rose and hobbled from the room as though already intent on some plan for Christmas.

Tessie washed the bowls and Kathleen dried them, as Mrs. Sanders slid the cakes into the oven of the huge black iron stove. Smiling to herself, Kathleen thought how she had enjoyed helping in the kitchen. It was far more interesting than sitting about waiting for the servants to do for you.

But the thought of Christmas made her sigh, not for herself, or Papa who would care little about it, but for Edward. Drying her hands, she stepped into the breakfast room. The sun had come out at last, and she lifted the curtains to look out on the drifts of snow sparkling like a million diamonds in the light. Across the yard, beside the tack shed, Ranse stood with Bradley, sorting through the used bridles. As always, her heart leaped at the sight of him, then settled into a steady ache.

The bridles! Of course! Edward had greatly admired Ranse's braided horsehair halter. From years of doing useless needlework, she knew she was clever with her hands. She would make a horsehair bridle for Edward for Christmas.

Following thought with action, she took her heavy wool

cloak from the hall tree, exchanging shoes for a pair of gum boots. The paths had been newly shoveled and were clean and frozen. She hurried eagerly across the yard.

The two men looked at her in surprised curiosity.

"Come out to enjoy the sunshine, Miss?" Bradley asked, doffing his worn stetson.

"Oh, yes!" she cried breathlessly, whirling around to take in the buildings piled with snow, the trees by the creek downed in white and dripping crystal icicles. "It's like a fairyland."

Ranse grinned indulgently as Bradley shrugged and said, "Long as you don't have to work in it, I guess."

"I've come to ask a favor, Ranse." She kept her eyes on his top shirt button, pleased that she was in control of herself, but certain that if she met his eyes all her carefully repressed emotions would tear her apart.

"Sure," he said, handing the bridles to Bradley, who nodded at Kathleen and trudged off toward the blacksmith shop.

"I want to make a braided horsehair halter for Edward for Christmas." The words tumbled out. "Will you help me?"

There was a long silence, before she heard him let out his breath slowly. "I guess I could. I'll have to get some hair for you, though."

"Can we start this afternoon?"

"All right. I'll come up to the house after I gather—"

"No." she interrupted. "Edward would see it, and I want to surprise him." She paused, terrified at the boldness of what she meant to say. "Could I come to your cabin to work on it?"

Again, there was a long silence. Kathleen's eyes moved upward to where his wool shirt stood open at the neck, fastening on the pulse beating hard at the base of his throat.

"If you want to," he said slowly, as though each word was dragged out of him.

"Two o'clock, then." Kathleen turned and ran back toward the house, feeling as though her feet never touched the icy path.

The hanks of black horsehair hung over the ladder-back chair. Behind the isinglass door of the Charter Oak heater, flames danced and gleamed. Ranse's cabin was one small room, with rough log walls. A bed, covered by a worn patchwork quilt, filled one corner, a camel-back trunk beside it. The walls were decorated with his gear: saddle, bridles and halters, chaps, his big hat, a sheepskin-lined leather jacket, all hanging from wall pegs. Before the stove, he had placed the one small oak table, with a chair for Kathleen on one side and for himself on the other. There was one window, with faded cretonne curtains of indeterminate color.

She had changed her gown three times, finally settling on a dark blue merino with pink ruching on the yoke and pink shell buttons down the front. Dampening her smoldering anticipation, she sat quietly, listening to Ranse's instructions.

Surely, she thought, he was as aware as she of the tension flowing between them. He seemed tightly coiled, carefully under control. Watching his big competent hands as he demonstrated the braiding, she wanted to take them in her own, kiss them until . . .

"It takes a strong hand," he was saying. "Horsehair is coarse and hard to braid tightly enough. I wonder . . ." He looked at her small white hands gently stroking the hank of horsehair.

"Let me try," she answered, reaching across the table.

Their hands touched, and the impact of his skin against hers rocketed through her with such intensity she gasped aloud.

Ranse jerked his hand away and stood up, turning away. "Oh, God!" he muttered. Then, turning on her, he said bitterly, "I shouldn't have let you come here."

There would be no other time for them, Kathleen knew. Standing, she faced him, not caring that all the months of waiting and longing showed in her face. "I love you, Ranse," she said.

Pain twisted his face, and he turned away again. "Kathleen . . ." Irresistibly drawn, she moved toward him. Slipping her arms about his waist, she pressed her face against his back, the wool shirt rough against her cheek.

"I love you, Ranse O'Neil," she said, her voice gathering

strength as her purpose became clear. "And you love me, if you'll only forgive me for being a jealous fool."

"It can't be." His voice sounded strangled as he shook his head in denial.

Her arms tightened about him, feeling the thunder of his heart beneath her hand. "Do you think I'm not good enough for you?" she asked, straining to make her tone light.

"Not good . . .?" He whirled around, clasping her shoulder in his hands, the dark eyes burning into hers.

"I love you," she repeated and was lost in the fierceness of his embrace. Hot kisses rained on her forehead, her cheeks, her ears, her eyes, and she lifted her face joyously to him.

Holding her against him, her breasts crushed to his hard chest, thighs straining close, Ranse drew back to look into her eyes. "Kathleen, my love, my darling. I've tried to tear you out of my heart and stop loving you . . ."

"Don't," she whispered, her fingers smoothing his cheek. "Love me always, Ranse. Love me now. I want you so."

She felt his hesitation, but the wild longing pouring through her would not be denied. Reaching up, she pressed her mouth to his. Ranse groaned softly, deep in his throat, his lips hotly possessive against hers. The flame that had smoldered since last they were together ignited, enveloping her in blazing passion.

"Love me," she whispered again, as his mouth burned against the curve of her throat.

"Kathleen . . . we can't." She silenced his protest with her lips, flicking her tongue against his until he opened to her. The salty, tobacco taste of his mouth evoked wild sensations in the very center of her being. Pressing closer to him, she felt his arousal and knew there was no turning back.

Ranse threw the bolt on the door, while she flipped the curtains closed. Quickly, they undressed beside the bed until her gown and the little underclothing she had worn lay heaped on the rough board floor.

For a long moment, he stood looking at her, then reached out, his hands gently moving over her body, cupping her soft breasts, tracing the curve of her hips. Carefully, she reached out to stroke him. Ranse drew in his breath sharply, his eyes blazing with passion. Gathering her close to him, he held her, hot skin against hot skin, pulses pounding in unison.

Quickly, he turned back the worn quilt, lifted her in his arms, and lowered her to the bed. They were together, limbs intertwined, hands stroking, caressing, building to an urgency that could no longer be denied.

When Ranse came into her, Kathleen cried out, lifting her hips to receive him, giving him her whole being in total surrender. The rapture spiraled up and up into an explosion of joy so intense she cried out, then wept with the beauty of it.

CHAPTER 27

Pale winter sunlight seeped around the edges of the faded curtains. The flames in the cast-iron stove gleamed through the isinglass, casting flickering shadows in the dim room. One braided length of black horsehair lay across the small oak table.

Raising herself on one elbow, Kathleen looked down into the face of the man lying beside her. A worn Hudson's Bay blanket and the faded quilt were pulled up to his chest. His eyes were closed, and she studied the lines of his rugged face, so vulnerable in repose. With a heart so full it seemed about to burst with love, she bent to gently press her lips against his eyelids.

She gasped in surprise as his strong arms seized her, crushing her against him, his mouth searching for hers, black eyes laughing.

When his mouth moved to caress the base of her throat, she managed to say, "I thought you were asleep."

"Darling girl," Ranse murmured, as he pushed back the blanket to nuzzle her breast. "I wouldn't waste my time with you sleeping."

Kathleen ran her fingers through his thick dark hair, closing her eyes in pleasure at the sensuous excitement of touching him. Bending, she pressed her lips against the top of his head. "I told Mrs. Sanders you were helping me braid a horsehair halter for Edward's Christmas." Lying back, she frowned at the ceiling. "Do you suppose she believed me?"

Ranse raised his head and grinned at her. "It's the truth, isn't it?" Suddenly, he sobered. Lying back beside her, he

253

drew her close and pulled the blanket up to cover their shoulders.

"Yesterday, after you left," he said, "I swore I wouldn't let this happen again. But this afternoon, when you stood there looking at me, your wonderful eyes so full of love . . ." He broke off to kiss her eyes lingeringly. Groaning, he turned on his back. "I'm weak as water with you, Kathleen. It's not right. I should be strong enough for both of us . . ." His voice trailed off.

Turning, she lay across his chest, looking down into his unhappy face. "Do you love me?" she asked softly.

"Oh, God!" he cried, his arms tightening about her as she touched her mouth to his and was instantly lost in his demanding kiss.

Holding her close, he sighed. "I love you more than I'd have believed it was possible to love anyone. Every minute we're apart you're there in my heart . . . sweet and warm and loving."

Kathleen took a deep breath. Laying her head on his chest, she said in a faltering voice, "I guess you'll have to marry me."

For a moment, his arms tightened, then she felt his hands moving gently on her back, soothing, caressing. "Do you know," he asked in a low voice, "just what it would mean to marry a Wyoming cowboy who owns nothing but his horse and saddle?"

"Ranse . . ." she tried to object.

"You were raised in a manor house in England, honey . . . with servants to do all the work, with fine clothes, luxuries. I've saved money to buy another ranch, but I'll be starting from nothing. It's a hard life." Cupping her face in his hands, he looked deep into her eyes. "Are you sure you'd still love me, living like that?"

"I'd love you in an Indian tepee," she announced, kissing him hard. Stroking his rumpled hair, she looked lovingly into his face. "Ranse, your mother was raised in a different way too. You said she went to fine schools in the East. Was her love for your father any less because they didn't live in luxury?"

His smile was wistful. "No, there was a lot of love in our

cabin when I was growing up, except for the sadness of the babies who died."

"Then I'll stay with you . . . always," she murmured, her lips against his.

"Always," he answered, and his mouth took hers in a deep kiss that awakened her body at once into urgent desire.

Her hand slid down his hard-muscled body, caressing his hard throbbing response to her touch. "Love me," she begged. "Love me today and tomorrow and forever."

Later, watching Ranse pull on his jeans and cross the room to make up the fire that had burned low, Kathleen stretched voluptuously beneath the blanket. Every dream of her lonely life had come true here in this tiny room, in the arms of Ranse O'Neil. As long as he loved her, she would never leave him.

He stood beside the bed, buttoning his wool shirt, smiling down at her with tender eyes. "Slugabed," he teased. "You'd better get back to the house before someone comes looking for you and we have a real scandal."

"Am I a scandal?" she asked, responding gaily to his teasing. Sitting up, she flung back the blanket and reached for her clothes.

"Oh God," he said hoarsely. She saw that the sight of her nude body had aroused him again.

She slipped the petticoat over her head and stood up. Pressing her hands against his chest, she looked up into his warm eyes. "I wish . . . oh darling, I wish I could stay with you and make love all day and all night."

Ranse drew her close, his face against her rumpled hair. "When we're married, we'll do nothing else for a month. Will that suit you, my wanton lady?"

When she was dressed, he drew her cloak about her, holding it beneath her chin and looking into her eyes. "My darling girl," he said, "I want everything to be right and honorable with us. I'll tell your father we're going to be married."

A faint chill ran down Kathleen's spine. Not Papa, she thought, yet she knew she couldn't marry Ranse without telling her father. In the past weeks, he had been nearly always in a drunken stupor, and she had come to ignore him as though he were not even present. "Let me tell you when, Ranse. When he's sober. Please."

"Soon," he urged, kissing the tip of her nose. "We can drive into Cheyenne."

"Yes," she answered, moving into his embrace. "Soon."

"Is winter always like this in Wyoming?" Kathleen asked, staring out the small window at the wind-driven snow whipping across the ranch yard.

"No," Ranse replied, looking up from the horsehair braid he was finishing. He sat at the oak table. Waves of heat radiated from the round iron stove. "The Indians say it will be a hard winter," he added gloomily. "Feed is already short on the range. All we can do is hope for a chinook soon."

"Chinook?" Kathleen looked at him, longing to gather him in her arms. They had not made love today, for her monthly flow had begun. Even that change in her body did not still the ache that only his loving could assuage.

"A warm wind from the south. It melts off the snow so the cattle can get down to grass." Wind rattled the window, blowing snow against the glass. "You shouldn't have come out in this weather," he added.

"I wanted to be with you," she told him, looking into his eyes. "Even if . . ."

"Come here." Ranse held out his arms, then drew her down onto his lap, cuddling her close against his chest. His mouth brushed softly against hers. She responded passionately, until, despite his efforts to hold back, their mouths melded and probed with frenzied longing.

"Oh, Kath," he murmured against her hair when they broke breathlessly apart. "Maybe you shouldn't come here anymore for a while." He drew a deep ragged breath. "For the first time in my life, I'm not in control. God . . . I lay here at night half-crazy with wanting you."

Smiling, Kathleen looked into his face, her fingertips softly tracing the weathered line on his cheek. "Do you know that I'm over there in my bed, half-crazy too?" She kissed him gently, then lay her head against his broad shoulder. Held close against him, she listened to the roar of the wind and the soft flutter of the flames in the stove, rubbing her cheek against the rough wool of his shirt.

"Ranse . . ." she began hesitantly. "Will it hurt you if I ask about your wife?"

She felt his lips against her forehead, and waited, fearful that she had opened an old wound.

"It hurt a lot at first," he began speaking slowly, as though examining his words. "But it's been ten years now . . ." His voice trailed into silence again. "She was seventeen," he said at last. "Hardly more than a kid. I was twenty, a randy age, and she was eager. With ten kids at home, she was anxious to get away." He sighed, and Kathleen remained very still, sorry now for stirring up painful memories. "We homesteaded this place and the future looked good. I did love her, and God, how I loved that little boy. He was six months old when . . ." His voice broke and he fell silent.

Longing to comfort him, Kathleen slid her arm up around his neck, pressing her cheek against his. Taking a deep breath, he continued doggedly, "Sandy found them. He used to have a homestead down the creek. I was working the roundup, and he came to tell me. Everything was gone . . . the cabin burned to the ground and no way to know what happened."

Drawing away, Kathleen looked into his eyes, dark with pained remembering. "Darling . . . darling," she said. "I'm sorry."

Ranse drew her against him in a fierce embrace. "That was long ago," he said quietly. "We have to let yesterday go."

It was an echo of the words that had filled her mind in the autumn meadow and sent her back to Ranse. Sitting straight, Kathleen took his face in her two hands, her fingers tangled in his thick dark hair. "I love you," she told him with all her heart in her eyes. "I want to make you happy, darling, for all the tomorrows we'll be together."

In a break between storms, Sandy had ridden to the foothills and brought back a piñon pine for a Christmas tree. From her own possessions, Mrs. Sanders provided decorations: tinsel, a tin star, and a few glittering glass ornaments. She and Tessie strung popcorn and baked gingerbread men to be tied to the tree with red knitting yarn.

Edward was entranced with the idea of an American Christmas. He bounced out of bed where he still slept in the sitting room before first light on Christmas morning, awakening the household and demanding that they open presents at once. Although the weather remained gloomy, a cheerful fire blazed in the huge fireplace, and Mrs. Sanders served sugared crullers and coffee. Even Papa was pleasant, for he had not had time to start on his drinking, although Kathleen knew he was not pleased to have the servants sharing the family Christmas in such a familiar manner.

Nevertheless, gifts were exchanged with gasps of surprise and much merriment. Kathleen had cut up a fine silk shawl to make scarves for Papa and Perkins and Sandy. Tessie and Mrs. Sanders each received one of the gowns she had put away when she first came to Wyoming. Delightedly, they held the dresses up to each other, plotting how they would alter them.

When Edward tore open the wrapped halter, Kathleen longed for Ranse to be with them. It was his gift too, for he had done more of the work than she. Crowing with delight, Edward threw his arms about her. "I always wanted one of these, Kathleen. How did you know? Is the hair from Blackie's tail?"

"Ranse helped me make it," she told him, enjoying his pleasure.

"Why isn't he here?" Edward demanded. "He should be here for our Christmas."

"He's coming for Christmas dinner," Mrs. Sanders answered, handing out the bags of candy she and Tessie had secretly prepared.

Edward took his presents from their hiding place beneath his bed. Kathleen kissed him and looked with loving pride at the picture he had drawn for her of her mare, Babe. Mr. Fraser had left behind a set of paints and art paper. From that, Edward had made all his gifts . . . a picture of Sandy's favorite horse, a drawing of the ranch for Mrs. Sanders, an unknown cowboy on a horse for Tessie, which made her blush and Mrs. Sanders eye her suspiciously. Perkins got a picture of the surrey and team, and Papa's was a fox hunt in full cry. Kathleen caught a glimpse of the one remaining and knew it was a drawing of Hawk, made for Ranse.

As he always had back in England, Papa gave each of the servants an envelope containing money. Pouring his first glass of port of the day, he turned to his children and said, "My present to the two of you will be a trip to England . . . as soon as this infernal weather clears."

Edward and Kathleen exchanged looks. She would not be going to England, Kathleen thought, and for the first time, felt a twinge at the distance that would then lie between her and Edward.

The Christmas dinner was nothing at all like those they had always known in England. Mrs. Sanders proudly served a spicy baked ham, with biscuits and gravy, mashed potatoes, buttered carrots, and candied yams. For dessert, there was a light and delectable dried-apple pie.

Ranse had arrived just before dinner, knocking the snowflakes from his hat and his leather jacket at the door. From beneath his jacket, he produced a pair of shiny spurs with tooled leather straps, and possession of them seemed to make Edward's Christmas complete. For Kathleen, Ranse brought a pair of soft beaded moccasins purchased from a wandering band of Indians encountered on the roundup.

Papa seemed to be making an effort to remain reasonably sober for the day. But when dinner was finished and the servants had retired, he continued to fill his glass with port. They sat beside the fire in the sitting room: Papa, Ranse, Kathleen and Edward. Ranse had duly admired his picture of Hawk, and Edward held onto his halter and spurs as though afraid they might disappear.

She saw Ranse's eyes following her father's movements as he filled his glass once more and returned to his Morris chair by the fireplace. After a short silence, Papa launched into a long, jumbled and rather maudlin account of his childhood Christmases with no one but the servants and his sister Martha.

In spite of her annoyance at his behavior, Kathleen found herself feeling sorry for the child her father had once been. Had all that neglect and loneliness made him into the cold and uncaring man he was now?

"Ah, well," he said, draining his glass. "Next Christmas, we will all be home again. My new son will be with us . . . and perhaps a husband for Kathleen."

She sat bolt upright, staring at him in shock. "What do you mean, Papa?"

259

He rose and moved unsteadily toward the port decanter. As he poured, a bit of the liquid slopped onto the table. Seating himself again, he smiled dimly. "Deborah writes that Griffin Sturgis's wife has died. He was always rather taken with you."

"Oh, Papa!" Edward objected disgustedly. "He's twice Kathleen's age and a rotten old devil besides."

"Well-off," Papa muttered. "Well-connected . . ."

"I'm not going to marry Mr. Sturgis, Papa," Kathleen said, trying to contain her dismay and anger.

Ranse reached over to take her hand in his. "I've asked Kathleen to marry me."

"And I intend to marry Ranse," she added, holding tightly to his big hand.

Papa sat bolt upright, spilling a bit of wine on his shirt, staring at them in amazement. Edward was bouncing up and down on the edge of the bed, grinning with delight.

"What bloody nonsense," Papa burst out. "Marry a common . . ." He waved his arms in desperation, as though unable to find the words. "A servant . . . no better than a groom . . . By God, I won't allow it."

"Papa, I've made up my mind to stay in Wyoming with Ranse," she told him firmly, returning the loving pressure of Ranse's touch.

"This godforsaken hellhole!" Papa cried, his face flushed with wine and anger. "You silly little bitch . . . acting like a mare in season . . ." He sneered at her. "You're as common as your slut of a mother."

Ranse leaped to his feet. In one long stride, he had seized Papa by the shirt front and dragged him up from the chair. "You'll not talk to her like that," he rasped, shaking Papa like a puppy. "You worthless drunken bastard." With a final furious shake, he shoved Papa back into his chair and turned on his heel.

Papa was silent, staring in open-mouthed astonishment. Edward curled on his bed, watching the adults fearfully.

Reaching out to draw Kathleen close to him, Ranse led her into the foyer. Pulling on his leather jacket, he looked down at her with serious eyes. "I don't know what to do, Kathleen. It's blowing a blizzard out there. We can't get to

Cheyenne." Gently he touched her pale, set face. "If you want to come to my cabin and stay . . ."

"No," she said, glancing at Edward, who sat watching them with silent tears running down his cheeks. "I can't." Impulsively, she flung her arms about his neck, holding him close. "Nothing's changed between us, darling. We'll go away as soon as the weather changes. Not Papa, nor anything on earth can take you away from me."

CHAPTER 28

The days after Christmas dragged. One storm followed on the other with little respite. Although Ranse came to the house almost every day to make sure all was well, he could not allow Kathleen to come to his cabin again.

"Wyoming is a small country," he told her. "Everybody knows everybody else, tongues wag and stories spread. I won't shame you just to satisfy my need for you."

"What about my need for you?" she murmured, running her hands across his broad shoulders. They had stepped into the darkened dining room, which was no longer used. Now, all meals were served in the breakfast room, to conserve the wood supply. It was here in the dining room they shared the urgent embraces and the tantalizing kisses that left them both burning with longing.

Ranse held her fiercely against his aroused body, bending to touch his lips softly to hers. "We can wait, darlin'," he said. "After all, we have all our tomorrows."

Sighing, Kathleen laid her head against his shoulder. "This winter has already lasted forever."

"The weather should break soon," he promised, tilting her chin with his fingers to look deep into her eyes.

The weather did break in early January. A warm wind came booming up from the southwest, melting the snow and blowing the exposed ridges bare. Cowhands ventured out on horseback to check the cattle.

Wearing the gum boots provided by Sandy, Kathleen and Edward ventured out into the brilliant day. The crystal icicles fringing all the buildings kept up a constant drip-drip in the warm air.

"A false spring," she said to Ranse when they met him at the stables.

"A chinook," he corrected. "If it lasts long enough . . . if there are no more heavy storms, then we're saved."

"Papa insists we should pack and leave at once," Edward interrupted.

Kathleen nodded affirmation at Ranse's questioning glance.

"He says he wants to get out of this blasted place," Edward added. Spotting his favorite horse inside the stable, he grinned. "There's Blackie." He slipped past Ranse into the dark odorous confines of the stables.

Free of the constraint of Edward's presence, Kathleen slipped her hand into Ranse's, looking up at him with loving eyes. "What shall we do about Papa?"

Ranse grimaced and shrugged impatiently. "I'll come to the house and talk to him. Right now, the mud on the roads would be up to the horse's hocks. You couldn't drive a vehicle a mile." Lifting her hand, he pressed his mouth against her fingers, his dark eyes hot with desire.

A fervent response surged through Kathleen. She moved closer to him, lifting her face for the kiss she longed for. Still holding her hand tightly, Ranse bent to brush his lips softly against her mouth.

"Darlin'," he whispered. "My darlin' Kathleen."

From the corner of her eye, she caught Edward's inquiring gaze and wide grin. Slipping an arm about Ranse's waist, she held out a hand to the boy.

"I'm going to marry Ranse and stay here," she told him.

Rushing to her, Edward flung his arms about her waist. "Can I stay too, Kathleen? Can I stay and learn to be a Wyoming cowboy?"

Dismayed by the boy's reaction, Kathleen looked imploringly at Ranse over Edward's head. "I'm afraid not," she said, stroking the bright blond head pressed against her breast. "You must go to Harrow this fall, get an education, and learn how to run the estate when you are Lord Hadley."

A wail of protest rose from Edward, his face smothered against her. "I don't want to be like Papa!"

"You could never be like Papa," she assured him, tears burning her eyes. Ranse laid a comforting hand on the boy's

263

heaving shoulders. "Oh, Edward," and she held him close, weeping at the thought of their parting.

Ranse turned the boy away from her, scooped him up and held him close while Edward clung to him, weeping against his shoulder. Love flowed through her in a burgeoning tide at this new evidence of the decency and compassion of the man to whom she had given her heart. Nothing would ever part them . . . not Papa, not even dear Edward. Nothing on this earth was more important at that moment than life with Ranse O'Neil.

Carrying Edward, Ranse walked back to the house with them as the sun disappeared behind clouds drifting in a windless sky. Over and over, he assured the boy that he could come back to Wyoming every year, that he must grow up to be a good man for Kathleen's sake and his own, that he was loved.

Papa had set Perkins to work packing. Half-drunk already, he flew into a rage when Ranse adamantly forbade their departure. Furiously ordering Ranse from the house, he retired to his study and the comfort of his wine.

The prudence of Ranse's decision became evident as morning dawned next day. Now the wind blew from the north, with the bite of arctic air. Clouds hung low and dark from horizon to horizon. The first flakes of snow whirled on the icy wind. There was a flurry of activity in the outbuildings as horses were stabled and fed, wood chopped and stacked against the outside walls after the woodboxes had been filled to overflowing.

"It's settlin' in to be a ring-tailed roarer," Sandy said gloomily, dumping another armload of wood beside the kitchen range. His wife hurried to slam the door where the gusty wind blew snow onto the mud-stained linoleum.

After supper, Kathleen slipped into the darkened dining room, staring out across the ranch yard toward the lights of the outbuildings dimly seen through the swirling snow. Sandy had said everything was snug at the bunkhouse, that Ranse was staying there to save wood. He was safe, she knew, but she wished him here in this dark icy room where they had shared so many kisses this winter.

All night, the wind beat against the house, unceasing. Windows rattled under its onslaught, snow pelting against the panes. Gray morning brought no surcease. Down from the north the blizzard roared, driving a snow so thick it was impossible to see across the ranch yard. The entire world seemed caught in the grip of a white and endless maelstrom.

Kathleen attempted to pass the time with Edward's lessons, but he was inattentive, as restless as the wind outside. By supper time they had quarreled and sat beside the sitting-room fire in cool silence. Papa was already drunk and in his bed upstairs. Sighing, Kathleen realized she had read the same page in her book three times. Rising to build up the fire, she was startled by a banging on the front door.

"It's Ranse!" Edward grabbed his cane and hobbled into the foyer.

Kathleen flung open the door, her heart wild with the hope that Edward was right. Ranse stood before her, his face covered by a wool muffler so that only his dark eyes showed beneath eyebrows whitened by snow. Taking off his hat, he beat it against his thigh to knock off the snow.

Quickly, he forced the door shut against the blast of icy wind. Discarding his frozen muffler, he grinned at them. "You two surviving the blizzard?" he asked.

"You shouldn't have come out in such a storm just to check on us," Kathleen admonished, helping him shed the now-dripping sheepskin coat.

"I'm glad you did," Edward interrupted. "Kathleen is mad at me because I didn't do my lessons. Now, I have someone to play cards with."

"What a brat you are," Ranse told him, ruffling the boy's hair affectionately, his eyes holding Kathleen's.

"I'll get the cards." Edward hobbled away into the sitting room, and Ranse drew Kathleen into his arms.

His face was cold against hers, but the warmth that rose from within dispelled the chill. "I had to make sure you were all right," he said. "I won't stay long."

Turning her face, she pressed her lips to his, not caring who might see, knowing only that his nearness and his strength were as necessary to her now as food and drink.

At the sound of Edward's demanding "I'm dealing the cards," Ranse slowly released her, his dark eyes smoldering as they looked into hers.

"I ran a guide rope from the bunkhouse so I can find my

way back," he told her, as they moved toward the sitting room.

"It's getting worse, isn't it?" she asked, as a blast of wind shook the house.

Ranse nodded glumly, then seemed to put aside his gloom as he and Edward embarked on a hard-fought game of gin rummy. Watching them with amusement, Kathleen struggled with the knitting she had undertaken to learn from Mrs. Sanders. It surprised her how quickly her unease had vanished when Ranse came into the house, how content she felt sitting across the fire from him.

Outside, the wind increased in violence, gusting against the house so that the windows shuddered and icy air seeped in through unseen cracks. When Edward began to yawn and lose interest in the game, Kathleen went into the kitchen to make hot chocolate for him. Sandy was banking the fire, on his way to bed.

"It's a whiteout," he said to her. "Ranse better not try to get back to the bunkhouse. Could get lost and froze to death tryin' to cross the yard."

"I'll tell him," she answered. "There's plenty of room for him to stay here the night."

Searching the sideboard, she found Papa's brandy and offered a glass to Ranse, repeating Sandy's warning.

"I'll have a look," he replied, downing his brandy. He shrugged on the heavy leather coat, then returned to look down at the sleepy Edward, already tucked in his bed. "Good night, cowboy."

"You can stay here," Edward mumbled. "Use my room upstairs."

Ranse glanced quickly at Kathleen, and she guessed his thoughts. The two of them together in the same house . . . how could they stay apart? Suddenly, she was pierced by such a longing for him, she reached out and grasped his arm. "Stay," she said.

His mouth tightened. "Better not."

At the door, he kissed her fiercely. The longing inside her burst into full flame. "Stay," she begged.

Shaking his head, Ranse broke away, opened the door and stepped out onto the porch. "Damn!"

Kathleen leaned out into the icy blast of the wind.

"Ranse, what is it?" Through the darkness and the swirling snow, she could barely see his figure across the porch.

"My guide rope blew away."

"Then you have to stay." Shivering in the cold, she seized his arm and drew him back inside, slamming the door behind them. "It will be all right," she promised. "You can sleep in Edward's room upstairs."

For a long silent moment, Ranse looked into her face. Kathleen felt the flame at the core of her being grow. The ache of longings denied these past long weeks pounded through her veins. Reaching up, she pushed the coat off his shoulders. "It's not worth risking your life to go back to the bunkhouse, Ranse."

"Are you staying?" Edward asked sleepily, as they stepped back to warm themselves by the fire. When Ranse nodded, he grinned. "Good. I feel better with you here." With a yawn, he turned on his pillow and closed his eyes.

"So do I," Kathleen said softly, her eyes locked with Ranse's, her hand still held tightly in his. It seemed a long time they stood there, drowning in each other's eyes, with only the low mutter of the fire singing below the raging wind.

"My love," he whispered at last, lifting her hand to kiss the fingertips.

"Bank the fire," she answered in a trembling voice and watched him do her bidding, love and longing sweeping through her with the intensity of the blizzard outside.

Hand in hand, they climbed the stairs. At the door to her bedroom, Ranse bent to brush her lips with his. "Good night, love." His voice was ragged with desire, his whole body taut with the effort to control and deny.

Kathleen opened the door, drew him inside, and slid the bolt.

"We mustn't . . ." Ranse's voice trailed off as her mouth covered his. Her arms tightened about his neck as she pressed hungrily against him. "Oh, God!" he muttered against her lips. Then he took her in a fierce embrace, his mouth claiming hers in a devouring kiss.

"Love me," she begged breathlessly, breaking their kiss. "I need you so, darling. Please . . . love me."

"Kath . . . darlin'." She stilled his protest with her lips, her hands unbuttoning his wool shirt.

In the icy bedroom, lit only by the small lamp she had carried upstairs, they undressed quickly. Between blankets warmed by the hot brick Tessie had placed there earlier, they turned to each other with an urgency that could not be denied.

Enveloped in the wild and feverish joy of loving, there were no words, only murmured names, soft gasps of pleasure. No world existed beyond this dim room, beyond this bed where they lay together at last.

Ranse's hands moved over her body, caressing, quickening her responses. His mouth claimed hers passionately, opening to a new and deeper closeness. Her breasts seemed to pulsate at the touch of his lips and fingertips. Beneath her own touch, she felt his flesh respond even as she reveled in the sensation of his muscular body enveloping hers. When they came together, the light of the lamp spun into star-shattered darkness. Her cry of fulfillment was smothered by Ranse's devouring kiss. Then he groaned, and she whimpered with joy at the rapturous sensation as he burst inside her.

Bodies entwined, they lay for a long time, slowly spiraling down from heights of incredible ecstasy.

"Kath," he said at last, turning on his side, but holding her hips against him so that he remained inside her. "My darlin', my love."

Embracing his hip with her leg, she tried to prolong their joining, wishing never to be parted from him. "Dear love," she murmured against his throat. "I've missed you so . . . wanted you so."

"I know." Gently smoothing back her tangled hair, he smiled at her. Turning on his back, he pillowed her head on his shoulder, one hand gently caressing her bare arm, the other hand cupping her breast. With a sigh, he added, "Even Wyoming winters don't last forever, Kath."

"We'll be married as soon as we can get to Cheyenne, won't we?"

"When spring comes." Ranse pressed his mouth against her forehead.

There was a silence in the room, the flame of the lamp

fluttering softly, the wind rattling at the windows. "Whose picture?" Ranse asked suddenly.

Kathleen opened her eyes, for she had been drifting on the edge of satiated sleep. In the dim glow of the lamp, the miniature of Fiona looked back at them. "My mother," she answered and found herself wondering if Mama had felt this same incredible happiness in the arms of her lost lover.

Unexpectedly, Ranse rose from the bed, stepped over to pick up the miniature. As she watched him standing there nude, studying the picture, Kathleen felt desire pulsate through her again. "You'll freeze. Come back to bed." Passion thickened the sound of her voice.

"You're like her," he answered, looking up from the portrait, as though comparing her with Fiona, "except for the coloring." He sat the miniature back, and smiled. "And you are more beautiful."

"Ranse," she chided, with a smile. "You're suffering from frostbite. Come here."

With a soft laugh he turned, his glance falling on the prayer book lying beside the miniature. "What's this?"

"Come here!" she demanded, aching now to hold that hard male body in her arms.

Setting the lamp on the bedside table, he slipped into bed still holding the prayer book. Kathleen took it from him, drawing him close to give her warmth to his cold body. His mouth found hers in a long kiss, and she felt him stirring with desire.

"The book?" he asked again, taking it from the table where she had placed it and opening the pages. At once, it fell open to the marriage ceremony where the flowers had been pressed for so many years.

"It was my mother's," she told him, drawing the blankets up about their shoulders. "The flowers were there when my grandmother gave it to me." Filled with a faint sadness for what Fiona had lost, and all that she had in the man who lay beside her, Kathleen murmured, "Perhaps her lover gave them to her before she had to marry Papa."

"It's the marriage ceremony," Ranse said, still studying the small book. And he began to read the words in a low, emotional voice.

As naturally as though she had rehearsed the words,

Kathleen made her responses. There in the pale lamplight, with wind and snow clawing at the windows, she looked at the dark-haired man bent over the words in the prayer book, lifting his head to look at her with burning eyes each time he sought her reply. It seemed a moment suspended in time, a ceremony preordained, complete and binding in itself.

When Ranse read the last words, he placed the book on the table and turned to take her in his arms. The dark eyes gleamed with moisture as he held her, looking into her face.

"My wife." The words in his deep, tender voice seemed fraught with truth and love everlasting.

"My husband," she answered, and gave herself to him with her whole heart.

·◦⊃I CHAPTER 29 I⊂◦·

It was the cruelest winter in Wyoming memory. Even after the great blizzard passed, the country remained locked in an icy cold. Unable to paw through the deep snow to scant feed, cattle drifted before the bitter winds, huddled together to die in the coulees and ravines, or piled against the southern fences where they had drifted in their aimless search for food.

All across Wyoming, men were forced to keep to the ranch houses for weeks, as bitter cold and high winds scourged the range. From beyond the corrals came the piteous bawling of dying cattle. Cowhands sat in grim silence, sick with their inability to prevent the tragedy. Old-timers talked of another chinook, but it never came.

Furious March winds piled snow in huge drifts. Wyoming remained in the icy grip of arctic weather until the second week of March at last brought relief. The sun came out, weak and pale in the cloud-filmed skies. Slowly, little by little, the countryside warmed. Melting snow ran in rivulets from beneath the snow drifts. Icicles edging the roofs dripped in a slow cadence.

"What's that I can smell?" Edward asked as he and Kathleen picked their way across the ranch yard. He had brought his cane only because the paths were slick with mud. They both wore heavy coats, even though the sun was bright. Their feet were clad in gum boots, with Kathleen's skirt tucked into the tops of hers.

In response to his question, Kathleen lifted her head. On the cold breeze there came a faintly sweet, sickening odor.

She shook her head. "We'll ask Ranse," she replied, catching sight of him coming from the bunkhouse.

"Dead cows," Ranse replied grimly to Edward's question. "I'm going out this morning with some of the boys to see how bad it is." His eyes met Kathleen's over Edward's head. Her heart jumped in response to the longing in those dark eyes. Since the night of the blizzard, their relationship had returned to fierce embraces and stolen kisses. The strain of that denial was there in his yearning face, and in the way her body leaped and pulsated at his look.

"Isn't it like this every year?" Edward asked, breaking the spell. "Papa said that's why it's such a profitable business, the cattle take care of themselves, winter and summer. The owners only have to gather and ship them as they increase."

Ranse gave him a rueful smile. "You sound like you'd memorized the prospectus for British and Far West Cattle Company. Sucker bait."

"What?" Kathleen gave him a puzzled frown.

Ranse grimaced and shrugged, reaching into his pocket for cigarette makings. "The great American cattle boom is over. The truth is, it never existed." He lifted his head and sniffed at the nauseating scent that hung in the air. "You can smell it now . . . the end of an era."

Troubled, Kathleen watched him light his cigarette. "Is the winter always like this?"

Blowing smoke into the air as though to dispel the odor, Ranse replied, "It was the worst winter in history, after a dry summer. Feed was short and the range overstocked." For a long moment, he studied his cigarette in morose silence. "Greed destroys most things, and now it's destroyed the cattle business."

"Ready, boss?" Three cowboys came from the stables, leading saddled horses including Ranse's bay, Hawk.

He nodded, taking the horse's reins. Ready to mount, he looked back at Kathleen. "I'll report to Lord Hadley as soon as we get back."

"Come have supper with us," she urged.

From his saddle, Ranse grinned down at her, giving a half salute. The dark eyes probing hers shook her as though he had touched her in the act of love.

Unexpectedly, Papa stayed fairly sober, for he was busy

planning his return to England, yelling at Perkins to get on with the packing, calling Mrs. Sanders into his study to give instructions for closing the house.

"The sooner we leave this bloody country, the better," he muttered, watching Sandy dismantle the sitting-room bed Edward had used all winter. "Living like peasants . . ." He moved off toward his study, still mumbling imprecations against Wyoming life.

A faint chill of apprehension ran down Kathleen's spine when Tessie came to say Lord Hadley wished her to begin packing the young lady's things. Shrugging off the feeling, she led Tessie upstairs to her room, telling herself that she must pack anyway to go away with Ranse, or even to move across the yard to his cabin. In her heart, she was certain that Papa would dismiss Ranse at once, and the apprehension returned as she wondered how the marriage was to be arranged over Papa's opposition.

Ranse's grim face at the supper table did nothing to allay her fears. However, Papa simply refused to discuss business at the table and cut Ranse off whenever he tried. When they had finished and Tessie was clearing the table, Papa strode off to his study, carrying a nearly empty bottle of claret and his glass. Kathleen gave Ranse a warning look, hoping he was aware how much wine Papa had consumed.

Almost at once, Papa's voice echoed from the study, loud and angry. "You bloody fool, how can you say we've lost 90% of the cattle? That's impossible."

"Step outside, Your Lordship." Ranse's voice was cold and contemptuous. "You can smell the loss. Every ravine is piled with dead carcasses. The cattle still alive are nothing but walking skeletons. It's been a long bitter winter, with no feed."

"It's not true!" Papa shouted, an edge of panic in his voice.

"It's true," came Ranse's grim reply. "British and Far West Cattle Company is broke, unless the investors can come up with enough money to restock the range."

"You know damn well that's impossible," Papa raged. "There was trouble when we paid only 20% last year."

Still sitting at the table, Kathleen and Edward pointedly avoided each other's eyes, ashamed for Papa's behavior.

"It was always a gamble," Ranse replied coolly. "Too many gamblers got into the game, and now the bubble's burst. You'll have to get out . . . and cut your losses as best you can."

"It's my hide they'll have," Papa bellowed. "It can't be as bad as you say. You're using the weather to cover your incompetent management."

"You son of a bitch," Ranse growled. "Only because of Edward, I'll help you get on your way back to England, and then I'm done with the whole rotten mess." He paused at the doorway to add, "Kathleen stays with me."

"Not bloody likely," Papa roared. When Ranse ignored him, stamping down the hallway angrily, he added, "You cheeky bastard!"

Quickly, Kathleen rose from the table, catching up with Ranse at the doorway, where he was pulling on his heavy leather coat. "Ranse, what's going to happen?"

In reply, he took a heavy shawl from the hall tree, wrapped it about her and drew her outside with him, closing the door behind them. His arms closed around her, warm against the cold night wind that chilled her face and ruffled her hair. Their mouths met hungrily in a kiss that left her breathless with longing.

Ranse held her close, her face pressed against his shoulder, one big hand smoothing her hair gently. "It'll be all right, honey." His mouth was warm against her cold forehead. "The old boy should be ready to leave by day after tomorrow. I'll take him into Cheyenne and put him and Edward on the train. You and me . . ." he held her away to give her a conspiratorial smile . . . "we'll find ourselves a justice of the peace." He sobered. "If that's still what you want."

"More than anything." She looked up into his face, barely visible in the darkness, her heart wild in her chest at the love glowing from his dark eyes. "I love you, Ranse."

Again his mouth claimed hers, his arms holding her fiercely against his tall strong body. With waves of desire pounding through her blood, Kathleen wondered, should she tell him now? No, she wasn't really sure. It was scarcely two months since the night of the great blizzard, and yet she was as sure as she had ever been of anything that Ranse O'Neil's child lay in her womb.

"I'll be riding out again tomorrow," his deep voice scattered her thoughts. "Need to cover territory we didn't get to today. I'll make a written report to the board of directors myself." His mouth twisted in a bitter grimace. "His Lordship will no doubt lay the whole disaster on my head."

"He can't do that," she protested.

"No matter, sweet Kath," he grinned and drew her close again. "Folks in Wyoming know my reputation, and I'm not likely to court any favors in England."

Looking out across the empty landscape, Ranse shook his head in despair. The horse picked its way along ridges where the snow had melted off, avoiding the drifts piled in every coulee and against every outcropping. Above, the sky was a dull cold gray, and the wind had a bite to it. Today, he'd ridden far from the ranch, hoping against hope to find some of the cattle herd sheltered in a draw. Instead, he found the draws filled with dead and rotting carcasses. Ahead of him now, his eyes took in a piece of fence left by some departed homesteader. Piled against it were dead cattle who had drifted southward before the storms, halted in the blind whiteness to die against a fence.

It was a sight to sicken the strongest heart. Ranse pulled his neckerchief up over his face, trying to shut the stench out of his nostrils. This was a disaster unlike any the West had ever known. The end of an era, he told himself. Never again could men convince themselves they could simply turn domestic cattle out on the range to fend for themselves in Wyoming's bitter winters. Cattle would have to be fed in winter, as saddle horses had always been cared for.

Spurring Hawk, he moved off toward some distant forms dark against the snow and sagebrush. Hunched in his jacket against the cold wind, he thought of Kathleen, so warm and yielding in his arms last night, her mouth responding passionately to his. God, how he'd wanted to take her to his bed and love her.

Suddenly, he grinned. Tomorrow night, they'd be in

Cheyenne, married and lying together in a hotel room . . . loving. His loins stirred at his thoughts.

Would she be happy here? He didn't want to think of that, didn't dare. She loved him, he knew that, and she wanted to be with him. He'd make her happy, and he could give her a good life. This awful disaster on the range had a good side. There'd be ranches for sale now . . . cheap . . . and he'd saved his money. They'd find a place, one she liked, and they'd restock it with cattle, build a home, have children, make a life together.

Filled with a wild unreasoning joy at his thoughts, Ranse spurred Hawk into a gallop. Those dark figures in the distance were moving. They might be cattle, still alive, in need of help.

Happiness poured through him. Tomorrow Kathleen would be his wife, tomorrow they'd be together forever. Jerking off his hat, he whipped it against Hawk's withers, shouting his delight into the cold wind.

Beneath him, the horse lurched, squealed in pain and stumbled. Unseated, Ranse fought empty air as Hawk rolled over and fell on him. His own cry of pain was sharp and startling in his ears. The dead weight of the horse lay on his lower body, pinning him to the rocky ground. Wild with pain, Hawk thrashed about, dragging Ranse with him in his struggles. Dimly, Ranse was aware of the rocky ground crumbling beneath them. Then they were falling, tumbling down the side of the ravine. Gray sky, gray snow, gray rocks . . . all dissolved into blackness.

CHAPTER 30

"The boys say Ranse ain't come back yet." Sandy brushed the moisture from his wide-brimmed hat. Icy air swept through the kitchen door, and in the dusk beyond, a cold sleet blew on the wind.

Mrs. Sanders frowned. "That ain't like him."

At the kitchen table, where she had been drinking coffee with Mrs. Sanders, Kathleen felt a sharp stab of fear. A moment ago, this kitchen had seemed so warm and comfortable. Certain that Ranse would be coming to the house as soon as he'd packed his things, she'd sat here talking with Mrs. Sanders about their departure. She hadn't mentioned her own plans . . . that tomorrow night she and Ranse would be married, in each other's arms in a hotel room in Cheyenne. Beyond that, she hadn't thought or planned, trusting Ranse for plans. This morning when she awakened, she'd been dizzy, with a faint sense of nausea in the pit of her stomach. The feeling passed quickly, leaving her elated and certain, anxious to share with Ranse the knowledge that their love had created a new life.

But now, anxiety tightened about her. "Why would he be so late?" she asked Sandy, who stood warming himself at the stove.

"Might have ridden farther than he intended," Sandy replied.

Turning from the stove, he met her frightened eyes. "Don't worry, Miss. Ranse knows this country. If he can't get back here tonight, he'll find a place to hole up out of the storm." He exchanged significant looks with his wife.

They all know, Kathleen thought, trying to smother the fear for Ranse that was gripping her throat, they all know about Ranse and me. Mrs. Sanders patted her shoulder comfortingly. "He'll be ridin' in here in the morning, big as you please. Just wait and see."

"Mr. Sanders?" Perkins appeared in the kitchen doorway, fluttering about uneasily. "His Lordship wishes to know if the storm will postpone his departure tomorrow."

"I'd say so," Sandy replied. "This wet sleet will turn the roads to mud . . . and they'd just started to dry out." He frowned at the older man. "Anyway, he ought to hang around until Ranse gets back. Better tell him that."

Perkins looked so appalled at the thought of telling Lord Hadley such a thing that Kathleen smiled wryly to herself.

"Supper's ready," Mrs. Sanders announced, pulling a beef roast from the oven of the big iron stove. She gave Kathleen a commiserating glance, then looked affectionately at Sandy. "You live scared a lot when your man's a cowboy," she said.

Sandy grinned at her. "Ranse'll be all right," he said, reaching over to pat Kathleen's hand. "He's the best hand in Wyoming, and he knows what he's doin'."

In spite of the Sanderses' assurances, she could not rest. All through the night, fear was a tight band about her chest. She tossed restlessly, listening to the rattle of wet sleet blown against the windows. Toward dawn, she finally fell into an exhausted sleep, only to awaken weeping from a vague dream filled with pain and death.

The storm slackened off next morning, but the skies were still low and gray with a cold wind blowing. Papa was furious at the delay in his departure, and even more furious at Ranse's absence.

"Blasted Americans . . . no sense of responsibility," he muttered, stomping to the sideboard to fill his glass with port. They'd only just finished breakfast, and Papa had started drinking already.

"If Ranse is delayed, there's a good reason," Kathleen protested.

"The bloody bastard's run out," Papa growled, staring at her. "He's put the company in bankruptcy, and he couldn't face it." His face twisted in an ugly sneer. "And he had the cheek to want to marry my daughter!"

"I am going to marry Ranse," Kathleen said, lifting her chin and staring into her father's eyes. "I won't be going back to England at all."

"You'll do as I say, you silly slut," Papa's voice rose. Behind her, Kathleen heard Edward gasp. She wished he hadn't come into the room, wished he need never know the kind of man who had fathered him.

"Your foul language won't change my mind, Papa. Ranse is an honorable man. He's asked me to be his wife, and we'll be married before you leave for England."

"Bitch!" His hand flashed out so quickly she could not avoid the blow that sent her reeling backward.

"Papa!" Edward flew across the room, pushing his father, pounding at his chest with doubled fists. Startled, off-balance, Papa dropped his wineglass. A scarlet stain spread on the white of the Navajo rug.

"Don't, Edward." One hand held against her painfully stinging cheek, she reached out with the other to grab Edward's arm. "He's drunk again." And she pulled the boy from the room with her.

"Bitch!" Papa shouted again.

Kathleen could hear the gurgle of wine being poured from the decanter. Her cheek burned where her father had struck her, but inside she felt cold as ice. Papa was a cruel and selfish man. Even when she was young and tried to love him, she had known that. Something in her own pain reached out to the long-dead Fiona, forced to marry this cold, unfeeling man she could never love. Tears stung her eyes with the certainty that the young Irishman had been a man like Ranse O'Neil.

"Everybody's gone out to look for Ranse," Edward told her, as they stood in the foyer donning their coats and boots.

"Sandy's sure he's all right," Kathleen replied, determined to force down the growing doubt that was as painful as her bruised face.

"He'll probably come riding in while they're looking for him," Edward said, confidently.

They walked beneath a sky filled with clouds breaking up,

blowing eastward on the wind. The ugly odor of rotting flesh was pervasive, and they tied their scarves about their faces to shut it out.

"You want to ride?" Edward asked, and she nodded, thankful to be free of the house, needing to do something, anything, to escape the weight of dread that seemed to grow with each passing hour.

Last night's wet storm had broken the ice on Cybille Creek. It roared and ground over the stones in the creek bed with the rush of water freed from winter's grip. Picking their way carefully along the bare banks of the creek, they rode in silence. They would not come this way again, Kathleen thought. Edward would be far away in England, at school in Harrow. She would be with Ranse. She forced down the fear nibbling at her mind. "Our own place," he'd said. Determinedly, she pushed her thoughts toward that place. Not a tiny room like the foreman's cabin, nor a place as huge as the ranch house, but a house filled with love and the sound of their child's voice. Tears spilled from her eyes, hot against her cold face.

"He's all right, Kathleen." Edward was regarding her with wide compassionate eyes. "He'll be here soon, and we'll have your wedding in Cheyenne."

"Yes," she murmured, loving Edward for caring, but fear enveloped her still, as pervasive as the stench of dead cattle.

"We'd better turn back." Edward pulled Blackie to a halt and looked questioningly at Kathleen.

Lifting her head, she stared up at the chalky cliffs of the Chugwater. Ranse's story of the Indian maiden who was denied her love filled her mind. Had she lost her love too, like the Indian girl and like her mother? Was it a kind of black fate following the women of her family that to love someone meant to bring disaster upon him? But for her, Ranse would have quit his job here long ago. He'd be safe somewhere . . . another ranch, anywhere but Cybille Creek.

Part of the searching party had returned when they rode back into the ranch yard. "No sign," they said, avoiding her eyes. "It's clearing up. We'll search again tomorrow."

But the next day's search was equally fruitless, and the day after that, and the day after, until Papa angrily called it off. Putting Bradley in charge, he demanded that the buck-boards be made ready to take him into Cheyenne tomorrow.

In her room, surrounded by her trunks and bags, Kathleen wept herself into exhaustion.

"Kathleen." Mrs. Sanders closed the door softly behind her. Sitting down on the bed, she laid her big capable hand on Kathleen's heaving shoulders.

Hope leaped in her as she turned to face Mrs. Sanders. "Did they find him?"

"No, hon." Mrs. Sanders shook her head sadly. Drawing Kathleen into her arms, she held her as she wept against the woman's stout shoulder. "Now, now," she soothed, stroking Kathleen's hair. "It's hard, I know. We all guessed how you and Ranse felt about each other. Sandy finally wormed it out of him that you meant to marry."

"He's dead, isn't he?" Kathleen interrupted, lifting her head to look into the sad broad face.

"We don't know that." Mrs. Sanders sighed, patting Kathleen's back. "But, Sandy says . . ." Her voice broke.

"What?" Kathleen demanded, her whole world poised on the answer.

"Ranse ain't the kind of man to run out on a job, and he sure wouldn't have run out on you, honey . . ." Her voice fell, and Kathleen watched the tears well and spill over from Mrs. Sanders's pale eyes.

"Sandy thinks he's dead, then?" Pain was building inside her, devouring her.

"Likely." Mrs. Sanders nodded, wiping her wet face.

"Oh, God!" The pain exploded. Her very heart seemed torn from her chest, as though a part of her must die with her love. It was a pain too deep for tears.

Dazed, she allowed Mrs. Sanders to help her undress, pull on her nightgown and get into bed.

"Would you like some brandy?" the woman asked then. When Kathleen shook her head, she looked sadly down at her. "Try to sleep, honey. Your pa says you're leaving tomorrow early."

Alone, Kathleen stared dry-eyed at the small lamp left burning on the bureau, stunned with the agony of loss. He was dead . . . the man she loved more than life . . . who had given her the only true happiness she had ever known. She wanted to die too, let life end now with him. But his child lay in her womb, his legacy doubly precious now.

"Mama," she cried to the miniature on the bureau. "Dear Mama, what must I do . . . where can I turn? Oh, Mama, if only you were here!"

When they checked into the Plains Hotel late next day, there was a message from Charles Vickers inviting them for supper. Kathleen had endured the miserable trip over muddy roads in dazed silence. A concerned Edward held her hand, while she sat numb with pain, unable to speak or think or make a decision. The stench of rotting carcasses piled in the ravines even permeated Cheyenne.

Bitter over the collapse of his hoped-for cattle empire, Papa intended to avoid the other cattlemen at the Cheyenne Club. They would be on the morning train eastbound, he said, and leave this godforsaken land behind them forever.

Forever. The word echoed in Kathleen's mind. She had meant to be with Ranse forever, all their tomorrows a glowing time of endless love. Now, forever meant death and loss and emptiness.

Sitting at Dr. Vickers's dining table, she picked at her food, staring into space, contributing to the conversation only when asked a direct question. Charles Vickers had been saddened by the report of Ranse's death. "He was a good man," he said. The words had such a ring of finality, Kathleen could barely maintain her composure.

Michael Fraser joined the dinner party, attempting to lighten the atmosphere by telling amusing anecdotes about his struggle to adjust to the disorder of the state attorney's office of Wyoming.

When Rachel cleared the table, returning to set a bottle of brandy on the table, Kathleen rose to leave the men to their after-dinner brandy and cigars. Glancing back, she saw Edward whispering urgently to Charles. As she stepped into the sitting room where a fire glowed in the iron fireplace, she heard Charles behind her.

"Edward says you've not been well, Kathleen. He wants me to check you out before you leave on your long journey home." Charles smiled, his dark eyes warm and kind.

Tears stung her eyes. "He's a sweet boy, but . . ."

"Come along." He took her arm to lead her toward his office in the front of the house. "It won't take long."

Seated opposite him, on the dark leather examining chair, Kathleen watched him pressing his stethoscope to her chest. Taking his hand, she pushed him away.

"I'm pregnant, Charles."

He sat back, regarding her in silence for a long moment. There was no censure in his kindly face. At last he sighed, and asked, "Ranse?"

She nodded, fighting the tears. "We were going to be married before Papa left for England. He'd saved the money to buy a ranch of his own. We'd planned . . ." Her voice broke as she bowed her head, dissolving into tears.

Charles laid the stethoscope aside, taking both her hands in his. "What will you do, Kathleen?"

"I don't know," she sobbed. "I can't stay here. Papa won't allow it. In England, I'll be disgraced forever. Papa will be furious, and Deborah will never forgive me."

Charles drew in his breath in a deep sigh. "I can persuade your father that you're not well enough to leave. We can do an abortion, and after a few days' rest you'll be able to travel."

Aghast, Kathleen stared at him. "No!" she cried. "No! Don't you see, Charles? This is Ranse's baby . . . all I'll ever have of him now. I won't give it up, no matter what."

"No matter the disgrace . . . no matter how you must live and bring up this child?" Charles asked gently.

"No matter," she affirmed. The compassion in his face brought fresh tears.

"You must have some kind of plan, Kathleen. Think of the child growing up branded a bastard." He held her hands tightly in his, looking into her eyes.

"I haven't been able to plan," she said, trying desperately to stop weeping. "All I could think of was Ranse being dead."

Charles fell silent, seeming deep in thought, his hands still clasping hers. "If you'll allow me," he began at last, "I may have a solution."

Kathleen looked into his kindly face, feeling for the first time a glimmer of hope.

"I'm very fond of you, Kathleen. You are a wonderful young lady. Perhaps you'd consider marrying me to give your child a name."

She gasped at the unexpectedness of his offer. "But I don't love you, Charles," she murmured sadly.

"That's of no consequence," he answered briskly. "We're considering the child here. Furthermore," he added with a smile, "I think I might enjoy having a lovely young person like you to grace my home."

Tears poured down her face, as she stared at him in disbelief.

"Don't worry, dear Kathleen." He patted her hand again. "I won't make any demands on you as a husband. We'll be merely friends . . . housemates, as it were."

"You are so dear and kind, Charles," she said in a low voice. "How can I take advantage of you?"

"Take advantage, my dear?" He smiled deep into her eyes. "I shall have the child I'd never have otherwise, dear Kathleen, the child of a man I admired. Perhaps it is I who's taking advantage."

Relief poured through her. It was a solution after all, unexpected, but certainly one she could live with. "Yes," she said softly, "I'll marry you, Charles."

As they walked together back down the dim hallway, she turned to him. "If Papa is terribly drunk, please, let's not tell him tonight. I don't want a scene."

Fortunately, Charles agreed, for it was necessary that he and Michael half-carry Papa to the carriage where Bill was waiting to drive them back to the hotel.

Alone in her room, Kathleen prepared for bed, glad that her months in America had taught her to do without the ministrations of a maid. Tonight, she wanted no one, as she attempted to quiet the turmoil raging inside her. She had lost Ranse, and grief tore through her again at the thought. Would there always be this raw pain inside her, as though a part of her own body had been torn away? Now, she had promised to marry a man she didn't love . . . but Charles was kind, and life with him would be far better than life at Hadley Hall, even if Deborah would allow her to stay there with her illegitimate child.

There was a knock at her door, and Kathleen sighed. It

would surely be the solicitous Edward checking up on her. She would have to tell him about Charles, even though she needed time alone to assimilate all that had happened this evening.

She opened the door to stare in shock at a pale and distraught Michael Fraser.

"Let me in," he demanded abruptly. "I have to talk to you."

"Do you realize the time, Mr. Fraser?" she asked in as severe a tone as she could muster. "And I'm alone here."

"I don't care," he said in a hard voice. Pushing her back, he stepped inside and closed the door behind him.

"Charles says he's going to marry you," he began without preamble.

"He asked me tonight," she replied, "and I agreed." She stared at him, horrified by the realization that Michael Fraser had been weeping.

"I won't allow it," he cried, an edge of desperation in his voice.

"That's Charles's decision." She stepped farther away from him, suddenly frightened by his behavior.

"You don't understand. He's doing it because he feels sorry for you."

"I know," she answered softly. "But I will be good to him and try to make him happy."

"You can never make him happy," Michael replied, his voice low and bitter. "You can't marry him and ruin his life . . . and mine." He grasped her arm tightly as though to emphasize his words.

"I don't understand . . ." His hand was tight on her arm, hurting her.

"Charles and I are lovers." Ignoring her horrified gasp, he continued. "We have been since we met at Harvard just before Charles finished medical school. He came out here to Wyoming, and I followed him. We've found a home here, a haven where no one knows or judges us." Grabbing her shoulders, he shook her roughly. "I won't let you ruin it for your own selfish reasons."

As suddenly as he had grabbed her, Michael released her. Slumping into a chair, he put his face in his hands and wept.

Kathleen stared down at the weeping man, a hot, sick

feeling clogging her throat. Charles and Michael . . . and she felt the bile rise. She was not so innocent that she hadn't heard of such things, but surely not Charles . . . It was true of course, or Michael wouldn't be so distraught.

Beyond the horror of his revelation, compassion welled in Kathleen's heart. Michael could not bear to lose his love, nor did she wish to be the cause of that loss.

Gently, she laid her hand on Michael's shoulder. "Go back to Charles," she said softly, as tears spilled from her eyes. Her own life was in a shambles, but no matter how she or the world might judge these two men, she was certain now that marrying Charles would only ruin other lives, perhaps even that of her child. "Tell him I said it won't work. I'll be leaving for England on the morning train."

The skies were as gray and ugly as they had been that day almost a year ago when she first stepped off the train into Wyoming. There were the same drab buildings, the same Indians begging, the same motley crowd milling about the station platform. A whistle sounded, and the train began to move. Seated beside the window, with Edward sitting opposite, Kathleen watched the station slip away behind them. Miles of gray sagebrush, still clotted with snow, lay ahead . . . as bleak as all her tomorrows. Wyoming was yesterday now . . . and lost forever.

CHAPTER 31

Brookfield, England, 1887

At first, it seemed that nothing had changed at Hadley Hall. The same stiff coachman met them at the station. Deborah greeted them at home in the drawing room, kissing Edward and remarking on how he had grown, with a cool kiss on the cheek for Kathleen. She gave her husband a decorous peck, watching him warily as though to assess his mood.

But the little girls seemed to have forgotten them, and now there was Thomas squalling in the nursery. It soon became apparent that Deborah herself had changed. She had a new assertiveness, and Kathleen guessed that she had thoroughly enjoyed being in full charge of the estate. How much in charge became clear when Papa realized she had sold off half his horses and most of the hounds. The entire staff could hear the quarrel that ensued, ending with the sound of Papa slapping Deborah as he demanded she keep her place.

What both Papa and Edward had considered *mal de mer* on the rough ocean crossing did not cease, and Kathleen found there was one person from whom she could not conceal her misery.

"You're pregnant, ain't you?" Francine asked, as she removed the basin to leave Kathleen pale and shaking in her bed.

The tears she had kept to herself for so long sprang from her eyes. Memories of Ranse and the love they had shared filled her with such pain she could scarcely bear it.

Francine sat down on the bed, gathering Kathleen into her plump arms. "Dearie, you can tell Frannie all about it."

Held in the comforting embrace of her one friend in all

the world, Kathleen poured out the story between broken sobs.

"Ah, poor love," Francine murmured, patting her mistress's shoulder. "I know your heart is broken, but we must decide what to do now."

"I've written to Aunt Elizabeth," Kathleen told her, wiping her eyes and trying to control her weeping. "She'll let me come for a visit, and after I'm in London, surely she'll help me find a place." Meeting Francine's sad eyes, she flung her arms about the girl. "You'll go with me, won't you?"

Tears rolled down Francine's plump face. "I'll never leave you, Miss Kathleen . . . not ever."

The dinner party for Edward's tenth birthday, prior to his departure for Harrow, was as joyless as most such occasions were at Hadley Hall. There were birthday gifts for Kathleen too, since it was her twentieth birthday, but it was Edward's day. His mother had made it so. Aunt Martha and Uncle Bertram were in attendance, both old and crochety, poor Uncle Bertram suffering now from some form of palsy, which annoyed his wife to distraction.

"Perhaps you should forgo the cake," Deborah said to Kathleen when the footman bore in the lighted birthday cake. "You certainly put on weight in Wyoming. Didn't she, Robert?"

Papa merely growled an answer. The mention of Wyoming always put him in a foul mood, Deborah should have sense enough to see that. When they'd arrived home, he'd been called down to London immediately by the board of directors for British and Far West Cattle Company. An accounting was demanded before the company declared bankruptcy. Kathleen knew Papa had blamed the company's financial disaster on Ranse's management as well as the fierce Wyoming weather. Holmes, the agent, had been here to confer with Papa, and the word "retrench" had been heard over and over.

"Blast it all," she heard Papa tell Holmes as the man departed. "I have a rich wife. To hell with your retrenchment."

So now they were living on Deborah's money, a fact she

never missed an opportunity to remind them of. She and Martha had quarreled over the subject before dinner. "Don't be so common, Deborah," Martha had said, and the two of them had marched into the dining room glaring at each other.

If only she'd hear from Aunt Elizabeth, Kathleen thought, as toasts were drunk to Edward. Deborah was right. The weight she was gaining was becoming obvious, and her condition could not be hidden much longer. Surely dear, kind Aunt Elizabeth would find a way to help her.

"Kathleen!" Deborah's sharp tones echoed across the table. "Mr. Sturgis was speaking to you."

With a sigh, Kathleen turned to the man seated beside her. "Sorry," she murmured politely, recoiling from the odor of his breath as he bent near her. Papa and Deborah had invited Griffin Sturgis for reasons all too obvious. They meant to marry her off to this ancient lecher.

Having buried two wives, he was in the market for a third. And having vast inherited land holdings, he had no need to look for a dowry. He was a jowly red-faced man, with thinning gray hair and sharp hard eyes which watched her with barely concealed lust. Feeling his knee press hers beneath the table, Kathleen moved away from him.

"I was asking if you'd care to ride with me tomorrow, Miss Kathleen," he said. Papa and Deborah watched expectantly.

"I'm afraid I've other plans, Mr. Sturgis," she answered, ignoring Papa's glare. "Perhaps another time."

A sense of desperation settled over her. When the dinner party finally ended, she sighed with relief. Papa, Mr. Sturgis, and Uncle Bertram were left to brandy and cigars. Avoiding her stepmother, who certainly meant to chastise her for not being more amenable to Mr. Sturgis, she hurried out to the stables, following Edward.

Tomorrow, he'd be off to Harrow with the new valet Papa had hired, and this might be their last chance to say goodbye in private.

"I didn't want to go to summer term, Kathleen," the boy said morosely, when she came upon him slumped on a bench beneath an elm tree in the upper garden.

"I know, dear." Sitting down beside him, she took his

hand in hers. When they would meet again, she could not guess, for she must go away from here, and her heart ached for this new loss. "Papa said you are too far behind after all those months in Wyoming. This will give you a chance to catch up with other boys your age."

"I'll miss you so." Tears started in Edward's eyes, and he leaned into her embrace, breaking into sobs. "Ranse is dead, Kathleen . . . he's dead."

It was the first time Edward had been able to acknowledge this awful truth. Trying to control her own pain, she held the boy close, her tears falling on his bright head pressed against her shoulder.

"Now, I'll lose you, too," he sobbed, looking imploringly into her face.

"You'll never lose me, dearest Edward." Smoothing back his rumpled hair, she tried to smile. "We're twins, remember? And twins can never really be parted."

"I'll see you when I come home on holiday between terms, won't I?"

He was too young to share the desperate secret she carried, too young to know that they must part now, perhaps forever. "I'll always write you, Edward. You won't lose me any more than you really lost Ranse. Please, dear . . ." Unable to control her feelings, she hugged him close and wept. At last, the pain subsided. She held Edward away, looking into his beloved young face. "Always remember the things Ranse taught you about being a man, and that way you'll never lose him. He'll be a part of you."

Edward nodded, reaching up to gently wipe the tears from her cheek. "When we say goodbye tomorrow, Kathleen, it won't really be goodbye. It'll be like the cowboys always said . . . 'so long.' Just 'so long' until we're together again."

"Yes, Edward," she lied and fiercely held him close to her.

There was a letter from James when the coachman brought the post from the village after he'd taken Edward to the train. Because she was in the foyer alone, Kathleen was able to conceal it from Deborah, and she ran upstairs to her room to open it.

Half the morning, she had wept over Edward's departure. Now, a new freshet of tears burst forth. Aunt Elizabeth had died last winter, James wrote in his fine precise hand. He was sorry she hadn't been informed. He and Serena and their two daughters were living now in the elegant Burnham House. They'd be delighted to have her come for a visit if her father would allow it. It had been far too long, and he would certainly never forget that because of her he'd found his adorable wife.

So Aunt Elizabeth was gone . . . and with her Kathleen's only hope of escape. How could she go to James and Serena and bring disgrace on them and their children? Never . . . never . . . Her mind raced in wild and desperate circles, searching for an answer. Certainly not Mr. Sturgis, for he'd soon know he'd been cuckolded, and the disgrace would be worse for having to marry such a man.

"Perhaps if you told Deborah, she'd give you the money to go away to spare herself the scandal," Francine offered when Kathleen confided her dashed hopes.

"I wouldn't take anything from her," Kathleen protested vehemently.

"Well, consider it," replied the practical Francine. "I've a little saved, but it wouldn't take us far."

"Us?" Kathleen asked, and received a hug in reply.

A disconsolate Kathleen wandered slowly downstairs late the next day. Early this morning, she'd been awakened by hounds and horses as Papa and Mr. Sturgis departed to hunt on the Sturgis estate.

As she passed the library, she saw a stranger sitting there, obviously waiting. She'd seen the hired trap from the village passing down the drive earlier.

The man glanced up, a trim and proper city man, she guessed. "Are you waiting for someone?" she asked.

"Lord Hadley," the man replied.

"Did someone tell you he's hunting and won't be home until late?" she asked, wondering where in the world Deborah had gone.

"I'll wait," came the reply in businesslike tones. "I'm Mr. Babcock, his solicitor from London, and it's important I see him about the Irish estate."

"Then you've had a long trip," she said, smiling politely as she concealed her curiosity. Papa owned no Irish estate. It had been her grandparents' and surely had gone to someone in the Browne family. "I'll have some tea brought for you."

He sighed and seemed to unbend slightly. "I'd be delighted."

When the maid had brought the ample tea she ordered, she sat down with Mr. Babcock, determined to ferret out the mystery of Papa's Irish estate. She asked for a bottle of claret, and kept the solicitor's glass well-filled.

"I was unaware Lord Hadley had holdings in Ireland," she said, as though making pleasant conversation.

Mr. Babcock gave her a superior smile, obviously intended to convey his opinion that women were not to be told men's business. "Why, Lady Hadley, I'm sure your husband wouldn't wish you to bother your lovely head with matters of business."

Since he had mistaken her for Deborah, Kathleen knew she could easily cajole the information from him now. With a simpering pout, she refilled his wineglass. "But Ireland, sir . . . really!"

"His first wife was Irish," the man said, then looked very uncomfortable.

Smiling sweetly, Kathleen pretended a sigh. "Yes, I know. A most unfortunate marriage." She watched him regain his composure, then asked, "Is this something to do with her estate?"

Babcock squirmed under her determined questioning, draining his wineglass, which she filled at once.

"It's been held in trust," he said, trying to inject a note of finality into the words, which were a bit slurred.

"For whom?"

"For his daughter, of course. The grandparents left the estate in trust for her until her twentieth birthday." He reached for the wineglass.

Silent, Kathleen struggled to control her shock. When she could trust herself to speak, she asked, "Then the estate is to pass to Kathleen now that she's twenty?"

"Quite right," he replied and drank. "This is capital wine," he added, draining the glass and setting it back on the table, watching as she filled it once more.

"You must understand, Lady Hadley," he continued, making an obvious attempt to speak clearly, his eyes a bit glazed now. "Your husband has been using the income from the estate since Mrs. Browne passed away. The stud there is well known, and the colts bring a fine price. It'll mean a considerable drop in his income."

Kathleen drew in her breath, trying not to cry out at the miracle this man had presented to her. There was a way out . . . a place for her. It was almost as though Fiona herself had reached out and rescued her lonely and despairing daughter.

"Yes," Babcock said, misunderstanding her reaction. "I'm sure that it's a shock to you. But perhaps the girl can be persuaded to let Lord Hadley continue to manage the trust until she marries. I feel that's what he has in mind."

Never, she told herself furiously. Papa had cheated her and lied to her all these years, and he would have continued to do so except for this fortuitous meeting. Now, she'd be free of him. She must go at once and write to ask that James handle the legalities necessary to bind the estate to her. And she must find Francine to tell her they had a place to go to now.

Mr. Babcock had departed soon after a wrathful Papa had returned from the hunt to find him sleeping off the effects of the wine on the sofa in the library.

Papa himself had gone direct to the library after seeing Babcock off. The butler had taken in a fresh decanter of brandy. Now, Kathleen thought, now she would confront him with her knowledge of his duplicity. He was her father, but she could summon no feeling for him.

"Papa," she said, determined to be strong and hard with him for what he had done. "I talked with Mr. Babcock this afternoon about my grandparents' estate in Ireland."

"What?" Papa sat up in the chair where he had been slumped before the fire, a brandy glass in his hand, still dressed in his riding clothes.

"The estate is mine now, Papa. I'm twenty, and Morning Hill belongs to me." She stood very straight, calmly returning his furious glare.

"The bloody drunken bastard," Papa sputtered. "He had no right to tell you anything."

"He told the truth, Papa," she snapped, "which is more than you have ever done. All these years, you've kept the money from Ireland. You've cheated me, and you've lied to me, and I won't have any more of it."

"You little bitch!" Papa rose unsteadily to his feet, glaring at her. "After what I went through with your whore of a mother, I damn well deserve anything she left. You'll not have it . . . not ever."

"You can't stop me, Papa," she replied, raising her chin defiantly.

"I'll stop you . . . slut . . . whore!" His voice rose as he lurched toward her. "Just like your mother . . . you bloody bitch . . . you won't . . ." His voice trailed off into incoherence.

Suddenly frightened, Kathleen saw that he had picked up his riding crop from the table. He advanced toward her, raising the crop threateningly. "Keep out of it . . . you hear me."

"You won't cheat me again, Papa," she cried. Raising her arms protectively, she tried to dodge the riding whip that cut across her arm and shoulder. "Stop it! Stop it, Papa! You're mad!" She moved away from him and felt the marble fireplace mantel press against her back.

"Damned mad!" he yelled, bringing the crop down again so that it caught the side of her face, stinging painfully.

"Stop it!" she screamed, as he raised the crop to strike her again. Beneath her hand, she felt the fire-poker, and she grasped its handle as the riding crop sliced her shoulder.

"I'll beat some sense into your silly head," he growled and raised the riding crop for another blow.

"No!" she cried. With all her instincts of self-preservation, she lifted the poker and swung it blindly.

Lord Robert Hadley stared dumbly at her, his mouth open, his eyes glazing as he fell heavily to the floor. Blood poured from a head wound onto the Oriental rug.

Stunned, Kathleen stared down at him. I've killed him, she thought and turned in panic. I've killed him. I have to get away . . . now . . . quickly . . . forever. Feeling almost disembodied, she walked from the room, closed the door, and ran up the stairs to Francine.

It would be an hour before the northbound train arrived, Francine reported after she had purchased their tickets to

Holyhead from her meager savings. "We'd best stay out of sight," she added, and they walked to the shadows at the back of the dim station. There, they sat on the two bags they had brought when Kathleen drove them in the gig . . . away from Hadley Hall, forever. The library door was still closed. No one would investigate until supper time, for Papa often drank in there alone all afternoon. By that time, if all went well, they would be on the ferry bound for Ireland.

Remorse caught up with Kathleen as they waited in silence for the train. She hadn't meant to kill Papa, and she prayed that he would live. Yet, she knew she could not stay to determine his fate. If he died, she would hang, maybe even in Ireland.

"Look!" Francine said and pointed. It was the carriage from Hadley Hall careening down Brookfield's high street.

Holding her breath, Kathleen watched as the coachman pulled the horses to a halt before the doctor's house. A groom leaped down and ran into the house. Within minutes, Dr. Alderson was in the carriage and the coachman was whipping the horses back toward Hadley Hall.

"I have to know if he's dead," Kathleen said. Francine nodded and rose to stroll across the station and the street to the doctor's house. A maid answered the door, and after a few minutes' conversation, Francine returned.

"He's not dead, love," she said, patting Kathleen's shoulder. "You couldn't kill the bloody bastard, he's so mean. The doctor's called to attend him. Fell off a horse, the maid said they told her."

Kathleen heaved a sigh of relief, touching the painful welt on her cheek. As much as she hated her father, she did not wish him dead by her own hand. Now, she could go to her new life free from guilt. The northbound train whistled, and puffed into the station, grinding to a halt. Kathleen rose and took Francine's hand tight in hers.

A sharp, fresh wind blew off the Irish Sea where whitecaps rolled in dark blue water. Far in the distance, Ireland seemed to float on air . . . a green and mystical island. Eyes straining toward this land of her mother's, a land she'd never seen, Kathleen felt strangely at peace . . . as though she were going home at last.

CHAPTER 32

Ireland, 1887

The jaunting car driver was a loquacious old fellow in a tattered tweed cap. He talked incessantly as the swaybacked gray mare trotted along the road out from Greystones. Behind him, in the cart, Kathleen and her maid, with the two bags between them, listened, occasionally exchanging amused glances. They had left the train at the seaside town, and after some bargaining, engaged the man to drive them to Morning Hill. A hired carriage was beyond their means.

"So it's Morning Hill ye're bound fer," he said, lighting his pipe while the mare guided herself. "A sad place now . . . a shadow of the old days when Cedric Browne ran one of the finest studs in all of Ireland."

"And why is that?" Kathleen asked, folding her cape to sit on to ease the bouncing of the cart.

"Absentee landlord," the man replied, with a trace of bitterness beneath his easygoing exterior. "After Mrs. Browne died, the place fell into the hands of the daughter's husband . . . an English lord. It's said he raised the tenants' rents beyond reason, and he sold off the horses until there's hardly breedin' stock left." Flicking his whip at the mare, he frowned into the distance.

"Who lives at Morning Hill now?" Kathleen asked, with a growing sense of apprehension about her anticipated home-coming to a place she had never seen.

"'Tis old Colin McLoughlin's kept the place goin' all these years. But now, it's said, he's had a stroke, and his son's come home to help him out."

Then there would be someone there who knew the place

and cared for it, Kathleen thought. With a sigh of relief, she settled back to feast her eyes on the green vistas of Ireland.

Sunlight gleamed on the mountain peaks, and there were cloud shadows chasing along the vales. A delicate wash of purple heather lay over the hillsides, and along the roadside yellow gorse bushes tangled with bracken and fern and whitethorn beneath ancient oak trees.

The cart slowed before the stone pillars of a gateway where the wrought-iron gate hung rusted and broken. "Morning Hill," the driver announced, turning in.

A long beech-shadowed drive led up to the house. The mellow brick of the manor house appeared above the oak trees surrounding it, an unusual house for its ellipse-shaped front wing with massed chimneys in the center of the building.

Windows were boarded up at the front of the manor house. Everything seemed gone to seed, with clumps of grass growing in the gravel of the drive, the whitewashed walls of the outbuildings peeling and stained. The gardens about the house looked overgrown and weed-choked. It seemed to Kathleen that the whole neglected place had an air of resignation, as though it simply waited to crumble into oblivion.

"We'll drive round to the kitchen," the man told them as they passed the stone gatehouse where the iron gate hung forlornly on broken hinges. "The house is closed except fer the kitchen, where ol' Nanny Quinn lives." He grinned and winked conspiratorially. "Good fer a cuppa tea, she is."

As he helped them down from the cart, and took out their bags, the curiosity he had barely contained during the journey overwhelmed him. "Beggin' yer pardon, Miss, but would ye tell me what yer doin' in this place?"

Kathleen looked around at the weed-choked yards, the empty stables with their peeling walls. It must have been a beautiful place once, and she thought of her mother growing up here, riding her horses out from those same stables, of her grandmother overseeing the gardens with her beloved fuchsias and the now-broken glasshouse, of her long-dead grandfather and his pride in the horses he bred. A sense of nostalgia came over her as though she were indeed returning home after a long absence. Morning Hill would live again, and so would she.

The kitchen door opened. A withered gray-haired woman looked at them curiously.

With a sudden lightening of heart, Kathleen turned to the questioning eyes of the jaunting car man. "I am the owner of Morning Hill now."

Nanny Quinn's mouth fell open. She stepped forward, staring into Kathleen's face. "Ye're Fiona's girl," she said at last. Tears poured down her wrinkled face. "The saints be blessed. It's Fiona's daughter come home." Still weeping, she seized Kathleen in a smothering embrace.

Overcome by such an emotional reception, Kathleen felt tears spring to her eyes. She returned the old woman's embrace, until Francine stepped forward to take charge.

"My mistress is very tired," she said in her most authoritative voice. "Please have some tea brought for her, and a room prepared."

Nanny Quinn dried her eyes on her apron, looking embarrassed now by her emotional outburst. "There's only meself here," she told them. "But I'll make tea straightaway." Turning back toward the kitchen, she added apologetically, "All the rooms are closed up. I'll ask Dierdre McLoughlin to come help clean a place fer ye."

Seated by the kitchen fireplace, they had hot strong tea with bread and butter. Nanny Quinn bustled about waiting on them. The cart man ate and drank his fill, listening avidly to the explanations Kathleen and Francine had concocted on their journey to Ireland. Kathleen was certain he would spread the story, just as he had gossiped on the way from Greystones. That was as well, for it would save her many an explanation.

"'Tis a sad thing to be a widow so young," Nanny Quinn said, tears of sympathy starting in her eyes as she gazed at Kathleen.

Kathleen stared into her cup of tea, fearful that she might weep too, as Francine told the story of a young English girl wed to an American rancher who had perished in a terrible blizzard.

"When Mrs. O'Neil returned to England," Francine continued, "she learned that Morning Hill was to come to her when she was twenty. The situation at Hadley Hall was difficult for her, and so she intends to make her home here . . . where her mother grew up."

"He's a bloody bastard," Nanny Quinn muttered under her breath, and the cart man's eyes brightened with curiosity. "Who?" he inquired.

"Lord Hadley." Nanny Quinn glanced at Kathleen, obviously aware that she had spoken out of turn. "Ye've had a bad time, missus," she spoke gently to Kathleen. "But we'll make ye welcome here . . . and the little one too, when it arrives."

Startled, Kathleen glanced down at her thickened waistline, wondering how this wise old woman had known so quickly that she carried a child.

Nanny Quinn packed the cart man off, with instructions to stop by the estate manager's cottage. Dierdre was to come help with the house, Colin to report to the mistress if he was well enough . . . if not, then Sean must come at once.

Dierdre, Colin's daughter, arrived shortly, a stout pleasant-faced woman. She and Francine were soon upstairs, dusting, cleaning, and preparing rooms for the new mistress of Morning Hill.

"I'll show ye the house, missus," Nanny Quinn told Kathleen, as she stacked the tea things to be done later. As they moved past the butler's pantry from the kitchen, the old woman added in a bitter voice, "It's a sad thing . . . so little left of what was once a fine house."

"Yer grandmama's desk was there," Nanny Quinn said as they stood in the morning room, graced only by its Connemara marble fireplace. "'Twas a lovely thing, from France. I kin see her now, sittin' there, workin' at her plant records." She gave Kathleen an appraising look, then said in a harsh, defiant voice, "He sold that too."

"Who?" Kathleen shivered. She had not expected to find the house stripped of furnishings.

"Lord Hadley!" Anger and hostility blazed in Nanny Quinn's face. "No sooner was the poor soul underground, than that agent came from England . . . Holmes was his name . . . with an auction man from Dublin. They brought wagons and hauled away everything that could be sold."

Kathleen drew in her breath, anger flushing her cheeks. Was there no end to Papa's greed?

"There . . ." Nanny pointed to the fireplace. "A painting of Mrs. Horace Brown, the wife of him who built this house, hung there. The auction man said it was done by a famous painter and would bring a good price . . . so they took it. And there . . ." her voice rose in full fury now. "All the fine Oriental rugs . . . all the silver. And here . . ." She stomped out the door and pointed down toward the great hall. "A chandelier of cut Austrian crystal—gone."

Kathleen sighed, knowing there would be no recourse against her father's plundering. They must somehow gather enough furniture to furnish at least one room downstairs. At least the bedrooms were intact. Nanny confided with a malicious grin, they hadn't been able to move the enormous mahogany sideboard in the dining room. There were a few chairs and odd tables left in the two half-round drawing rooms.

"They didn't get around to the attic," Nanny said comfortingly, seeing Kathleen's growing dismay. "There's furniture there. When ye've rested a bit, we kin go look at it."

Kathleen set her lips in a determined line. Morning Hill was denuded of furniture, neglected and run-down, but it was her home now . . . hers alone.

Dierdre called Nanny from the top of the stairs with a question. She must show Dierdre and Francine where things were stored, the old woman told Kathleen, and she labored slowly up the beautiful curving staircase.

Wandering aimlessly through the house, Kathleen stepped into the shrouded dining room. Here the windows were not boarded up, and the tall French doors looked out across the dusty, empty conservatory, over the neglected garden. Honeysuckle and roses and geraniums . . . all tangled together, spilling over the broken wall, strangling the fuchsia bushes. A sundial was barely visible through the thick growth of dock and nettles, the walks overgrown with plantain and sedge.

It would all be again as it had once been, Kathleen promised herself. She forced open the rusty hinges of the French doors and walked slowly down the stone steps to inspect the forlorn and neglected garden she knew had been her grandmother's pride.

A step sounded behind her, the heavy tread of a large man. Turning, she looked into a pair of eyes as sapphire blue as her own. He was tall, with broad shoulders, and the fit muscular figure of a man used to physical labor. His hair was a salt-and-pepper gray above a face that was handsome still, even in middle age. There was something in that face . . . the deep lines incised on his cheeks, the harsh set of the mouth, that suggested a pervading sadness lay beneath his outward composure.

"I'm Sean McLoughlin," he said, taking off his tweed cap and staring at her.

"I'm Mrs. O'Neil." She held out her hand, and it was enveloped in his big calloused one. He held the hand longer than seemed necessary. Looking up, Kathleen saw that the intense blue of his eyes glittered with moisture.

"Kathleen . . ." He said the name in a low voice, rolling the syllables as a lover might. "Kathleen."

Shaken by his behavior and by the odd sense of familiarity she felt toward him, Kathleen slowly withdrew her hand. Sean McLoughlin straightened, seeming to regain control as she watched him curiously.

"Pardon, Mrs. O'Neil." He cleared his throat. "Me Da, Colin McLoughlin is the manager here. He's been ill, but he's gaining now. Would you come along to the cottage and talk to him?"

"Have you been running the estate in his illness?" she asked.

"Aye, ma'am," he answered, almost reluctantly. "I'm a horse-trader, meself. Buy and sell horses at the country fairs all over Ireland. When I got word me Da was down, I come along here to help out."

"I'm grateful to you," she said. "It seems this place has been sadly neglected."

Sean frowned, and the blue eyes darkened. "Not by me Da, not him . . . it was Lord Hadley who drained off every shilling fer his own use, raisin' the rents, sellin' off the horses till there's scarcely breedin' stock left." He paused for breath, obviously holding his anger in check. "You know what that means? All the offspring of the fabled stallion, Agincourt, gone to pay the bills of some bloody English . . ." The words seemed to choke in his throat. "Beggin' yer pardon, Miss."

"Never mind that," Kathleen replied in a spirited tone. "I'm well aware the kind of man my father is, but Morning Hill belongs to me now by the terms of my grandparents' will, and Lord Hadley has no more power here."

Sean smiled for the first time. "If ye're Fiona's daughter, then Morning Hill will live again." He took her elbow in his hand. "Come along now, and we'll tell Da the news."

The McLoughlin cottage was in need of whitewashing, although the thatch was tight and well-repaired. Inside, a turf fire muttered in the small fireplace. Everything seemed bare and clean and well used, from the table and three chairs to the bureau against the wall.

"This is me Da, Colin McLoughlin," Sean told her as the old man turned to face them from his chair by the fire. He looked worn and ill, his hair completely white and the blue eyes faded and dim. A wool blanket was draped over his knees.

"It's Fiona's daughter," Sean said. His voice fell, and Colin stared at her. "She's Mrs. O'Neil now . . . a widow, Da. And she's inherited Morning Hill."

"Thanks be to God," Colin's eyes widened, and his face broke into a grin. "Then Lord Hadley won't be here agin?"

"Never!" Kathleen promised in a firm voice.

"Ah, missus," Colin said, "it's welcome ye are. Sean, lad, fix some tea. Dierdre's gone down to the big house to help."

When Kathleen finished telling how she had learned of her inheritance, Colin regarded her in silence for a long moment. "Are ye sure he'll not take it all away from ye?" he asked, shaking his grizzled head. "Lord Hadley's a hard and greedy man."

"I know." Kathleen looked down at the hands she had clasped together in her lap, wondering whether she should tell them everything. The ugliness of that last confrontation with her father lay like a weight on her heart. "I struck him with the poker," she said in a low voice. "I could have killed him. But he'll not be inviting me back to Hadley Hall." She looked up, surprised to find the two men grinning at each other.

"There's a bit of Fiona Browne in you, missus," Colin said, clearly pleased at the idea of Lord Hadley being attacked by his daughter.

Kathleen tried to quell the pain that rose in her chest as the ugly memory overwhelmed her. "It was wrong of me. After all, he is my father, however wicked he may have treated me."

There was a long silence, broken only by the murmur of the peat fire and the faint faraway call of a dove. Sean McLoughlin's intense blue gaze burned through her. Colin stirred himself, his eyes going from Sean to Kathleen until he caught Sean's attention. There was a question in his face, Kathleen thought, but when Sean shook his head, the old man shrugged and turned away.

"I'm going to write to James to make sure everything is legal and secure," she said, unsure what had just passed between the two men.

"James was a great help to your grandmother," Colin said. "Sure, an he's a man ye can trust." Picking up the stick beside his chair, he held it between his knees as though he intended to rise and be about his work. "What'll ye be wantin' done?"

Kathleen smiled. "Your daughter's helping us open the house, but we'll need someone to take the boards from the windows. I'd like to have a man clean out Grandmama's garden. I know how much she loved it, and I can't bear to see it so overgrown."

"I'll have a man there tomorrow," Colin answered.

She sighed. It sounded so easy, but reality must be dealt with now. "I have no money to pay him. My maid, Francine, had to pay our passage from Holyhead."

A muttered oath escaped Sean. Colin gave him an unfathomable look.

"Some of the rents are in arrears since that rackrenter Hadley set 'em up so high," Sean growled. Then he brightened. "But the tenants might work off the rent fer ye."

"Good thinkin'," Colin grinned.

"Only if the rents are lowered," Kathleen interjected. The man beamed at her.

"Will you stay, Sean? I can't pay you now, or perhaps for a long time."

"I'll stay," he said. Again, there was the questioning look from Colin, again Sean's negative shake of the head. Then, the two men plunged into a discussion of tasks to be done and tenants to contact.

"It's yer comin' done it," Nanny Quinn said as she served breakfast in the kitchen next morning. "There's Colin, up and about at dawn, like the old days. You've given him new heart, Mrs. O'Neil."

"And being here at Morning Hill has given me new heart." She smiled at Nanny and, setting down her teacup, rose from the table. Somehow, coming home had assuaged her grief, although she knew the emptiness in her heart that Ranse O'Neil had filled would remain empty now, forever. "If you'll lend me an apron," she said, rejecting that painful thought, "I'll help Francine and Dierdre with the cleaning."

"You'll do nothin' of the sort!" Nanny Quinn looked at her sternly. Kathleen nearly laughed, remembering Papa's complaints that Irish servants were nearly as incorrigible as American.

"Ye'll not chance the bairn, doin' heavy work, missus. Get on with ye. Young Phin Sweeney's workin' in the garden. Ye might be watchin' him to make certain he does it to suit ye."

It was lovely and sunny in the garden. Sweeney brought out a wicker chair for her, and Kathleen sat bathed in spring sunlight, the scent of roses and honeysuckle and warm earth all about her. Perhaps Nanny Quinn was right, she thought. A deep sense of calmness filled her, as though the child growing inside brought hope and the certainty of contentment.

She heard Colin speaking to Francine and Dierdre as he came through the dining room and the conservatory. Leaning heavily on his stick, he made his careful way down the stone steps, then sitting on the stone wall beside her chair.

"Top o' the mornin'," he said with a smile. "Is Sweeney pleasin' ye?"

Sweeney, pulling weeds nearby, saluted the old man.

Filling his arms with weeds, he carried them to his wheelbarrow across the garden.

"Saints above, look what he's uncovered," Colin said, reaching over the stone wall.

Kathleen drew in her breath sharply at the sight of the green shrub, revealed now that its shroud of tangled weeds had been removed. The small round scalloped blossoms gleamed like jewels . . . purple, lavender and white.

"Yesterday-today-and-tomorrow," Colin was saying. "A pretty thing, ain't it? Yer mum quite fancied it."

"The flowers are pressed in her prayer book," Kathleen told him, watching as he plucked one of each color, holding them out to her. Taking the blossoms from his hand, she held them to her nose, inhaling the faint sweet fragrance. A feeling of communion came over her, as though she were repeating an act Fiona had long ago performed in this very garden.

Colin sighed heavily and passed a hand over his brow. "I've sent Sean out for the horses . . . the ones I hid from Lord Hadley when he was sellin' everything. They'll be breedin' stock fer ye t'start agin." He slanted an inquiring look at her. "If ye won't have me sent up fer horse-stealin'."

"Not likely," she answered, and they laughed together.

Colin sobered, staring at the flowers she held. "He said I wasn't to tell you. He didn't want to burden you with the past. But ye need each other now, with you alone . . . and him . . ."

"Tell me, Colin," she urged softly.

"Sean . . ." he said, as though each word was an effort. "He's yer true father, little one. He and Fiona loved each other, though God knew I told him no good could come of it. They ran away together when her parents wanted her to marry Lord Hadley, but Sean was set upon and shanghaied in Dublin. We thought him dead. She was carryin' you when I brought her home agin, and there was nothin' to be done then but marry Lord Hadley to give you a name."

Spring sunlight lay golden across the garden. Bees mumbled in the honeysuckle. A flight of pigeons wheeled down to the earth Sweeney had newly turned. Kathleen sat quite still, staring at the flowers in her hand, the tears pouring hot down her face. This was why she had felt so drawn to the man whose sapphire eyes stared back from her own face. He was her own blood . . . her father.

There in the golden light, she felt the memory of another sunlit garden stir in her mind. A tall, dark-haired man who dandled her on his knee and carried her on his shoulder across the garden . . . both of them enveloped in the aura of her mother's happiness. The man had been Sean, she was certain of it now, putting the story together with what Aunt Elizabeth had told her.

"I brought the horses, Da." It was Sean, standing on the stone path. "Do you want to see them, Mrs. O'Neil?"

"I told her," Colin said abruptly, rising from the wall and moving as quickly as his old legs would allow, past Sean and up the steps to the French doors.

"Told what?" Sean looked at her questioningly, and seeing the tears coursing down her cheeks, said, "Ah . . ."

Sitting beside her in Colin's place, he took her hands in his and looked long and searchingly into her face. "I'm sorry, Kathleen love." His voice broke, and his blue eyes swam with tears.

"Here," she said and held the blossoms out to him. "These were her token to you, weren't they?"

Unable to speak, Sean nodded. Taking the flowers in his big hand, he bent his head, his tears falling on the multicolored blossoms.

He grieves for her still, Kathleen thought, and wondered if she too would grieve so long. Surely it was over now . . . all the years of loneliness and pain. Father and daughter would comfort each other for the lost loves of yesterday. Rising, she put her arms about Sean and held his graying head against her breast. His arms came about her waist.

The evil Robert Hadley had done would be ended now. James would sever for her all financial and economic ties. With Colin's words, the last shred of emotional commitment had faded into nothingness. The man she had given her loyalty as a father, who had never loved her, was not her father. He had never held her in his arms and comforted her as Sean did now. The kinship she had felt at once was true and good.

The jewel tones of the yesterday-today-and-tomorrow

gleamed in the shadows. Yesterday was gone. Today she had found her father, and tomorrow belonged to the child in her womb, the child of Ranse O'Neil, her one and only love.

Sean drew away from her, smiling as he reached into his pocket for a kerchief to wipe his eyes.

With her hands still resting on his shoulders, she looked lovingly into his face. "What shall I call you now?" she asked with a warm smile.

Disconcerted by the question, Sean frowned. "Why, Sean, I suppose."

"No," she said softly, laying her hand gently against his worn face. "You are my own Da."

BOOK III

CHAPTER 33

Morning Hill, Ireland, 1895

Megan O'Neil urged the white Connemara pony faster and faster over the obstacles set up in the training paddock. Impatient, she raised her riding crop again. Why wouldn't Granda let her try the jumps set up for the trainers, the ones he himself used? She was tired of the easy one- and two-pole hurdles.

Glancing up as Granda called to her to stop, she saw the wide jump the trainers used. It was her favorite, with a low hedge and enough water to lure ducks to its surface. She loved it when the trainers surprised the ducks, jumping the water and sending them quacking into the air. With a burst of determination, she turned the pony and brought the riding crop down hard on its flank.

White Cloud seemed to become his name . . . floating into the wind, his hooves thundering across the paddock. Megan's knees tightened and the horse responded, stretching for the jump. She thought for a moment they'd made it and grinned with pride. Then his hind legs came down in the water, and he stumbled in the mud. Megan was unseated . . . jolted as she hit the ground, splashed with mud and water as the pony scrambled to his feet and ran off. Shaken and dizzy, she stared up at the misty blue sky, aware that in the distance her Granda was shouting.

Sean's blue eyes glistened with fear as he bent over her. "Are ye all right, lass?" Carefully, he lifted her, smoothing back her dark hair which had fallen loose in her wild ride.

She gave him a triumphant grin. "I almost made it, Granda."

311

"Bloody hell," he growled, lifting her to her feet, his eyes flashing with anger as his fear faded. "Yer seven years old and tryin' to ride like a steeplechaser. I've told ye t'keep to yer own jumps."

"I almost made it," she repeated, hoping to tease him out of his anger at her disobedience.

"Aye," he said sternly. "And now yer afoot, lass." When she wailed in protest, he frowned at her. "Ye'll not ride agin till I think you've learned a lesson."

"I've learned, Granda," she pleaded, appalled at the thought of not riding. "Please."

"No more," he snapped. "Brush yerself off."

Megan looked down ruefully at her mud-splattered clothes . . . corduroy trousers and a thick wool sweater. Her eyes followed Sean as he walked across the paddock to pick up the pony's reins and lead him back. She could tell by his long stiff strides that he was angry, but with a flash of insight guessed it was because he had been frightened for her. Smiling, she went to meet him and take his hand in hers, certain she would not be afoot for long.

"Someday," she confided as they walked back toward the stables, "I shall ride as well as they say my Grandmama did."

"Aye," he agreed, and she saw his eyes cloud with sadness as they always did at the mention of the legendary Fiona. Releasing her hand, he took her by the shoulders and drew her close to his side, looking down at her with love. "Aye, little one . . . it's like her spirit came to dwell agin in you."

Sean gazed pensively down at his grandaughter's dark head, and his thoughts flew back across the years to when he and Fiona had last been together.

For two days he'd paced the ferry docks at Holyhead, afraid to leave for fear of missing her. The whistles of the departing boats became a wail of pain inside his head. Something had happened to her he was certain, and his soul filled with a sense of dread.

There was little money left in his pocket, but he bought a train ticket back to Brookfield, determined to take her away with him this time. When the conductor came through the car and took his ticket, he nodded in recognition.

312

"Well, sir, going back to Brookfield, I see."

Sean merely nodded, for he was too disturbed to engage in idle conversation.

"Quite a sad thing there," the conductor continued, unperturbed by Sean's coolness. "Her Ladyship fallin' from a horse like that."

Sean sat bolt upright, his heart freezing within him. "What?"

"Lady Hadley," the man said, his face settling into properly mournful lines. "She was killed . . . and her a fine horsewoman, too."

Sickness washed over Sean. It was all he could do not to cry out with the grief that tore through him like a sword. "Her daughter?" He barely managed to make the words intelligible.

"Oh yes," the conductor answered. "Quite right . . . there is a child. She's with her aunt, so I hear."

Something in Sean longed to go there, to tear his daughter away from the despicable Hadleys. Yet he had nothing . . . no home, little money, and no prospects. How could he drag her away and make her into something like a tinker's child?

The conductor moved on and Sean sat with bowed head, thankful that the darkened car concealed the tears pouring down his face. At last, he bestirred himself. There was nothing to go back to Brookfield for now. Sunk in despair, he could only think of Ireland and Morning Hill, where he had been with Fiona long ago.

Leaving the train at the next stop, he went back to Holyhead, turned in two of the tickets to Ireland and boarded the ferry.

Morning Hill was already in mourning when he arrived. The Brownes had departed for Brookfield for their daughter's funeral. They would not have welcomed his presence in any case, Sean knew, but his family wept with joy to learn their son lived. It was certain he could not stay at Morning Hill. Colin sold him two older horses, on the cuff to be paid for later, and he set out for the horse fair at Inniskerry where he became a horse-trader.

"Am I really like my grandmother?" Megan asked now, looking up at him as they walked. She never tired of hearing stories of the beautiful girl whose miniature stood on her mother's bureau.

"Aye, that you are." Granda gave her a teasing smile and began to sing the words, "Oh, Megan O'Neil was an Irish colleen. A sweeter neater lass I never have seen . . ."

Megan laughed with pleasure at her name set in the old ballad.

"Everything your mama is not," Sean said, pretending severity as his song ended, "Spoiled, willful, impetuous, wild . . ."

With a rueful smile, Megan considered her mother's endless patience and love. It was always Nanny Quinn or Frannie who spanked her bottom when she misbehaved, never Mama. Yet Mama's disapproval carried more power than all the spankings in the world.

Now that Nanny Quinn had grown quite crippled with the aching in her bones, she spent most of her time beside the kitchen fireplace while Frannie ran the house. Granda ran the stud and the training stables since old Colin had died.

They never socialized with their neighbors. Aunt Dierdre and her husband, Padriac Murphy, sometimes came to visit from their tavern in Greystones. But having married late, she had no children for Megan to play with. Granda's other sisters lived far away. Aunt Maeve and her large family were settled in Cork, and Aunt Grainne had emigrated to Canada, where she had found a husband.

Once, two years ago, Cousins James and Serena, who were somehow related to Mama, had come from London with their children for the summer holiday. After the first shyness, she'd loved playing with Elizabeth and Anne and the chubby toddler named Reggie. There were no other guests at Morning Hill except the people who did business with Granda. Until lately . . . Unthinking, she sighed, and felt Sean's hand tighten on her shoulder.

Frannie said that their neighbor, John Fitzpatrick, had been a widower for a year now, and he was looking for another wife. But not my Mama, Megan protested silently, wishing he would not come so often to take supper, or to ride with Mama, or to argue politics with Granda. She wanted no changes and no intruders in this bright and perfect world that made up Megan O'Neil's Morning Hill.

That night at supper time, Mama seemed filled with repressed excitement. They had scarcely seated themselves at the table when she burst out, "Edward's coming for a visit." Her eyes sparkled with anticipation as she held the telegram up to show them.

Glancing out the dining room windows where dusk lay over a garden bursting with spring, Megan gave an exaggerated seven-year-old sigh. "Must he?" Somehow, Edward was a presence in this house where he had never been. Mama spoke often of her brother, her twin she sometimes called him. There had always been letters from him, and presents for Mama, but only Francine and Mama had ever seen this legendary person. When her mother looked at her in astonishment, she protested sullenly, "He'll have to ride with you and Granda, and then what will I do?"

"That's very selfish of you, Megan." Mama's voice was sharp and indignation flashed in the blue eyes that were exactly like Granda's.

From the corner of her eye, Megan saw Granda looking down at his plate, trying to suppress a grin. Across the table from him, Frannie frowned at Megan.

"You will be polite to Edward, young lady," Frannie said severely, "or you won't be able to ride, for I'll see to it your bottom is too sore."

Knowing she could not win against the adults, Megan concentrated on smashing her potatoes into a buttery soup.

"Does he know about . . ." Francine inclined her head toward Megan.

"No," Kathleen answered in a low voice. "I could never think how to tell him. I was afraid he'd think less of me, and I couldn't bear . . ."

"Bloody hell!" Sean swore, while Frannie stared at Kathleen in unbelieving astonishment.

"It'll be a bit of a shock, won't it?" Francine's voice was disapproving. Having seldom heard her mother spoken to in that tone, Megan looked up, once more interested.

"You'd best write him," Sean said.

"But he'll be here tomorrow," Kathleen replied, refusing

to acknowledge their fears or her own. "He's to go from here to London to meet his friend and their tutor to begin the Grand Tour. Lord Hadley . . ." she stumbled over the name, "would never let him come here if he knew of it." Tears welled in her eyes.

"He was a wonderful little lad." Frannie spoke in a soothing tone. "I hope he's grown into his early promise."

"Yes." Kathleen's voice was faint. Megan stared at her mother, aware that once more she had withdrawn from present company, gone far away into a land of memory where she could only go alone.

Ever since Edward's telegram had arrived that afternoon, Kathleen had been overwhelmed by memories. She and Edward had shared so much, the dreadful years at Hadley Hall, the year in Wyoming that had changed her life for all time. The memory of that year was still strong in Edward, for he often spoke of it in his letters, bringing alive again for her the image of Ranse O'Neil. He knew she had rejected the name of Hadley and was known as Mrs. O'Neil . . . but a tremor went through her as she wondered whether he could accept her illegitimate daughter as easily.

After all the years, her grief for her lost lover had never really healed. She'd covered it over with the hard work of restoring Morning Hill. The background of Hadley Hall, with servants to do everything, had faded quickly as she scrubbed floors, washed windows, grubbed in the garden, and helped exercise horses. Money was so short that they'd done with a minimum of furniture in the house. Only recently had she been able to complete the furnishings and replace the silver.

With Sean to guide her, they'd built up the horse herd. Agincourt's line bred true, and the fame of his fast, strong offspring brought buyers from as far away as England. The "mouse in the corner" at Hadley Hall had proven herself. Through hard work and perseverance she'd brought the house and the stables back to a semblance of former glory. She had her true and loving father, her daughter, and she told herself she was content.

The hired carriage from Greystones rolled up the drive, spinning gravel behind the wheels. Kathleen watched from

316

behind the lace-curtained windows of the half-circle drawing room. Apprehension tightened her throat, while her heart pounded with anticipation. Once, Edward had been her dearest friend, her brother, her birthday twin. Surely, he wouldn't have changed and become like his father, arrogant and cruel. His frequent letters to her always sounded like the Edward she had known . . . warm and caring, interested in everything. If he had grown into a different kind of man, he wouldn't have come here at all, she reassured herself.

Smoothing the folds of her dark blue faille gown, she turned toward the door. A smile curved her mouth when her eyes fell on her daughter sitting stiffly on the sofa. Nanny Quinn had dressed her in ruffled pink muslin and curled her long dark hair into soft ringlets. The lovely little face was pensive. The arrival of this stranger troubled the child, Kathleen knew, for visitors were unusual in the safe little world of Morning Hill.

Megan's dark eyes met her mother's, and such a pang went through Kathleen that she pressed a hand to her heart and drew in her breath sharply. Some days, just looking at his child could bring Ranse back to her, the image of him so sharp, the love they had shared so fresh and real that she wanted to cry out in anger at the gods.

Struggling for control, she held a hand out to Megan, praying that Edward could accept and love her child. Together, they walked to the great carved front door. The new maid, Violet, opened it. Watching Edward's manservant leap from the carriage to take down the luggage, Kathleen allowed herself a wry smile. In this private enclave of hers, she had almost forgotten how obsequious English servants were.

Morning Hill was a scandal among the neighboring gentry, she knew, because the housekeeper and the estate manager ate at the same table with the owner. Nor did they like it that she insisted on fair rents for her tenants and fair wages for her workers. The fact that she had acknowledged Sean as her father had put her beyond the social pale. Kathleen loved the world she had created here out of hard work and loneliness. She would never be invited to the great houses of Powerscourt and Currancourt and Russborough, but the shallow social scene held no attraction for her.

Glancing down at Megan, she pushed away the thought that perhaps one day it would matter to her daughter.

Edward jumped down from the carriage, and instinctively, Kathleen held out her arms. How tall he'd grown . . . as tall as his grandfather, Mr. Macabee, and with that same commanding presence. His thick fair hair had darkened to a light brown, but those wonderful eyes were the same . . . an ever-changing myriad of colors, green and gold and brown.

"Edward!" she cried, and was enfolded in his arms.

"Kathleen." He held her away to look into her face. "Oh Lord, it's been far too long. But you're as beautiful as ever."

"Still the flatterer," she teased, smoothing back her hair, pleased by his words.

"Mama." There was a tugging at her skirts as Megan demanded attention.

Dead silence fell as Edward stared incredulously at the child. Even the horses were still, and the breeze fluttering through the oak trees died.

"Ranse O'Neil," Edward murmured, his eyes intent on Megan. Then he looked at Kathleen, and his voice was accusing. "Why didn't you tell me?"

"Don't judge me, Edward," she said softly, her voice breaking. "Not until you know that kind of love."

"But I could have helped you," he protested, his eyes drawn to the wide-eyed child staring at him.

"I've helped myself, Edward," Kathleen replied, drawing Megan close to her side. "With my father's help, I've made Morning Hill into a profitable estate, and I'm happy here." Her voice trembled and she looked down, not wanting him to see the moisture in her eyes. "As happy as I'll ever be without Ranse."

His face twisted, and for the first time she realized the depth of Edward's own grief. "There was a man," he said softly. "There was a *man.*" For a brief moment, he held her close in a comforting embrace.

Drawing a deep breath, he turned to the child who stood watching with wide eyes. "And who is this beautiful young lady?" Edward asked, smiling down at her.

"My name is Megan O'Neil." She dropped such a proper curtsey that Kathleen stared in pleased surprise. "I ride with my Granda every day," Megan continued in positive tones, "and you are not to say I can't go along."

Edward laughed aloud. "Already, she gives orders as well as her father ever did." Kathleen smiled, pleased by Edward's reaction to her willful daughter.

Letting go of Kathleen for the first time, Megan touched Edward's arm and looked pleadingly into his face. "Did you know my father?"

To Edward's questioning look, Kathleen replied, "We talk about him often. Megan loves to hear about Wyoming and the American West. Mrs. Sanders gave me some photographs before I left Cybille Creek, so she even knows what he looked like."

Bending down, Edward scooped the little girl up into his arms, and started up the stone steps. "Your father was my dearest friend," he told her. "I still have a horsehair halter he and your mother made for me one Christmas when I was about your age. That was the Christmas we spent in Wyoming . . ."

Smiling, Kathleen followed him, leaving Violet to help the manservant with Edward's baggage. While Edward's deep voice continued the story of Christmas in the Wild West, Megan's arms crept about his shoulders, her eyes intent on his face as he talked, totally enraptured by this new tale of her father.

Lunch was served in the garden, with the scent of roses all about them, and the soft sound of doves cooing in the distance. Gratefully, Kathleen watched Edward accept Sean's presence with total ease. It was only after Sean had departed for the stables that he confided the news that the scandal of her illegitimacy had spread to England.

"So I am a scandal like Fiona?" she asked with a laugh, not caring for the opinion of unknown aristocrats in distant England.

"Scandal or not," he said affectionately. "I hope you still consider me your brother."

"Always," she answered. Smiling into his warm eyes, she knew that the bond between her and Edward, the bond she had vowed on the day of his birth, had held. It seemed they had been interrupted in the middle of a conversation, taking it up years later as though they had never been parted. He'd grown into the man she'd hoped for, Kathleen told herself, only now realizing how terrified she had been that he might have become a replica of his father.

Edward kissed her hand, and held it as silence fell between them. They were interrupted by Nanny Quinn arriving to take a reluctant Megan upstairs, for her tutor had arrived from the village to begin the day's lessons.

"Mrs. O'Neil," Edward said in a low, emotional voice when they were alone. Kathleen smiled ruefully at the title she had become so used to, grateful for Edward's discretion. "Have you never contacted anyone in Wyoming? Never tried to learn whether," he faltered but did not stop, "whether Ranse's body had been found?"

Kathleen shook her head, tears welling in her eyes. "It was such a terrible time at first, Edward. I nearly killed your father."

"So he told me," Edward answered wryly. "I didn't believe it."

"It's true, but only to defend myself from him." She wiped away the tears and continued in a low voice. "I had no money when Francine and I ran away to Ireland. Morning Hill was run down, the house closed, nearly all the horses sold." Lifting her head, she gave him a shaky smile. "But with the help of my cousin James, my father and I have brought it back to life. Then Megan came . . . and I had a bit of Ranse again. I guess I never really wanted to hear that . . . that he'd suffered . . . or how he died. I just wanted him back alive." She could no longer hold back the flood of grief and pain. Edward's arms were about her, and she felt the warm wetness of his tears against her cheek.

Megan could scarcely breathe as she waited for Uncle Edward's eyes to meet hers across the table. Each time she caught his glance, his beautiful mouth curved in a smile and his golden eyes gleamed, encompassing her for a moment before his attention turned elsewhere.

It was the loveliest dinner she could remember, although they often had flowers and silver on the table. Candlelight glowed softly. Mama, dressed in a rose-colored silk gown trimmed with gauzy ruffles, sat at the head of the table with Granda opposite. Edward was at her right, and beside him Francine, dressed in one of her black silk gowns heavily ruffled with fine lace. Megan had been seated opposite Edward. Beside her, and she frowned as she glanced at him, was John Fitzpatrick.

He was a powerfully built man of medium height, with curly gray hair and pale blue eyes. Francine said he wanted to marry Mama, but that was not the only reason for Megan's dislike. She had heard Granda say Fitzpatrick was too free with his advice, criticizing the way Morning Hill was run, telling Mama how she could increase her profits and that she was too generous with her help. Megan wished he would go away, and that Uncle Edward would stay forever.

Kathleen suppressed a sigh, sorry now that she had invited John Fitzpatrick to dinner before Edward's telegram arrived. John was a man of strong opinions, and he liked to dominate the conversation. He'd bought Windward some years ago, after Mr. Reynolds was murdered. A desperate evicted tenant, his cottage tumbled and burned, his family homeless, had shot Mr. Reynolds. Mrs. Reynolds had returned to her family in England. A tragedy, but according to Sean, one that should have been foreseen by a landlord who treated his tenants with vicious disregard.

As Violet served the caramel custard for dessert, Kathleen listened in amusement to the deft manner in which Edward steered the conversation. John's heavy-handed pronouncements on the state of the economy in England and Ireland included unstinting praise for Charles Parnell, the "uncrowned king of Ireland," who had worked for Home Rule and separation from England.

"Parnell's dead these four years," Sean growled impatiently. "The English still hold the yoke of Ireland. It'll take revolution . . . like the Americans." He glanced at Edward's interested face and fell silent.

Edward diplomatically changed the subject. He spoke of the war in China, of the infamous Dreyfus treason case in France, of the newly introduced death-duty tax in England, then of his trip.

"You're going to Paris first to begin your Grand Tour?" Frannie asked, and sighed at Edward's affirmative. "I left France a mere child. I wonder, shall I ever see it again?"

Somehow she would, Kathleen promised silently, as Edward outlined his itinerary for them. He was to meet his friend from Oxford, Binky Wharton, and Professor Darcy, who would be their guide and tutor, in London. The tour was to cover all of Europe, lasting several months.

"Mama insisted on it," Edward said. "She thinks all young men of the nobility are required to take the Grand Tour at the age of eighteen." He laughed self-consciously. "Of course I didn't object. I love to see new things, new places."

"You will write to us," Kathleen asked, "and tell us all about the countries and peoples you see?"

"Certainly," Edward answered with a smile. "And I hope to end the tour in Ireland if you'll invite me."

"The invitation is always open," Kathleen replied warmly.

"Edward," Megan's childish voice demanded attention.

"Yes, pretty Megan?" The tall handsome young man leaned across the table toward her, smiling his blinding smile.

"You must not find anyone to marry on your tour," she told him emphatically.

Grinning, Edward sat back in his chair. "And why not?"

"Because you must wait until I'm all grown up, and then you will marry me." Megan felt her face burn as the laughter of the adults echoed around the table.

"I shall be old and gray then," Edward answered in a teasing tone, "and you won't want me."

"Promise you'll wait," she begged, her heart pounding.

"Ah little Megan . . . I promise." But she knew it was not a promise, only an adult being indulgent with a child. She stared at him with fierce concentration, engraving his image on her heart for all time.

CHAPTER 34

Portofino, Italy, 1895

Silk gauze curtains billowed in a warm breeze laden with the heavy scent of exotic flowers. From behind the curtains, Edward could see, through tall windows, the brilliant blue of the Mediterranean, the fishing boats bobbing in the harbor, the warm terra-cotta tones of the square tile-roofed houses clinging to the cliffs above Portofino.

The fragrant air touched his nude body like a caress. At the thought, he felt his loins stir again with desire. Turning, he gazed at the woman sleeping in the tumbled bed across the large airy room. Crossing through shafts of sunlight spilling onto the bare floor, Edward paused beside the bed to look with longing at the figure lying there.

Angela's dark hair lay spilled across the white pillow. Her perfect, olive-skinned face might have been that of a goddess, carved from marble, and her long dark lashes lay fringed along her soft cheeks. That flawless beauty was marred only by the fine lines at the corners of her eyes. It was the only indication to him of the difference in their ages.

He'd met Angela Crocetti at a ball in the English embassy in Rome. Her husband was in the Italian diplomatic corps, and she was, beyond doubt, the most beautiful woman he'd ever seen. Just waltzing with her had aroused him. Wisely, she'd known it, and drawn him out onto the balcony until he could recover his composure.

She had kissed him there in the hot Italian night, a kiss unlike any he'd ever known. The barmaids and whores who serviced the wild young bloods from Oxford's Christ

Church College merely spread their legs. This woman pressed her full red mouth to his in a way that ignited an unquenchable fire in the very depths of his being.

"I'm going down to Portofino next week," she murmured in her engagingly accented English. Turning from him, she wandered along the balcony, her long slender hands on the marble balustrade as she moved. Her voice was like velvet, seeming to touch him in intimate places. "Every year I have a month to myself in our house at Portofino." She turned to give him a meaningful smile. "My husband indulges me, you see . . . a month alone, away from the children, and household concerns."

She paused for a long moment, looking out at the lights of Rome below. Edward waited, unsure what to say or do, his whole body throbbing with sexual desire. Almost stunned by the intensity of his longing, he'd watched the flow of the ivory satin ball gown about her generously curved body, inhaled her heady perfume. Her opal necklace had glowed like fire against her smooth throat.

Angela's dark eyes claimed his, and Edward had known nothing would keep him from her if she wanted him. The fact that she was a married woman with children was forgotten in the urgent need that blazed between them.

"Take the train down on Tuesday," she'd said. Her voice was low and intense. "Ask for Villa Crocetti. I'll have a room for you."

Someone had opened the tall French doors onto the balcony. The rich full strains of a waltz poured out into the night. "Come," she whispered, laying her hand on his arm and giving him a practiced social smile. "We must go back to the dancing before we become a scandal."

Now, Angela stirred under his intense scrutiny. She came awake as she had done every morning for the past month . . . smiling, holding her arms out for him.

"Angela," Edward murmured and sank into her embrace. She was like no other woman he had ever known and his love for her was near to madness. Her full, soft breasts burned against his chest as he kissed her, inhaling the warm intoxicating scent of her, probing the moist depths of her sweet-tasting mouth.

With languorous kisses and caresses, they led each other

along a rapturous path that had become familiar, yet was forever new. Angela's sensuous enjoyment of the act of love, to which she gave herself with complete abandon, brought Edward to heights he had never dreamed possible.

Their movements quickened, growing more frenzied until she cried out and arched against him. Edward surrendered his whole being to the depths of her body in a joy so complete the world seemed swept away.

With a soft, satisfied sigh, Angela settled her dark head on Edward's shoulder. "I taught you well."

He laughed aloud in pure pleasure and drew her closer.

Kissing his throat, Angela continued in a light tone. "But then, you had all the right inclinations. So many Englishmen don't even like women."

Edward's mouth twisted wryly as he thought of his traveling companions. The Grand Tour had come to an abrupt end that night in Rome when he'd returned early to their rooms to find Binky and Professor Darcy locked in a shameless embrace. They'd sailed for Greece without him. No doubt they were now emulating the ancient Greek heroes somewhere beside Homer's wine-dark sea.

Propping herself on an elbow, Angela looked down into his face. One finger softly traced the outlines of his face, lingering on his mouth. "You have a beautiful mouth, Edward. You must never grow a moustache and hide it."

He took her hand in his and kissed it, so overwhelmed by love he could not speak.

"And your wonderful eyes," she went on, smiling down at him. "Like the opals I wore the night we met . . . ever-changing, filled with unexpected lights."

With a long sigh, she fell back on her pillow, staring up at the ceiling where the light from the sea moved and changed. "My husband will be here on Saturday with the children and the nurse. You must leave today, darling Edward."

"Leave you!" Devastated by the thought of being parted from his love, Edward sat bolt upright in the bed. Reaching down, he seized her in a fierce embrace. "I can't leave you, Angela. I love you."

"Darling Edward," she soothed, stroking his hair tenderly.

"No!" Cupping her face in his hands, he looked into her

calm dark eyes. "I love you, Angela. You must leave your husband and go with me."

"Edward . . ." she tried to interrupt.

"Pack your things and come with me today," he begged. "I can give you a good life. When my father dies, I'll inherit the title and his fortune. Please, Angela. I can't live without you." Even in his desperation, he hated his own lies, for his mother controlled the fortune, and the title would bring with it only enormous debts.

Gently, she pushed him away, smiling sadly. "How young and dear you are, Edward. But you must know I can't leave my husband and children." Her tone lightened, as though she were trying to break the intensity of his mood. "I am very lucky to have a husband who indulges all my whims."

He looked at her in silence for a long time, the truth gradually filling his mind. "There have been others before me," he accused, chagrined by the knowledge of how callow and youthful his bitterness must seem to her.

"None so beautiful," she murmured, laying her palm against his cheek. When he could not reply for the pain that filled his whole being, she continued. "This has been a wonderful time, darling Edward . . . an enchanted time. How few people in the world ever know such a time?"

"Angela!" Again, he seized her hand and pressed his mouth into her palm, not wanting her to see the tears that stung his eyes. He had found paradise, and now he was being cast out. If he had been experienced, older than eighteen, a man of the world, perhaps the loss would not be so painful.

Angela rose from the bed and walked across the room toward the bath. Watching her move sensuously away from him, Edward knew it was ended. Furiously, he wiped the moisture from his eyes. He must move on, and there was no other place in the world he wanted to be. Certainly not with his erstwhile traveling companions.

Back to Ireland, perhaps, to the warmth and comfort of Kathleen's well-ordered household. Not to Hadley Hall. His mother had been bitterly resentful of his trip to Ireland. She had written him an angry letter reminding him that her younger son, Tom, would never have shamed her so.

A gust of wind whipped the silk curtains, and suddenly he was transported to another land. The curtains billowed in a fierce Wyoming windstorm . . . and his mind was flooded with the memory of distant mountains, great open spaces, and a sense of freedom. Wyoming had been the touchstone of his life, changing him forever. He would go back there, forget Angela, and find himself again.

Looking up from the square oak Irish-built desk where she was working at the household accounts, Kathleen eyed Francine speculatively. Frannie was wearing one of the black silk gowns she affected as housekeeper at Morning Hill, the silk fitting snugly over her plump breasts. She stood beside the fireplace studying the week's menus they had just worked out, humming softly to herself.

Above the Connemara marble fireplace hung the portrait of Agincourt they had found in the attic, overlooked by Lord Hadley's plunderers. It had been painted by an unknown itinerant artist and, in spite of the proud lift of the stallion's head and the powerful lines of his body, Sean claimed the untrained painter hadn't done justice to the great horse.

Beyond the windows of the morning room, late summer lay lush and green over the land. Horses browsed, hock-deep in grass. Bees hummed furiously in the geraniums beside the window.

Covertly, Kathleen studied the woman who had become her dearest friend in the years since their escape from Hadley Hall. They called each other Frannie and Kathleen now, ran the house together, and sometimes disagreed over the discipline of Megan. From the flighty maid she had once been, Francine had become an efficient housekeeper, handling the other servants with firmness and dispatch. She had even begun growing herbs and exotic vegetables in Margaret Browne's restored glasshouse. She'd been beside herself with excitement over the two orange trees Edward had shipped to them from Spain.

And yet . . . for all the love and gratitude she felt toward this woman, Kathleen's insides roiled with an unspoken anger this morning. Out of the mouths of babes, she thought, for last night as she had tucked Megan in and kissed her good night, the child had confided, "I saw Frannie at Granda's cottage today. They were kissing."

Sean lived alone in the estate manager's cottage, since Colin had died two years ago. After Dierdre's marriage, he began to take his meals at the main house. Kathleen knew that strange men came and went at the cottage in the dark of night, yet she refused to know. If Sean felt he owed an allegiance to the Fenians for what they'd done for him in America, he would do what he must.

But it was not those shadowy fugitives she was concerned with now. Megan felt free to go to the cottage anytime to see her beloved Granda. What if . . . Kathleen thought, and felt a new surge of anger, what if Megan had found them in bed together? Had it gone that far?

Glancing out the window, she saw Sean walking a horse in front of the stables. Sunlight gleamed on his thick gray hair. He held himself straight and tall, as strong and virile-looking as . . . Oh God, she thought, how could she expect such a man to remain forever faithful to a memory, even that of a woman as beautiful as the legendary Fiona. Surely, he'd had other women in the years he'd traded at the country fairs.

Frannie had had other men, legions of them to hear her tell of it. A bungled abortion had left her sterile and safe from the price most women might pay. Yet, Kathleen knew of no man since they had come to Ireland, except . . . A surge of emotion poured through her, and she recognized it at last. Pure jealousy, mixed with envy for the friend who had love when she did not.

Memory of the physical joy she had shared with Ranse O'Neil rose in her, the loss made more painful by the knowledge that it was forever. The early years at Morning Hill had been so filled with work, with caring for Megan, she had denied those longings. But now . . . there was time to think, to feel . . . to envy.

Through the open window, she could hear Sean singing as he worked, an old ballad, beloved by the Fenians:

*"For many a year our weary race have tilled the mountain
   side
Have smoothed Glenveagh's old rugged face
Have steamed the Atlantic wide
Full fifty homes he has leveled all, and wild sighs fill the
   air
Full fifty thousand curses fall . . . on cruel John Adair . . ."*

"On cruel John Adair . . ." The last words echoed from
the upstairs window in Megan's clear young voice. She was
supposed to be at her lessons with Mr. Riley, the tutor from
the village, but in spite of that, Kathleen laughed and
exchanged amused glances with Frannie. Did the gift of
music skip a generation, she wondered, for she had never
had that true sweet singing voice that Sean and his grand-
daughter shared? She delighted in hearing them sing together, even when they teased her with, "Kathleen Mavourneen,
the gray dawn is breaking . . ."

"There's John Fitzpatrick," Frannie's voice broke into
her thoughts.

Kathleen glanced out the window, glad Megan hadn't
sung "cruel John Fitzpatrick," as she had done at other
times. Her eyes lingered on the strong muscular figure of
John Fitzpatrick, who was dismounting to greet Sean and
shake his hand. Turning, she met Frannie's significant
glance.

With a chuckle, Frannie added, "His estate must be going
to rack and ruin while he spends all his time here. You
should marry the man, Kathleen, and put him out of his
misery."

Kathleen frowned; even for Frannie, the words were too
free.

Undismayed, Frannie swept from the room, saying, "I'll
tell Cook there'll be one more for supper."

Sighing, Kathleen decided she must somehow impress on
Frannie the need to be more circumspect. An ache deep
inside reminded her of desire long suppressed and hidden.
Her eyes went again to the masculine figure of John Fitzpatrick. He was a fine-looking man. If he was convinced
that all women need the guiding hand of a man, she could

perhaps disabuse him of that. He wanted to marry her . . . she was certain he would propose soon.

Deliberately, she made herself think of lying with him in intimate embrace. But her mind flooded with memories of a sunlit meadow in a faraway land, and a dark-eyed man who had made her body sing with rapture.

Laying her head down upon the desk, she wept for all the empty years.

··❧ CHAPTER 35 ❧··

From the sewing room window, Kathleen looked out on the cold misty day. Even though the trees had not yet begun to change color, she knew it was the beginning of autumn. Across the years there came a memory of golden cottonwood leaves fluttering down through the wine-crisp Wyoming air and she was stabbed through again with longing for Ranse O'Neil.

The dressmaker tugged at the skirt of her gown. Startled into awareness, Kathleen glanced down at Mrs. O'Hara's gray head. Her lips tight about a bundle of pins, the woman studied the drape of the pale blue watered silk, then began pinning up the hem once more.

Kathleen sighed for the golden memory quickly gone. This blue gown could be her wedding dress if she consented to marry John Fitzpatrick. The doubts she had fought to suppress rose inexorably. John was a fine man, she told herself sternly, upright and honest, well thought of in the countryside, and Irish to the core. He'd courted her for over a year now, until his patience had worn thin. Tonight, he'd be coming for supper, and she'd promised him an answer. Even now, she was unsure what that answer would be.

"You need a man," Frannie had said sternly. "A memory can't fill your bed or put its arms about you when you need comfort. He's a good man, Kathleen. Marry him and give yourself some happiness."

John was a good man, Kathleen thought now, watching the seamstress move around her to measure up the hem. And yet, the doubts kept surfacing, doubts she hardly dared admit to herself, let alone her family. In spite of his kindness, John Fitzpatrick was an overpowering man who liked his own way. She knew he found it difficult to discuss business with her. Perhaps it would be impossible for him to overcome his deep-rooted feeling that a woman could not make decisions and must be taken care of by the superior and more powerful male.

The uneasiness she'd felt from the beginning began to eat at her. So far, John had refused to discuss where they would live. She didn't want to leave Morning Hill now that she'd restored it to its former glory, but she knew John would never leave his estate at Windward. Too much remained unresolved between them, and Kathleen fiercely decided she must settle everything before she could consent to marry him.

"I'd finish the young miss's gown today," said Mrs. O'Hara, "if I could measure her hem."

"She's out riding with her grandfather," Kathleen replied. "Perhaps she'll be back before Sweeney takes you to the village. I'll have Cook give you some tea."

"Thankee, ma'am." The woman replenished the pins between her lips and moved on around the hem.

Kathleen allowed herself a small smile, knowing that her daughter was as scandalous to the locals as her household. Sean dressed Megan in trousers and taught her to ride astride, something the gentry simply did not do. Yet Megan was already a fine horsewoman. Again Kathleen sighed, wondering whether she really wanted to change this life she'd made just for the pleasure of a man in her bed.

Weary of standing, she glanced out the window where the grounds of Morning Hill sloped down to the high road. From out of the mist, a team of horses appeared, and the hired carriage from Greystones. Because no guests were expected, Kathleen watched in idle curiosity, expecting the carriage to roll on toward one of the estates farther down the road. She drew in her breath in surprise when the horses slowed, making the turn through the stone portals of Morning Hill.

"We have company," Kathleen announced, running to the window, leaving Mrs. O'Hara staring after her in frustration, her lips tight over her pins.

The carriage halted at the front entrance, wheels crunching on the wet gravel of the drive. She could see only the back end where the baggage was piled in the boot, but she did see the new young footman Francine had hired hurry out with an umbrella. Smiling, she thought Frannie had already trained him well.

A man in a gray wool cloak, wearing the silk hat of a gentleman, appeared in her line of vision, pointing out the luggage to the footman. When she could see his face, Kathleen cried out joyfully, "It's Edward!"

Turning to Mrs. O'Hara, who still waited on her knees with a mouthful of pins, she demanded, "Get me out of this at once. My brother's just arrived."

"But ma'am," the seamstress protested, "I'm nearly through."

"You can finish without me," Kathleen told her, already struggling with the gown. When the woman hesitated, the eagerness to be with Edward put an edge to the words, "At once, Mrs. O'Hara!"

Straightening her hastily donned wine red merino gown, Kathleen descended the stairs. She wanted to hold Edward and look into his dear face, no matter that her hair was rumpled . . . and she reached a hand to smooth it.

Francine was there already, instructing the new footman to take the gentlemen's hats and cloaks. Gentlemen . . . yes, there was another man with Edward. As he came into her range of vision, dim in the gray light of the great hall for the new Waterford chandelier had not been lighted, Kathleen froze on the last step. Her hand clamped convulsively on the bannister. She could not see his face, for he had turned to let the footman help him shed the tweed greatcoat he wore. Even in that unfamiliar garment, with a tweed cap on his head, there was something so like Ranse O'Neil that a tearing pain filled Kathleen.

The man turned then, and the dark eyes of her lost love looked into hers. All the vain dreams of the past years seemed to have come true. It flashed through her mind that loneliness and longing had made her mad. Edward was grinning at her, his hands outstretched, saying something. But his words were unintelligible, coming from a great distance. She knew nothing but the face of Ranse O'Neil, floating in a mist that gathered there in the great hall. Even his face was lost in that mist as her knees gave way, and she crumpled into darkness at the foot of the stairs.

A peat fire muttered softly in the drawing room fireplace. Outside, the autumn mist had turned to rain and drops pattered against the tall windows. All the lamps had been lit against the dark afternoon, so that the room glowed with warmth and light. Violet was setting out tea on the table in front of the fire.

Megan sat stiffly in a straight chair beside the fire, staring intently at her mother. Francine's bottle of smelling salts still stood on the table beside the sofa where Mama lay. But it was not the fact that she and Granda had returned from their ride to find Mama had fainted that troubled Megan. It was the strange man who sat so close to Mama now, holding her hands and looking into her face. And it was Mama, who had scarcely noticed Megan, or Granda, or even Edward, her eyes feasting on the stranger's face, her hands reaching to stroke his cheek, her voice softly murmuring his name, "Ranse . . . Ranse . . ."

Megan wriggled in the chair, unhappy at being shut out. Even Edward scarcely noticed her as he sat with a satisfied grin on his face watching Mama and the stranger. Granda and Frannie were exchanging pleased glances. Sliding down from the chair, she crossed in front of the fireplace to lean against Edward. At once, he lifted her onto his lap and squeezed her shoulders. Megan sighed with relief, looking up into his beautiful beloved face. Edward still loved her, even if Mama had forgotten she existed.

"I've brought your father to you, Megan," Edward whispered in her ear.

She liked being on Edward's lap with his arm holding her, so she would say nothing to offend him. But she did not like this stranger having her mother's undivided attention. With hot eyes, she watched as the man said something in a low voice and bent to kiss her mother's forehead gently.

"Have some tea now, dear," Frannie urged, holding a steaming cup out toward Mama. With a smile, Mama sat up, the man helping her, then moving to sit beside her.

Megan kept her unwavering stare on the stranger. How could they say he was her father? Her father had died, long ago, in the hard winter in Wyoming. Surely, this man was a liar and an impostor. Critically, she took note of his dark thick hair, graying above the ears, the dark eyes that never left her mother's face. He was tall, even taller than Edward, but thin beneath the tweed jacket, and his dark weathered face was seamed with lines as though he had been ill. He was not her father, she told herself, her stomach roiling with jealousy as Mama rested her head against the man's shoulder and smiled into his eyes.

"I was in Italy," Edward told them, and Megan snuggled closer to him. "Suddenly, it came to me that the only place in the world I wanted to be was Wyoming."

"Thank God for that," Ranse said, his voice deep with emotion. "I might have died an old man, thinking Kathleen had left me for an easier life in England."

Tears stood in Kathleen's eyes as she set down her teacup and covered both his hands with hers. "They told me you were dead, that you couldn't possibly have survived. I had no choice but to go back to England."

"Tell them what happened," Edward prompted.

"My horse stepped in a prairie-dog hole and broke his leg," Ranse began. "I was thrown and knocked out cold. Finally, I came to enough to shoot poor old Hawk, but I'd broken something and couldn't move. Kept passing out all night, hugging that poor dead critter for warmth. The next afternoon, a band of Indians came by. They were gathering what beef they could from the frozen cows." He fell silent for a moment, staring at the floor, then continued. "They loaded me on a travois and dragged me back to the reservation with them." He looked up, his face drawn with remembered suffering. "I've no idea how long they kept me there, nursing me until my bones healed and the lung fever went away. It was late summer before I got back to Cybille Creek."

"And we were gone," Edward interrupted. "The ranch was deserted except for a caretaker. Even Dr. Vickers was gone . . . he'd moved to California. So there was no one to tell him what had really happened."

"I bought the ranch," Ranse said, smiling at Kathleen. There was a long silence as memories flooded between them, their eyes locked.

"At bankrupt prices," Edward grinned. "You should see it now, Kathleen. Ranse made a going concern out of my father's failure."

Kathleen and Ranse seemed unaware of the presence of others in the room. Edward smiled indulgently and turned to address his remarks to Sean and Francine. "The ocean voyage was hard on Ranse. When we landed, he had lung fever again, so I sent him down to Brighton to get well while I went on to Hadley Hall."

Kathleen turned to look at him, her eyes brilliant with tears. "Dear Edward," she said. "How can I ever repay you?"

"Be happy." Edward's voice was gruff. Megan gave him a puzzled glance.

"We're forever grateful," Ranse said, with a warm look at Edward. "It's a second chance at life that I never expected to have." His voice fell as his eyes rested on Megan. "And my daughter . . ."

"Come here, Megan." Mama held her hands out toward her.

Megan wriggled closer to Edward, both arms tight about his neck, shaking her head. With a firm grip, Edward loosened her hands, lifted her down on her feet. Giving her a pat on the bottom, he urged her toward her mother.

"This is your father, Megan," Mama said, drawing her close, an arm about her shoulders. "I thought he was dead, but he's alive, and now he's come back to us to love us and live with us forever."

Megan stared back into the man's dark, wary eyes. He smelled of tobacco and wet tweed, and he was a stranger. "No!" she cried, pulling away from her mother's embrace. "No!" And she ran up the stairs to her room, locked the door, and flung herself, sobbing, onto the bed.

"She's a wee bit spoiled," Sean said, as the door upstairs slammed. "Give the lass time and she'll come round." He grinned to allay Kathleen's obvious dismay over Megan's reaction. His daughter's happiness meant more to him than his own. Secretly, he'd worried over the possibility of her marrying Fitzpatrick. He could be an overbearing man, and Sean knew that beneath Kathleen's quiet, gracious exterior there lurked all the fire and independence of his beloved Fiona. The love he saw flowing now between Kathleen and this American filled him with a secret joy. He'd liked Ranse at once, and he was the father of the adored Megan. Sean sighed with satisfaction, giving Frannie a smile. Her eyes were warm, and he knew she would lie in his arms this night.

"Bloody hell," he said as a sudden thought struck. "Fitzpatrick's comin' fer supper."

Silence was thick in the room until Kathleen spoke in a firm voice. "It's just as well he knows right away. I'll speak with him alone when he comes."

To Ranse's questioning look, Sean said, "John Fitzpatrick was wantin' t'wed me daughter."

"That would be bigamy," Frannie added with a giggle, although she knew very well that it would not.

When Ranse turned to Kathleen, she touched his face gently and smiled. "I'll tell you about it later, darling."

Rain streamed down the bedroom windows. The leaves of the great oak rustled in the wet autumn wind.

"Do you remember a night like this?" Kathleen asked, turning from the window, the thin linen negligee floating about her slender figure.

"That was a snowstorm, darlin'." Ranse sat on the edge of the bed removing his boots. The dark eyes that met hers were filled with love.

"The night we said our marriage vows," Kathleen murmured, yielding to his embrace as Ranse rose to take her in his arms.

"My wife." His mouth closed over hers and fires long banked within her sprang into an inferno. "We'll make it legal as soon as we can," he told her as he drew away, his eyes devouring her face. "For our daughter, we have to."

"Yes." Kathleen's smile faded as Ranse released her and began unbuttoning his shirt. "I'm sorry she behaved so badly to you, love. As Da said, she is spoiled . . ." Her voice trailed off as she watched him remove his shirt.

"She'll come around," Ranse said, but he did not look directly at her. "Edward's nurses gave me this," he told her with a laugh as he took a nightshirt from his bag and pulled it over his head. Kathleen laughed too, for the garment did not suit him at all.

Ranse sobered. "Was it difficult with Fitzpatrick? He looked like he'd kill me if he could get away with it."

"He was angry and upset, of course," she answered. "But I could hardly marry him when I already have a husband." Putting her arms about his waist, she laid her head against his broad shoulder, so familiar, and so dear.

Ranse's arms tightened about her. "Did you love him?" he asked as though the words were pried out of him.

"Why, no, of course not." She looked up at him, surprised by the question. "I was lonely, and he kept asking."

"What if I hadn't come this week?" His embrace was so fierce she could scarcely breathe.

"But the miracle did happen today, love," she said. Taking his face in both her hands, she reached up to touch his mouth with her own. All the half-forgotten sensations flamed through her as his tall body strained against hers, his arms pressing her close, his lips hot against hers.

His discarded nightshirt lay with her nightdress on the floor. As Kathleen's hands moved hungrily over his body, she realized how thin he was and remembered Edward had spoken of an illness. The thought was lost in her wild response to his caresses, to his mouth burning against her throat, her breasts, his knowing hands moving over her body until she was intoxicated with passion. Still, he did not come into her to relieve the ache that grew until it possessed all her being.

Suddenly, Ranse collapsed on top of her, his face buried against her neck. "Oh God, Kathleen," and the words seemed torn out of him. "Oh God, darlin' . . . I can't . . . I can't."

Kathleen lay very still. There was a wetness on her throat where Ranse's face was pressed, and tears sprang to her own eyes. Her arms tightened about his shoulders, one hand softly smoothing his hair. Within, her whole body clamored for release until she wanted to cry out her frustration.

A need to comfort overwhelmed her own pain. She pressed her lips against his hot forehead. "It's all right, love," she soothed. "You've been ill, and you're exhausted from the trip."

Ranse shook his head in angry denial of his own impotence.

"Darling, darling," she murmured, holding him close against her. "Tonight, I just want you to hold me and make me know you're really here in my arms." Pushing back his rumpled hair, she bent to look into his unhappy eyes. "We have tomorrow, love. We have all the tomorrows in the world now."

·▹[CHAPTER 36]◃·

He should never have listened to Edward . . . never have come to Ireland with a dream of love recaptured. In Wyoming, he'd have lived out his days as the old bachelor rancher, respected by his peers, but all alone. He wouldn't have failed the woman he loved as he had done last night.

Ranse lay on his back, his eyes deliberately closed tight, unwilling to awaken into reality. He sensed Kathleen's absence from his side although she'd lain in his arms all night, holding him until they both fell into exhausted sleep. A faint sickness clogged his throat when he recalled how passionate she'd been last night, how eager to surrender to his lovemaking . . . and he'd failed her.

"Damn," he muttered and turned on his side. Morning sun glowed through the mist, gilding the windowpanes. Lace curtains blew gently where the window was ajar. When the door opened, he did not turn around.

Kathleen came to sit beside him on the bed. She wore a robe of softest spun wool in shades of lavender, and her eyes were as blue as the deepest ocean . . . as blue as Wyoming mountains. When he forced himself to meet those eyes, there was no blame in them, only love. Ranse drew in his breath, lying back on his pillow as she bent to kiss him. Her mouth lingered on his, her tongue soft and warm against his lips.

"Kathleen," he murmured, his arms holding her close.

Slowly, she drew away. "Look, darling." She held Fiona's prayer book. "Remember the flowers my mother pressed in the book on the marriage ceremony." Opening the pages, she showed him the faded blossoms crumbling there. Ranse looked at her, aching with the need to love her.

Smiling, she lifted her hand to show him the three fresh blossoms she held ... purple, lavender and white. "I was afraid they'd all be gone this late, so I went downstairs to look. See ... Sean gave them to Fiona long ago. Yesterday-today-and-tomorrow it's called." Pausing, she looked into his eyes and Ranse felt himself enveloped in her love. "I wanted to give them to you, darling. Our yesterdays ... today, and most of all, our tomorrows together."

Moisture stung his eyes as he drew her down into his embrace. "My love ... my love." Their mouths met and clung, opened and joined. A wave of desire swept through him, and he cried out with joy as his manhood stirred and came alive.

Robe and nightclothes discarded, Kathleen came into his arms, her soft white body responding to his touch. Her hands spread fire everywhere they touched until his whole being cried out for her. She arched against him, wanting him, yet she winced when he entered her, for it had been so long. His body seemed to melt into hers until they were fused together, one being soaring on a cloud of endless rapture.

"Your Ireland is a beautiful land," Ranse said as they strolled through the rain-wet gardens that afternoon.

The blue eyes that met his still glowed from a morning of lovemaking. Smiling, she teased, "Didn't I tell you that the O'Neils were once the kings of Ireland?"

Ranse laughed. "Maybe that's why I feel as though I'd been here before."

Kathleen leaned to press her cheek against his shoulder, a gesture that filled his heart. "The king has come to claim his throne," she murmured, tentatively adding, "Could Ireland be home for you, Ranse?"

Taking her shoulders in his hands, Ranse turned her to face him, his entire being overflowing with love. "Home, darlin'," he told her, "is wherever you are."

"But you can't just give up the ranch you've worked for so long," she protested.

"I don't intend to." He drew her close, pressing his lips

against her forehead. "Maybe we'll go back there to live . . . you and me and Megan."

"Perhaps," she murmured, lifting her face for his kiss.

They said he was her father and she must love him, but Megan didn't love him. Disconsolate, she kicked at a pebble on the gravel drive. How could she love that man when he'd taken her Mama from her? She always thought of him as "that man" even though she had been told to call him Papa. Mama was still loving to her, but now her eyes were only for that man, all her efforts were to please him.

For the last month, since his arrival, they'd shared the bedrooms that had belonged to Grandfather and Grandmother Browne. The thought made her stomach roil in a peculiar way. She'd heard the stableboys' talk. It was something like what happened between a stallion and a mare . . . but surely not Mama!

Megan gave a little private groan of protest. She'd listened outside the bedroom on one of the afternoons they'd gone up for what Mama called "a rest." The sighs of pleasure told her Mama liked whatever it was they were doing. But it was the two of them in there with Megan outside, alone. At least she knew that man didn't hurt Mama. But she'd looked at Mama with hard, resentful eyes when she came downstairs, her hair carefully rearranged, her face glowing.

Leaning against the trunk of the oak tree, Megan glanced up at the bare, empty branches. Beyond the gravel sweep, she could see her beloved Granda showing that man how they worked the horses in the training paddock. The two of them were always talking horses. Even Granda had deserted her.

Tears rolled down her cold cheeks, and the autumn wind seemed bitter. And the worst thing of all had been Edward's departure. Word came that his father was ailing, and he was needed at home. Dear Edward had kissed her when he left and promised to come back as soon as ever he could. That promised return was the only bright spot on her small horizon.

She wasn't sorry Mama hadn't married Mr. Fitzpatrick, who was far too bossy for Megan's taste. At least, that man wasn't always reminding her to keep her place for she was only a child, or shaming her because she was allowed to dress in trousers. That man was always kind, but distant. Sometimes, she caught him watching her with a puzzled look as though he too could not believe they were related.

"Come in to tea, Megan," Frannie called from the drawing room window.

Megan sighed and kicked up a shower of pebbles. Frannie had Granda, although they seemed to think no one knew it. Mama had that man, and now that Edward had gone away, Megan had no one.

Wearily, Ranse sat down on the stone wall. Elbows resting on his knees, he buried his face in his hands. It was quiet in the bedroom above now . . . the long night of pain ended, only loss and disappointment remaining.

With a tired sigh, he straightened, brushing his rumpled hair back from his forehead. Spring had come to Morning Hill with a kind of lush beauty he'd never known in the stark land that was Wyoming. For a moment, he was struck by a pang of homesickness for the wide sagebrush plains, the towering blue mountains, and the sharp clarity of atmosphere he often longed for here in misty Ireland.

Multicolored blossoms spilled over the rock walls in a glorious profusion of colors. The fragrance here in this garden was almost intoxicating . . . roses and heather mixed with the orange trees blooming in the conservatory. Yet, in all that glory a peculiar stillness reigned. Even the doves were silent in the dovecote.

From the corner of his eye, he saw a small figure appear at the open French doors of the dining room. He drew in his breath, waiting, scarcely breathing. In the fear and tension of last night and this morning, they'd all ignored Megan. She must be scared to death by all the goings-on she couldn't understand, yet he dared not make the first move. Their relationship was too precarious.

The one flaw in the happiness he'd found here with Kathleen had been Megan's unswerving resentment. Throughout the winter, he'd cautiously tried to win her acceptance, only to be rebuffed again and again. The nearest he'd come had been at Christmas time, with the horsehair halter he'd made for her. Then, the child had made it clear she treasured the halter only because it was like the one he'd made for Edward so long ago.

Now, he turned to watch as she moved hesitantly toward him through the conservatory . . . the daughter he'd found so late, perhaps too late to really win her love. At eight, she had grown tall, with long coltish legs. Her coloring, dark eyes and hair, were so like his own he could not have denied her had he wished to, even though Sean still insisted she was Black Irish.

When she stood before him, hiding the painful uncertainty of childhood behind a determined face, he saw that her eyes were red from weeping. It was all he could do to restrain himself from taking her in his arms, knowing she would at once push him away.

"What's wrong with Mama?" she demanded, and her voice broke.

Ranse cleared his throat, for it had grown tight. His voice was thick. "She's very ill, Megan." How much could he tell her, he wondered? Just how much could a child understand? He hoped she hadn't seen the bloody sheets or heard Kathleen's cries.

"Why?"

Ranse sighed, seeing a bit of himself in this skinny girl, determined, straightforward. He clenched his hands into fists, for he wanted so much to put a comforting arm about his daughter. Searching for the right words, he began speaking slowly.

"Your Mama was going to have a baby. She wanted a family, a little brother or sister for you, but . . ." Ranse's voice trailed off as the memory of Kathleen's anguish overwhelmed him.

"She aborted?" Megan's voice was high and scared.

Startled, Ranse stared at the child, amazed at the earthy knowledge behind that innocent face. Yielding to his instincts, he reached out and drew Megan to his side.

Looking down into her frightened eyes, Ranse explained gently. "The baby miscarried, Megan. Your Mama was very sick."

"That's why the doctor came," Megan stated, as though reassuring both of them. "That's why Frannie's rushing about so, and why Granda is out at the stables, staring at nothing, and not talking."

"Yes, Megan." Ranse's voice was low. "We're all pretty worried."

"She won't die, will she?" Megan's face was white, her dark eyes wide with fear. When Ranse hesitated, she cried out and flung herself into his arms.

Holding the sobbing child close in his arms, Ranse felt his own sorrow at the loss of the baby, and his pain for Kathleen's suffering melt away. At last he had his daughter. Murmuring words of comfort, he patted the heaving little shoulders, stroked the dark mane of hair, and tentatively kissed the top of Megan's head.

When her weeping had eased, Ranse lifted her chin in his fingers to look into her eyes. "My little Megan," he said, looking at her with eyes of love. "Your Mama won't die." He managed a reassuring smile. "We won't let her. Between us, we'll love her enough to make her well."

Through tear-blurred eyes, Megan studied the face that was almost a mirror image of her own . . . the same eyes, the same dark hair. There was love for her in those eyes, and a flood of warmth filled her small aching body.

"Oh, Papa!" she cried, and her thin young arms tightened about his neck. "Papa!"

When the child's sobbing had waned into sniffles and he had dried his own eyes, Ranse smiled at her. "Maybe we could see Mama now, just for a minute."

"Could we?" Her dark eyes gleamed with hope.

He nodded and Megan slid down from his lap. Reaching across the stone wall, she picked a handful of flowers, purple, lavender, and white. They gleamed like jewels in her small brown hand.

"This is yesterday-today-and-tomorrow," she told him seriously. "Shall we take them to Mama?" Her voice fell and her eyes studied his face. "Will you be here tomorrow, Papa?"

"Always," Ranse answered in a voice choked with emotion. "Always, my little Megan."

·❦[CHAPTER 37]❦·

London, 1898

A chill late summer fog pressed against the windows of Burnham House. As Kathleen watched, a lamplighter moved across the park opposite the house, heavily muffled, carrying his ladder on his back. The faint sound of carriage wheels rose from the street. Perhaps it was Edward, for Serena had invited him to dinner tonight.

Smoothing a stray lock of hair into her neat coiffure, she smiled at her daughter who was staring intently into the bedroom mirror. An adolescent child is like a gangly newborn colt, she thought, all arms and legs and uncertainty. Having finished dressing in a gown of pale blue tulle, Megan had come to her parents' bedroom for inspection, but now she was absorbed in inspecting a pimple on her chin.

"I look absolutely hideous," she wailed, turning from the mirror. "I can't bear to have Edward see me all blotchy and ugly."

Ranse lit his cigarette and leaned back in the chair beside the fireplace, regarding his daughter with an amused grin. "You look quite presentable to me," he said in a teasing tone, "considering I usually see you in a pair of corduroy pants."

"Oh, Papa!" Megan stamped a foot and returned to her perusal in the mirror. "If only Frannie were here, she'd know what to do to cover this."

"Well, Frannie is visiting her family in Paris," Kathleen frowned, a bit exasperated with all this adolescent emotion. "Anyway, Edward isn't the kind to judge a woman by the state of her complexion."

"I'll ask Serena," Megan replied in a haughty tone and flounced out the door.

Shaking his head, Ranse looked after his departing daughter. "She's not at all like you," he said, reaching to take Kathleen's hand and pull her down into his lap.

Yielding to his embrace, and to the touch of his firm mouth against hers, she sighed. "No, but perhaps being loved as a child makes one dare that kind of independence."

He smiled lovingly and kissed her again. Kathleen laid her head against his shoulder, content to be here with him until the maid came to call them down to dinner.

Three weeks since they'd returned from Wyoming, she thought, three weeks of James and Serena's hospitality while Ranse recovered from a severe case of lung fever contracted on the ocean voyage. When she'd realized they'd be here until Ranse was well enough to travel to Ireland, she'd sent for Frannie to bring Megan to London. They were both lonely for the daughter they'd been away from so long, and it would give Frannie the opportunity to go to France and see her family at last.

Somehow, the months and years had slipped away, with Ranse's American business handled by letter and cablegram, until James had decided it was necessary to check on the Wyoming property in person.

Like honeymooners, Kathleen and Ranse had sailed for New York, leaving Megan with Frannie and Sean. They had traveled up to Boston to see Sean's old friends, the O'Briens. The inhabitants of that substantial house on Beacon Hill greeted them with open arms, anxious to send back the word that Fergus O'Brien had prospered in America and now owned a successful freight business.

America had changed. There were more people everywhere, settlements and farms dotting the vast plains their train chugged through. Even Cheyenne had grown, with brick buildings, and trees, and a fine new courthouse. It was there they said their marriage vows before a justice of the peace . . . legal at last. They had never dared risk a ceremony in the small world of Ireland, where there were no secrets. It would only have added Megan's illegitimacy to the many scandals already attached to those who lived at Morning Hill.

The big house at the ranch had been boarded up, but was opened for their arrival. The cottonwood trees had grown as tall as the house they shaded. A heavyset woman who was the foreman's wife had cleaned, made up beds and stocked the pantry.

"Remember . . . remember . . ." they said to each other as they wandered about hand in hand. But in all the nostalgia, they never spoke of Robert Hadley or of the painful days when their lives had been torn apart.

On a sunny summer day, Ranse saddled horses and they rode along Cybille Creek. As they crossed the gravelly creek bed and made their way through a thick stand of willows, Kathleen realized where he was leading her.

It was the same . . . that private flowered meadow . . . as though it had been preserved under glass, awaiting their return.

"Remember?" Ranse asked as he lifted her down from the saddle into his arms.

Tears stung her eyes as she looked into his tender face. "Make love to me, Ranse," she whispered. "Just like the first time."

When they lay together in the flower-starred grass, with the horses munching noisily nearby, and quails calling in the distance, it was as though time had turned backward. Once more, they discovered and explored each other's bodies. Every touch, every response held the same breathless wonder as the first time. Together, they soared to dizzying heights of ecstasy, made more intense now by long and intimate knowledge of each other.

Sated with love, Kathleen pillowed her head on Ranse's bare shoulder. In that searing moment of climax, they had achieved a oneness more complete than they had ever known. Looking up into the dark smoldering eyes of her love, Kathleen gently smoothed back his rumpled hair. She dared not share the dream that burgeoned in her mind. If fate were kind, they would have, in this perfect joining, created the son she had waited and prayed for so long.

Now, in this elegant room with its dark blue damask hangings and thick Persian rugs, she looked again into the dark eyes watching her, gleaming in the firelight.

Reaching up, she laid her palm softly against his cheek.

"Are you sorry we came back, Ranse . . . sorry we didn't stay in Wyoming?"

With a hesitation so brief she might have imagined it, Ranse turned his face to kiss her palm. His eyes were warm with love when he looked at her. "Ireland's home now, darlin' . . . yours, Megan's . . . and mine."

Silently, Megan blessed Serena for arranging the table so that Edward sat next to her. Watching him under lowered lashes, with quick sidewise glances, she thought he looked thinner than she remembered. There were shadows under his wonderful glowing eyes, but that dazzling smile was the same as the one in her memory.

He had brought champagne for his hostess, and Mama had allowed Megan a glass. She closed her eyes in pleasure as the wine bubbles burst inside her mouth.

"That's a lovely gown," he said, smiling down at her, and the champagne bubbles seemed to burst all through her body.

"Thank you," she managed to reply, wanting to die because she was not all grown up and beautiful and clever at conversation, hating being twelve years old with a pimple on her chin.

"Your father tells me you've become an excellent horsewoman," he said.

Did he care? she wondered in an agony of uncertainty . . . or was he just being polite?

"Tell me about your mare," he urged, his multicolored eyes smiling down at her as though he wanted to hear about the mare more than anything in all the world.

"Her name is Cybille," she began, and found herself telling him how she had named the horse for her father's ranch in Wyoming, and how pleased Papa had been, and how Granda had helped her train the mare . . . and now, if only Mama would consent, she might ride her in the competition at Dublin next year.

"Megan, you mustn't monopolize Edward," Mama said with an indulgent smile.

Suddenly, Megan was twelve again, deflated, no longer Edward's equal in discussing horsemanship. With a sigh, she nodded and looked down at her plate. Beneath the table,

Edward's hand took hers, squeezing it sympathetically. Megan's head swam, and her heart seemed about to leap from her body. She felt bereft when his hand released hers. Lifting her head, she looked into the warm eyes of the young man beside her, her face glowing her adoration, not caring who knew that she loved Edward with all her heart, and always would.

The butler set brandy and cigars before the library fire and discreetly departed. Ranse drew in the smoke of the fine cigar, savoring the taste before he exhaled. Through the film of smoke, he considered the other two men . . . James, so successful and contented . . . Edward, too thin, nervous and seeming at loose ends.

Edward needed to talk, for he began to pace before the fire, his brandy glass in his hand. Along with the title, he told them, he'd inherited enormous debts. He was trying to cope with that burden by selling off his father's hunters and dogs and equipment. His Aunt Martha had died, and he sold the dower house, where she had lived for so long. His mother's fortune was untouchable, as were the trust funds his maternal grandfather had established for each of the children. But his father's creditors were pressing. He'd come down to London to sell the shooting preserve his father had created at enormous expense.

Pausing, he looked at Ranse. "Seeing you and Kathleen has been the only bright spot in my life for . . . I can't remember when . . ."

"You shouldn't be so down about the mess your father left," Ranse told him. "Sounds like you're making progress." He paused to cough into his handkerchief. Damn ocean voyages . . . they always seemed to bring back the lung fever. He hadn't expected to spend three weeks recuperating in London. James and Serena were charming people, but still he felt a burden. That James was a financial genius was proven by the way he'd carefully nurtured Kathleen's little money for her.

"Better ask James to take over managing your estate," he said. James nodded and smiled, sipping his brandy.

"I did that after my father died." Edward lit a cigarette and resumed his restless pacing. At last, he paused before the marble fireplace, staring down into the glowing embers.

"It's just that my life doesn't seem to make much sense anymore, Ranse."

"Too much wenching and drinking?" Ranse asked, only half joking.

"That too." Edward blew out a stream of cigarette smoke, giving Ranse an ironic look. Flipping his cigarette into the fireplace, he stared down at it. "As Lord Hadley, I'm expected to be a part of the social scene along with the rest of the nobility." His head jerked up and he said vehemently, "I hate it! The silly, shallow . . . stupidity . . ."

"Then get out of it," Ranse replied mildly.

"I don't know how." Edward's voice was tired.

"That doesn't sound like the old Edward. He always knew what he wanted." Ranse watched the troubled young man with sympathetic eyes. James smoked his cigar in silence.

Edward shrugged, turning the familiar dazzling smile on Ranse. "Maybe it's more wenching and drinking I need . . . not less."

Next morning, Edward came to say goodbye, for he was taking the noon train north. There was a Scottish lord in Edinburgh who might be interested in buying a shooting preserve.

"You'll come to Ireland soon, won't you, Edward?" Megan asked, staring adoringly up at him.

"Soon." He gave her an indulgent smile and kissed her hand as though she were a real lady. He embraced Mama and kissed her gently on the mouth, then hugged Papa and strode down the long marble hall of Burnham House.

He was gone . . . and the tears burst from Megan in a flood.

CHAPTER 38

Ireland, 1901

"You're quite mad, girl," Frannie cried distractedly as Megan sent the maid back to the clothespress for a different gown. "Edward has seen you in trousers, for pity's sake. What difference does it make which dress you wear when he arrives?"

Megan frowned at the teal blue silk her maid held up, shook her head, and reached again for the pale gold faille she had just discarded. "He hasn't seen me since we were in London three years ago," she replied, turning so that Rose, the mousy little maid from Inniskerry, could do the buttons down the back of her gown. "I was all arms and legs and blotchy skin. I've grown up since then."

Frannie rolled her eyes and threw up her hands. Glancing at the pile of discarded gowns littering the bed, she turned to leave the room. "Sweeney was to pick him up at Dun Laoghaire this morning. If you change one more time, you'll likely not be dressed when he arrives."

Frannie didn't understand how important this meeting was, Megan thought. All these years, she'd waited to grow up for Edward. Now, at last, it had happened. The rest of her life might depend on today.

Studying herself in the pier glass, she plucked at the shirring on her bodice. She was as tall as Mama now, but her figure was too slender to be really fashionable. Despite the dressmaker's protests, she'd insisted on the shirring to emphasis her round young bosom. Mama had allowed her to put her hair up for the occasion. Rose had done it in a psyche knot with a cloud of dark hair framing her face and a tiny curl in front of each ear.

"Do I look grown up, Rose?" she asked the maid, suddenly despairing. Would Edward think her still a child playing at grown up? She had always lived only with adults, and she wondered sometimes if she had ever really been a child. Could Edward understand that she was old beyond her years . . . that she loved him, and had loved him since the day he picked her up in his arms and told her of her father.

She had not seen him since their meeting in London. She had been so blinded then by her own adoration, she was surprised when Mama said later that Edward looked pale and miserable. She'd added that he drank far too much, and she'd taken him to task for that, asking him if he intended to be like his father.

At the thought of London, Megan frowned. Serena had told Mama she must bring Megan to the city for a season when she was seventeen, to find a suitable husband. Well, she told herself, whirling before the mirror, pleased with the way the wide skirt emphasized her slender waist, she simply would not go. Why be displayed like a mare at auction when she would never accept any of those young men? The one man who would be her husband was on the way to her now, in the Morning Hill carriage coming up from the ferry.

Kathleen slid the ledger into her desk drawer and stood up. Absentmindedly, she bent to inhale the fragrance from the bowl of roses standing on her desk. She was glad Edward was coming to Morning Hill for their mutual birthday. June was the loveliest month of the year. Smiling, she glanced at her reflection in the gilt-framed mirror on the wall of the morning room.

Through the years, her hair had darkened, auburn lights that had only been noticeable in the sun, became more and more pronounced until Sean swore her hair was nearly the color of her mother's. She wore it parted in the center, looped back over her ears in soft waves to an intricate knot at the back of her head. Smoothing her hands over the bodice of the pale blue muslin blouse with its deep ruffled yoke, she admired the fit of her blue faille skirt. Her figure had changed little, although she was well into her thirties.

The old sadness welled in her then. Perhaps that figure

remained girlish because she had borne only one child. She'd badly wanted more, especially the son she envisioned in Ranse's image. The specialist she'd seen in London after their return from Wyoming had told her that awful miscarriage had damaged her so she could never again carry a child to term. Ranse refused to mourn over that circumstance. A thousand times, he'd assured her that Megan was all they needed. She'd watched the love between her husband and her daughter grow and deepen, and only seldom did the unfulfilled dream rise to haunt her.

Just then, Ranse came along the hallway, shrugging on his tweed jacket. The Wyoming cowboy had truly become the Irish country gentleman, she thought, watching him affectionately.

"He's here," Ranse announced, peering through the doorway.

At once, Kathleen went to him, slipping her arm about his waist, lifting her face to meet his kiss. This was enough, she told herself with a sigh . . . this beloved man, and the willful young lady upstairs who was made in his image.

His arm still about Kathleen's shoulders, Ranse stepped into the great hall, watching as Connors, the footman, opened the front door. The carriage, its door discreetly adorned by the ornate letters "MH" painted in gold, crunched to a halt, the horses stamping and blowing.

"Welcome home," he called as Edward's eager face peered from the carriage window.

It occurred to Ranse then, that this place was indeed home. He loved this old, graciously ordered house, loved spending his days working the horses in the lush green meadows. He'd even astonished Sean by training a promising filly as a cutting horse. No matter that occasionally he ached for the sight of Wyoming's endless expanses and its sky-piercing mountains. Even though he knew Kathleen would have stayed in Wyoming had he asked, he had chosen Ireland. This was home . . . where his daughter had grown into a beauty and an expert horsewoman . . . where each night he lay in Kathleen's loving arms and forgot that he had ever been lonely.

"Edward!" Kathleen cried, as she rushed to greet the tall young man descending from the carriage.

Ranse's heart sank when he saw that Edward was in uniform, a khaki-colored tunic with scarlet officer's tabs on the high collar, his trousers tucked into polished boots. Going off to Africa to fight the damn Boers for the bloody Empire. Ranse cursed softly to himself, then sighed, thinking that if he were Edward he might have done the same.

Edward looked around the dinner table and drew a contented sigh. The best loved faces in his life were around this table, warm in the glowing candlelight. He had changed into black broadcloth dinner clothes, wryly acknowledging to himself that he had worn the uniform to impress.

At the head of the table, Ranse sat at ease in his dark dinner clothes. My brother, father, mentor, Edward thought, giving him an affectionate glance. A faint sadness touched his heart as he realized there were deep lines in Ranse's weathered face, lines that even candlelight could not erase.

Kathleen sat at the other end of the table, smiling at him. My sister, my twin, my dearest friend . . . Edward returned her smile and lifted his wineglass in salute. She was more beautiful now than she had been as a young girl, he thought, beautiful because she was loved and content. And still as efficient. He grinned to himself as she turned to give instructions to the maid and the footman serving the table.

Flanking Kathleen, across the table from each other were Sean and Frannie. He treasured Sean's friendship and approval, knowing it must have been difficult for him to accept the son of the man who had stolen his beloved Fiona. And Frannie . . . he chuckled to himself, thinking how outraged his mother would be to see a former maid sitting at the same dinner table with Lord Edward Hadley.

Almost reluctantly, his eyes met those of the girl sitting opposite. Megan wore a gown of cherry red tissue silk, cut low so that her creamy throat gleamed softly above the ruffled neckline. Her hair was a dark soft cloud framing a perfect oval, olive-skinned face.

Luminous dark brown eyes gazed warmly into his. The scene blurred and faded. The scent of roses from the centerpiece seemed as thick and intoxicating as the fragrances floating on the air in Portofino long ago. Dark eyes held his, reviving a longing unassuaged in all the years since Angela had held him and taught him the real meaning of lovemaking.

In Wyoming, where he had escaped to forget her loss, he had told Ranse about Angela.

"You're lucky," Ranse had said. "She gave you a gift few men ever know. Be thankful for it."

"Edward."

Startled from his dream of the past, Edward looked into Megan's questioning face. This was no voluptuous Italian matron, eager for passion. This was a girl . . . his sister's child . . . just beginning to grow up. Not his sister's child, some voice within reassured him, for he and Kathleen were no blood relation. Somehow, that knowledge seemed important.

"Surely," Megan was saying, "you didn't have to go into the army and go so far away . . . to South Africa."

"No, of course not," he replied, adding wryly, "I could have continued in the silly aimless life I was living."

A small frown appeared between her wonderful eyes, as though she chose not to believe he could live a silly life.

"We thought the war was over, with the relief of Mafeking and the taking of Pretoria," Ranse said. "Does it go on because the old Queen's dead and King Edward is too busy wenching to run the country?"

"No." Edward grinned, knowing Ranse's distaste for royalty. "The Boers refuse to surrender. They keep fighting . . . guerrillas and commandos. Lord Kitchener asked for reinforcements, and I thought I should go, should have gone long before now. Kitchener's a great hero in England, you know." He smiled reassuringly at their somber faces. "It will be an adventure."

No one answered, their fear for him there in their eyes. Thankfully, he heard Frannie announce, "Here's the birthday cake!"

The maid set a huge round cake, lavishly decorated, before Kathleen. She smiled across at him. "Your favorite, Edward. Chocolate."

Taking the glass of champagne the footman poured, Edward stood up. Raising his glass, he looked lovingly at

ALWAYS TOMORROW

Kathleen. "To my sister, my twin, my dear friend," he said. "Happy birthday!"

"Happy birthday, Edward darling," she replied, reaching to touch his glass with her own.

All the old rapport was there, all the bonds that bound them, a warm current of love and caring flowing between them. He would never again be so long away from her, Edward swore to himself.

The others stood, and there were toasts around the table. Edward felt wonderful, happier than he had been in years, and it was not just the champagne. Yet, a faint sense of guilt nibbled at the edges of his mind as his eyes were drawn irresistibly to the adoring face across the table.

·❊[CHAPTER 39]❊·

How quickly the fortnight had flown, and tears stung Megan's eyes at the realization that Edward would be leaving tomorrow. It was as though selfish fate simply snatched the time away. Even Mama had helped snatch it, telling her firmly, "Edward simply can't spend every minute with you, Megan. He enjoys Papa's and Granda's company. He's having such fun teaching them to play polo. Don't hang after him so."

She'd tried so hard to be sedate and aloof and grown up. It was just that every glance from his wonderful everchanging eyes was precious to her. Every one of his dazzling smiles filled her heart with indescribable joy. Yet, she sensed a kind of wall between them as he attempted to treat her like a child.

"I'm no child," she announced to the mirror, startling Rose, who was arranging her hair. When Rose stepped back to admire her handiwork, Megan rose, shrugging off the jacket of her dove gray riding habit. The day was warm, her pale pink handkerchief linen shirtwaist would be quite enough.

Studying her reflection, she thought she looked wan, and wondered whether she dared sneak into Frannie's room and use a bit of her carmine. No, she decided, once she and Edward were riding, the fresh air would bring up her color. Taking up the bottle of "Attar of Roses" toilet water Serena had given her, Megan splashed the scent at the base of her throat.

Dismissing Rose, Megan stood for a moment at the door

of her bedroom. A faint tremor shook her deep inside, for she had made a momentous decision. Tomorrow, Edward would be gone to faraway South Africa. She had only today to share her heart with him, to somehow bind him to her, forever.

In the kitchen, she picked up the picnic basket Cook had packed for her, peering inside to make sure there was wine for Edward.

Frannie gave her a suspicious look. "Edward spoils you as much as everyone else does," she said sternly. "Have you thought he might rather play polo or hunt with Sean and Ranse today, than picnic with you?"

"He promised," Megan replied airily, "and this is his last day at Morning Hill."

"Just remember you're not yet fifteen and Edward is a young man," Frannie called after her. Megan's heart thumped. It was as though Frannie had read her intentions.

Edward was waiting with the saddled horses. Megan's heart seemed about to leap from her chest at the sight of him. The dark green moleskin riding breeches fit his tall frame to perfection, and the open-necked white linen shirt accentuated the tan he'd acquired at Morning Hill.

"Are you ready for our picnic, sir?" she asked, smiling up at him.

"At your service, ma'am." He grinned, his teeth very white in the tanned face.

Megan laughed for sheer happiness as he lifted her into the saddle. But when she looked down at him, his face had changed somehow. It was as though a shutter had closed over his myriad-colored eyes. His hand trembled a little as he handed her the reins.

Spurring her horse, she called for him to follow. She'd chosen the spot already. The larch woods her great grandmother had planted years ago were tall now, the branches interlaced to create a hundred secret places.

The sun was so bright everything seemed gilded . . . the meadows they raced across, the stone fences they leaped. Breathless, she reined in at the edge of the woods.

"This is where we'll have our picnic," she told him. "Isn't it beautiful?" With a wave of her hand, she took in the lush

359

green meadows, the tall larch trees murmuring softly in the slight breeze, and in the far distance the cloud-rimmed Irish Sea.

"Beautiful," he said as he dismounted, but his eyes were on her.

"Edward," she murmured. At once, he looked away.

On a blanket spread in the low-hanging shade at the edge of the woods, they shared the lunch Cook had packed . . . cold ham, and beef and tongue, and bread spread thick with fresh butter. There were sweet little red plums from the garden, and Edward poured half a glass of wine for her.

Edward finished his wine, set the glass in the basket and lay back on the blanket, his hands beneath his head. He felt strangely detached, as though time had stopped and the two of them were cut off from reality. Megan tossed a bit of bread to a voracious squirrel and laughed aloud at the creature's scrambling. God, he thought, did she even guess how enchanting she was with that musical laugh, her perfect face, and that exquisite young body?

Stop it, he commanded himself. Deliberately, he looked away from her, staring contemplatively out to sea . . . a sea that would soon take him far away from here. Unexpected pain struck him at the thought. All he held most dear was here in this green land.

Megan moved across the blanket, setting aside the picnic basket, so that she was close beside him. She smelled of roses and horses, he thought, an incongruous but strangely exciting scent.

The dark eyes studied him, and Edward found he could not bear to look into them.

"When will you come back?" she asked.

With a sidelong glance, Edward smiled and shrugged. "When the Boers surrender, I suppose. The Dutchmen can't win against the British Empire . . . but who knows how long they'll keep trying?"

Watching his quiet, tanned face, so handsome above the white linen shirt, Megan felt desire wash through her, as inexorable as the tide. "I shall miss you terribly, my beautiful Edward." She leaned across to look directly into his eyes.

At once, the shutter closed in his eyes. "Dear little

Megan," Edward said indulgently, reaching up to stroke her cheek. "I shall miss you too."

Bending her head, Megan deliberately touched her mouth to his, softly at first, then, as passion possessed her, harder . . . wanting . . .

With a start of surprise, Edward took her shoulders in his hands and roughly pushed her away. "Don't!" His face was white and shaken. "Don't, Megan!"

As though reading his thoughts, Megan cupped his face in both hands, looking deep into his eyes. "I'm not a child, Edward. Not any more. I'm a woman." Taking his hand, she held it against her full young breasts. He felt the nipples harden beneath his touch. Covering his hand with hers, Megan held it there. "I love you," she murmured, "and you're going away. Please . . ."

"Megan . . . don't . . ." His words were lost in the eager mouth possessing his again, warmer now, more urgent. Without thought, he caressed the sweetness of her lips with his tongue. Hesitantly, she opened to him, and the taste of her aroused him beyond control. Their mouths melded together, straining, wanting more.

Her hands were everywhere, as though a thousand years of womanly instinct guided them . . . unbuttoning his shirt, caressing his back, slipping open his belt, sliding gently along the hot, throbbing evidence of his desire for her. Somehow, her shirtwaist was gone, her camisole pulled up above the soft breasts that burned like firebrands against his naked chest.

Lost now, beyond thought, beyond anything but the blinding force of his need to possess the exquisite, abandoned creature in his arms, Edward returned her caresses. He kissed the pulse pounding at the base of her throat, teased her breasts until they were hard peaks of desire. His mouth trailed kisses downward as her skirt and pantaloons were discarded. In the moist throbbing next between her thighs, he kissed and stroked until she arched against him, moaning softly.

"Love me . . . oh, please love me, Edward." Megan clutched him fiercely against her as their mouths met and devoured each other.

When he entered her, she cried out softly in pain as her

maidenhead gave way. He began to move gently against her, and she cried out again, this time in pleasure.

Edward thought his very flesh and bones had melted into hers. They were one being caught up in a cosmic wind, no longer earthbound, no longer aware of anything except the ecstasy of this moment. When she cried out his name, arching against him, taking him deep into her soft warmth, Edward heard his own cry of rapture echo hers.

They lay in spent silence, holding each other close.

"Darling, darling Edward," Megan murmured, kissing his ear, her breath still coming rapidly. She hadn't guessed it would be like this—man experience so intense she knew she would never again be the same. The love she had borne for Edward for so long had flowered into something new and wonderful beyond belief. Raising on her elbow, she looked down into his face. His eyes were closed, and she leaned to kiss his eyelids. "My love . . ."

"Oh, God!" His eyes closed tightly, and a look of unbearable anguish filled his face. "What have I done?" Abruptly, he sat up, his back to her.

"You've made love to the woman who loves you, dearest Edward," Megan murmured as she sat up too, leaning her face against his bare shoulder.

"You're a child!" he cried, his voice filled with pain. "God! Your father would have me gelded if he knew of this."

Megan smiled, pressing her lips against his shoulder. "He won't know . . . nor anyone. Edward, please look at me."

Reluctantly, he turned to face her, and the regret in his eyes pierced her heart. She'd quite deliberately and selfishly brought him here to seduce him. How could she have known that their marvelous joining would hurt him so afterward?

"It was all my doing, Edward," she said quietly, laying her palm gently against his cheek. "I wanted us to love each other before you went away tomorrow. It seemed to me that if we did, I could be sure you'd come back to me."

"Ah, Megan . . . it was wrong." He shook his head doubtfully.

"It was wonderful," she corrected with a radiant smile.

"Tell me," her voice was low and throaty. "Wasn't it wonderful?"

"Magical . . ." Edward's voice was muffled as he turned his face to kiss her palm. Then she was in his arms again, their mouths hungry against each other.

"Shall I fix your bath now, Miss?" Rose asked.

Megan sighed as she let her rumpled skirt slip to the floor at her feet. She didn't want a bath, for that would wash away the touch of Edward's hands, the imprint of his body on hers, even his semen, dried now between her legs. Ignorantly, she'd thought once would be enough just to bring them together. Now, she found herself wanting him again with an intensity that was like a fire burning inside.

"Yes, Rose . . . the bath," she said absently. When the girl went to the kitchen for the pails of hot water, Megan bundled her discarded clothing together, hoping Rose wouldn't notice the stains.

They would have each other again, Megan told herself fiercely. She would be old enough to marry when Edward came back from South Africa, and they would have each other forever then.

"Oh, God!" she cried aloud, suddenly aware how many days and nights lay between now and that much-desired resolution.

If only Edward hadn't been so guilt-stricken. It had broken her heart to see the pain in his face when he pulled away from that last fierce embrace in the darkness of the stables.

"Forgive me, Megan," he said. She saw that his eyes were a clear green when he was unhappy, just as they turned to gold when he kissed her and loved her.

"I love you, Edward," she said, looking steadily into those unhappy eyes. "I'll wait for you to come back to me, and no one else will ever know about today."

They parted then, for Sean came into the stables. How much more needed to be said, she wondered, and would there ever be time enough to say it?

"Your bath's ready, Miss." Rose's voice startled Megan from her thoughts. "Shall I help you?"

"No." In spite of herself, Megan's voice was sharp, for she could not bear the thought of any hands but Edward's touching her body. "Lay out the red tissue silk," she said. Tonight was Edward's farewell dinner, and he had told her how beautiful she looked in that gown.

Stretching out in the warm soapy water that filled the long tin tub, Megan looked down at her pale body. It seemed almost the body of a stranger. Tentatively, she touched her flesh as though to prove she and the body were one. Closing her eyes, she let a rush of desire pour through her. Her hands moved of their own volition, touching where he had touched. Her nipples hardened, and her whole being ached with frustrated passion.

Trembling, Megan leaned back in the tub, knowing now that she had opened a Pandora's box that could never be closed.

CHAPTER 40

Could he possibly survive this night, Edward wondered, and tomorrow's farewells? It was all made a thousand times more painful by the presence of the exquisite creature sitting across the table from him. The cherry red gown added a charming flush to her olive skin, and he ached to kiss the laughing mouth. But there were shadows in the dark eyes that never met his . . . shadows he had put there.

Beyond the guilt that lay like a sick lump in the pit of his stomach, Edward knew he would never really leave this girl behind. The love he felt for this child-woman bore no resemblance to what he'd felt for his other loves . . . not even to his infatuation with Angela. Somewhere in the blank days of the future, he knew they would be reunited. Those enchanted moments in the larch woods had welded their very souls together.

Kathleen rose from the table to lead them into the drawing room. In this unorthodox household, there was no separation of the sexes after dinner. They all gathered together, the men to enjoy their brandy and cigars, the women to join them in good conversation.

"Edward." Ranse's hand was on his arm. "Could I have a few minutes alone with you . . . in the library?"

Edward froze, his heart sinking. Had Megan somehow revealed to her father his friend's betrayal of trust? Dear God, he thought, I can't bear for him to know what I've done. He waited in agony as Ranse took a decanter of brandy from a cabinet in the library and poured two glasses.

Handing one glass to Edward, Ranse sat down, indicating Edward should take the chair opposite. "I need to talk business with you," Ranse said, and Edward suddenly realized he'd been holding his breath.

He waited as Ranse studied his glass, seeming to steel himself for what he had to say.

"I'll never make old bones, Edward," he began abruptly.

"Nonsense." Edward said the proper thing heartily. He knew at once from Ranse's piercing look that hypocritical platitudes had no place in their relationship. "Tell me about it," he added softly.

"We've brought Morning Hill to where it's a going concern," Ranse told him. "But it'll never be a big money-maker. Since the war started, we've been able to sell the cull horses to the army at a good price, but that's a one-time proposition."

"Everything appears to be going well," Edward remarked, puzzled as to Ranse's intentions.

"Everything but the old man here," was the ironic reply. After a moment's silence, he looked directly at Edward. "When I first came to England with you I had that bout of lung fever, remember?"

Edward nodded.

"It wasn't the first time. All those weeks I spent with the Indians . . . always cold, never enough to eat. The poor bastards did their best for me, but they were cold and hungry too. When I finally got back to Cybille Creek, I spent a month lying around and trying to stop the damn coughing. Thought I was over it, but somehow those ocean trips started it up again." He paused to accept a light for his cigar from Edward, who lit his own cigarette. "Since Kathleen and I went to Wyoming, it's never really gone away."

"Have you seen a doctor?" Edward asked, everything inside him denying what Ranse was telling him.

"Oh, yes." Ranse cocked his head, and grinned. "All he can do is agree with me."

"Bloody hell!"

"It's Kathleen and Megan's future I'm thinking about now," Ranse continued. "I've got the Wyoming ranch leased on a profit-sharing basis . . . with damn little profit. I need to sell out and have James invest the money for them." He fell silent, staring at the glowing end of his cigar.

Denial rose strong in Edward with the refusal to believe his boyhood hero could ever die. Mention of the Wyoming ranch brought memories of the wide and beautiful country where a boy had once found who he really was, where a young man had come to mend a broken heart and found himself again. He had lost that self for a while in the hectic scramble of English-noble society. Now, he hoped he'd found it for the final time.

"Let me buy Cybille Creek," he burst out, and laughed aloud at Ranse's incredulous face.

"My grandfather left me a fortune in my own right . . . apart from the Hadley estates. With James's help, it's grown considerably. I can afford it, and you know what the place means to me."

Ranse's dark eyes gleamed with moisture, his face working to repress emotion. "No charity, Edward."

"Damn it, Ranse," Edward protested. "I want that property."

"It's yours." Ranse held out a hand.

Edward clasped the hand in both of his. "I'll make the arrangements with James before I leave for South Africa."

"Ranse." Kathleen opened the library door and peered in. "Have you forgotten I had the photographer come out from Greystones to take pictures tonight?"

Edward crushed out his cigarette and rose to meet Ranse's level gaze.

"Don't mention this to Kathleen," Ranse said in a low voice. "No need to trouble the time we have left."

The maids were finishing clearing up breakfast in the dining room. Edward's bags stood waiting in the great hall. Megan paused at the foot of the stairs, staring at the bags, fighting against the pain that rose in her throat.

How could she bear to wait again? It seemed her whole life had been spent in waiting . . . waiting to grow up, and now waiting to marry, waiting to lie in Edward's arms once more. Tears ached behind her eyes as she turned and went out through the French doors of the dining room into the garden. She knew Papa had gone to the stables to make sure Sweeney had hitched the horses up correctly. He really trusted no one with the horses except Granda.

All the breath went out of her when she saw Edward's tall figure standing there in the garden. She hated the uniform that was taking him far from her, but he looked incredibly handsome in his well-fitted khaki tunic with the leather strap across his chest, the scarlet fastenings on the high collar, and the buttoned epaulets of a lieutenant. He was smoking a cigarette, staring off into the distance where the blue Wicklow mountains swam in a summer haze.

"Edward," she spoke softly.

Quickly, he turned, flipping his cigarette onto the gravel pathway. "Megan." His voice sounded choked.

For one searing moment they stood, drowning in each other's eyes. Then she was in his arms, and the warmth of his embrace set her flesh aflame. In blind need, their mouths sought each other. She clung to him, thigh to thigh, breasts crushed against the brass buttons of his uniform.

Breathless, their lips parted. Megan's eager tongue caressed the perfect mouth she loved so much. With a groan, Edward took her into his mouth, and the taste of him, pungent with tobacco, aroused a wild excitement in her. His arms held her fiercely against him, his mouth hungry on hers.

She felt him gathering his strength then, and just as suddenly as they had come together, Edward pushed her away.

"Don't!" he said in an agonized voice.

"Don't you like it?" she asked, amazed at her own daring.

"I like it far too much," Edward replied hoarsely, turning away.

"Wait!"

"Megan, you promised." Edward looked at her, his eyes green and filled with misery.

"Dearest love," she said. "That was goodbye. I won't kiss you again until you come back to me."

"Dear God," he murmured, gazing intently at her, his eyes golden now. "I have no right to love you like this."

Megan let out a long breath, forcing herself to refrain from touching him. "You love me, Edward. That's all I need to know."

Quickly, she bent to the green shrub growing beside the path, its blossoms gleaming in the morning sun. She plucked one of each . . . purple, lavender and white. Straightening, she held them out to Edward.

"It's an old tradition in our family to give these flowers as a token of faith and everlasting love." Looking into his golden eyes, she continued breathlessly, "My grandmother Fiona gave them to Granda, and pressed them in her prayer book. Mama gave them to Papa when he came to us here at Morning Hill. Let me give them to you, dearest Edward . . ."

When Edward did not move, simply devouring her with his eyes, Megan stepped close to him and tucked the blossoms into the breast pocket of his uniform tunic.

"Don't forget me," she begged, suddenly terrified that she might never see that loved face again.

Taking the hand that still lingered where she had placed the flowers, Edward pressed his lips into her palm. "You're in my heart, sweet Megan," he said in a choked voice. "You will always be there."

Sun-dappled shade from the great oak tree lay over the gravel sweep and the stone steps. Sweeney loaded the last of Edward's bags, slammed the boot closed and came around to climb up into the driver's seat.

No farewell in all his life had been as difficult as this one, Edward thought as he hugged Francine and thanked her. Next, he shook Sean's hand, and the older man clasped both his hands over Edward's.

"Take a care, young Edward," he said in a husky voice. "Come back to us."

Turning to Ranse, Edward felt a terrible aching pain rise in his chest, and his throat clogged with unshed tears. Ranse's dark eyes were bright with moisture as he held out his hand. Edward seized his shoulders and held him in a fierce embrace, torn by the bitter certainty that he would never see this beloved friend again. At last, they parted, and Ranse turned away, pulling out his kerchief to wipe his eyes and blow his nose.

"Dear Edward," Kathleen said and came into his arms. "How I wish you could stay with us always." Her voice was muffled against his shoulder. She felt a jolt as she saw the blossoms in Edward's breast pocket, and a faint chill came over her as she guessed who had placed them there.

"Sweet sister." Edward kissed her gently on the mouth and smiled into her tear-stained face. "I have to go now, but I'll be back." She would need him when Ranse was gone, he thought, and he must be there for her. With tender fingers, he wiped the tears from her cheeks. Kissing her forehead, he knew that he must go now, or he too would weep.

Megan stood a little apart, watching. When her dark tear-filled eyes met his, Edward drew in his breath, knowing this would be the most difficult parting of all. For a moment, they looked at each other, then she flew across the space between them, flinging herself against him, wrapping her arms about his neck like a child.

Edward steeled himself, yet his arms tightened around her slender body of their own volition. Bending, he pressed his mouth against the top of her head, knowing that if he kissed her lips, he was lost. Taking her shoulders in his hands, he gently held her away, turned quickly and climbed into the waiting carriage.

"Goodbye," he said, leaning from the window, struggling to hold back the tears. "Goodbye." The dazzling smile that had been Edward's special gift since childhood shed its warmth upon them. Sweeney touched the whip to the horses, and the carriage rolled down the beech-shaded drive. To those who watched, it seemed some of the brightness had gone from the day.

CHAPTER 41

Ireland, 1902

Megan wandered restlessly into the kitchen, hoping Sweeney had brought the post with one of Edward's infrequent and long-delayed letters from South Africa. Spring sunlight lay across the well-scrubbed wooden floor, blending its warmth with the peat fire muttering low in the grate. It struck her how empty the kitchen seemed, now that Nanny Quinn no longer rocked beside the fireplace. Since last winter, she lay in the hillside near the chapel . . . her bones aching no longer.

Megan didn't want to think of loss and grief, she wanted a letter from Edward to bring him alive again for her. Tears stung her eyes as she thought of the homesickness that came through in the letters addressed to the whole family. Strange to think that spring began in South Africa in September with icy rains that Edward said turned the veldt into a quagmire, and Christmas was in midsummer. The British had thought the war over, but Jan Smuts and his commandos had refused to stop fighting through the burning South African summer. Now, the war was truly over, for the surrender had been signed at Pretoria this very month. Surely, Edward would be home soon.

If there were no letter, she told herself, she would take the old ones from Mama's desk and read them all again. As many times as she had searched through them, she had never found a message meant for her alone. Why had she thought Edward would write love letters to her? Obviously, he still thought of her as a child, even though she had given him a woman's heart and a woman's love.

371

He was as far from her as though he were on the dark side of the moon. She had only his picture, taken that last night of his visit at Morning Hill. It stood on her bureau, gilt-framed, looking out at her with that radiant smile curving his fine mouth. His eyes looked dark in the photograph . . . golden brown, she thought, and his thick hair was a bit mussed. Sometimes, when she looked too long at the beloved image, her whole body seemed to scream with longing.

Frannie's step startled Megan. Turning from the fire where she had been absorbed in her thoughts, she saw Frannie hurriedly try to conceal a bucket from her. Looking over Frannie's shoulder, she gasped. Soaking in the bucket of cold water was a bundle of bloodstained handkerchiefs.

"Papa's," she choked. Frannie nodded, her plump face tight with pain. Megan's safe and beautiful world began to disintegrate.

"Oh Frannie!" She burst into sobs, turning to the comforting arms held out to her. "I should have known . . . I should have helped . . ."

"There's nothing you can do, love." Frannie patted her heaving shoulders.

But she should have known. If only she hadn't spent her days mooning for Edward, she would have guessed. Signs came back to her . . . Mama's perpetually worried frown, the hollow coughing in the night from Papa's bedroom, the way he'd given over more and more of the training of the horses to Sean and the new trainer, Tobin.

"Is he going to die, Frannie?" she demanded through her tears.

Frannie sat down heavily at the kitchen table. "We all have to die someday, Megan," was her evasive answer.

Then it was true. Megan sat down opposite, burying her face in her hands, tears streaming from her eyes. She remembered that long-ago day in the garden when she had first accepted Papa. How dear he had been with her then, comforting her in her fear for Mama. For the first time, she realized how deeply she had come to love him. And how she'd taken him for granted, certain that he would always be there when she needed his strength and his warmth.

372

"It's not fair!" she sobbed, looking at Frannie. "We haven't heard from Edward in weeks. Maybe he's been killed in the war . . . and now Papa . . ." Grief was a terrible, hideous pain. "Oh Frannie, what can I do?"

"Megan, love," Frannie began, reaching across the table to take her hands in a comforting clasp. "I've been with you since the day you were born. I know you're a bit willful and spoiled, but I know that you are sweet and strong too."

"I can't bear it, Frannie." A new freshet of tears burst from Megan's eyes as she looked into her friend's sympathetic face.

"We bear what we must, dear." Frannie sighed thoughtfully, then continued. "I've been your mother's friend since her unhappy years at Hadley Hall. She's good and loving and strong, but I fear not strong enough for this. I see her watching him constantly, urging him to eat, yearning to make him well and comfortable again." A sob caught in her throat, and it was a moment before she could go on.

"You'll have to give her your strength, Megan. Help her bear this loss, because she loves Ranse with all her being, as though he were a part of her, body and soul."

Reaching out, she cupped Megan's tear-stained face in her plump capable hands. "Love them both, dear heart . . . and be sure they know it."

From the day the specialist in Dublin had given them his fateful verdict, Kathleen had hoped only that there would be no long and destructive illness. Months of invalidism for a man who had always been strong and active seemed more than either of them should have to bear. She kept her own grief within, maintaining a cheerful facade for the sake of the household and for Ranse. Yet, she knew that no one at Morning Hill could be unaware of the inexorable progress of his disease. The servants, the stable hands, even the tenants, could not miss seeing his strong body slowly wasting, the skin across his rugged face shrunk to the bone.

She was thin and hollow-eyed herself from rousing to change the bed after the terrible night sweats, propping him up to ease the coughing. Now, the doctor had given them the dreaded drugs to ease his pain . . . an indication to her that the end was near.

Spring came in a rush that year. One day, it was still dismally winter; the next, the countryside burst forth in verdant green. Trees leafed out, roses and fuchsias perfumed the garden, hosting a swarm of mumbling bees. The soft mating cries of the doves echoed through the warm air.

"I'm glad to be here for the spring," Ranse mused as he settled into the wicker chair set for him in the garden.

Kathleen plumped his pillows and tucked the blanket over his knees. Her throat ached and tears burned her eyes. She had known one day he would insist on speaking of the reality she had tried so hard to deny. Slowly, she sat down on the rock wall beside his chair, letting him take her hands in his dry, wasted ones.

"My love," he whispered hoarsely. The dark eyes holding hers were soft, even with the fever that burned so brightly there now. "My forever love . . ."

When she leaned across to kiss him, Ranse turned his face away. "You mustn't kiss me anymore. I don't want to leave this damnable thing with you."

Clasping his face in her hands, Kathleen pressed her lips to his. Pain lanced through her as she tasted the sourness and the salt of old blood on his mouth. Forcing a smile, she told him brightly, "You're my husband, and I have the right to kiss you whenever I please . . . for as long as . . ." Her voice trailed away. Hot tears stained her face.

At once, he drew her close, holding her face against his shoulder as she wept, smoothing her hair with his thin fingers. "For as long as I am here to kiss," he murmured in her ear. "Yes, darlin' . . . what can it matter now with so little time?"

"I can't bear it!" she burst out. "I can't bear to live without you."

Ranse sighed, lifting her chin to look into her tear-filled eyes. "What is . . . is, dear love." His fine chiseled mouth trembled, but he forced himself to continue. "I have to go, and you must accept that . . . and let me go." His arms tightened about her. "We'll be together again. I know it. Somewhere, I'll be waiting for you to come to me."

She had always prided herself on being strong. Now, that strength seemed to have disintegrated. It was her dying love who provided strength even while his body failed. In the time left to them, she must not burden him with her grief. She must allow him to prepare with her for the future and, as he had asked, let him go.

When the end came, it was as though Ranse had planned it. All the necessary business papers had been signed. All the things he had wanted to say to those he loved had been said.

"I'm lucky," he told Kathleen wearily. "Some people never have a chance to say goodbye."

She found him in the garden when she came to bring him a morning cup of tea. His head was leaning to one side, and she thought he had fallen asleep from the drugs. But when she touched his gaunt face, it was cold as ice. Dry-eyed, she sat beside him, holding the loved hand to her lips for the last time.

It was Megan who wrote the messages . . . to Edward in distant South Africa, to James in London . . . for Kathleen could not seem to even contemplate the task. She sat for hours, staring at nothing, neglecting all the household tasks that had once kept her days filled. Megan and Sean and Frannie exchanged worried glances, urged her to eat, begged her to rest although she never slept at all. She never wept, and watching her, Megan thought her mother was frozen in grief . . . frozen tears, frozen feelings.

The day of the funeral was calm and clear, with a serene and flawless blue sky arching over the green hills. A minister came up from Greystones, for there was no Protestant clergyman in the village. He read the service from the Book of Common Prayer. Megan saw that Mama held her own copy, its leather cover cracked and worn . . . Fiona's prayer book.

Tears burned Megan's eyes, and her throat felt clogged with grief. Taking her mother's icy hand in hers, Megan felt the hot tears spill down her cheeks and fought down her wild sobs, for it seemed to her the black-clad woman beside her had died too. Kathleen stood very stiff, her empty burning eyes staring straight ahead, her face expressionless.

The minister's low voice was accompanied by the soft click of beads telling the Rosary, for all the tenants had come, and the villagers Ranse had traded with, and all the horse breeders and buyers from the county. The kindness of the straightforward American cowboy had won the hearts of his Irish neighbors.

At the graveside in the old family burying ground, the dark fir trees rustled and sighed in a sudden breeze. Megan felt a tremor shake her mother as she withdrew her hand from Megan's grasp.

She watched as Mama stepped forward, trembling as if in pain, and laid upon the coffin three small blossoms . . . purple, lavender and white.

"Tomorrow . . ." she whispered as the box was lowered into the earth. "Until tomorrow, darling."

James and Serena arrived from London two weeks later. Serena was elegant in her Paris gowns, and she wore an enormous hat with a black ostrich feather. James was as briskly kind as always, growing a little paunchy now, his hairline receding. They were a welcome diversion for her mother, who seemed so lost and unable to cope with the slightest task. James at once took over the desk in the morning room and set about putting the financial affairs of Morning Hill in order.

"Time will heal," Frannie had promised, but watching her mother wander through the house like a pale ghost as though she were looking for Papa, Megan wondered.

Now, with James and Serena here, Mama was forced back into reality. There were guest rooms to be put in order, meals to plan. At the end of the first week, Mama seemed more herself. It was then, James asked the two of them to meet with him in the morning room.

"My dear Kathleen," James began, peering at them with his dark, bright eyes. "I'm delighted to be able to tell you that your financial position is excellent."

When Kathleen merely stared at him in silence, Megan asked, "Just what does that mean, Cousin James?"

"I didn't know your father well, Megan, but I did know how deeply he cared for his family's welfare. He asked that I not tell you this at the time, to spare you worry, but he sold the ranch in Wyoming. I've invested the money in a trust fund that will be more than adequate, even without any income from Morning Hill."

"He sold Cybille Creek?" Kathleen sat up straight, staring at James in consternation. "Who bought it?"

"I'm not at liberty to say," he replied, not meeting her eyes. "Rest assured it's in good hands, Kathleen. And be thankful your husband cared enough to make you and Megan financially secure after his death."

Kathleen collapsed into violent weeping. Quickly, Megan rushed to embrace her, thankful that the dam had burst at last. They had all watched her dry-eyed stoicism fearfully, knowing that somehow she must weep to cleanse her wounds and heal her grief. That Papa had sold his beloved Cybille Creek to care for them had opened the floodgates. In time, Mama would be herself again.

The letter from South Africa arrived only a few days before Serena and James were to leave. It was written in an unfamiliar hand . . . a short note of condolence written, it said, by a nurse in a British hospital. "The only thing worse than knowing Ranse is gone is my not being there to comfort and help you." The words were so like Edward, she could almost hear his voice, but fear burgeoned in Megan's heart as she read them. Edward was surely wounded or ill to be in a hospital, yet nothing was said in the letter about his condition.

At once, she sat down to reply, demanding that he let them know the state of his health and when he would be home. Posting the letter did not ease the fear that nibbled at the back of her mind. With all her heart, she longed to fly across the miles separating them, hold Edward in her arms and make him well.

"Leave off the bandages when you get home," the doctor in London had said. "The wound is suppurating and needs air to dry up the pus so it can heal."

Edward glanced around the vast echoing hospital, filled with khaki-clad wounded back from England's most expensive and ugly war. "The last battle of the war," Edward muttered, grimacing with pain at the doctor's touch.

"That right?" the doctor had said disinterestedly. "Well, see your own doctor when you're home." Wiping his hands on a grimy towel, he'd moved on to the next patient.

Standing now before the mirror in his own room at Hadley Hall, Edward slowly removed the bandages he had worn on the trip up from London. When the last strip of blood- and pus-stained linen lay on the dresser, he stared at the man who was now Lord Edward Hadley.

His family hadn't seen his face yet . . . only the bandages. His mother had welcomed him with her usual cool kiss on the cheek, his sisters had cried and said he was very brave. Sixteen-year-old Thomas had stared at him as though he scarcely remembered him. They would have to see it now, and he winced at the thought.

The face looking back from his mirror might have been two different men . . . one the old Edward . . . the other, a scarred monster. His wound, still red and ugly with infection, had destroyed the left side of his face. From the wide red slash on his forehead, down through the swollen, weeping hole that had been his left eye, the smashed cheekbone, the huge gash ended just above his chin.

"The last battle of the war," he muttered bitterly. "The last bloody battle."

The April morning had been cool and sunny, as the British, under Colonel Ian Hamilton, advanced on Rooiwal. Major Roy had chosen Edward, with forty other men, to ride in the advance screen. They had pushed their tired horses forward across the implacable veldt, daring the Boer commandos to show themselves.

Suddenly, they were there . . . an eerie sight, as a thousand slouch-hatted figures on horseback swept knee to knee up the hillside toward them. There was no cover, or camouflage, no trees or farms to hide the British scouts.

The Boers opened fire from the saddle, cantering slowly at first, then breaking into a wave that swept over the British.

Edward's horse fell beneath him. Quickly, he took protection behind the animal's body, firing his rifle at Boers descending from every direction. The magazine was empty, and he hurried to reload. In that brief pause, a huge bearded Boer drew rein beside him. Dismounting, he stared at Edward with wild, furious eyes.

"Burn me farm," he shouted, unsheathing the saber at his waist. "Rape me wife, murder me babes! Die, Khaki pig!"

As he lifted the saber and swung, Edward threw up an

378

arm in defense, taking part of a blow that might have cut his skull in two. The Boer lifted the saber for another stroke when a bullet caught him in the chest. His huge body fell across Edward, spurting blood.

Covering his face with his hands, Edward wished he might wipe that scene from his mind forever, along with all the other ugliness of war: the flogged Africans lying unconscious in the unmerciful sun, the stinking camps where Kitchener, once his hero, had gathered the Boer women and children to starve and die so that he might scour and burn the countryside, the dams full of rotting animals, the veldt covered with slaughtered Boer herds, tired hungry horses falling beneath their weary riders . . . and the dead . . . so many dead. He'd gone to fight for his country, searching for some focus in his purposeless life, only to return disillusioned and heartsick.

He heard a quick indrawn breath behind him and looked up to meet the eyes of the valet his mother had sent to attend him.

"Pretty sight, eh?" he asked, his mouth twisting bitterly. The man lowered his eyes and hurried to lay out Edward's dinner clothes.

He'd lost weight, Edward thought as he descended the stairs to the dining room. The dinner clothes seemed too large, or maybe they were simply strange after all the months in filthy khaki.

The family had already gathered in the dining room, waiting for him, and Edward steeled himself for what was to come.

"Good evening," he said pleasantly, taking the chair left for him at the head of the table.

Horrified silence fell as they stared at him. He heard one of the maids gasp. A low wail broke from his mother's throat, rising into anguished screaming. She tried to stand and fainted into the arms of a footman. Victoria grasped her young husband's arm and buried her face against his shoulder. Georgiana burst into sobs, covering her face with her hands. Thomas stared at his brother, in both revulsion and fascination.

"Sorry." Edward rose, knowing he should have replaced the bandages, and knowing there was no one at this table who cared about the man behind the ugly wound. "Bring a tray to my room," he told the footman.

The fire had burned low. Edward sat slumped in his chair, the untouched dinner tray beside him. Sunk in misery, he pictured the painful scene in the dining room reenacted at Morning Hill . . . Kathleen fainting in horror, Megan hiding her face in revulsion . . . Oh God, he thought, why didn't I let that Boer cut my head open?

There was a timid knock at the door. His mother came in, looking pale, supported by Thomas, whose glittering eyes fastened at once on Edward's wound. Somehow, the boy reminded Edward of his father.

Staring at the fire to avoid looking at him, Deborah asked in a faint voice, "Will you always look like this, Edward?"

I'm your son, he wanted to say, does it matter? Instead, he answered in a flat voice, "The wound will heal eventually."

"Georgiana is so upset." His mother's voice wavered. "She's nineteen and hasn't been offered for. She thinks . . ."

"She thinks having a monster in the house will ruin her chances?" Edward looked at her dispassionately, feeling nothing for her, and nothing for the staring brother beside her. He didn't belong here where there was no love for him . . . had never belonged.

Deborah paused, seeming to steel herself. "We'd planned quite a busy social schedule. The title carries responsibilities, you know." She stared fixedly at her hands. "We all think it would be better if you went away . . . for a while."

All the agony of the past months, all the loneliness and pain, rose like a bitter tide, overwhelming reason. In a violent movement, Edward stood up, sending the dinner tray crashing to the floor. Deborah gasped. Thomas grinned.

"Take it all, damn you," he shouted. "Take the bloody title and everything that goes with it!"

Deborah drew back with a gasp, sniveling, never meeting his eyes.

With a tired sigh, Edward turned away. It was over . . . his life ended by a blow on the African veldt in a way more agonizing than death itself.

"I'll be gone tomorrow, Mother," he said in a low hard voice. "I'll be gone."

* * *

Afternoon sunlight streamed warm and golden through the windows of the guest room where Megan lay across the bed watching Serena pack. From the paddock, they could hear the voices of James and Sean calling as they watched the trainer put a hunter through its paces.

"You have such beautiful gowns," Megan sighed. "I didn't realize before how unfashionable and dowdy we dress here in the country."

Serena glanced at her with a soft musical laugh. "Fashion isn't all that important, Megan. I must dress well because of James's position, although I must admit I love fine clothes."

Turning on her back, Megan stared at the ceiling. It occurred to her suddenly that she had much to learn. If she were to marry Edward, she would have to know how to dress for his position as Lord Hadley, and how to behave in society. A long sigh escaped her, as she was certain she would not like society. Perhaps Edward would live here, and everything could go on as it was now.

"You must come down to London for the season next year," Serena said as she carefully packed and rolled her jewels. Her maid moved quietly about the room, folding clothes into the open bags. "We'll be presenting our Elizabeth to society. There'll be wonderful balls and parties." Smiling, she glanced at Megan. "You have a lovely figure, dear. I'm sure my dressmaker could do wonders for you." Eyebrows lifted, she gave Megan a meaning look. "And I suspect you'd charm more than one eligible young noble into offering for you."

Megan drew in her breath, remembering now that the London season was simply a marriage market . . . and she was not in the market. Yet, she could learn things there, manners and ways of dressing that would please Edward.

"I shall have to ask Mama," she answered, smiling back at Serena.

Later, the carriage swept through the stone pillars at the end of the drive, and the gatekeeper hurried to close the iron gates behind it.

"I shall miss them, Da," Kathleen said, watching the carriage disappear along the roadway.

"Aye. Fine people . . . for aristocrats," Sean answered, with a grin.

"Let's have tea in the garden, shall we?" And she turned to give instructions to the maid.

As usual, she sat in Ranse's wicker chair. Sean drew up another chair opposite, with the wicker table between them. She wanted to talk, he thought, needed to talk, and he waited.

"Serena wants me to bring Megan down to London for a season next year," she began without preamble.

Sean nodded. "To find a husband?"

Kathleen drew in her breath in a long sigh, not wanting to contemplate the thought of losing Megan just now.

"It's best, Kathleen." Sean's voice was low. "She's as restless as a mare in heat already. If ye don't find a man fer her, she's likely to be rollin' in the hay with one o' the grooms."

"Da!" Kathleen protested, shocked.

"Tis God's truth," he continued doggedly. "She's too much like her grandmother. Tobin already has hot eyes for her."

Kathleen was silent, staring across the garden, where the fuchsias lay over the stone wall like the ruffles on a lady's gown. "She had her heart set on Edward," she said in a low sad voice. "Now, we don't know whether he's alive or dead." She swallowed the sob that rose in her throat.

"Blast his mother," Sean growled. "She could've answered yer message and let ye know whether the boy was all right."

The maid approached with the tea tray, and Kathleen sat up, gesturing to her to place it on the table. When the girl had gone, she turned to Sean with an ironic smile. "You must remember, Da, that she always hated me. Just as she hated the memory of my mother."

Sean did not reply, staring down at his big brown hands. She thought perhaps he was lost in memories of Fiona. Again, she sighed, not only for herself, but for all the women of her family, who seemed destined to love only one man in all their lives.

CHAPTER 42

London, 1903

London was both fascinating and frightening, Megan thought, as James's carriage took them from Victoria Station to Burnham House. The house itself was even more intimidating than she remembered, replete with gilt and marble and fine satin brocade. She thought of the easy comfort of Morning Hill and doubted she could ever find happiness among these English aristocrats.

Mama had written again to Hadley Hall for news of Edward, and again there was no reply. James was asked to check on him, for members of the nobility did not simply drop from sight. If Edward had been killed, or had died, there would have been a notice in the Times. But James replied ambiguously that he no longer managed the investments of the Hadley estates.

Doggedly, Megan continued writing to the South African hospital until a bundle of her letters was returned, marked "Unknown." It was horrifying to see that word written across the package of letters . . . as though Edward had never existed at all.

"Perhaps we'll never know what happened, love," Kathleen told her weeping daughter. Gathering all her strength, she added with finality, "Edward would want us to get on with our lives and be happy. Perhaps London . . ."

Megan was not to be consoled. It was only for Edward she had meant to go to London at all. Restless in the house, she rode every day . . . long and hard. Watching her, Sean remembered another girl who had spent her repressed passions in the same way.

"It's best ye go to London," he told Kathleen.

"Yes," she agreed, and asked Serena for lists of what they must bring. They would go two weeks before Elizabeth's ball so they could make use of Serena's fashionable dressmaker. When James offered to present Megan at a ball along with his own daughter, Megan was terrified by the idea. Remembering her own unhappy London season, Kathleen suggested a small reception for Megan so that the ball would be Elizabeth's own.

Elizabeth, named for her maternal grandmother Kathleen remembered with such affection, at first looked askance at these country cousins. But soon, she and Megan had revived the childhood friendship. They shared plans, squealing with delight over gowns and kid gloves and satin dancing slippers. Megan was relieved that her mother had refused to let her share the great ball with Elizabeth, for she was certain her cousin would have resented it. The days flew with fittings, dancing lessons, and etiquette lessons from Serena.

On the night of Elizabeth's ball, Megan stood before the mirror as Rose buttoned her gown. It was cherry red silk, the color chosen because it had been Edward's favorite. Tears started in her eyes as she realized again that he would not be here to take her hand and whirl her in a waltz. She had planned to come to London to learn to be the kind of wife he would want, and now there was no need, for he seemed gone from the earth. No, she told herself vehemently, Edward was alive somewhere, and when he could, he would come back to her.

Serena had impressed upon her that to find a husband she must dance well, say little, and never, never talk about breeding the mares. With a sigh, she thought that now she was caught up in the whole thing, she must go through with it.

Behind her, she heard Rose sniffling. Picking up the garnet necklace James had given Mama from his mother's jewels when he had realized they had only the pearls Papa had bought when he and Mama were in London, she turned to the maid. "What is it, Rose?" she asked, seeing the girl's eyes were too filled with tears to fasten her necklace.

"Nothin', Miss," came the broken reply.

"Do you always cry over nothing?"

Rose wiped her eyes on the hem of her starched white apron, trying to control herself. Then she burst out, "It's Connors. He, he . . . well, he's been offered a post here in London and he's like to stay."

Eyeing her speculatively, Megan recalled the warm glances that had passed between maid and footman on the journey from Ireland. "Mama will be furious," she pronounced.

"Aye," came the muffled answer. "Mayhap, I'll stay too."

"With Connors?"

Rose shook her head violently and burst into fresh tears. "Mistress will turn me out anyways when she knows."

"Knows what?" Megan stared at the girl weeping into her hands. Slowly, understanding dawned. "The bloody bastard's got you pregnant," she burst out.

A long sorrowing wail came from Rose.

Megan drew the girl into her arms, unmindful of her elegant ball gown. "Now, Rose," she comforted, patting the heaving shoulders. "Mama would never turn you out for that. And she'll deal with Connors . . . I'll see to it."

Rose lifted her tear-stained face, hope growing in her pale blue eyes. "Oh, Miss. I was near out of my head to know what to do."

"Do you love Connors?" Megan demanded bluntly.

"Aye." The girl's face softened, and her eyes glowed. "Oh . . . aye, I do, Miss."

An ache began somewhere in the depths of Megan's heart as she looked at the face of love. Her love was gone from her, perhaps forever, and suddenly the ball seemed a terrible and tedious pretense, for she would find no husband here or anywhere on earth.

The days flowed one into the other, filled with calling and receiving callers, riding in the park, shopping. Nearly every night, there was a dinner party, or a reception, or a ball. Serena announced that the Irish cousin was a great social success and would certainly be offered for by some eligible young gentleman.

But Megan found the young gentlemen indistinguishable in dress and looks and conversation. Often, she forgot their names and stumbled along until she could ask Elizabeth whom she was talking to. The balls were best, she thought, for there, whirling in the arms of some young man, she could pretend she danced with Edward. He had been here once, she was certain, in all these great houses, dancing, flirting, drinking. And he was always with her in her thoughts. His picture was the last thing to fill her eyes at night and the first when she awakened. When she casually mentioned his name in conversation, no one seemed to know of him.

"Wounded in South Africa, so I heard," one ancient colonel harrumphed in reply. But he knew no more.

Serena's prediction came true, for the night came when Megan went into her mother's bedroom to tell her that Charles Allen wanted to see her tomorrow to offer for her daughter's hand.

"Which one is he?" Kathleen asked in astonishment.

They fell into each other's arms, howling with laughter over poor Charles, who looked like every other young man. Serena would know his pedigree, as well as the family assets, for she took the business of marrying off daughters seriously. Two young men had already asked for Elizabeth's hand and been summarily dismissed by James, who thought their prospects poor.

When their laughter died, Megan looked imploringly at her mother. "Can we go home, Mama? I can't accept Charles . . . and you know that I'm no more fitted for this life than you. No wonder Edward tired of it."

Kathleen's face sobered. Reaching out, she gently pushed a stray lock of dark hair back from her daughter's face. "Edward," she repeated the name softly. When she lifted her chin in the old decisive way, Megan could only smile. "We'll go home next week," Kathleen said. "And we'll go by way of Hadley Hall."

They took a hired carriage from Brookfield, leaving Rose and Connors ensconced in their own private room at the inn. They had been safely married in an obscure Catholic church in London, with Kathleen and Megan standing as witnesses. Rose glowed with happiness, and Connors was subdued, as befitted a man about to be a father.

Nothing seemed changed as the carriage approached Hadley Hall's steep gabled facade. Tall windows still peered down through ivy-colored walls, and the beech trees were heavy with the green of summer. Even the same hounds bayed at the approach of a carriage.

"The hounds . . ." Kathleen said, frowning. Edward had sold the hounds, and most of the hunters, and the shooting preserve, in an attempt to pay his father's debts. But there were hunting hounds again at the hall.

"He's not here," Megan said, as the driver, in his rusty tail coat and top hat, jumped down to open the carriage door. Kathleen stared at her, puzzled, until Megan added defensively, "If he were here, I'd know it." She hurt inside with the certainty of his absence, and she was grateful when her mother took her hand sympathetically.

The maid took Kathleen's calling card and disappeared, leaving them standing in the hall. Redecorating was under way at the manor, for the rugs were rolled up on the stairway where she had waited for Edward to be born, and there were painter's ladders in the drawing room.

"My lady's not at home," the maid announced as she returned, the silver card tray still in her hand . . . empty.

Anger blazed in Kathleen's eyes, and the maid shrank back. How dared Deborah do this? she thought furiously. Whatever grudges she had borne all these years, surely she could not refuse to grant Kathleen some knowledge of Edward.

Pushing the maid aside, she sailed down the hallway, certain that Deborah would be in the ladies' sitting room at this time of day. The door was discreetly closed, and Kathleen flung it open.

Deborah rose to her feet, dropping her embroidery. Beside her, a young woman stared in amazement.

"How dare you!" Deborah gasped, and Kathleen smiled.

All that plum cake, she thought, for Deborah had grown uncommonly stout, the pale flesh of her face hanging in porcine folds, the fine silk gown straining at the seams.

"I won't trouble you except for one thing, Deborah," she said in a cool tone. "Just news of Edward."

Deborah's head jerked up, making her jowls tremble. Her eyes flashed. "We no longer speak that name in this house."

"You will speak it to me," Kathleen's voice rose, and Megan stared at her mother in astonishment.

"Edward has disgraced his family by the unsuitable life he leads," Deborah cried harshly. "He's renounced one of England's oldest titles, for . . . for . . ." Her words dissolved into inarticulate sputtering.

"Mother . . . your heart." The girl rose to place a placating hand on Deborah's arm.

"At least, my son Thomas knows his place as a gentleman and an aristocrat." Deborah's eyes held a gleam of pride now, but it faded into cold hatred as she added bitterly, "Edward is dead to me."

"Where is he?" Megan cried, no longer able to restrain her anxiety.

Deborah gave her an icy look. "In that godforsaken place where my husband lost his fortune."

"Wyoming," Kathleen exclaimed joyfully, turning to smile at Megan.

Deborah jerked at the bell pull, and a footman appeared in the doorway. "Show these two . . ." and she seemed at a loss for a word to describe her unwelcome visitors. "Show them out at once."

Megan leaned on the rail of the ferry, watching Ireland rise out of the sea. A cold wind blew from the north, but nothing could drown the warmth of the knowledge she hugged to herself. Edward was alive! In Wyoming, that distant land that had been the focus of so many of her father's tales.

She had begged Mama to let her take the first boat from Liverpool to America, but Kathleen had been adamant. "We know where he is now," she said firmly. "We'll write, and if he wants to see us, he'll say so."

"Something has happened to him," Megan protested. "Something more than his mother told. If only I could see him, I know I could make it right."

But now, as she stared at Dublin taking shape on the shoreline, she wondered if her seduction of Edward had sent him away from her, forever. He had loved her, wanted her, but his guilt had been terrible.

388

From her reticule, she took the gilt-framed picture and stared into the beloved face. There was a sweetness about the finely chiseled mouth, a warmth and depth in the eyes that was more than photographer's art. A bit of Edward's soul was captured there.

"Dearest love," she whispered to his image. "We'll be together again. Even an ocean can't keep us apart."

··❧ CHAPTER 43 ❧··

Ireland, 1904

Tobin kissed her. Megan had known he wanted to, for she'd felt his hot eyes watching her for weeks now.

She'd just come in from a long morning ride, across the stone fences and the brooks, around the larch woods to the cliffs above the sea where an ancient round tower crumbled into the grass. Whipping the horse, she rode wildly as she always did, trying to escape the demons inside.

Spring had come again to Morning Hill, and still Mama would not let her go to Wyoming. The letters sent to Edward at Cybille Creek remained unanswered. They had even contacted Mr. Carlson, the lawyer who had once handled Papa's business in Wyoming, to no avail.

All winter, she'd felt it building inside her, this need for which she had no name. Again and again, in the darkness of her bedroom, she'd rehearsed all that had happened that long-ago summer day in the larch woods. It terrified her to find the memory growing dim. She felt bereft when she could not quite conjure up Edward's face without the aid of his photograph.

This morning, she'd ridden like a wild gypsy through the golden sunlit meadows, where mating larks called. Taking the fences at a gallop, she wondered whether she was riding toward something or escaping from something.

Her horse had been sweating when she'd brought him into the stable for one of the grooms to rub him down. Tobin was there alone, and he took the reins from her, staring at her.

Then he roughly pulled her against him and kissed her hard. Tobin was a muscular young man with curly brown hair and close-set blue eyes. Granda said he was a top trainer. He was handsome enough that the village girls welcomed him, but Megan had never felt any particular attraction to him.

Yet, when his hard masculine mouth claimed hers, a wave of heat swept through her body. An ache began between her thighs. Out of all her loneliness and longing, she returned his kiss for a moment. Then full realization dawned, and she shoved him away.

Tobin grinned triumphantly. Megan turned and fled. How could she condemn his behavior when she felt that somehow she had invited it? Not only that, she had kissed him back.

Granda was walking across the gravel sweep toward her, and she began to tremble, wondering whether he could tell from her face what had happened. What was this madness that possessed her and seemed to grow stronger day by day?

"I can't possibly go to Wyoming now," Kathleen said at supper when Megan tentatively broached the subject once again. "There's a buyer coming over from Sussex, and the Master of the famous Quorn Hunt. There's the auction next month in Connemara . . . and then the Dublin Horse Show. Tobin's going to ride Crécy for the Breeders Cup. I've always wanted to win it, and this year we've a good chance."

"There'll always be something, won't there, Mama." Megan's voice was low and resentful. Pushing back her dish of trifle, she decided she must consider how to run away and go to Wyoming by herself. Perhaps Mama simply didn't want to go without Papa. Or maybe she feared what they might find . . . even feared Edward's rejection. Megan only knew she had to go.

"I think Megan should go to America this summer." Having made this pronouncement, Sean leaned back in his chair. His dark blue eyes were steady on Megan's face.

It was as though he read her heart and understood the insatiable yearning that drove her night and day. He'd so often said how like Fiona she was. Perhaps that was why he understood her better than Mama . . . better than anyone.

"I'll go with her," Frannie made her own announcement. She exchanged glances with Sean, as though all this had been agreed upon beforehand.

"I don't . . ." Kathleen began doubtfully, to be interrupted by Megan's joyful laugh as she reached to squeeze Frannie's hand in gratitude.

"She needs to go." Sean's eyes held Kathleen's. "Whatever she finds there, she can't get on with her life until she goes."

For a long moment, Kathleen stared at her father, then slowly nodded. Her willfull and passionate daughter seemed a reincarnation of Fiona, Da's great love. Perhaps that accounted for the strong rapport between them.

"You're right, Da," she conceded.

"When?" Excited, Megan turned to Frannie, ready to make plans.

Granda cleared his throat loudly. When they all looked at him, he smiled. "It's my feelin' it would be best fer Megan to travel with her Grandmama . . . and we'll make it that, if Frannie will wed me afore she goes."

Frannie looked startled. One plump hand pressed against her black silk breast, as a slow smile lit her face. "Why not, old Sean?" she said with a soft laugh.

"Why not, indeed?" Kathleen interrupted briskly. "You two have been a scandal long enough."

Every moment of the trip was excitement for Megan. She paced the deck of the ocean liner, breathing the sharp sea air and counting the days until Wyoming. Meanwhile, Frannie lay moaning with *mal de mer* in their stateroom, audibly wishing she had never agreed to this trip.

An old friend of Sean's came down from Boston to meet them at the dock in New York. Fergus O'Brien was a stout, white-haired man with a round Irish face. He saw them safely aboard their westbound train, promising to telegraph Mr. George Carlson in Cheyenne of their imminent arrival.

The vastness of America astounded them . . . the immense forests, the huge farms, and finally the unending plains rolling away to the horizon.

"A lonely sort of place," Frannie said, staring unhappily out the train window.

"Papa used to joke that in Wyoming you could stand on a hill and see forever," Megan replied, determined to buoy

Frannie's spirits. She suspected her new grandmama already missed Sean and wished herself safely back at Morning Hill. It was not as though they were newlyweds after the small family wedding in St. Kevin's church in the village. They had been together for years.

And she had been apart from Edward for three long years. The thought brought a sense of urgency rising in her. She had been tense and high-strung ever since the trip began, forcing down this same need with the knowledge that she was on her way to Edward at last. Yet, even as she enjoyed the sights, the trip seemed interminable.

"How far to Cheyenne?" she asked the conductor strolling through the car.

"Tomorrow, Miss," he answered, touching his cap.

Megan's heart leaped and raced like a wild thing. Tomorrow, she would be with her love . . . hold him in her arms again. With a smile, she reached down to open the carpetbag at her feet so that the small potted plant inside might breathe. Yesterday-today-and-tomorrow, nurtured all the way from Ireland just for Edward. Now, tomorrow was almost here.

George Carlson was a tall, heavyset man, his bald head covered by a derby hat. He wore a huge, drooping moustache which was stained at the edges by tobacco juice. His wide face was set in a frown, although he tried to conceal his dismay with carefully polite manners.

He had been there waiting when Megan and Frannie walked from the train into the echoing cavern that was Cheyenne's railroad station. The derby hat was doffed only long enough to introduce himself. Replacing it square on his head, he stared at them with a distracted air.

"I telegraphed the ship. I telegraphed your hotel in New York. I can't believe you didn't get my messages." He struggled to cover the annoyance in his tone.

"What messages?" Megan inquired innocently, glad that she had intercepted those telegrams and Frannie had not seen them. No one was going to keep her from Edward, not this man . . . no one.

"Mr. Hadley has refused to see you, Miss. There was no point in your coming to Wyoming at all." There was a final ring to the words. Mr. Carlson looked stern then . . . like a judge to whom there is no appeal.

Megan hesitated for only a moment, before she announced defiantly, "He'll see me." Picking up her carpetbag, she started through the station.

Frannie threw up her hands, then bent to pick up her bag. She knew Megan too well. If she had made up her mind to see Edward, not this Mr. Carlson, nor the devil himself, could stop her.

The unhappy Mr. Carlson signaled a redcap who gathered their baggage and followed Megan to the front of the station.

Exhilarated, Megan looked around at the bustling town. Mama had called it a raw boom town, but Cheyenne had grown up. Brick stores lined the streets where streetcars and carriages and motor cars moved back and forth. There was a little park with green grass and tall cottonwood trees. Cowboys, in wide-brimmed hats, rode by. Hitching racks stood before many of the business places, and waiting horses were tied there.

"I'll bring my automobile around," Mr. Carlson announced with unconcealed pride. "I'm sure I can get rooms for you at the Plains Hotel, Cheyenne's best . . ."

"Why not just go direct to Cybille Creek?" Megan protested. When she saw his hesitation, she urged, "We'll gladly pay you for your trouble."

The troubled frown returned to his face, and he drew a deep breath. "I have been told by Mr. Hadley that, under no circumstances, am I to bring you to his ranch." When Megan stared at him in surprised dismay, he shrugged. "Really, Miss, there's nothing I can do."

"Well, I shall do something." Her voice broke on the words, and unwelcome tears stung her eyes. How could Edward do this? It was so unlike him.

"There's a telephone at the ranch." Mr. Carlson was obviously upset by her reaction. "After you're settled at the hotel, perhaps you could telephone Mr. Hadley and speak to him yourself."

"Capital idea!" Frannie agreed. "Right now, I just want my room, with a soft bed and a hot bath."

"Oh, Frannie," Megan said remorsefully, hugging her

friend. "You must be tired . . . I'm sorry." Turning to Mr. Carlson, she smiled her most dazzling smile. "We'd be so appreciative if you would give us a lift to the hotel."

It was their first ride in an automobile, though neither of them would have admitted it to Mr. Carlson. Frannie sat very stiff, clutching the edge of the seat as though she expected the thing to explode. Horses shied from them as the auto chugged down the main street to the hotel. Mr. Carlson seemed inordinately proud of his auto, but Megan thought it stank, and it was noisy, and she'd never trade a good horse for such a contraption.

As the bellboy disappeared into the elevator with their baggage, Mr. Carlson gave her his card and explained that the hotel operator would place a call if they should need to get in touch with him.

"Just let me know when you're leaving," he said, "and I'll be delighted to take you to the station."

"We're not leaving until I see Edward," Megan replied in spirited tones, frowning at the man, wondering why he was so difficult to convince.

Mr. Carlson opened his mouth as though about to speak, then snapped it shut. With a sigh, he drew another card from his card case and handed it to Frannie. "If you need anything, please call me."

"Cheyenne isn't the place I'd choose for a holiday," Frannie announced with a sniff. A carriage passed them, rolling up a mixture of dust and dried horse droppings.

"It's exciting," Megan protested, looking about as they strolled down the main street. "Look at the Indians." She frowned. "They don't look like the pictures." Although their black hair was in long braids, they wore white man's clothes beneath the colorful blankets wrapped about their shoulders, but no feathered headdresses or bows and arrows.

She felt exhilarated this morning, for already she'd called Cybille Creek Ranch, astounded and delighted by the miracle of the telephone. A Mrs. Tompkins, the housekeeper, had answered. Mr. Hadley wasn't in, she said in acerbic tones. Would she have him call Miss Megan O'Neil at the Plains Hotel this evening? Megan asked. "I'll tell him," was all the woman said before she abruptly hung up.

Tonight, she'd hear Edward's voice on that telephone. She'd tell him how she still loved him, and everything would be all right. By tomorrow, they would be together. She was certain of it.

Today, she and Frannie explored the town. The shopping did not compare with Regent Street in London, or even with Dublin, but everything was new and different. In a small shop that catered to tourists, she bought a beaded Indian purse of soft white doeskin for Mama. She had a mad impulse to buy a feathered headdress, but it cost far too much. In a dressmaker's shop, she gleefully purchased a dark brown divided riding skirt, which the proprietor assured her was the fashion for ladies in Wyoming. It should have been a fashion long ago, Megan told Frannie.

Before they ate dinner in the hotel's restaurant, Megan made sure the desk clerk knew where she was, so he could call her to the telephone at once. But no call came, although Megan stayed awake until midnight, hoping. He's out with the cattle, she consoled herself, remembering Papa's stories. He didn't come back to the ranch at all today. But he'll call tomorrow, or I'll call him.

By evening of the next day, she could wait no longer, and she called Cybille Creek once more.

"Hello," Mrs. Tompkins's gruff voice came on the line.

"This is Megan O'Neil again," she said. "Did you give Mr. Hadley my message?"

"I gave it to him," the woman said.

"But he didn't call," Megan protested.

"That's his business," came the short reply.

Dismayed, Megan stared at the phone. Edward knew she was here, and yet he hadn't answered her call.

"Will you please tell him I'm waiting to hear from him?" she asked, struggling not to be angry with the woman.

"Sure."

Megan sighed. Mrs. Tompkins was a woman of few words. "Thank you," she said, and the receiver at the other end clicked.

Walking slowly back up the stairs, Megan did not know whether to be angry or sad, or simply amazed that Edward would behave in this manner. It wasn't like him to be rude or uncaring. Something terrible has happened, she thought, and the tears started.

Next day, her conversation with Mrs. Tompkins followed the same laconic lines. But now, anger blazed in Megan. How could Edward treat her like this . . . how dared he!

"Tell him I'm coming out to the ranch to see him if he doesn't call." She almost shouted the words into the telephone.

"Oh, no, Miss . . . no." She'd struck a nerve, Megan thought, for the woman was obviously upset by her threat. "Mr. Hadley doesn't see strangers."

"I'm not a stranger!" Now she was shouting, and weeping at the same time. Because she was crying too hard to talk, it was she who hung up.

"Maybe we should listen to Mr. Carlson and just go home," Frannie said, her strong competent hands massaging Megan's shoulders. Having wept herself into exhaustion, Megan lay prone across the bed, her eyes closed.

"Not until I see Edward," she muttered stubbornly.

"Ah, love," Frannie sighed. "He doesn't want to see you. He's made that more than clear. Whatever his reasons, believe me, dear . . . you can't ever force a man to love you."

"But I love him, Frannie," Megan answered with soft certainty. "I always have, and I always will. I won't go home until I've seen him and know he doesn't love me."

Mrs. Tompkins's voice began to take on an exasperated tone at the daily announcement that Miss O'Neil was calling for Mr. Hadley. A week of daily rejection and Megan looked worn from the bouts of weeping. Mr. Carlson came around to see how they were, if they were ready to leave for England. He took them to dinner at one of Cheyenne's finest restaurants, but he still refused to offer an explanation for Edward's peculiar behavior.

The next night, Megan sat in the little wood-paneled booth, waiting for the operator to complete her call. If she were refused again tonight, she decided, tomorrow she would hire a carriage and go to Cybille Creek Ranch anyway. She had waited all these years, and she would not be denied now.

There was a long sigh at the other end of the telephone when she gave her name once again.

"Mr. Hadley said to tell you," Mrs. Tompkins stated, "that you may come to the ranch tomorrow, and he'll see you for a few minutes." She paused, and a curious note crept into her voice. "He also said that you haven't changed a bit."

·◦】 CHAPTER 44 【◦·

Wyoming, 1904

Cursing heartily, Mr. Carlson struggled to change the flat tire on his automobile, pausing occasionally to wipe his sweaty face and mutter an apology to his lady passengers.

Unable to idly stand and watch, Megan strolled through the sagebrush. When Carlson observed that there might be snakes out there, Francine took a firm stance in the middle of the dusty road and refused to move. Ignoring his warning, Megan moved away, bending to pick the flaming red flowers Carlson said were called Indian paintbrush.

On every side, the sagebrush plains stretched away, a woolly blue-gray blanket over the landscape. To the west, immense blue mountains rose from the plain, with one tall peak still snowcapped in midsummer.

Jubilant that her journey was ending, Megan loved it all . . . loved the pungent fragrance of sage perfuming the crisp clear air, the sense of infinite space and freedom. She knew now how much Papa had loved her mother . . . to leave this wide inviting land behind him, forever.

It would be over soon, the long agonized waiting. Today, she would be in Edward's arms again, and there would be n more waiting . . . ever.

Mr. Carlson rose, vainly trying to brush the dirt from his light gray summer suit. Picking up the discarded tire, he quickly tied it to the spare frame bolted on the side of his auto. Cranking the machine into thundering life, he helped his passengers board, and they moved off once more, down the rutted dirt road.

Slowly, a line of green grew into trees and willows along Cybille Creek. The landscape rose into rolling hills, with limestone outcroppings, and in the far distance, pale limestone cliffs.

When Mr. Carlson turned off the road and jumped down to open a pole gate, Megan gave a soft cry of recognition. Her parents had brought photographs of Cybille Creek Ranch from their last visit, so she knew the shape of the huge log house. But the black-and-white photos did not depict the silvery sheen of the weathered logs, or the deep green of the tall cottonwood trees surrounding the ranch house. From the hours spent with her father, she could almost name the outbuildings . . . cookhouse, bunkhouse, stables, tack shed, the corral where Edward had been injured all those years ago. There was a huge barn, obviously new, for the lumber had not yet weathered.

With a long sigh, Megan stared at the reality of a lifetime's dreams. Only when Mr. Carlson spoke her name twice did she realize he had stopped the engine and parked beside the front of the house.

Almost at once, the front door opened, and a tall, rawboned woman walked toward them. She wore her gray hair in a tight knot at the top of her head, and her dark calico gown was covered by a voluminous white apron.

"Good day, Mrs. Tompkins," Mr. Carlson said jovially. "These are the ladies I've brought to see Ed . . . Mr. Hadley. May I present Mrs. McLoughlin, and Miss Megan O'Neil."

Even while responding with pleasantries, Megan was aware of the hostility in the woman's eyes.

"Well," she began in her harsh American accent. "It's too bad you come all this way. Mr. Hadley was called out to one of the line camps this mornin'. One of the boys got hisself hurt."

Dismayed, Megan protested, "But he'll be back soon, won't he?"

"Cain't never tell how these things go," the woman snapped. Then she seemed to relent. "C'mon in. I'll give you a cup of coffee 'fore you head back to town."

Mr. Carlson cleared his throat as though to say, I told you so. With a frowning glance at him, Megan turned to Mrs. Tompkins, determinedly donning her most innocent and pleading face.

"I'm sure Uncle Edward wouldn't want us to leave." Behind her, she heard Frannie choke at the title she hadn't used since childhood. "We've brought our luggage, you see." And she waved a hand at the back seat of the auto stacked with bags.

"He said . . ." Mrs. Tompkins began.

Quickly, Megan stepped to her side, laying a hand softly on her arm and looking at her with wide innocent eyes. "I wonder if you knew my father, Ranse O'Neil?"

The hard face softened, and her faded blue eyes gleamed. "Everybody in Wyoming knew Ranse. A good man through all his troubles . . . and no better cowman ever lived."

"Do you suppose," Megan asked, deftly turning the woman about to walk up the veranda steps with her, "that I could have my mother's old room? It would mean so much to me . . ." She let her voice trail away on a sorrowful note and saw that she had won the woman completely.

"Why sure, honey." Mrs. Tompkins patted her hand. "I'll have to make up the beds for you, and I'm the only help Mr. Hadley keeps in the house." Over her shoulder, she called, "C'mon in and get your coffee, George. I'll have one of the hands bring the bags in later."

With a quick backward glance, Megan caught a glimpse of Mr. Carlson's astounded face, and Frannie rolling her eyes heavenward.

The room was just as Mama had described it, although the blue chintz draperies were faded now, the heavy mahogany furniture had a faint sheen of age, and the room smelled closed and musty. She had been conceived in that bed, Megan thought with a smile as she laid her cape across it . . . during the worst blizzard of the century. Mama had told her that once in a fit of exasperation, as though trying to explain her daughter's wildness.

Frannie was in the room next door with a small dressing room between. Just now, she was helping Megan unpack.

Mr. Carlson had downed his coffee and a huge ham sandwich, then cranked up his auto and headed back to Cheyenne. Saying goodbye with a doubtful expression, he urged Megan to call him if she needed him.

A knock on the door made Megan's heart leap. Perhaps

401

Edward was back. But it was Mrs. Tompkins reporting that Mr. Hadley would see them at dinner . . . seven o'clock.

"I'll have a tray in my room," Francine said quickly, adding when Mrs. Tompkins raised her thick eyebrows questioningly, "I'm quite worn out from the trip."

"Why can't I see him now, if he's back?" Megan demanded.

"Miss, please." Mrs. Tompkins looked distraught, as though being a go-between had worn her out.

With a sigh, Megan conceded. It would give her time to bathe, fix her hair, and dress carefully for Edward. She must look perfect for him on this most important night of her life.

Lifting the china pitcher from its stand, she poured a bit of water into the potted yesterday-today-and-tomorrow. Should she give it to him tonight, or wait until she knew exactly how she would be welcomed?

They had searched the Dublin shops for the exact shade of cherry red silk Edward had once admired on her. It had been worth it, Megan thought, studying herself in the mirror above the bureau. The tiered sleeves fell in soft ruffles to her elbows and the low, softly ruffled neckline accentuated her round bosom and her creamy throat.

Frannie fastened Aunt Elizabeth's garnet necklace and smiled at her in the mirror. "You are so beautiful, love. No man could resist you."

Doubts assailed her. She fought back the tears, determined not to ruin the effect by crying. "Do you really think so, Frannie?" What if Edward didn't like her at all? What if he loved another woman? She had waited and dreamed so long. Now, reality waited downstairs, and she was terrified the dream might be shattered.

"Go now," Frannie said. "You mustn't keep him waiting."

Megan's heart pounded so violently she could scarcely breathe. Her hands on the smooth bannister were cold and damp, and her knees felt like water.

The stairs curved down into the stone-paved foyer which opened through a wide archway directly into the sitting room. It was all as it had been described to her . . . the colorful Indian rugs on the pine floor, the rustic furniture, the huge stone fireplace.

All the breath went out of her at the sight of a tall man standing beside that fireplace. He wore a dark suit and his back was to her, but she would have known him anywhere. One hand rested on the mantel, the other held a glass of whiskey. His proud, aristocratic head was bent as he stared into the blazing fire.

"Edward!" All the years of longing and waiting burst forth in the joyous sound of his beloved name.

Quite deliberately, he turned toward her so that the light from the lamp fell across his face. Shock stilled her running feet, and she felt suddenly cold as ice. The sound torn from her throat was half horror and half protest. For a hideous endless moment, they stared at each other, then she ran to throw her arms about him. At once, she knew that moment of hesitation had been too long. Edward stood very cold and stiff in her embrace.

Taking her by the shoulders, he held her away so that she had no choice but to look into his face. It was still the loved face she remembered, but the left side was distorted and ravaged. A huge white scar crossed the side of his forehead, descended through the puckered remains of his left eye and down his cheek.

When he spoke, the voice was harsh, and bitterness colored every word. "Always determined, weren't you, Megan? Now, you've had your way. You've seen the Cyclops of Cybille Creek."

Overwhelmed by pain for him, her eyes swimming with tears, Megan reached up to touch his face. Edward jerked away from her angrily.

"Darling Edward," she cried as the tears spilled over. "I can't bear it that you should have been hurt so terribly."

"A Boer saber," he said in a dispassionate voice, turning away to pour a glass of sherry for her from the decanter sitting on the sideboard. "They said I was lucky to be alive." He handed her the glass, his face cold and distant. "A questionable conclusion."

"Why didn't you come back to Morning Hill?" Megan asked softly. All her being longed to comfort him, yet she knew instinctively that he could not bear her sympathy. "We've written you over and over . . . and we've asked about you everywhere."

"At Hadley Hall?" His voice was bitter. When she nodded, he continued. "My reception there convinced me there was no place in society for a man who looks like this. My mother and sisters wanted to hide me in the attic . . . the family monster. So I threw it all over and hid myself in the wilds of Wyoming."

With trembling hands, Megan lifted the glass of sherry to her lips and sipped, hoping the wine would steady her. "Your mother is a dreadful woman," she burst out.

A semblance of the old smile twisted Edward's still perfect mouth. She wanted to seize him and kiss that dear mouth, but she stood still and waited.

"You're quite right," he said, and suddenly he seemed composed, in command of himself. "Here." And he drew up a Morris chair upholstered in dark red corduroy. "Sit here by the fire. Even in summer, Wyoming nights are cool."

They might have been two casual acquaintances, she thought in anguish, rather than two lovers destined for each other.

As Edward sat opposite her, he drew something from his coat pocket. Megan forced herself to look directly into his face, composing her features, determined not to be repelled by his disfigurement. Lifting his hands, Edward slipped a black leather eyepatch over the lost eye.

"I usually wear this to spare the world," he said sardonically. Then his jaw tightened. "Tonight, I wanted you to know it all."

"It's very dashing." Megan forced a smile, trying to lighten the mood. "You look like a wild buccaneer from a pirate ship." She looked at the wide white scar on his forehead and cheek gleaming in the firelight, determinedly keeping the teasing smile on her face.

"Indeed." Edward's voice was sarcastic. He took a drink from his glass, then turned to her, once more the polite and proper Edward.

"Tell me about Kathleen. Is she well? And good old Sean? I thought Francine was with you. Where is she?"

Megan laughed. The tense atmosphere in the room evaporated as the words tumbled out of her, trying to answer all his questions at once. She told him about Sean and Francine's wedding, about James and Serena's visit after their daughter Elizabeth's marriage, about her season in London.

"Mama is too involved in her horse business to come with me," she said.

His eye met hers, and she remembered then how she had known his eyes were green when he was unhappy. "Perhaps she didn't want to be here without Ranse," he said softly.

"Yes . . ." Megan held out a hand toward him. "Oh, Edward, I know Papa would be pleased to see you running Cybille Creek."

Edward's mouth compressed, and he turned away, fumbling for a cigarette. When he spoke, his voice was low and each word seemed to cost him pain. "Ranse told me he was dying before I left for South Africa. That's when I bought the ranch." He drew a deep breath. "I meant to be there with Kathleen when it happened. I thought she'd need me . . . but I failed her. I hope she'll forgive me when she knows why."

Megan's eyes stung. She longed to touch and comfort him. "Mama loves you as she always has, Edward. It's been hard for us, not knowing what happened to you."

"I'm sorry for that." Edward stared down at his cigarette. "It just seemed to me I had no other choices."

You could have trusted our love for you, Megan thought and started to reach out to take his hand. He looked up then as Mrs. Tompkins announced dinner, and the moment was lost.

There was fine linen and china on the dining table, with a silver candelabra shedding its warm light over them. The meal was simple American fare, Edward told her, roast beef, potatoes and gravy, buttered carrots, with apple pie for dessert.

Megan ate little, her throat aching, her mind preoccupied with wondering what she might say to reach Edward's heart. He plied her with questions . . . about her trip . . . about her time in London . . . about the goings-on at Morning Hill.

"We have a new trainer," she said. "Granda thinks he's very good." Her face warmed at the memory of allowing

Tobin to kiss her . . . a poor substitute for this beloved man across the table. She thought he was studying her face, and she dared not meet his look.

At last, he rose from the table and took her arm to lead her back into the sitting room. Replenishing the dying fire, he poured two brandies and offered one to her. As before, he sat opposite her before the fireplace, but now there seemed no more questions. Silence fell between them as they sipped the brandy.

Watching his brooding face, Megan thought how she had always loved that gentle curve of his mouth, the proud set of his head. Surely, he must know that she loved him beyond his outward appearance. She had to make him know that.

"Do you remember," she asked softly, "the day before you went away to war . . . in the larch woods?"

"I remember." His voice sounded strangled. Abruptly, he stood up, setting his glass down hard on the mantelpiece.

"You've had your way, Megan." His voice was low and bitter. "You've seen me. Now, you must go back to Ireland and get on with your life. I'll have one of my men drive you into Cheyenne in the morning."

Trembling, Megan rose from her chair, willing him to meet her eyes. When he would not look at her, she reached out to touch his arm. In spite of her efforts, her voice wavered when she spoke. "I've waited and searched for you so long, Edward. Please don't turn me out now."

The once gentle mouth hardened into a grim line. But there was something, a flickering along his jaw, something that ignited a faint spark of hope inside her.

"I won't go," she announced, her voice rising, her chin up in the old willful way. "And you're too much of a gentleman to throw me out."

Distractedly, Edward ran a hand through his thick light brown hair. Looking at the floor, he shook his head. The flame inside her blazed when she thought she detected the ghost of a smile on his lips. Then he turned on his heel and strode from the room. Pausing at the foot of the stairs, he glanced at her, then looked away.

"Very well, Megan. You win for the moment. My house-keeper will look after you. Good night." Without a back-ward glance, he disappeared up the stairs.

In spite of the blazing fire, Megan felt like a pillar of ice as she stared after him. Such anguish rose in her that she wanted to cry out against cruel fate. She had come to Wyoming searching for her lover, only to have her dreams shattered against the wall of his bitterness. Behind that wall, and behind his disfigured face, she was certain the old Edward dwelt in loneliness and pain. She had seen glimpses of him tonight at dinner. Somehow, she would find a way to tear down that wall and teach him to love again.

CHAPTER 45

At breakfast, Frannie greeted Edward with a composed face and a warm hug, for Megan had prepared her for the sight that awaited her.

"We've missed you at Morning Hill," Frannie told him as she took her place at the table in the breakfast room.

Edward took another sip of coffee before answering in a slightly unsteady voice. "I've missed all of you, too." Abruptly, he stood up, and forcing a hearty tone, said, "Well, I have work to do. I trust you can entertain yourselves." His glance passed quickly over Megan's startled face before he turned toward the doorway.

At once, she was on her feet, hurrying after him, to stop him with a hand on his arm. "I'd like to ride with you today, Edward. It's such a lovely morning."

"I'm afraid I don't have the time," he answered gruffly, not looking at her.

"What nonsense," she said, and grinned impishly up at him. "You're the owner here. You have time to do anything you really want to do." Her voice fell, and she waited, fearing his refusal. "Please, Edward."

He let out a long sigh. "You're still very good at getting your way, Megan. Very well, come down to the stables when you're ready."

Edward felt a faint sense of chagrin as he tightened the sidesaddle on the chestnut mare. He was well aware that the cowhands were watching him in open-mouthed amazement. Ignoring their stares, he saddled his own tall black gelding, then led the horses up to the hitching rack in front of the house.

He had scarcely tied them when Megan appeared at the front door, smiling, seeming to float down toward him. Dear God, she was beautiful, and he felt pain stab through him, knowing he could never claim that beauty for his own. She had fulfilled every promise of the enchanting child-woman who had given herself to him in love so long ago.

A neatly tailored riding habit swirled about her, accentuating her slender waist, the jacket cut in a low scoop neck so that her full young breasts gleamed through the thin material of her shirtwaist. She had tied her dark hair back on her neck like a girl, but soft curls escaped to frame her smiling face.

Edward looked away, struggling to subdue the longing that seemed about to overwhelm him. He wanted her this moment as much as he had wanted her young self that Irish summer day that now seemed a lifetime ago. Now, he'd never have her, he told himself, furious at this weakness of his.

After all the pain, he'd made a life for himself here in Wyoming. The cowhands no longer noticed his disfigured face. Once in a while, some stranger turned to look when he was in Cheyenne. But he couldn't forget that his mother and sisters had treated him like some hideous ogre to be hidden from society. His brother Thomas had stared at him as though he were a carnival freak. He couldn't bear that from Megan or Kathleen, certain that even if Megan's love had been more than a girlish infatuation, she would only pity him now. So he'd fled to Wyoming, and once he'd run from it, the fear of rejection grew until he was afraid to risk it even with those he loved most.

"Beautiful Edward . . ." The memory of her voice saying those words filled him with incredible pain.

"What a lovely mare," that voice said now as Megan ran her hand down the horse's neck, inspecting the set of the ears and the liquid eyes.

Edward closed a door in his mind, nodding seriously at Megan's words. "Yes, isn't she? A quarter horse . . . nothing to compare with your Irish hunters, but she'll breed good cow ponies . . . maybe even some racing stock."

"And for today I shall ride sedately sidesaddle," Megan

tossed her lovely head. "I won't shame you by riding as wildly as I do at home."

"At least until you know the country," Edward cautioned, and helped her mount. A flame spread from the hands clasping her firm uncorseted waist. Quickly, he turned to mount his own horse, hoping she did not guess how that brief contact had shaken him.

As they rode, Edward pointed out the landmarks, delighting in Megan's joy as she cried, "Oh, yes, I remember Papa telling me. Yes, I remember."

He reined in his horse at the rapids where Cybille Creek poured into the Chugwater River. Above them towered the pale chalky cliffs of Squaw's Leap. "There's an Indian legend about those cliffs," he told her, swinging down from the saddle and dropping the horse's reins to the ground. He drew a cigarette from his vest pocket and lit it.

"Tell me." Megan had dismounted without his help and stood looking eagerly up at him.

"Well," he said, blowing blue smoke into the warm summer air and staring up at the cliffs. "It seems there was an Indian maiden who loved a poor brave who hadn't enough horses to buy her for his bride. The brave went away to make his fortune stealing horses from other tribes, and while he was gone, the maiden's father gave her to a wealthy old chief for a bride. On her wedding night, she learned that her lover had been killed in a horse raid, so she threw herself from the cliff there . . . and died to be with him."

Megan's eyes devoured the tall figure standing with one booted foot propped on a rock, smoking his cigarette, staring up at the cliffs. She had seen Edward in black formal dress with ruffled shirt front, and in a pearl gray morning coat with striped trousers and silk hat, dressed as an English gentleman dresses. Yet he stood before her now clad in blue denim jeans, a worn leather vest over his blue cotton shirt, a gray wide-brimmed hat square on his head. In old photographs, she'd seen her father dressed in this manner, and he had seemed quite at home in the tweeds of an Irish country gentleman . . . just as Edward seemed at home in the simple clothing of an American cowboy.

The perfect right side of his face was turned toward her,

marred only by the string holding his eyepatch in place. All her being yearned toward him with such intensity she could scarcely keep from crying out.

When he glanced toward her, she carefully composed her face.

"Kathleen was fascinated by the story," he told her. "She seemed to think it was the story of her own mother . . . and of her own lost love."

Megan protested. "Fiona lost Sean, but sad as it must have been for Mama when she thought Papa dead, you brought him back to her. They had some wonderfully happy years together in Ireland."

"Yes." Edward's voice was distant, lost in the rushing sound of water pouring over stones. Above the distant cliffs, two hawks swirled in a graceful mating dance.

"Let's go," he said, and almost roughly, lifted her into the saddle. Mounting his own horse, he spurred the animal into a trot.

Inside her chest, Megan's heart felt bruised as she gazed longingly after him. She had promised herself she would go slowly and patiently with him to win his trust. But the need that had driven her across the ocean to find this man grew more urgent with every passing day. "I don't intend to lose my love again," she said, knowing he did not hear.

When she came down to supper, Megan carried the small potted plant she had nurtured all through her journey. Carefully, she sat it before Edward's place. He looked puzzled and gave her an inquiring look.

"Yesterday-today-and-tomorrow," she said, a tentative smile wavering on her lips. "Remember, Edward . . . in the garden at Morning Hill?"

At once his face changed . . . set and cold. "It appears to be drooping." His voice was flat. "I doubt it'll survive Wyoming."

Drawing her breath in hard, Megan swallowed the sob rising in her throat. She wanted to scream at him, to beat her fists against the shell he'd grown around himself. The old Edward would never have said such a hurtful thing.

In the next three days, the open-mouthed amazement of the cowhands changed into meaningful glances as Edward and Megan rode together. He was, as on the first day, unfailingly polite, only occasionally unbending. In those rare moments, he became the person she remembered and hope flared inside her. She would win him again!

Today, as she had insisted, she rode astride a western saddle, wearing the divided skirt she had bought in Cheyenne. Flinging a challenge over her shoulder, Megan raced him across the sagebrush plain, reveling in the clean air rushing past her face, tossing her hair. Above them, and that endless expanse of sagebrush, the skies hung low and gray. Distant storms appeared like india ink smudges on the horizon. Megan gulped in the sweet scent of wet earth borne on the wind, exhilarated, certain now that this was where she belonged.

"You're near a match for the boss," a grizzled cowhand said with a grin, taking the reins of her horse from her when they returned to the stables.

"I intend to be," she told him with a toss of her head, and the cowhand laughed aloud.

Walking back toward the house with Edward, she said, "Mama told me once how the people here disliked Lord Robert for trying to force English customs on them." A thrill of pride went through her as she looked up at him. "Mrs. Tompkins says you're tough but fair, and the cowboys obviously respect you."

Edward frowned. His tone was sardonic. "I have never aspired to be like my father. Quite the contrary."

She had said something wrong again, she thought miserably. Would she ever be able to reach him and make him love her? Tightening her mouth, she told herself she would stay until she did.

They had been playing three-handed whist before a low fire that smelled of pine and sweet mountain air. Frannie nearly always won, playing with fierce concentration, knowing her two opponents were too distracted by each other's presence to play well.

Kerosene lamps lent a soft glow to the sitting room. Once again, Megan wore the cherry red gown, her hair in a soft psyche knot that framed her face like a dark halo.

Edward's brandy glass sat empty at his elbow on the card

table, and the blue smoke from his cigarette in the ashtray curled slowly upward. Leaning back in his chair, he smiled at Frannie. "I'm thinking of setting you up in a card parlor in Cheyenne. We'd make a fortune."

"Only if everyone in Wyoming plays as badly as you two," she chuckled. With a yawn, she rose to her feet. "You've worn me out, following your bad plays. I'll say good night now."

When she had gone up the stairs, there was a long silence in the room. Megan felt wound so tight she feared her whole being might spring apart. She'd waited so long . . . waited and waited.

"I'll teach you how to play gin rummy," Edward said, shuffling the cards.

Fiercely concentrating on the game, Megan managed to submerge the tension clutching every part of her body. When she added up the score and announced that she had won, Edward burst into laughter. The sound of that laughter filled her with such an intense joy she could scarcely contain herself. Dear God . . . she had made him laugh again. Surely now, she could make him love again.

"You're the wildest player I've ever seen," he said, still chuckling as he gathered up the cards. "Absolutely without logic . . . and yet you win."

"Instinct," she told him, smiling up at him as he rose to empty the ashtray into the fire. It was instinct then, that brought her to her feet and around the table to face him.

Immobile, they stood before the fire. Before he could compose his features, she saw the vulnerability reflected there, and beyond that, the longing. Very deliberately, she slid her arms about his shoulders, moving so close that her breasts pressed against his hard chest. Standing on tiptoe, she touched her mouth to his, gently at first. Sense fled as a wild excitement surged along her veins. Her lips opened, and her tongue tasted the half-remembered sweetness of his mouth.

Edward moaned softly, as though in protest. Then his strong arms tightened about her so fiercely she could scarcely breathe. His mouth devoured hers as though he were starved for her.

413

Incredible joy poured over her until she seemed drowned in passion. As suddenly as he had embraced her, Edward pushed her away from him. Megan gasped.

"I don't want your pity!" he cried in a voice that was harsh with bitterness.

He turned away. Recovering from her shock, Megan reached out to touch his arm. "I don't pity you, Edward," she said softly. "I love you." When he shook off her hand and moved away from her, her voice rose. "Damn your stupid pride. I proposed to you when I was seven years old, and I intend to marry you."

With his back turned to her, Edward started across the room. Suddenly he turned, pulling off the black eyepatch, staring full into her face. "You're still that foolish child," he said bitterly, "if you think you could live with this face the rest of your life."

"I love you, Edward," she cried, tears welling in her eyes. "I love you . . . not merely a handsome face."

"Don't stay here and torture me, Megan." His voice was cold and under control now. "Go home. Go back to Ireland. Go tomorrow."

In a few long strides, he was gone from the room, up the stairs. She heard his bedroom door slam, and cried out again, "I love you."

"Megan, love . . . what is it?" Francine leaned over the bed, summoned from her room next door by the sound of abandoned weeping. From the pillow where Megan lay face down sobbing, Francine retrieved the torn fragments of Edward's picture. "Oh God, love, what's happened?"

Held in Frannie's comforting arms, Megan choked out an incoherent version of the scene downstairs. "He said I must leave tomorrow" . . . she ended with a wail of misery.

"Now, now," Frannie soothed. "Don't cry anymore. I'll get a cold cloth for your eyes."

Lying there with the cold cloth over her face, and Frannie stroking her hand sympathetically, Megan felt utterly defeated. Edward had been interwoven with every dream of her life, and now he had rejected her.

"I thought that because I love him so much I could make everything right for us," she told Frannie miserably. "It's like he's locked himself in a prison . . . and he won't let me inside."

"He's very unhappy," Frannie told her gently. "And he loves you very much."

"No," Megan said and felt the tears rise again.

"Yes," Frannie said decisively. "I've seen him looking at you with such a hunger." She took the cold cloth and gently wiped Megan's tear-ravaged face. "His family hurt him so . . . you have to understand that, Megan."

"I hate them," she burst out.

"That'll gain you nothin'," Frannie told her. For a long moment, she stared thoughtfully at Megan, then rose briskly. "Here now, wash your face, and fix your hair." She opened a bureau drawer and searched through.

"Why?" Megan stared at her in puzzlement. "What are we going to do?"

"We . . . I mean you," Frannie answered, pulling a dainty lace and silk nightdress from the drawer, "are going to seduce Edward."

"Frannie!" Megan stared at her in disbelief.

"It'll be easy enough, my dear. He's a true gentleman. Afterward, he'll do the right thing and marry you." Frannie turned her around and began to unbutton her gown. "After you're in his bed, you'd best take off the gown," she continued as though instructing one of the maids how to set the dining table. "Most men like their women bare."

Megan choked.

Taking the discarded gown and petticoat, Frannie continued in the same dispassionate tone. "Stroking arouses men quickly . . . particularly down . . . uh . . . well, you know, you were raised on a stud farm."

Megan began to laugh hysterically, tears pouring down her face at the same time. "Frannie," she gasped. "I can't . . ."

Ignoring the protest, Frannie slid the silky gown over Megan's head. Then she took the bottle of Attar of Roses toilet water from the bureau, splashing it on Megan's throat and wrists, and in the cleft between her breasts. Picking up a brush from the dresser, she began to smooth Megan's disordered hair until it floated about her shoulders in a soft cloud.

"Now, Megan love." Her voice was gentle. "It will hurt when he first takes you, but you mustn't cry out or let him know." Frannie stood before her, arranging the loose dark hair about her face. Her smile was loving, woman to woman. "What comes after will be well worth the pain, I promise you."

If Frannie only knew, Megan thought. But the love she had shared with Edward was a golden treasure for the two of them alone. She was not afraid to be loved now, she only feared he would not love her.

Slipping her feet into her silk slippers, she embraced Frannie quickly. Trembling in every limb, she made her way down the dark hallway to Edward's door.

CHAPTER 46

"Who's that?"

Oh God, Megan thought, as she closed the door behind her and slid the bolt. She'd hoped he'd be asleep so that she could lie beside him and kiss him into wakefulness and passion.

Without answering, she stood beside the bed where Edward sat bolt upright now. Sliding the shoulders of the silken gown over her arms she let it fall to the floor.

"Megan!" His voice sounded choked. "For God's sake . . ."

Lifting the sheet, she slid into bed beside him, forcing him back against the pillow, her mouth seeking his. A sound of protest was smothered by her lips, her warm sweet tongue's insistent caress. For a moment, he responded, his mouth hungry on hers. Then his strong hands clamped on her shoulders, and he held her away.

"Don't!" The word was a cry of pain. "Just leave me to my misery."

"Darling Edward," she whispered, sliding out of his grasp to lie across him, her soft breasts crushed against the rough hair of his bare chest. Remembering Frannie's words . . . remembering a long-ago day scented with larch woods and summer and love . . . her hands slid along the length of his body. A sense of pure joy flooded through her when she realized he was already fully aroused, and she was certain she had won.

Her mouth moved hot across the broad shoulder, the strong cords of his neck, and back to the dear sweet-tasting mouth. As though against his will, Edward's arms came slowly around her. When the kiss deepened, sending searing flame to the very center of her being, those arms tightened fiercely about her.

Breathless from his kiss, Megan pressed her lips to his ear. "I love you so, Edward. I need you to love me the way you loved me long ago, on the most magical day of my life."

"You always smelled like roses," he murmured, his mouth tracing the line of her throat, lingering on the pulse beating madly there. When his hands cupped her breasts, his face buried in their softness, Megan knew he had surrendered.

Her fingers tangled in his thick hair, pressing him against her, reveling in the sensations aroused by his tongue caressing her breasts, circling her navel, tracing the hollow beneath her hip bones. As his kisses moved downward, she felt the need that had driven her for so long pounding insistently between her thighs.

"Edward," she cried softly, pleading. His mouth took hers again, devouring, savoring. Her hands slid down along his back, clutching at his hips with wild urgency.

When he entered her, she arched against him, taking him deep into the aching depths of her. She let out a long soft sigh, knowing that at last she was whole again.

They seemed one being, melded together . . . mouths and breasts and hips . . . moving in the age-old ritual. Wild with passion, Megan responded with frenzied urgency, caught up in a soaring ecstasy that transcended time and place. With a hoarse cry of fulfillment, she took him deep into her. Edward gasped her name, and they were lost in a blind, whirling rapture.

"Megan . . . my darling, my love," Edward murmured, brushing back her tumbled hair, his face against her throat.

"Dearest Edward," she answered, sleepily content, lying with his arms about her, one long leg embracing her hips. "I love you so." The long waiting was over. They would never be apart again. Sighing, she drifted into fulfilled slumber as raindrops broke softly against the windowpane.

Pale morning light filled the bedroom as Megan's eyelids fluttered open. Stretching sensuously, she closed her eyes again, delighting in the delicious soreness of her body. Startled, she realized she lay alone in the bed. Relief flooded through her at the sight of Edward standing before the window.

He wore a dressing gown of maroon velvet, and he was smoking a cigarette, staring moodily out the window. Love filled her as she watched him, until she thought she might burst with the wonder of it.

"Edward," she called softly.

Almost hesitantly, he turned toward her, as though reluctant to show the scarred face without his eyepatch. He waited, crushing out the cigarette, searching her face as though not sure whether he would find love there . . . or revulsion.

Megan lifted her arms to him. The face was Edward, the man she loved. Another Edward, from long ago, was gone now with the picture torn to bits in despair last night.

"Come here, darling," she said, all her love and longing mirrored in her face. "I need to be loved."

Smiling, Edward sat on the bed beside her. "Insatiable creature," he teased, reaching to smooth her tumbled hair.

"But I've waited such a long time for you," she answered with mock severity. Untying the sash of his robe, she took his arm in her hands and drew his face down to her.

His kiss was eager and possessive, and she yielded to it joyously. Breathless, they broke apart. Megan cupped his face in both her hands. "You have the most beautiful mouth," she whispered, running her tongue softly over his lips. "And it still tastes wonderful."

Edward's body tensed. A sadness came into his eye. "Sweet Megan," he said doubtfully. "Can you make love to a face like this in the daylight?"

In reply, she drew him close, her lips gently tracing the wide white scar down the side of his ravaged face . . . forehead, blinded eye, and down his cheek. There was wonder in his expression, and love beyond measure.

A tremor of desire shook her. Megan's hands moved down his body, stroking sensuously along his back, around his waist to push the robe aside, between his thighs to the burning length of his erection.

"The most important part seems to be undamaged," she said, giving him an arch look.

Edward laughed aloud. Clasping her close, he rolled over so that the long lean length of him lay on top of her.

A tremulous smile curved Megan's lips as her fingers tangled in his thick hair. "It's so good to hear you laugh, darling."

"Megan . . . Megan . . ." His voice was muffled as his lips caressed the pulse throbbing at the base of her throat. "You've given me back my life."

Urgent need boiled up inside her, and she closed her eyes as it flooded through her, building in intensity. Reaching down, she urged him inside her. He moaned, thrusting deep as she arched to meet him. Joined together, they moved into an exquisite delirium that burst at last into a crescendo of joy.

Spent from lovemaking, Megan lay contentedly in Edward's arms, her head pillowed on his shoulder. Beneath her hand, his heart still thundered wildly.

Last night's storm has passed, and the morning sun lay its golden light across the room in a bright rectangular pattern. Through the open window, a breeze brought the fresh scent of sage and rain-wet earth.

Megan saw for the first time that Edward had placed the struggling Brunfelsia plant on his bedside table. She knew then what it must have meant to him . . . brought all the way from Ireland, with love.

With a soft cry, she turned to Edward. "Look, darling . . . look, it's blooming." And she pointed at the one tiny purple blossom gleaming among green leaves. "Yesterday-today-and-tomorrow."

Pressing his lips against her forehead, Edward smiled and reached one long arm out to gently touch the purple blossom. "And which is that?"

"Tomorrow," Megan whispered, looking into the beloved, ruined face. "It's an omen . . . and a promise, my love . . . for all the tomorrows we will be together."

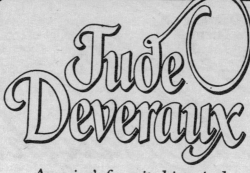

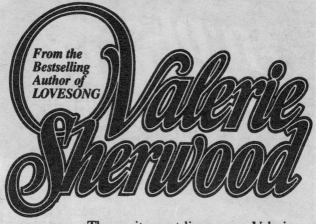

JUDE DEVERAUX

A Unique New Voice In Romantic Fiction

Jude Deveraux is the finest new writer of historical romances to come along since Kathleen Woodiwiss.

The Montgomery Annals

_____**The Velvet Promise** 54756/$3.95
_____**Highland Velvet** 60073/$3.95
_____**Velvet Song** 60076/$3.95
_____**Velvet Angel** 60075/$3.95

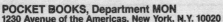